ENIF

Russ Berg

JONES MEDIA
PUBLISHING

Jones Media Publishing
10645 N. Tatum Blvd. Ste. 200-166
Phoenix, AZ 85028
www.JonesMediaPublishing.com

Printed in the United States of America

ISBN-13: 978-1-945849-69-5 paperback
JMP2018.2

DEDICATION

I would like to dedicate this book to my wife, Melody,
whose encouragement prompted me to write this journey
of words and thoughts.

ACKNOWLEDGMENTS

I want to express my gratitude to Janet Humphreys whose literary expertise guided my footsteps.

CONTENTS

CHAPTER ONE

THE CHALLENGE

It had been two months since Jerry Humphreys promised the stars of heaven to Mandy Miller. Life had reached a frenzied pace since he had proposed. A nervous excitement raced through his blood as the two sat cuddled on a wind-carved boulder in the Santa Catalina Foothills, looking into each other's eyes, letting the world melt away under a cloudless sky. A warm August wind whipped through the Tucson desert, rich with the scent of chaparral and mesquite. Jerry pointed to the heavens. "Mandy, what do you see?"

"Well, there's Orion's belt ... and there's the Big Dipper."

"No, I mean what do you really see?"

"I see God's hand in an ever-expanding universe filled with wonders beyond our comprehension."

"One day, those wonders will be yours. And you and I ..." Jerry squeezed her hand as he gazed into her eyes. "We shall dance among those stars, leaving a path of stardust in our wake." Jerry moved closer to Mandy, inhaling her fresh, clean scent, laced with a hint of orchids. His thoughts slipped into the flames of desire, embracing her as though he would never see her again. "I only wish I had the means to take you there now."

"Jerry, you're too impatient. Things are going to be fine."

"As a geologist, you'd think I could change the hoard of pyrite I found into the real thing."

"Your past is behind you. You've made it!"

"Have I?" Jerry looked away.

"Do you love me?" Mandy gently touched his face.

"What do you think?"

"Then relax. You've just started your business."

"I know, but ..." Jerry drew her close as their eyes met. "I need to show you how much I really care for you." The awful embarrassment of being found lacking terrified him.

"Our love is perfect. I don't need riches to make me happy. I just need you. Besides, my job at Geophysics is secure."

Jerry looked at Mandy and smiled. She was everything he had hoped to find in a woman. After his mother had died in a car accident, he had been so depressed, trying to get through college but unable to pull it together. He thought God had abandoned him until Mandy showed him life could be good again.

A few cirrus clouds had gathered, dimming the stars. Jerry glanced at his watch. It was ten o'clock. "It's late, and I know you have to get up early."

Mandy nodded. Her employer was sending her into the field to investigate potential sources of natural gas near Arizona's southern border.

Jerry took her hand and lifted her from her rocky chair, lacing his fingers between hers. Together they headed back toward their cars. Coyotes' yipping and barking echoed through the desert's darkness as they followed the trail of saguaros to Mandy's Jeep.

"I wish tonight would never end." Jerry's heart burned like fire.

"Me, too." Mandy sighed.

With a gentle touch, Jerry lifted her chin and kissed her. "Call me when you get back."

"I will, but it may be late."

"I'll be up. Love you."

When Jerry got home, he was emotionally drained and got into bed without taking off his clothes. He lay there suspended in darkness, drifting into a blissful sleep.

Eight o'clock ticked around, and the morning brought with it the usual routine. Determined to do his shopping before going to the office, Jerry jumped out of bed, showered, threw on a pair of clean Levi's and a short-sleeve blue deck shirt and hit the road. He rushed around town and finished his chores in time to grab a Big Mac and a Coke before meeting with the previous owner to discuss a different strategy for his newly acquired business.

The humidity had ramped up, and the sun was struggling to break through the clouds. The smell of rain filled the air. A typical monsoon was brewing when Jerry escorted Mr. Stubal into his office.

"I see you've remodeled the old place." Mr. Stubal glanced around, squinting through his round-framed glasses. "It looks like a museum, with all these minerals." Colorful rock displays bordered the plainness of his office, along with a computer on an oak veneer desk and several stacks of maps and unfiled reports.

"I've collected rocks ever since I was a kid. My veins bleed ore."

"I'd say so."

"Before my dad died from cancer, we'd go rock hunting, hoping to find gold." Jerry reached into his pants pocket and squeezed a piece of iron pyrite. "It was one of the simple pleasures I looked forward to as a youth. I guess that's where my obsession with geology started."

"I'm sorry to hear that about your father."

"I was ten. My mother never remarried."

"Is this her?" Mr. Stubal picked up a picture of a middle-aged woman with graying hair.

"Yes."

"She's an attractive woman."

"That she was."

"Was?" His forehead wrinkled.

"My mother sacrificed everything for me, including her life."

Mr. Stubal stood silent, gazing at the picture.

"It's been three years since she passed away from her car accident." Jerry's eyes teared and his voice cracked. "She was driving home late from work one night and fell asleep, hitting a concrete barrier head-on."

"Your life has been filled with tragedy."

"Nothing came easy." Jerry's heart ached. "After my dad passed away, we struggled financially. When I wasn't working, my entertainment entailed studying geology books, burning the midnight oil, and falling asleep with my face plastered on the open pages. I promised Mom after I finished college, she'd never need to work again."

Mr. Stubal placed his hand on Jerry's shoulder. "Son, let's see what we can do to make sure her sacrifice wasn't in vain."

Moments later, they sat down to review Jerry's desire to change the direction of the company.

"You know"—Mr. Stubal lifted his glasses and rubbed his eyes—"most of my contracted work involved prospecting for new mineral deposits."

"I know, but I feel the future is in green energy." Jerry sensed his concern but continued. "I mean, I'll still follow up on the existing contracts, but my real passion is in preserving our ecosystem."

"Son, you've chosen a tough environment to compete in."

"I know, and I can't tell you how much I appreciate you carrying my loan."

"I know all too well the suffocating grip a person experiences when taking on a lot of debt, and I'm concerned about your ability to pay your bills."

"Mom often quoted the Bible, telling me that whatever was born of God can overcome the world. Then she would add, 'This life is full of battles, and you are a survivor.'" Jerry stared into his eyes. "She shared my tears, she shared my fears, and, well ... here I am. Plus my two-year stint at Arizona Geothermal has provided me with significant insight."

"Son, a little advice." Mr. Stubal leaned back in his chair. "It's easy to get caught up in the nuances of this job. It nearly cost me my marriage."

"Don't worry. My fiancée is in the same field. She'll understand." His words were meant to ease Mr. Stubal's doubts as much as they were meant to comfort himself.

After several hours of discussion, Mr. Stubal shook Jerry's hand and excused himself. "A severe storm warning has been issued for this evening, and I'd like to get home before it hits."

"Sometimes, nature exhales a mighty breath, threatening vengeance for disrespecting its benevolence."

"Might be." Mr. Stubal headed for the door but then turned. "Oh, I almost forgot." He reached into his satchel and pulled out a large egg-shaped rock. "I found this geode when I was examining an open pit mine in Rio Grande de Sol, Brazil. These specimens have some of the most incredible features I've ever seen—mainly dendritic inclusions that resemble trees or bushes. I left it uncut. That privilege goes to you."

"Thanks. I'll add it to my collection." Jerry rotated the stone, his eyes wide. "It's like another world lost in time, trapped inside a shell just waiting to get out. I'll treasure it forever." "I'll be around if you need a consult," Mr. Stubal said as he opened the door and stepped outside.

"I can't tell you how much I appreciate your help. I'll be in touch."

Minutes had ticked into hours. Jerry checked his watch. He was late. It was eight p.m., and he'd planned to meet with a few friends at Joe's house for a night of banter and camaraderie.

He grabbed his satchel off the oak desk, stuffed his clipboard and field reports into the bag, and stepped outside. After locking his office, he paused to inspect the sky. Angry black clouds crisscrossed above him, preparing to unleash their fury. The air was thick with humidity. He hurried to his old Chevy truck, holding his handbag tightly, his thoughts on autopilot. *My debt is strangling me, but if I can find just one source of thermal energy, I may be able to untangle this financial web I've spun.*

The wind had kicked up, blowing from the east, and, with it, dust. Power lines had toppled over, and swirling walls of dirt blurred the streets as Jerry left the parking lot. Highways ordinarily bright with light and filled with cars on a Tuesday night were dark and deserted.

Suddenly, the air crackled and a bolt of lightning flashed, snapping the limb of a tree not more than twenty feet in front of him. His muscles tightened as he slammed on the brakes, swerving to miss the fallen branch. Jerry's heart raced. *Wow, that was close. Just like life, the weather is no respecter of persons, and if you get in its way, look out.*

After dodging flying debris and fallen tree branches, Jerry turned left on East Broadway and found his way to Joe's driveway. When he exited his truck, a stray black cat shot under his feet, trying to find refuge from the storm.

Whoa, that was creepy. Sure glad I'm not superstitious.

Narrow steps led to a covered porch. He found the door ajar and knocked. No answer. The wind raged hard and furious. Jerry pulled his shirt over his face as a wave of rain mixed with dust descended, pummeling him with drops of mud. Desperate to find shelter from the stinging deluge, he pushed the weathered white entry open. "Hey, anyone home?"

A voice echoed through the hallway as he stepped over the threshold. "We're in the kitchen."

Warm, sticky air saturated the room, and the smell of pizza met his nose. Mark and Joe were there, but Stan had canceled due to the power outage. The two were huddled around a grimy glass-top kitchen table where a single candle flickered, creating a muted glow against the room's shadowy darkness. Domino's pizza boxes and empty soda cans cluttered the counter.

"Cokes are in the fridge," Joe said. "We were talking about the area south of Tucson where all that weird stuff's been happening.

"What weird stuff?" Jerry said as he grabbed a Coke.

"You know. That area in the Chiricahuas where those hikers disappeared."

"Pizza?" Mark held out a cold slice.

"No, thanks," Jerry said, his palm facing out. "You mean that remote section off of Highway 186?"

"Yup. That's the one," Joe said.

"Oh, that's a bunch of superstitious bunk," Jerry said, sitting down. "People get lost there all the time."

"There's talk of people becoming possessed and seeing strange things," Joe said.

"Maybe you should check it out." Jerry's face reflected a hint of mischief.

"Huh-uh. Not me. No way!" Joe's eyes twitched while he flipped his curly brown hair out of his face. He cleared his throat as his wiry frame shifted in his chair. "You know, that particular area has a nasty reputation for being dangerous, but even more so since the quakes started."

Suddenly, a jagged flash of white light ripped through the atmosphere, piercing the night's blackness like a strobe. A loud thunderous groan shook Joe's house, causing the dishes in the cupboards to rattle and clink against each other.

Joe scooted his chair next to the kitchen window, placed his hand on the glass, and stared out into the darkness. "See, even the gods agree with me."

"Oh, you're just a scaredy-cat. I bet you still sleep with the lights on."

"Whatever."

"It's kinda like this." Jerry blew out the candle. "Just like this lingering smoke can create illusions in your imagination, people see what they want to see. The real monsters out there may be in the form of thermal energy."

"Knock it off," Joe said, fumbling to relight the candle. "I'm not going!"

"I'm just saying—"

"Cheap talk. That's all I hear," Mark cut in, snatching the last slice of cheese pizza. His preference for baggy white T-shirts, faded Levi's and Nike sneakers complemented his overweight frame and onyx black hair. Mark had an infectious grin, and when he spoke, he sprayed spittle and sounded like he had an asthmatic wheeze. "What about you, Mr. Geologist?"

"Yeah, right!" Jerry's gaze shot to Mark. "I don't see your boots blazing a path into the unknown."

"Got too many rocks on my tectonic plate as it is."

"Yeah, yeah, yeah. You'd have trouble hiking the Aspen Trail, let alone anything in the Chiricahuas." Mark exaggerated everything, especially his geological skills.

"I'll bet you ten bucks you can't find your nerve," Mark said and drained the rest of his Coke with a sloppy slurp. "That is if Mandy—"

Just then, Jerry's phone rang. It was Mandy.

"Hey, gorgeous," Jerry said, settling back in his chair.

"Where are you?"

"I'm with the guys."

"I just walked in the door."

"Everything all right?"

"Yes, but I'm exhausted. I'll tell you more about my trip later." Jerry could hear Mandy yawn. "Are we still on for tomorrow night?"

"Yup, wouldn't miss it." Jerry nodded as though she could see him.

"Okay, see you then."

"Love you." Jerry hung up while checking the time on his cell phone.

Mark laughed and shook his head. "I don't think Mandy will let you off your leash."

"You're just jealous," Jerry said, jutting his feet out, crossed at the ankles.

"I don't know ... Mandy can be pretty stubborn."

"It's her Irish heritage, but I can handle her."

"Prove it!" Mark said, fanning a ten-dollar bill in the air.

Jerry leaned forward over the greasy table, his shoulders even with his ears, his eyes intent. "All right, Hog"—Mark's nickname—"you're on."

Mark just smiled.

Jerry blinked—then blinked again. Had he just got sucked into another one of Mark's insidious bets?

The evening continued with spirited taunts and fiery debates. Outside, the storm had calmed. Eucalyptus limbs swayed in the wind, scraping against the faded brown exterior of Joe's house like fingernails screeching on a blackboard. At half past midnight, Jerry excused himself.

"You know, I've got a wedding to help plan," Jerry said, yawning. "I'll ping you tomorrow."

"May the quartz be with you," Joe teased giving a high-five slap.

On the drive home, Jerry worried about Mandy's reaction to his decision to explore a site where safety was an issue, but he hoped she would understand once he had pled his case.

Jerry woke to the early rays of light creeping through the bedroom window, rubbing his tired eyes. He lay quiet, reflecting on the geological reports that had to be finished before he could relax with Mandy. Today he would work at home. Exhaling a weary groan, Jerry pushed himself up, fired up the computer, and resumed the never-ending task of regulatory filings.

It was close to three o'clock by the time he finished his last report and stepped outside. A few dark clouds still clung to the sky, and the hot August air was thick with humidity and bugs. Jerry glanced around at the red brick buildings, the local thrift store he frequented as a youth, and the roads filled with cracks and potholes.

He stood silent, watching and listening to the kids who hung out at the thrift shop, seeking acceptance and inclusion by their peers. *Yeah, things haven't changed much at all.* Nothing had changed in Tucson since he was a kid except for a few more tall buildings and busier streets framed by the majestic Catalina Mountains. He paused to inhale a breath of fresh air left over from the night's storm, his stomach churning with hunger. After grabbing a late lunch, he jumped into his truck and drove to Mandy's home, fighting his fatigue. First on the side streets, winding around loose debris left by the monsoon, and then on the main throughways, which were already cleared. Power outages in several neighborhoods remained, making travel difficult without traffic lights.

Amid the screeching of tires and honking horns, Jerry negotiated his way onto East River Road. Dirt, gravel, and an occasional downed tree cluttered the street, but finally, he made his way into her driveway.

A tired sun drifted low while the shadows of saguaro cactus stretched their arms, lengthening their reach across the desert mountain's face. A moist, warm breeze whirled around him as he jumped out of his truck. Mandy owned a gray condominium on the east side of Tucson near the Catalina Foothills. When he opened her white French doors, she gestured to him from the dining room.

Jerry detected the soft fragrance of sweet orchids as he sprang over the threshold and made his way to her. He recalled the intoxicating scent he'd first encountered the night they'd met at a University of Arizona dance. When she flashed that cheerful Southern California smile, his heart melted. Now he couldn't wait to hear the words "I do."

Bright yellow walls echoed gleaming light from a crystal chandelier, showcasing a row of family pictures, including one of Jerry kneeling at her feet, proposing. Detailed lists of photographers, caterers, party favor suppliers, and other service providers were mapped out on her polished oak dining table. "Love Story," by Taylor Swift, saturated the air in the background.

Jerry met her gaze as she sang along in harmony. Mandy swung her shimmering honey-blond hair to the side, raised her arms, and embraced Jerry. Her hot pink dress of lightweight cotton flowed freely around her as they waltzed around the table. They were about to go over their wedding program when Jerry announced, "Hog challenged me to a duel."

"What are you talking about?" Anger flashed in Mandy's face. "What do you mean 'a duel'?"

"You know that mysterious place in the Chiricahua Mountains? Well, Mark challenged me to go there." Jerry's grin touched his dimples.

"Aaaand?"

"Hey, I bet him ten bucks ... and I've meant to check it out anyway." Jerry bit his lip. "I'm convinced underground thermal emissions are causing the weird accounts. If I can tap into just one, I may be able to pay for our honeymoon."

"Oh, Jerry, that's ridiculous." Mandy turned to her computer and clicked on the gift registry at Nordstrom's. "I've heard too many strange stories about that place, and I don't expect to lose you before I get that ring on my finger."

"What stories?" Jerry picked up some samples of wedding invitations.

"I don't know. Some claim to have seen sightings of creepy apparitions, while others complained of a sudden onset of cold and nausea."

"Doesn't sound life-threatening to me."

"I've heard of missing-person reports, too, but I don't know the specifics."

"I don't want to upset you, but I need to find out if thermal emissions are causing these weird accounts."

She met his gaze, her eyes narrowed and curious. "I didn't realize that area was open for exploration."

Jerry smiled but didn't comment.

"Why are you doing this?" Mandy's tone had changed.

"You don't understand. There may be new evidence of sustainable thermal gases. You know the hot sulfur spring that everyone avoids?"

"Yes." Mandy stood motionless.

"Well, Mr. Stubal received a tip of recent seismic activity exposing pockets of steam in that quadrant." He placed his arms around her, his face crinkling in a smile. "Plus, I'm not superstitious. I don't believe in the boogeyman."

"I don't know what's going on down there, but you're not going." There was a hard determination in her voice.

Jerry paused. "You know, your work takes you to some pretty dangerous places."

"True, but none are life-threatening."

Jerry flexed his muscular arm. "Did you forget that I received the Jagged Pitch award from the mountaineering course I took?"

"I'm not questioning your abilities. It's the unknown that worries me."

"Must you always give me such a hard time?" Jerry focused on the picture with him proposing on one knee.

"Are you serious?" Mandy turned off the computer. "Really?"

Frustrated, Jerry turned and mumbled, "Do I need to get on my knees again?"

"What'd you just say?"

"I'm sorry." It wasn't until the words left his mouth that he realized how they'd sounded, offensive and disrespectful. "I didn't mean—"

"Is that how you feel?"

"No! That's not what I meant." Jerry's face reddened with shame. "I'm tired, and it's just that ... It's just that I feel choked with all my debt."

"I told you not to worry. My job is secure."

"I know, but ... I need to feel like I'm helping."

"That place may be dangerous, and I don't want to lose you." Her look was meant to chastise, but love was reflected in her eyes. "You need to take my feelings into consideration."

Jerry slumped in silence.

"You know what I think?" Mandy took his hands in hers and gently squeezed them. Her touch was warm and reassuring.

"What?"

"I think your fear of failure is going to drive everyone around you crazy."

"You don't understand." Jerry stared into her deep blue eyes. "You've never wanted for anything. Sometimes, I think that all the bad things that ever happened in my life are paybacks for the wrongs I've committed."

Mandy's countenance softened. "Oh, Jerry ..." Her voice broke as she embraced him with tenderness. "I love you. Isn't that enough?"

"It's hard to forget the past."

"I know, but you need to move on."

"I keep thinking ... if I'd taken more time off from school, mom wouldn't have been so tired from working all those double shifts, and she'd still be alive."

"Jerry, you've got to stop blaming yourself."

"It's easier said than done."

"Trust me, your mother would be proud of your accomplishments."

"Okay, okay." Jerry smiled and tried to lighten the mood. "Can I borrow ten bucks?"

He reached into his pocket and squeezed the chunk of iron pyrite. The pale brass-yellow mineral was a constant reminder of where he came from. In the back of his mind, he'd already committed to the trip, but he wanted to avoid further confrontation. *I'll load my truck tonight and sneak out of town and be back before she notices.*

CHAPTER TWO

THE CAVE

Jerry didn't sleep well after his little spat with Mandy, and it wasn't until midnight that he dozed off amid the constant chattering in his mind. Startled by an annoying beep, he woke from a deep slumber in the early morning darkness. Jerry groaned, hit the "snooze" button, and flopped back onto his bed. Then he remembered his mission.

Within moments, he'd slipped on a pair of Levi's, his favorite scuffed green hiking boots, and a University of Arizona T-shirt. His stomach grumbled, signaling it was time to start his day. "Hold on. I'm going to feed you." He hurried to the kitchen and grabbed a cold jelly muffin off the counter and then dashed to his truck.

Jerry drove south on the I-10, his silver-blue eyes fixed on the road, his hands gripping the black, three-spoke steering wheel of his dad's creaky old Chevy truck. *With all the rain we've had, the humidity is going to push the heat index into the triple digits.* Jerry turned on the air conditioning and wiped the beaded sweat from his forehead with the back of his hand.

The sun peeked its face over the horizon as he sped past Murphy High School, evoking strong memories of humiliation from wearing secondhand clothing that didn't match, along with a few bruised fists. Behind-the-back laughs had always irked him, but that was behind him now, wasn't it? *As God is my witness, I'll never be poor again. Never!*

Jerry refused to indulge in the past that threatened to engulf him. With Mandy at his side, his life found new purpose and meaning. Even though times were tough, excitement surged through him with the thought of finding a source of thermal energy.

"Maybe it's the drive people fear more than the actual site. Especially in my old truck. Right, Old Faithful?"

Jerry had named his faded-green '56 Chevy truck after the Yellowstone geyser. Every time he turned on the air conditioning, the engine overheated, causing the radiator to spew water. Jerry dreaded the two-hour trip across the blistering Arizona desert, but he was determined to act on the tip about a possible dry steam application. However, driving during the hot, humid month of August wasn't much of a joyride, with temperatures hitting a hundred degrees or more. Shadows even slumped in the searing heat, and without proper hydration, a person would feel like a shriveling piece of bacon.

Blurred columns of rising heat rippled through the air. Every minute that passed, the outside temperature rose. Now at a boiling point, the highway shimmered, causing a mirage of water to materialize. Sure enough, after several minutes into his mission, the heat gauge surged.

"Aw, come on. Ugh, I wish I could trade you in for a young and reliable model. One that didn't hiss back." After his father had died, his mother kept the truck in remembrance of the countless memories they had shared. When Jerry was old enough, she passed the icon on to him to memorialize his father's life.

Jerry shut off the air and rolled the squeaky window down all the way. A blustery wind whipped his scraggly brown hair, tossing it wildly, while sweat streamed down his forehead, stinging his eyes. The last thing he needed now was to find himself stranded in the middle of the scorching desert, especially if he had to call Mandy for help.

Within a few hours, the rugged mountain range in southern Arizona came into view. Paved with desert grasslands, thorn-scrub bushes, and saguaro and cholla cactus, the Chiricahuas' rocky terrain included steep slopes that presented a serious threat to the unskilled. A sulfur hot spring ran through it, and due to the rotten-egg smell, most people shunned the area.

Jerry's old pickup shimmied and rattled as it crawled up a narrow dirt road, bouncing on the corrugated washboard trail as though he were in a rock tumbler. Thirty minutes later, his truck slowed to a stop, the gravel road terminating in a dead end.

The eyes of the mountains squawked above him. He looked up. Red-tailed hawks circled high on the updrafts, screeching at each other.

He paused to reflect on the mountain's majestic beauty, a wonderland of rocks, a cradle of stillness where superstitions and legends contended with ghosts from the past. Throughout his life, he'd been fascinated by the supernatural lore, but the truth remained a mystery. Would this be the day he unlocked their secret, a secret that could help free him from his past?

After shutting the engine off, he sat in silence. He spotted a lonely sycamore tree that had grown crooked, hunched over from years of struggle. *Nothing in life is ever easy. Adversity shouts insults at every turn, but like so many withered trees, survival may be but a raindrop away.*

Jerry's excitement boiled as he flew out of his truck, holding his hand over his wrinkled nose due to the rotten-egg smell. A hot oven breeze creased his face, feathering his thick brown hair. Red ants scurried across the sizzling desert floor while cicadas sang in unison. The harsh terrain was harder to access than first imagined.

A partially surveyed rocky trail led away from the sulfur hot spring across a scrub-covered desert scattered with chaparral and cholla to an abandoned site at the mountain's base. The Forest Service had halted all maintenance in this region for the past several years, and significant erosion had occurred, exposing an assortment of thorny bushes, a lot of sharp sticks, and a few piñon pines. Jerry ran his fingers through his hair and exhaled a long breath. *No wonder this place repels people. This may be where my survival training comes in handy.*

Within the hour, Jerry had graphed the area of reported seismic activity and begun drilling to obtain a soil sample. Just as the drill head pierced the topsoil, the earth shook under his feet, causing a boulder to break away from the hillside. Startled, Jerry dropped hard to the ground, braced for impact.

Moments passed, and he peeked out from under his arm. *Okay, that was way too close.* The boulder had shattered into pieces, but Jerry remained unharmed. He stood and brushed the dirt off his clothes, his hands still trembling. *I'm glad I don't have to explain this to Mandy.*

After the dust had settled, a cluster of curious-looking rocks caught his attention. Jerry inched his way toward the formation, wary of a rockslide. *Okay, this wasn't here before.* As he approached the intriguing dark structure, his keys, dangling from his pants pocket, started to jingle and then, without warning, shot through the air like a missile, attaching themselves to the unusual stones. His muscles jumped. His pulse quickened.

Is this some kind of rock cairn? If so, who placed it here and why? Jerry stood silent, trying to sort out his thoughts. *Maybe I am in a Bermuda Triangle of sorts.*

Seven magnetic stones, oblong-shaped like a football, were positioned in a circle on a mysterious blue crystal platform. Each one revealed a smooth, shiny black surface with violet streaks coursing through it. While the surrounding structures radiated a blistering heat from the sun, these strange forms felt like they'd been refrigerated.

"Okay, this is odd," Jerry said as he felt their coldness. "I haven't experienced anything like this before." Jerry squinted in the bright midday sun, scanning the area, looking for answers. Confused about what had transpired, he wiped the sweat from his brow. "Is anyone here?" he shouted.

A warm desert breeze brought a whiff of the nearby sulfur springs while two red tail hawks screeched above him. His uncertainty caused him to focus on the strange artifacts. *The pedestal's shape reminds me of the Star Trek insignia. I wonder if we have some Trekkies around here.*

Curious, Jerry removed a stone from the blue crystal platform. *Whoa, this feels like it's made of lead.* His gaze shifted to the pedestal. *What's this?* He had uncovered part of a geometric pattern inscribed on the platform. Intrigued, Jerry stripped more of the unusual rocks from the asymmetrical, arrowhead-shaped structure, exposing two peculiar petroglyphs. *These are similar to the solar markings of Fajada Butte, in New Mexico. I wonder if these spiral engravings have the same ability to record the equinoxes and solstices.*

The air crackled with static electricity, causing the hair on his arms to rise. *Okay, this is weird. I feel like I'm in an electromagnetic field.* He documented what he'd seen and snapped pictures with his phone.

Jerry glanced around and then proceeded to return the intriguing objects back onto the crystal-like platform. In his haste, he placed one of the magnetic rocks in the opposite direction. *Wait, that's not right.* Just as he reached to turn the stone around, its reversed polarity created a chain reaction that caused the others to spin simultaneously. Jerry jumped back, splaying his arms. *Whoa, this is crazy. Maybe the rumors about this area are true.*

Without warning, a towering, convoluted shadow appeared against the mountain's rocky slope a few feet from him. A rush of adrenaline zinged through his body and left him motionless. Within moments, the tendrils of darkness faded, replaced by a light brighter than noonday.

Jerry staggered away from the anomaly with his hand shading his eyes. The sound of rushing water rippled through his ears, followed by a feeling of bliss. As this strange event unfolded, a cave materialized, the brilliance gone. Numb and bewildered, he stood in disbelief.

"What the ... No way!" Jerry scanned the breach in the mountain for answers. "This is incredible."

The desert's heat percolated up through the soles of his boots, warming his feet with a moist sweat. Something urged Jerry to enter the cavity, an essence that seemed foreign but alluring. Curiosity outweighed his fear, and he stepped into the shadowy, portentous cavern. *I can't believe I'm doing this. Mandy will kill me if she finds out.*

A damp, musty smell met Jerry's nose. Loose debris grated under his feet. The mouth of the tunnel led to a dark underground corridor. Faint marks were visible on the interior walls, but the cave's dimness made it impossible to view, let alone interpret. Jerry's mind raced. *What is this place? Who could've made these symbols?* Soon after his descent, the cave's blackness swallowed the insipid light.

"I can't see anything," Jerry murmured, groping to find his way out. Enveloped in a euphoric tingle, he made his way back to the entrance, his pulse humming.

Elated about his discovery, he struggled within himself about whether to return and share the news with Mandy or forge ahead. *Should I or shouldn't I?* A sudden dread surged like fire through his veins when he thought what Mandy might say. *But I never said I wouldn't go.* If he shared his secret, he might never find his prize.

His thoughts shifted to the cavern's enigmatic symbols hidden beneath the Earth's flesh. What were these strange markings, and where did they come from? Why hadn't he come across them in his studies? Was this an ancient religion from a forgotten time? Did the ruins of an old civilization lie hidden deep inside?

Jerry's mind raced with expectation, hoping to find a new discovery that would place his name among the greats. *I don't know what this is, but my gut tells me it has significant value ... maybe even something that would make others take notice.* After reflecting on the cavern's inscriptions, he decided to hike back to his truck for the rest of his gear.

Thirty minutes later, Jerry had set up camp. Shadowed from the heat in his brown nylon tent, he prepared to enter the mysterious cavern. Delusions of grandeur consumed his thoughts. *Wouldn't everyone choke if I found something really amazing? Hey, maybe I'll get written up in the Journal of Geology and Geophysics.*

Before proceeding farther, Jerry meticulously checked his supplies. "Let's see, got my backpack, energy bars, canteen, flashlight, knife, rope, gloves, plastic bags ... Oh, I can't forget my testing equipment. Looks like I'm good."

Once inside the chamber, the cave exhaled a stale, musty breath as though it were alive. Chills pierced his gut. *Whew, that was eerie. I feel like I'm in the belly of a whale.*

Jerry pulled his tactical LED flashlight from his pack, turned it on, and waved it back and forth in an arc. Mottled grayish-white rock framed the interior. It was a small enclosure, not much bigger than the Colossal Cave, in Tucson. Loose sedimentary rocks crunched under his feet as he made his way into the depths of the cavern.

Now with the proper lighting, several distinct engravings emerged. Scattered on the walls was a series of stark and evocative symbols of unknown origin. Jerry craned his neck to a darkened grayish rock in a curved recess to a spot near the ceiling a few feet above his head. Fine lines coalesced into two spiral images similar to the markings on the pedestal outside. *How long have these etchings been hidden deep inside these dark chambers, waiting to be discovered?*

Jerry touched one of the strange impressions on the wall, slowly tracing it with his index finger. *What do these symbols mean?* He paused as the light passed over the engravings. *These look like star patterns similar to our constellations.* Jerry focused on one particular grouping. *In fact, this one is Aquarius, my zodiac sign. Is this an archaic astronomical center, and if so, how old is it ... and who were its creators?*

Jerry pulled a penny from his pants pocket and tried to scratch the wall's surface near the engravings but couldn't. *Strange. Calcite is one of the softer minerals and should scratch easily, but this carbonate has a high degree of hardness. Whoever inscribed these symbols had to use a tool harder than copper.*

Caught up in the moment, Jerry grabbed his phone and snapped pictures of the inscribed symbols. *Maybe I can connect to the Internet and tap into an online library of stars.* Try as he might, he couldn't get a signal. Frustrated, he found his way back to his campsite and tried again. Still, no signal. *Man, I wish I would've paid more attention in my astronomy classes.*

In the solitude of his tent, Jerry pulled out his notepad and began sketching the star patterns he had taken on his phone. *Just think of the hands that left these images who knows how many years ago. What were they like? What were they thinking?*

Minutes bled into hours as the day slipped by. Slowly, the desert terrain relinquished its scorching heat to the night's soothing sounds and smells. After completing the last sketch, Jerry closed his eyes and inhaled the scents of the evening's sweet earthy residents—chaparral, sage, and the local desert cacti, with their clean floral fragrance. The sun had dipped into a purple sunset, and a shimmering curtain of light had materialized near the cave's mouth not more than twenty feet from Jerry's tent.

The strange phenomenon burned sapphire blue at its center and white at the edges. Its glistening color beckoned to him. His breath was short. His pulse hummed. Was it a dream or a nightmare? It seemed so real. *Is this one of those supernatural events Joe was describing? There must be an explanation within the laws of nature or physics. Like the aurora borealis, nature has its quirks.*

When he approached the ominous curtain, he hallucinated, or so he thought. A five hundred-pound grizzly rose onto its hind feet, ready to pounce. Jerry stood petrified. It released a low guttural growl, its eyes locked onto Jerry's. Wide-open jaws flashed gigantic carnivorous teeth. Without warning, the massive creature lunged at him.

Terrified, Jerry jumped backward, his adrenaline surging. The beast's warm, moist breath tickled against his neck. Just as he was about to be devoured, the vicious threat dissipated into a gentle mist.

"Aagh ..." His voice quavering, Jerry was unable to speak. His face blanched, and he held his hand over his pounding heart. *Is this someone's idea of a sick joke?* He stumbled around as though he were going to pass out. *How could something so real vanish into thin air?* He sat down, his legs wobbling. *Someone has gone to a lot of trouble to scare people off. But why?*

He rose slowly, turning his head, trying to locate the source of the prank. But silence met his ears except for the distant gurgling of the sulfur spring. After collecting his senses, he approached the shimmering curtain once again, but this time he readied himself for an attack.

For a moment, he froze at the sight of a huge mountain lion just feet from him, crouched and ready to pounce, its gaping jaws wide, its scream bloodcurdling. Fierce, saber-tooth fangs drooled. Beady black eyes just stared. In an instant, the vicious cat sprang toward him.

Jerry squeezed his eyes closed and cringed, his adrenaline surging for the second time. Just when he thought he was the cat's dinner, the phony terror dived through him and evaporated into thin air.

With his teeth unclenched, Jerry stood motionless. Once again, a sparkling curtain of blue light materialized. It seemed permeable. Soaked in sweat, he approached the strange archway with trepidation, his hands trembling.

I don't know what just happened, but there's got to be a logical explanation. I need to record this and follow up when I get back.

He eased his arm through the misty blue doorway and looked around. Compelled to see what was on the other side, Jerry slipped through the glimmering entrance, his heart thumping. A slight tingling sensation shot through his body, and in that instant, an amazing display of the universe burst into view.

"Incredible!"

It was as though he had opened the hatch from a spacecraft and stepped outside into the vast depths of space. Shivers spiraled up his spine. His breath quickened and his blue eyes darted about, soaking up the cosmos's serenity. Filled with the night's residents, a microcosm of constellations bathed Jerry in a spectrum of color. Never had he felt so insignificant.

Spinning neutrons glowed while eerie-looking masses unleashed wisp-like waves, causing a spectrum of light to expand. It was as if he were standing in an IMAX 3-D movie theater debuting the universe's twinkling stars. The stellar patterns presented an orderly arrangement that bordered the constellation Pegasus.

Jerry stood there for a moment, staring at the celestial images in stunned silence. Then, after snapping out of his daze, he quickly took several pictures with his phone, capturing the unique designs offered before him. His head buzzed with questions. *What are you trying to tell me?*

The stars blinked as though they were exposing their divine secrets. But what secrets? What was hiding behind those shining masks of mysteries? Moments later, the simulation faded, and Jerry found himself standing at the cave's entrance like nothing had happened.

Silhouettes of saguaro cactus dotted the horizon like giant pitchforks stabbing the sky. Jerry felt the warm desert breeze on his face. In the momentary pause, his thoughts disappeared into the sulfur springs' distant bubbling and splashing while he listened to the tranquil ambience of chirping crickets.

Jerry lifted his face toward the heavens, the star's brightness reflecting in his eyes, dreaming of a life without financial worries, a life full of happiness, a life free from the chains of debt. *Mandy, I can't wait to bring you here and show you the boogeyman.* Out of the corner of his eye, a streak flashed across the darkened sky like a fireball falling to Earth. *Ahh, a shooting star, a fortuitous sign, one to wish upon. Just maybe my luck is about to change.*

The glint of moonlight shared the heavens with its family of twinkling stars. The curtain of nightfall had descended, the mountainous sounds had changed, and the night's whispers were drifting softly by, signaling that the day had closed.

Mental exhaustion from this extraordinary event stole his excitement. *I can't keep my eyes open.* Yawning, he retired for the evening. *Tomorrow is another day. Maybe I can piece this thing together after a night's rest.*

The next morning, Jerry Humphreys woke to the long sharp song of a pair of vermilion flycatchers. The distinctive bright red birds were a common guest that inhabited the scrub and riparian areas around the Chiricahuas. He rubbed his sleep-deprived eyes and gazed out of the tent flap for several minutes until his thoughts had gathered. It was a hot August morning, and he lay quiet, wanting to sink back into the delicious bliss of sleep, aware of an acute weariness from the previous night's struggle to understand all that had occurred. Exhaling a weary grunt, he pushed himself up and stepped outside his balmy tent.

Jerry paused as he felt the day's warmth surging, filtering down, touching his face. Possessed with a resilient resolve, he focused on the task of discovery. He looked at his watch. It was already ten o'clock. *Man, I guess yesterday really kicked my butt.*

With his notes in hand, he reviewed each sketch and compared it with the images he'd taken with his phone. *My battery is almost gone, and I don't want to hike back to the truck to recharge it.* Jerry drew a deep breath and focused his gaze on the celestial patterns. *There's something here, but what? People have wondered about the stars for thousands of years. Is there a reason for their arrangement in the universe? When we connect the dots, they become constellations.*

Then an impression popped into his mind. *Can it be that simple?* Using his pencil, he placed the constellations he had sketched from the cave in the order seen in the veil, starting with Centaurus at the top and ending with Pegasus at the bottom. *I don't know all the names of these constellations, but if I'm correct, I won't need to.*

Without warning, he became dizzy and nauseated. In his excitement, he hadn't eaten since yesterday afternoon. Jerry wiped the beaded moisture from his face as his stomach churned in protest. *Maybe I should eat before going farther. I feel a little weak.*

The sun blazed overhead while flies buzzed around him, trying to quench their thirst with his dripping sweat. He munched on a dry peanut butter and jelly sandwich, his mind teeming with excitement. After resting for a short time, he fantasized about the cavern's possibilities. *I can't wait to rock the scientific community. Who knows what rare and exotic discoveries await me that will shock the world. I wonder what my friends will say when I unearth some incredible find, especially Mandy.*

Tumbleweeds, alive with the breeze, rolled aimlessly across the dusty desert floor. A lone coyote howled in the distance while the desert's warm breeze brushed against his face. Unable to rest and feeling better, Jerry wrapped himself in a lightweight camel-brown fishing vest that had a lot of room and numerous pockets and then collected the gear he'd need for a safe return.

Armed with his flashlight, he found his way back into the cave, hoping to unravel the code of the mysterious symbols. He hadn't traveled far before his hike brought him to his previous location. *If I'm right, the solution may rest in the order of alignment seen at the veil. But what to do now?*

Jerry ran his fingers over the star patterns inscribed on the gypsum wall, seeking a trigger or some palpable way to manipulate the symbols. When his hand passed over the engraving of the constellation Centaurus, the entire grouping illuminated a bluish hue similar to what he'd seen at the veil.

Startled, he stepped back to assess the situation. *Okay, that was weird.* Jerry pulled his list out and found that Centaurus was the first star pattern seen at the veil. *But of course, all I need to do is follow the order of progression to the last constellation, which is ... Pegasus.*

Jerry touched the engraving once again, tracing it slowly with his finger. A warm tingling shot from the tip of his first digit to the inside of his head as though an unknown intelligence were exploring his thoughts. A euphoric rush surged through him, creating a feeling of intense bliss. *This is incredible ... powerful.* With each touch, the celestial illustrations glowed and pulsed until he had contacted the last constellation, Pegasus.

Suddenly, a blinding blue light erupted from the symbols, projecting a three-dimensional holographic image suspended in midair. Free from the wall of glowing symbols hung a translucent but detailed object that resembled a world globe, and it had irregularities like a topographical map. *What in the geode ...*

Jerry leaned forward and examined the holographic sphere. An interactive grid revealed a series of spatial corridors and subterranean chambers throughout the entire mountainous system. *This is incredible, but what is it for?*

With one bar left on his phone, he pulled out his notepad and proceeded to sketch a one-dimensional diagram detailing the underground channels as they appeared in the hologram. After its completion, Jerry studied the chart and found he was close to another chamber. *Should I go back and get help to excavate this site? By now, the rumor of geothermal gases must be raising suspicion, and soon others will be descending on this place. Man, I wish I had cell service.*

Jerry was torn by indecision. Tomorrow was Saturday, and he could spend the entire weekend reviewing what he'd found. But who was he kidding? There was no way he'd be able to rest knowing that someone could stumble upon his discovery. He had to go now. The last thing he wanted was to return with empty pockets and in need of a bath. *What if I find something noteworthy? No doubt, word would leak out and others would flock to it. This could propel my career into the stratosphere. Finally, I could prove myself and shed the chains of my past.* Once he decided to continue, he inventoried his backpack and was off.

The deeper Jerry traversed the cave, the more unlevel the ground became. Cooler temperatures were met with dampness that hung in the air, making it a bit chilly compared with the blistering heat outside. A foul odor of organic decay filled the passage, giving his throat a nasty taste. Jerry's heart tugged at his chest in excitement.

He found himself scrambling up and over broken piles of loose rock, squeezing between large blocks of stone, trying to remain alert for loose debris that might shift and cause him to slip and fall. Cold sweat dripped from his face.

His flashlight flickered. "Aw, come on. Don't go out on me now." He tapped it against his leg; the beam brightened. *Maybe I should've brought a backup.*

Mice scurried away from his feet, and bats swooped down, startled by his presence. Jerry's footsteps echoed as he marched down the narrow twisting corridor, crunching cave crickets and venomous spiders trying to flee from his path.

A damp breeze smelling of bat guano tempted Jerry deeper into the cave, where he hoped a larger chamber awaited him. It wasn't long before his hike came to an abrupt halt. The trail terminated at what seemed to be a solid wall of weathered rock, suspending his quest. Jerry wiped the beaded moisture from his brow with his forearm and waved the flashlight's beam back and forth.

Encrypted on the stone barrier were the same geometric patterns etched on the pedestal outside the cavern. The skillfully drawn spiral lines, detailed and naturalistic, radiated warmth. Jerry pulled out his notepad and reviewed his impressions. *This is the third time the solstice and equinox symbols have appeared. But why?*

He traced the fine line engravings with his finger, but to no avail. *What do they represent? The summer and winter solstices are six months apart, but so are the spring and autumn equinoxes.* Then a thought flashed through his mind. *They're like the yin and yang of nature, a balance of life, but opposites do attract.*

Jerry touched the two spiral carvings at the same time, using a finger from each hand. Energy shot through him as though he had completed the loop of an electrical circuit. Within moments, the engravings illuminated a bluish hue, and like with the veil outside, a misty blue archway appeared.

He let out a triumphant yell that echoed in the empty corridor, bouncing off the jagged walls and ceiling. A subtle breeze whispered through the cavern, instilling a sense of peace and tranquility. Jerry reeled with excitement and a warm glow immersed his body. Standing at the threshold, he couldn't wait to discover the secret inside the next chamber. Chills rushed over his skin when he inserted his arm into the shimmering mist, feeling the same electrical tingling he'd experienced before. *Yes, just like outside.* Jerry glanced around, drew a deep breath, and stepped through the glimmering curtain.

CHAPTER THREE

THE TREE OF TRANSFIGURATION

The veil quickly faded and returned to its original state of solid rock, sealing his escape. Jerry felt a sudden rush of panic; he'd been so absorbed in his discovery that he hadn't considered the things he may have set in motion, let alone having violated one of the cardinal rules of caving: never go alone.

"Oh no!" His gaze darted around, his hands trembled. Jerry closed his eyes and thought hard. *Why didn't I see this coming? There's got to be a way to reopen this doorway.* His throat tightened while drops of sweat trickled down his nose. *My phone ... my phone.* Jerry tried to call out, but the battery was dead. His thoughts flashed to Mandy. *I've got to get a message to her, but how?*

Jerry swept the room with his light. The rock barrier remained impassable, with no seams or triggers to activate it. Musty air permeated his lungs as he continued to search for signs that would help him escape. Dread cut through his gut like a bad case of food poisoning. *I can't believe this is happening.*

He pounded on the rock wall. His pulse quickened. God wouldn't abandon him again, would he? If only he had confided in Mandy. But how could he have known? How indeed?

"Is anyone here?" Jerry shouted louder, "Please, answer if anyone is here."

A chilling silence infused the chamber, silence except for the lonely echoing of his voice and that of dripping water whispering in the cool, dark cavern. *I'm such an idiot! Why didn't I trust Mandy? If I had left her on the other side, I wouldn't be trapped alone.* Had he engaged in some reckless journey spurred by a sense of adventure, or was it something deeper?

Jerry dropped down on the cold hard ground, his thoughts shooting through his mind like speeding bullets. Ashamed of himself, angry at his stubborn pride, he sat there, arms wrapped around his knees, numb with misery, staring at the sealed stone wall. It was like entering a closet of the earth, slamming the door shut to the outside world.

An hour passed. His legs cramped under him, and his head throbbed. In the quiet solitude of that dingy space, he was lonelier and more miserable then he'd ever been in his life except for the time following his mother's death. Nothing could compare to that. A hopeless shiver rippled through him. Would God demand his life next? The only thing he could do now was to move forward and pray for a miracle.

The combination of stress, lack of sleep, and the sting of remorse merged into a sickening ache in his gut. He shone his light into his pack and rummaged around, hoping to find something that could ease his dilemma. *What's this?* Jerry grabbed the geode Mr. Stubal had given him. Human features embellished the egg-shaped stone. Two small slits resembled eyes, while a curved ridge projected a half smile and a conical-shaped nodule posed as a nose. "What are you looking at?" The half-opened eyes just stared, watching.

Like the geode, Jerry had become trapped in another world, waiting for someone to break him out. He tossed the stone back into his pack and zipped it tight. In his disturbed state of mind, his thoughts could settle on nothing. Jerry swallowed and shook his head, trying to clear his mind. *Maybe I can find another exit, but first I need to leave a message.* He tore a piece of paper from his notebook and with a trembling hand wrote:

Mandy, if you are reading this you know what I have done. Words will never express how sorry I am, but I truly thought this was an answer from God. Unfortunately, it was wrong and stupid. You don't deserve any of the grief and anger I have caused you, and I can only hope you will find it in your heart to forgive me. I will die if I stay here, so I have decided to move forward in the hope of finding a way out. If I get out, I'll never leave your side. I love you so much.
Jerry

He placed a rock on the note, flashed the light into the dismal narrow passage, and started his descent. He had no idea where he was going, only that he had to find a way out, somehow.

A veil of darkness cloaked his capture. It was like walking down a dark and creepy alley without knowing what was waiting. With the blackness came a sense of foreboding, and time, marked by ambient sounds, passed with agonizing slowness.

Incessant dripping echoed like a leaky faucet. Jerry became concerned about the batteries in his flashlight and tried to conserve their power. He fumbled his way through the phantom corridor until an illumination farther down the channel materialized. It was as if someone had flipped a switch.

Where'd that come from? Hope rising, he thought maybe he could find an exit. *Please, let me find a way out.*

His heavy footsteps interrupted an unnerving silence as he hurried toward the light, slipping on loose debris. When he stopped at an incandescent tunnel, his heart sank. It was just an extension of the same passageway. Had he really expected to find a way out? A bitter groan escaped his mouth.

The air was thick and moist, and the interior projected a muted orange glow. A strange odor filtered through his nose. The place was so ominous and foreboding that he could feel it crawling under his skin. Jerry stepped back, unzipped his backpack, and stuffed the flashlight inside. He reached out and ran his fingers over the passage's eerie lining. *It feels like a snake's skin, smooth and scaly.*

Suddenly, the interior came alive. It was as if a den's worth of serpents were slithering inside the walls. His throat tightened, and he gave a vacant stare. What warning did it portend? The channel was just large enough for him to pass through, but did he dare?

Not knowing what to expect, he crept down the spooky corridor, holding tight to his pack. His feet wobbled with doubt. His heart pumped faster and faster. Then, without warning, snake-like appendages shot out from the rippling walls, triggering a rush of adrenaline, fueling his steps through the subterranean channel.

The ground quivered, the muted light pulsed. He sprinted through the passageway, straining to escape injury from the serpentine extensions, his legs becoming heavy. The snake-like projections lashed out at him, striking his backpack. He yanked his knife from his belt and slashed through the deadly tentacles as he ran down the earthen hallway.

Jerry was gulping down breaths, his eyes wide. *Faster. Got to go faster.* An opening appeared toward the end of the tunnel. He leaped forward, tumbling into a chamber with a vertical ceiling of a hundred feet or more.

"Holy geode!" He lay facedown, sprawled out, gasping in relief. Jerry shook as he sat up, brushing the dirt off his vest. He felt cold and lightheaded, his hands moist. Specks of sweat beaded his forehead, dripping into and stinging his eyes. He took a long drink from his canteen, wiped his mouth with the back of his hand, and sighed. "Man, I feel like I'm in a waiting station, one marked for death."

The reality of his decision to enter alone hit him so hard he couldn't breathe. He was lost in a world so foreign he didn't know what to do. What sort of place was this, and what were those horrible things that tried to kill him? Was it a forgotten secret, a way to test or execute people? If so, why? He'd escaped death, but now what?

Helpless and trapped, his mind prickled as though a thousand ants were stinging his brain. He sat silent. His eyes were distant, transfixed on the cavern's shadows. He didn't want to think anymore; he just wanted to go back to his life as it had been before everything had changed.

A faint breeze brushed his face. The hard ground was cold, but still Jerry sat for a long time with his pack held tight, wondering what was to become of him. Mandy couldn't help. She didn't know where he'd gone or that he had even left town. His heart surrendered to hopelessness. It was no use. He would never get out.

His loneliness grew, and his regret ... That was even worse. He had reenacted the events of the day in his mind endless times, thinking how he'd do it differently if he could, making sure this time Mandy stood at his side. Guilt racked his thoughts. She'd warned him not to go, but he was too stubborn. He had to prove he was right. Now he had paid the price ... They both had.

An ambient light beamed down from the cavern's roof as though a natural skylight permitted the sun to penetrate its chamber. A faint pulse echoed drip by drip. Away from the desert's sounds, Jerry resided in an underground world with gigantic subterranean chambers, fanciful cave formations, and amazing features. Slow corrosion had carved out the damp, moldy interior, eroding the calcareous rocks. The limestone, dolomite, and gypsum landscape dominated the enclosure that gave form to his imprisonment. *This can't be real. It just can't be. Man, I feel like I just stepped into the Twilight Zone.*

In spite of his circumstances, Jerry appreciated the natural beauty that emanated from the cavern's life force. Remnants of lava tubes abounded. Stalactites drooped from above like frozen icicles. Mineral-laden water seeped down the inclined ceilings, creating decorative folds that resembled glistening draperies, while delicate soda straws hung like massive chandeliers.

Finally, with his heart calmed, Jerry set up camp and calculated how he was going to proceed. *I should have stayed at the entrance, but now my only choice is to move on, and hope I find a way out.* Time dripped by slowly as he plotted a path to the next chamber detailed on his hand-drawn map.

Passages interconnected between many points, creating an endless succession of obstacles and dead ends. *I need to stay on the main trail so I don't get lost.* His stomach grumbled, complaining about the lack of nourishment. *Ugh, I've guzzled more than half of my water, and I only have one energy bar left.* Sweating hard, he made a plan to conserve his rations.

With a grunt, Jerry pushed up off the ground and put his map into his back pocket. After gathering his things, he stowed them in his pack and pressed forward, drifting along as though he were dreaming, unable to wake up from the horrible nightmare he had entered.

The chamber ran deep underground and had narrowed to the size of an outdoor amphitheater. Slow steps sank into a sandy surface, one after another. Hours later, he stopped when the pattering of a soft rain penetrated his ears. He perked up and listened. Water! Was he imagining that sound? Jerry hustled to the gentle splashing, his shoes flicking silt everywhere.

A waterfall had erupted from the cavern's roof, showering down streams of fine droplets that fed into a colorless spring. He loved the way the spray settled on his arms, like sparkling beads of diamonds clinging to his skin. The clear liquid flowed past the speleothems, reflecting their majestic beauty. It was breathtaking, a natural beauty emerging from nowhere, and it filled Jerry with a powerful urge to explore its route. *Surely, the water must lead to an outside source. If I can find where it empties, I may be able to find a way out.*

Cool, damp air slid down his trachea, filling his lungs with hope. The stream hummed and gurgled as it coursed to an area where unusual flora flourished, but he became disappointed when the precious liquid mysteriously vanished back into the ground just as it appeared. The pangs of hunger seized him as his discouragement deepened. Jerry gazed quizzically at a perfectly manicured garden of trees and shrubs. *Is this some kind of secret underground lab that's not supposed to exist? And where are the people who oversee it?*

Unusual trees flourished in this secluded retreat, some tall, some dwarfed. Almond-brown trunks, patched with orange-tinged lichen, framed the arboretum with a serenity that bathed it in a warm glow. The branches flared and were laden with strange fruit. Heart-shaped yellow leaves illuminated the trees as if splashed with dewdrops from the sun. Cheerful magenta bushes stood in orderly manicured rows. A silky-smooth layer of blue silt caressed each step.

The reflective silence, broken only by the faint whispering of the huddled trees and the gurgling of a tumbling stream, touched a chord of serenity. *How could this incredible world be hidden beneath a few mountains, lost in a time of technology?*

He paused. The air was still ... Nothing moved. Sweat slid down his face, prickling his skin. *I feel like I'm living a fairy tale.* A tightness tugged at Jerry's stomach as he scanned the indoor orchard. He paced back and forth, running his fingers through his hair. *Things keep getting stranger and stranger.* He continued to pace the area, searching for something—anything—that could help him escape.

He spotted a small branch that had broken off one of the trees and lay next to the gurgling spring. He strolled over, picked up the lightweight limb, and removed the twigs and knots with his knife. *Man, I could've used a hiking stick earlier to help with those steep descents.*

Before placing his knife back on his belt, he glanced inside his pack. The geode stared at him with those thin slits. "Are you going to monitor my every move?" He grabbed the stone. *I could use some company.* Using his knife, he stripped a few stems from the surrounding bushes and used them to bind the geode to the yoke of his staff. "Well, Mr.—" Jerry hesitated. "Mr. G, you don't happen to have a key to get us out of here, do you?" Jerry stared, waiting. "Yeah, I didn't think so."

Several hours had passed by now, and Jerry was ill-prepared for a lengthy stay in the subterranean cavern. His food and water had dwindled to nothing, along with his patience. He placed his hands against his throbbing temples, his dry tongue stuck to the roof of his mouth. Jerry sniffed the strange fruit, his stomach growling. *Are these edible? If so, I may not need to worry about my survival, at least for the time being.*

Jerry plucked one of the unusual fruits. They were round like a baseball and had a bluish-green hue. The aroma of a freshly baked apple pie tickled his senses as he passed the enticing piece under his nose. "Wow, Mr. G, I've never smelled anything so inviting." He used his knife to carve it into four pieces. Inside was a green, fleshy center dotted with black seeds. "This looks like a kiwifruit, but is it safe?" He held out a piece. "Want a bite?"

Jerry waffled until he built the courage to taste the sweet-smelling flesh inside. He placed a slice between his teeth and nibbled on the plump fruit.

"Oh, my." His mouth exploded with an insatiable desire for more. "This is amazing. Sure you don't want to try a piece? I don't know if I have ever tasted anything so sweet and delicious." Consumed with an insatiable appetite, Jerry feasted.

"Whoa! What's happening?" An excruciating pain suddenly shot through his head like someone had jabbed a white-hot poker into his eye. "I can't see. Everything is blurred." Bright lights filled the darkness behind his eyes, causing him to stumble and fall. Nauseated, he was about to vomit when the symptoms vanished.

Jerry sat gasping and rubbing his head.

The cavern suddenly darkened and a majestic show of elegance erupted, exposing the shimmering constellation

Pegasus. *What in the geode?* Sixteen stars detailed the noble steed, sharing their bluish-white brilliance, illuminating the cavern with a waterfall of light that stretched across the entire chamber's ceiling. The quivering starlight radiated a warm glow and, with it, a strange feeling of peace.

Jerry sat—watching—unsure what was happening. "How is this possible?" He stood. "Mr. G, I ... I must be dreaming."

Moments passed, and his vision came back into focus like a camera, except now he had enhanced detail and resolution. His body glowed with a radiant aura. Perspiration ran down his cheeks. Everything was sharper and brighter, more so than ever before.

His awareness was enhanced, and his mind was pierced with an influx of data. He sank to the hard ground with his back against a large stalagmite, giving in to the energy that now coursed through his veins. Light returned to the cavern as the star's twinkling brilliance faded. "Oh, my ... It's like ... it's like I have Blue-Ray eyes. The color ... the detail ... My vision is incredible. I guess I won't need my reading glasses anymore, Mr. G."

His mind had expanded beyond anything he'd ever experienced. He wiped his eyes with his fingers. Amazed at the images now seized in his consciousness, he raised up, stupefied. The real world looked washed-out and dull by comparison. Pores in limestone deposits were sharp and clear. Microscopic sediment of calcite crystals trapped in water droplets reflected a yellow tinge. Within seconds, his body changed. Even his smell and taste had morphed into something different. Fresh sensations sanctioned by his mind gave way to strange emotions.

What's happening? I feel like I've been drugged ... Really weird ... Like a euphoria. I need to stop and assess my condition before—

Suddenly, several humanoid creatures materialized, perhaps a dozen or more. Jerry leaped backward, stumbling to get out of their way. "Whoa!" he said, staring at the motionless band of beings. *Can things get any stranger?*

They were about Jerry's height, six feet tall, and dressed in gleaming metallic jumpsuits. Their hair, cut short, varied in color, and expressionless faces exposed empty stares. An icy chill engulfed his body. He stood silent, holding his walking stick out as a weapon. *Am I hallucinating, or is this real?*

A sudden, echoing of a foreign language erupted throughout the cavern, sparking the beings to come alive. The sound was quiet at first but then grew louder, like the volume on a radio was being turned up. His heart raced. *Voices! There must be others down here.* With flesh-like "skin," the automated androids looked and acted like functional, realistic humans except for their misshapen ears and eyes that didn't quite line up. He scanned the chamber. His legs wobbled. "Hey! Anyone here?"

Teams paired up and began caring for the unique refuge, digging and pruning with tools that mysteriously appeared in their hands. A synchronous rhythm and tone accompanied this strange dialect. Jerry watched as he continued to shout. "Hey! Can anyone tell me what's going on?"

The tenor of the speech changed, and the humanoid creatures tossed glittering golden dust into the air, instantly rejuvenating the foliage. Wilted leaves and hanging branches lifted as though a new life flowed through them. Jerry shook his head in disbelief. *This is weird. I feel like I'm in some freaky sci-fi movie.*

As he approached one particular animated being, it exhibited no response. "Excuse me. Is there a way out of here?" Struggling to communicate, he shouted, "Where did you come from? Can anyone help me?" He waved his hand in front of their eyes without any reaction. The automated units continued their work uninterrupted as Jerry shook more fruit from the unusual trees. "Well, at least I have some company for the time being." He continued to scan the area for help, but his hope grew dim.

Now he craved the effects of this peculiar food. Each round treat continued to tantalize his taste buds. The more he ate, the more his mind expanded. Facts that were once difficult to understand now proved simple. His neural synapses sizzled with energy. Information inundated his mind, and his gray matter became supercharged as if he were accessing the universe's conscience. It was a magical moment, a magical moment of change. But into what?

The gurgling spring reminded him he had no drinking water, which immediately deepened his thirst. Jerry grabbed his digital H2O device to check the stream's purity. "Well, let's see how dingy you are." After dipping the unit into the babbling spring, he blinked in amazement. "No way." The device displayed a zero. "Can it be, Mr. G? The liquid is pure, not a trace of contaminants."

Jerry bent down to give his sticky, dry mouth relief. He cupped his hands, dipped them into the cool inviting liquid, slowly brought them to his lips and took a long sip. Even the clear beverage had a unique flavor. With each swallow, his visual and auditory acuity intensified as though he were consuming nectar from the gods. Like a synesthete, he had the ability to link all five senses to his recall.

He now understood the unfamiliar language. As he listened to the synchronized speech, he heard different commands barked out. With each directive, the androids altered their movement, as if programmed to perform specific duties.

All of a sudden, the talking ceased. The humanoid creatures became motionless and then faded from view. "Mr. G, that was weird." Jerry sighed. "Well, here we are, alone again."

For the first time, he felt a connection to time and space, a plethora of possibilities, wherein the slightest action could send a ripple across the universe. A sense of danger flooded his mind, a fear of lost memories, a desire to hold tight to the present.

Despair hardened to a grim resolve as Jerry pondered his dilemma. "Well, Mr. G, I think it's time we camel up." After filling his canteen, he picked several fruits and stowed them in his pack. Then he pulled out the map and plotted a path, hoping to find a way out. Filled with curiosity and equipped with a heightened sense of awareness, he pressed forward, wondering what would happen next.

CHAPTER FOUR

JULEAN, FIRST CONTACT

A steady airflow circulated through a twisting labyrinth of limestone artwork. Thousands of stalactites and stalagmites created a network of beauty in a chamber that could fit two cathedrals inside its cavernous walls. A soft overhead light continued to pour into the cavern from an unseen source. *I don't get it. The ceiling is considerably darker than the floor, yet a certain brightness fills the entire cavern.*

Within minutes, the landscape had changed again, extending deep into the underground cavern. The fresh smell of a bakery turned into a sweaty locker-room odor. Jerry now found himself hiking through a desolate environment, having left an oasis of wonder and beauty.

The ground became uneven, and his steps grated and slipped on a loose, gritty trail. Without color or life, the terrain had converted into a rocky surface, making the path difficult to traverse. Hot gases spewed from the cave's pores, popping and sputtering as though he were inside a living cauldron. A dreary draft raced by him. Harsh shadows made Jerry wonder what dark secrets were lurking.

Headaches, fatigue and aching legs set in after an hour of trudging through the rugged landscape. He stopped, grabbed a bluish-green fruit from his pack, and ate it. Within seconds, increased energy replenished his strength, exhaustion easing out of his sore muscles.

"Mr. G, I feel like I just downed an energy drink packed with caffeine." Jerry shook his head. "I feel incredible, but I sure would like to know what's going on."

He stood, scanning the passageway and wondering if he would ever find a way out. His inability to contact Mandy weighed on him, plaguing him with doubt and hesitancy. Then a sudden strange movement farther down the trail shot an uneasy dread through his mind. *Great. Now what?*

Jerry tried to quiet his shaking but couldn't help feeling a cold chill ripple through his body as the clattering of rocks danced ahead of him. Old lava flows that reminded him of a Chinese shar-pei's wrinkled skin paved the path. He tightened the straps of his pack and crept toward the frolicking figures, avoiding quick movements.

Several black stone-like puppies were romping about with each other. The pups raised their hind ends in the air and slapped their front legs down on the ground, snarling and growling. Exaggerated bouncy movements accompanied silly open-mouthed grins. *No way! They act like regular puppies, wrestling and biting each other. How can this be?*

They appeared to be friendly. Jerry knelt on one knee and stroked the back of one pup, watching its tail whip the air as the others licked his hand. He tried to pick it up, but the stone puppy rolled onto his back, wanting his stomach to be scratched. After rubbing its tummy, he gently lifted the shiny pup and held it in his hand.

Black onyx eyes reflected a naïve trust. On inspection, he determined its geological matrix was fine-grained lava, similar to glass in texture. In the world of geology, obsidian was a common occurrence, but he was baffled by the way they behaved with an organic quality. *How can something made of an inorganic mineral demonstrate properties of a living organism?*

"Mr. G, I guess this is what you would call an authentic rock hound."

From the shadows, two massive creatures emerged about twenty yards away. Finely chiseled rock-shaped wolves with pinned-back ears and curled lips now confronted him. Teeth drooling viciousness were waiting to crunch through bone and sinew.

Standing about three feet in height and flashing razor-sharp teeth, they inched forward, growling and snapping. Their glowing red eyes exuded outrage, and with each intimidating step the menacing canines became fiercer.

Jerry's eyes opened wide. His mouth dropped. "Uh ... O—okay. I meant no harm. Here. You can have the little guy back."

He set the small puppy down and shifted away from the ferocious creatures, wanting to avoid fast or quick movements. At once, the two rock guardians raced after him. Jerry turned and ran. His footsteps pounded the hard rocky path as he rushed to escape the vicious jaws of death.

The hostile creatures sprinted across the dried-up old lava flow, closing in on him like a pair of starving animals, their slobbering jaws nipping at his heels.

Muscles burned, stung, and cramped. Jerry forced his exhausted quads to push harder. Stunned and breathing heavily, his heart felt like it was going to explode. Then he fell.

Huddled in a protective ball, he cringed in anticipation. Suddenly, music flowed from all directions, penetrating the cavern's silence. Like a hypnotic drug, the slow tempo of Celtic flutes and stringed instruments drifted through the chamber, weaving their harmony into the souls of the ravenous creatures. The rock beasts stopped dead in their tracks and lay down.

Jerry uncurled and pushed himself up from the hard ground. He stood bent with his hands on his knees, sucking deep breaths into his lungs as though he'd just run a marathon. The sleeping beasts lay at his feet. He looked around but was unable to detect anyone in the vicinity. A hopeless shiver rippled through him, weakening his legs. Would he ever escape? Come morning, would he be alive?

"I don't know where this music is coming from, but I'm not staying around to find out. Right, Mr. ..." He paused as he spun around. "Mr. G!" His voice shook. "Where are you?" Jerry had been in such a hurry he had dropped his staff.

He rushed back the way he had come, wary of the sleeping wolves. Within moments, he'd found his companion lying on the ground next to a broken stalagmite with glowing red ants crawling all over it. "We okay? Huh?" He picked up the staff, careful not to get stung, and brushed off the swarming insects with an old tissue he'd pulled from his pants pocket. "Were you scared?" he asked as he started back. "Me, too. You know it was the only option I had at the time, so just forget it, okay?"

Jerry's heart was still motoring when he passed the sleeping canines on his way to the main path, clutching his staff tightly. Swirling undercurrents of indecision flooded his mind as he resumed his journey toward the second chamber. He desperately wanted someone to talk to about what had happened. Mandy had always been there to comfort and console him, but now ... he was alone. "Well, Mr. G, it looks like it's just the two of us. Got any advice?" Jerry stared at the geode's thin-eyed slits. "I thought not."

An hour later, the dreary surface had transformed into a soft texture easy on the feet. The air was fresh and clear. Water dripped and echoed throughout the cavern. Roots dangled from the sheer rock walls like long lifeless snakes just waiting to come alive.

A narrow path of smooth cinders and silvery crushed powder ushered the way to a large chamber, its floor reflective like a mirror. Several massive stone columns that resembled the pillars of Stonehenge formed a circle. A strange aura emanated from them, pulling him closer.

Jerry crept toward the unusual structure, glancing around, wondering what other creepy things lurked in the shadows. *This place just keeps getting scarier and scarier.*

Inside the circle of stones, a small beam of white light projected from the cavern's roof down to the glass-like surface. Never in his life had he felt such a gentleness permeate his inner soul. He raised his hand, and his finger gently touched and then penetrated the soft ray of light. *It feels so warm, so inviting ... as though it was alive.*

He looked around and then passed his hand through the beam, breaking its connection. The light flickered and then disappeared, replaced by a tall robed figure. Jerry stumbled backward, his eyes wide.

The man pulled back his hood, revealing long wavy hair as white as a dove and skin that radiated a silvery sheen. His glimmering blue robe displayed the same symbols found at the cave's entrance.

Jerry stood there in stunned silence. His pulse raced while a pair of twinkling steel-blue eyes fixated on him. Finally, he cleared his throat and asked, "Uh ... who are you?"

"My name is Julean. I come from Enif, a celestial body found in the constellation Pegasus." The man's words were tailored and very precise as though rehearsed.

"Enough ... what?" Jerry rubbed the back of his neck, something he always did when he was nervous.

"It's pronounced *E-nif*. A faraway place where lives are changed."

Jerry's throat tightened and his breath shortened. "Ca—can you help me find a way out of this ... nightmare?"

"There are forces outside the perception of reality that are beyond the scope of your mortal understanding." Julean's hands moved in rhythmic gestures as he spoke. "Long ago, our people mastered the powers of the ancients, learning their secrets, secrets that had been hidden for eons of time. Our scientists placed this transition station here specifically to find individuals ... those qualified to learn these powers ... to make the trip back to our realm."

Jerry stood silent.

Julean leaned forward, his eyes fixed. "I help travelers complete the transcendence of their mortal experience to a higher level of life, balancing the scales of their journey with training and assistance when applicable."

Jerry did his best to hide the intimidation he felt. "Whatever," he said, shifting his weight. "I just want to know how to get out of this place. I never signed up for this transcendence stuff."

"You have embarked on a mission that will change your life." His voice was firm and sure. "Seven chambers exist. You must find and break their seal. Each one offers variable degrees of opportunity to improve your overall attributes. You have already noticed numerous improvements in your knowledge and sensory capacities. You must find the seventh seal to transcend to the next level." With an unnerving stare, Julean added, "The only way out is to reach the last chamber. No other solutions exist."

"Wait a minute! What if I don't want to pursue your ... whatever?"

But before he could ask more questions, Julean disappeared, leaving behind a golden pedestal with added symbols and unanswered queries.

"Wait. Don't go. Please come back. Argh. Come on!"

Jerry kicked the ground while a nervous knot took root in the pit of his stomach. Was this his destiny or was God playing another cruel joke on him? He had never ventured far from

Tucson, where he'd been born and raised and lived his twenty-five years, let alone been to someplace called Enif. His body tingled in fear and his hands trembled, reacting as if a snake had bitten him. *Why did I ever enter this hole? I had to be right, didn't I? Jerry sighed. Maybe I can still find a way out.*

Though Jerry was tired and cold and alone, if he was going to find an escape route, it looked like he'd have to go through the necessary steps to find the seventh seal. His gaze was drawn to the images engraved on the gilded pedestal. *Strange—I've never seen these symbols before, and yet I feel a connection ... like I've known them my whole life, but how?*

After reviewing the ciphers, he gathered his things and checked his food and water supply. *I'm okay for now, but what's to keep me from dehydrating or starving to death before I find the seventh seal?*

The shimmering stars, trapped beneath an earthen ceiling, illuminated the chamber with a bright yellow hue. It felt surreal, as if he were dreaming. He had often wished for an adventure to unlock the mysteries of the universe, but he never thought it would be like this—a fight for his freedom, and possibly his life. He was stranded in a world of dirt and rock with little hope.

CHAPTER FIVE

HOUSE OF ILLUSIONS

White calcite crunched under his feet as he traveled deep into the bowels of the earth, wondering if he would become the next missing-person story. With each daunting step, the flicker of hope grew fainter.

Several hours after Jerry had left Julean, an ominous rumbling interrupted the silence. A deep booming sound filled the air, vibrating the earth beneath his feet, causing him to lose his balance and stumble. Stalactites above him shifted and crumbled as though he were caught in an earthquake. He clung to his staff while dodging falling debris.

Then, without warning, an enormous structure erupted from the ground, bursting into view. Before him stood a spacious building layered in gold and silver. He squeezed his eyes shut and then opened them. Was he trying to see things that weren't there? Perhaps it was a residual effect of the fruit he had eaten earlier.

Jerry remained unmoving, open-mouthed. What was this place? He couldn't fathom how an elegant structure like this could exist in a world so far removed. The windows shimmered with the brilliance of polished diamonds. Majestic golden scrollwork enticed and seduced him. The door hung from platinum hinges and opened to a floor that radiated a pearlescent shine. His pulse quickened, and he rushed into the lavishly decorated edifice.

Inside, he stood breathless.

"No way!" He picked up a heavy golden necklace laced with sparkling sapphires, his legs wobbling. Jerry turned, his eyes soaking up every detail. "Mr. G, is this real?"

Enormous amounts of gold, rubies, emeralds, and diamonds packed the spacious interior. Opulence stared him straight in the eye, daring him, flaunting its elegance. Growing up, Jerry fantasized about being rich as a way to escape the harsh reality of being poor. Now he envisioned what life would be like with all these riches.

He shivered as he touched the ornately adorned columns that rose to a cathedral ceiling. With his eyes fixed upward, he marveled at the lifelike artwork that rivaled that of Michelangelo's masterpieces.

Before Jerry left the main room, he stuffed as many jewels and gold pieces as he could into his pockets while he gazed in disbelief at the fortune that was his. With wide eyes, he made his way down a red mahogany hallway ornamented with solid gold candelabras. His footsteps echoed on an elegant white marble floor that led to another richly decorated room, exposing another captivating bounty of beautiful items.

Engraved ivory walls with golden inlays were coupled with stained glass windows portraying floral motifs. "Mr. G, with all this wealth, I'll never need to work another day in my life."

Jerry hustled down another passage, his boots squeaking on the marble floors as he rushed impatiently to the next room. Every time he opened another door, vast treasures besieged his senses. The idea of becoming rich was addictive as the allurements kept coming.

Then Mandy's face filled his thoughts, her long blond hair, her deep blue eyes and thick lashes. A sudden deep sense of loss penetrated his heart, so forceful, infused by so many memories. He stared at all the sparkling jewels, his chest aching. A lonely, empty feeling swept over him.

All the wealth in the world meant nothing if he couldn't share it with Mandy. A tear leaked from the corner of his eye and trickled down his face. He couldn't wait to get away from this barren and desolate emotion.

After locating an old decrepit stairwell, he made his way up a set of rickety wooden steps to a locked door. After a quick glance around, he spotted a gray skeleton key lying on the warped and creaky floor. Jerry picked it up and rubbed his thumb against an engraving that read "Illusions of Reality." *Sounds like an oxymoron, but what else is new?* The key stuck when he placed it into the opening, but after he jiggled it, the lock clicked and the plain unassuming door swung open. A cool silvery light spilled into the enclosed chamber from a louvered window. Cracks and scuff marks marred an old polished wooden floor. Silence muffled the room.

Jerry entered the small cubicle, peeking around. The only item in the room was a mirror positioned directly in its center. *No gold ... no silver. How strange.*

Handcrafted with high-relief carved details, the frame displayed gilded pairs of doves transporting the laurels of peace, a duo of sphinxes beneath a date palm, and a set of griffins. He circled the elegantly designed looking glass, unsure what it meant. His eyes were drawn to a plaque at its base with an inscription that read "Annaei Tempore."

Ugh. Latin. It was my least favorite subject in school. Jerry rubbed the back of his neck. *Though I struggled with the language, I think it says something about reflections of time. But what does it mean?*

Jerry looked hard into the decorative mirror but was unable to see anything. He leaned closer, his face just inches from the smooth, clear glass, staring vacantly. Gradually, the image of a woman materialized. Jerry fidgeted about to get a better view. He froze, his heart racing.

"Mandy!"

She lay in bed, her eyes wetting her pillow. It was obvious she had been crying for hours. Jerry dropped Mr. G and ran his hands over the glass. "Mandy ... what have I done?" Even now he could smell her scent, feel the softness of her face. His stomach knotted in pain and his head throbbed. "What am I going to do?" He rubbed his neck, kneading the muscles at the base of his skull. It had been only a few days since he'd last seen her, but to him it seemed like an eternity.

His lips pressed against the mirror, his knees buckled, and he slumped to the floor, wracked with remorse. Tears fell like drops of rain.

He sat, staring, his mind numb. He craved the closeness they had shared, hiking hand in hand, seeing her bright smile and hearing her laugh. His fist clenched as he let out a strangled moan. "Oh, Mandy ... if I had only listened, you'd still be by my side."

Jerry pulled his gaze away from the mirror, feeling guilty about his actions, but when he turned back, Mandy was in the arms of another man. Unable to bear the thought that the girl with whom he was smitten might actually love another person, he leaped up and threw the mirror violently on the floor. He grabbed Mr. G and sprang from the empty cubicle, feeling nauseated and lightheaded, and hustled toward the exit. *No way was that real. No way!*

Once outside, he doubled over, dry heaves wrenching his gut. Now that he was away from the misery, the impressive edifice started to fragment. All the alluring enticements were crumbling before his eyes, vanishing into nothing. Now, with hope fading, he wondered if he would ever see Mandy again.

He slumped against a smooth stalagmite, putting his head in his hands. "What have I done?" Jerry listened to his own breathing, feeling the dampness seep into his lungs. It was always the same story, the same fate, so close to finding happiness only to have it snatched away.

A sense of loneliness swept over him. His thoughts turned backward, recalling all the years of toil and sorrow. He closed his eyes, angered and stung by the mockery and humiliation fate continued to deal him. Slowly, he opened his eyes and grabbed a fistful of sand. Like so many past hopes, it trickled through his fingers, powerless to hold on to it.

He rose up, clutching his staff tight, his nausea easing. "Well, Mr. G, at least you're real, but now what?" A throbbing head and an aching heart still plagued him. Jerry stared, waiting for a reply. "I know. I know, but I really don't have much to lose at this point, and I can't go back."

He reached into his pack and grabbed a bluish-green fruit and ate it. Within seconds, his head had cleared and he felt rejuvenated. "Man, this stuff is better than aspirin. I only wish it could show me the way out of here."

Summoning every ounce of courage he could, he turned on his heel and rested his eyes on the trail ahead of him. "Mr. G, it's time we resume our trek for freedom." He pulled the map from his pack and glanced around. Within a few minutes, he'd found the path that led to the next chamber.

The floor was a mosaic of colorful stones, a winding trail of red and yellow tiles bordered by massive stalagmites. A natural light continued to emanate from a ubiquitous source, illuminating the way.

Within a short time, Jerry stood at the second sealed door. Would this be the door that would help him escape? A waft of warm air drifted through the cavern but did little to dispel the ache in his heart. If only he could get a message to Mandy.

In front of him was a series of symbols. He was quick to recognize them from Julean's golden pedestal. Jerry hesitated, but without any real options, he touched the inscriptions, one at a time, each emitting a bluish hue.

After he had touched the last inscription, the secured entrance morphed into a misty blue veil. Jerry took a deep breath and stepped through the shimmering curtain, feeling a strange combination of dread and hope.

CHAPTER SIX

ANDROMEDA'S ENCHANTED STAFF

Once he was through, the misty veil converted back into its original rock composition, sealing the passage behind him. A rank, ammonia-like stench similar to urine singed his nostrils. His eyes darted about; he strained to see in a developing darkness that rolled in like a dense fog, cloaking the corridor in a thick pervasive blackness that seemed to permeate every pore of his skin. The air was damp and chilly. Jerry pulled his vest tight, wishing it had been fleeced-lined. His pace slowed to a crawl.

"Great, who turned out the lights? Mr. G, I can't see anything, and now my flashlight won't work." Jerry slapped the flashlight against his leg, but try as he might, the light would not turn on.

Jerry felt disoriented. He reached out his hands and felt his way in the darkness, taking short steps. Gravel crunched under his boots. The distinct squeaking and scurrying of rodents provoked strong memories of the home he grew up in. A chill in his bones made him shiver. *I hate mice!*

He struggled to find his way through the tortuous corridor. Each time he touched the rocky interior, the limestone crumbled in his hands. Tentatively, he groped his way along the disintegrating interior, and after he'd plodded but a short distance, the walls started to vibrate. A low rumbling sound bounced and ricocheted throughout the corridor. Suddenly, the passageway began to collapse around him.

His adrenaline kicked in; panic rippled through him. Jerry broke into a staggering run, rushing through the hallway, tripping over fallen debris along the way. The walls shook and crumbled as he dashed through the corridor. Rocks pelted his body as the ceiling rained down around him; the floor quaked. A visceral, terrifying primal fear seized him: being buried alive!

Jerry banged his head on a low ceiling and fell. In an instant, he jumped up, clutching Mr. G, and took flight once again. Pebbles slipped and scattered under his boots. The billowing dust and the dampness were overwhelming. Dirt flew up his nose and into his eyes. Then a faint light at the cavern's end came into view. With his adrenaline surging, he leaped forward from the death chamber just as the rubble sealed the exit. He landed hard, slamming his head into the ground.

"Holy geode!" Jerry's hands shook and his muscles quivered. He lay on the cold ground with his head throbbing, his eyes closed. *That was way too close.*

A faint light permeated the chamber. Jerry rose up and brushed the dirt off his clothes, confused by what had just happened. In his haste, his phone had slipped out of his pocket, lost beneath the fallen debris. *No matter. Without a charged battery, I can't call out anyway.*

His legs felt weak, a cold shiver shook his body, and his chest burned from inhaling the swirling dust. Fear turned to anger. "Julean, if this is what you meant when you said I would improve my overall attributes, you forgot to add 'if you survive'!"

His face scratched and bruised, Jerry stared into a chamber dominated by stalagmites, stalactites, vertical cracks, and sinkholes. Underground water seeped through porous walls, clinging to and running down the sandstone barriers like a series of capillaries pumping blood.

The cavern's incredible creations helped numb his mind, but he couldn't turn his thoughts off. Like watching an old movie rerun, he revisited his decision to enter the cave over and over, wishing he'd waited for help.

He thought back to his friends, to their smiles and laughs. Would he ever see them again? He recalled the moments he'd spent outdoors, the sun and the hot, dry air on his face, thinking that those days would never end.

"I wish I knew what was going on. I couldn't make this stuff up if I tried." Jerry's gaze turned to Mr. G. "Talk about being born under a bad sign. It's been one crappy thing after another." Mr. G's expression seemed almost human. "Don't give me that stone-cold look. We could've died."

Suddenly, the dimness of the cavern faded and a pervasive mist of darkness seized the chamber. *Great. Now what?* Stagnant moisture hung in the air. A stale taste caused him to clear his throat. The idea of facing more danger made his stomach turn.

In the quiet of his mind, he stood in stunned silence, the cavern's fluids dripping like a ticking clock. Was an alarm about to go off that would wake him from this awful nightmare?

Dread and despair filled his heart. Then he remembered how he had felt after eating the fruit in the last chamber. He fumbled around in his pack, pulled out one of the bluish-green treats, and ate it.

Within moments, his confusion evaporated like a clearing fog. The foul taste in his mouth vanished, and the darkness dissipated, giving way to an infusion of pure crystalline light radiating from the hanging stalactites. Jerry's facial muscles tightened. "No way! This can't be real." He stroked his chin. "Mr. G, how is this possible?"

An aura of awareness preceded him as he resumed his journey. *How bizarre. It's as though I can feel every pebble under my feet like the earth is trying to communicate with me.*

Intuitively, he stopped in his tracks. *What's this strange feeling? Am I reacting to the fruit or—*

Suddenly, the ground collapsed in front of him, forming a large open pit. "Whoa! Now I get it. Mr. G, it's like having a sixth sense."

Jerry tiptoed around the huge cavity, only to fall into a collapsing hole on the other side. He fell headlong down a ten-foot shaft and struck a stone floor with a crash that rattled his senses. Blood tinged his hand when he swept it across his forehead. *So much for a sixth sense.* His head throbbed as debris trickled down on him. He looked about, blinking in the dimness. It was hard to see, but he appeared to have fallen into a small cramped chamber.

His dry, dusty throat made him cough, causing him to flinch in pain. *Ugh, that's going to leave a mark.* He pushed himself up, grabbing his side, and washed the dirt down with a gulp of water. Within moments, he felt his thirst quenched, but now his stomach tightened as he worried about his new dilemma. In the chamber above were endless shafts in which a person might get lost. Had he been swallowed up and devoured by a single mistake?

He pulled the flashlight from his pack and pushed the button repeatedly. Finally, a stream of white light pierced the darkness, illuminating the confined enclosure. *This thing is so unreliable. I should've bought a new one long ago.* He swept the beam back and forth, up and down, until it rested on the pit's ledge where he'd fallen in.

A drop of water splashed against his face as though a tear had just been shed. After wiping his face with his hand, he whipped the light toward the ground, walked over, and picked up Mr. G. "Humph. I should be the one crying, but I am a survivor." Jerry looked up. "Julean, do you hear me? I will survive this!"

Jerry was powerless to climb out of this compact space, but he would not allow hesitation to steal his courage. His flashlight beam extended into the darkness, flickering off the damp stone walls and evoking a feeling of uneasiness. A light breeze brushed his cheek, carrying with it a sweet scent. *Mmm, that smell. It reminds me of the fragrance Mandy wore the last night we had dinner together. She always said a woman without perfume was like a flower without a scent.*

Without warning, a boulder broke loose from the ceiling. "Argh." Unable to speak, he dropped to the ground, his arms wrapped around his head. The massive stone hurtled toward him. He thought himself a dead man, but at the last second the boulder disintegrated, spraying him with a fine mist. He slowly opened his eyes and peered around. Jerry sighed to himself. *This is insane. I don't know what's real and what isn't.*

He rose up, his legs shaking, wondering how he was going to get out. But before he could take a step, a short passageway materialized less than ten feet from him. *Okay, is this real?* The narrow path, lined with huge boulders, led to a set of stone stairs on the other side. He paused to take a deep breath and then forced himself forward. *I've got to get out of this place before it's too late.* Each rickety stone rumbled and shook as he passed by. The thought of being crushed crept into his brain. Then the ground quaked under his feet.

All of a sudden, vines sprang from the ground and began crawling toward him. Tendrils stretched and reached like an octopus, entangling themselves around his leg. He seized his knife and hacked his way through the knotted mass. Once free from their death grip, he leaped toward the stone stairway, securing his safety.

Now, perched on the first step, the roots vanished as if they'd never been there. He scratched his head. "Mr. G, it's becoming clear that things are not always what they—"

His words choked when he saw his staff lying on the ground several feet away. Panic surged inside of him. He lunged forward, grabbed his walking stick, and leaped back to the security of the stairs. "You owe me. I just saved your bacon from an illusion, I think, but now what?"

Mr. G's slit-like eyes seemed to look past him, focusing on the stairwell's outlet. Jerry turned and glanced upward at the sudden appearance of light at the top of the steps. "Okay, let's go." Jerry shook his head. "I can't believe I'm taking advice from a rock."

Up and up he sprinted, taking the steps two by two. But the faster he climbed, the more his escape eluded him. "Ugh, I feel like I'm on an escalator going in the wrong direction."

Fatigued, Jerry slowed his ascent, and much to his amazement, he found that the slower he climbed, the quicker his exit advanced toward him. When he emerged from the stairs, a sudden shock froze him.

Before him stood a woman dressed in a long flowing gown as though she had just stepped out of an old English movie. She was gorgeous, her features perfectly formed and smooth. Her emerald-green eyes had a radiant glow, and her long hair, black as the night and layered and full, fell in loose waves around her shoulders.

Am I dreaming? How could anyone with such beauty live in the depths of these malicious caverns?

Jerry stood in stunned silence, unable to take his eyes off her. The soft fragrance of sweet orchids that he had detected earlier infused his lungs. Her scarlet gown, layered in black with long, rich silk sleeves, flashed mysterious combinations of symbols as she moved. Her countenance radiated a soft, warm glow that transcended anything he'd ever seen. He stared in awe, forcing out every breath. *Am I going mad or is this another illusion?*

"You are neither mad, nor am I an illusion."

"Uh ... um, did you just read my mind?" he said.

"Yes. You will understand in time."

Jerry remained shocked but strangely thrilled at the sight of another person stranded this far down in his dungeon of nightmares. Jerry cleared his throat. Barely able to breathe, he just stared. "I'm Jerry, but who are you, and how'd you get in here?"

"I didn't mean to frighten you, but I am the overseer of illusions." Her eyes locked onto his. "I have good news. You are not cursed or ill-fated, and you're certainly not doomed. My name is Andromeda, and I'm here to assist you in your travel to the seventh seal."

"Overseer of illusions?" Jerry's face twitched.

"Yes, and as the overseer of illusions, I'm here to warn you." Her movements were slow and graceful as she spoke. "During your journey toward the seventh seal, you'll encounter much danger, but also much enlightenment."

"Much danger?" Jerry gave a vacant stare.

"When you unlock the entry of each chamber, you will have the opportunity to progress beyond your wildest dreams."

"I don't understand anything you're saying. Please, I just want to go home."

"Imagine a life free from all worries." She leaned toward him, her eyes narrowed. "Where your imagination is limitless."

"I don't know. So far, all I've encountered are things that have tried to kill me."

"Your life will be free from all wants and needs."

"All wants?" Jerry turned and looked at Mr. G. "No needs?"

"Where your imagination knows no limits."

Jerry laid his head back and closed his eyes. For several moments, he stood in silence. Then he huffed out a breath, "Do I really have a choice?"

Andromeda held out her hand. "I will be assisting you on your journey to the seventh seal."

"You ... assisting me?" Jerry grasped her soft hand in contemplation of her offer. "So, what is it that I have to do?"

"You'll need help in conquering the challenges ahead of you, so please, take this staff and learn its use." Andromeda reached behind her, and with outstretched arms she placed the staff in Jerry's hands. "It's made from the enchanted alder tree, and over time it will become an extension of your mind and body, allowing you to overcome the most difficult trials you may face."

Vanilla streaks ran through the motley brown staff, and its spiraling form reminded Jerry of a DNA strand. Etched into the shoulder-high shaft were intricate symbols and star patterns, and when he grasped the scepter, each one illuminated. The staff felt smooth, and a warmth embraced his hand as he wrapped his fingers around it.

"Oh, that's weird. So, what does it do?" Jerry stared at the glowing images.

"Imagine the connection between a witch and her wand—"

"Is it a magic wand?" Jerry was excited by the thought of possessing magic. "I mean ... uh, you know, it ... it looks like a carved piece of wood I bought at a renaissance festival."

"Perhaps to some, but to you it will become part of your life force. Without it, you will not be able to progress or succeed in your adventure to the seventh seal. The power you will develop and wield is not magic, but a force so strong you will have the ability to do things only imagined in your dreams."

"What do you mean?" The staff felt light, as though it were made from air. Jerry studied the strange markings along its shaft. "How do you turn this thing on?"

"It's called an aether, and the engravings are called anuns." Andromeda pointed to the strange markings on the staff. "They stem from a primordial source that has been in existence since the beginning of time, which is the breath of our being, the very heart of our essence. You will be taught in the order of this power as you progress and learn the Enifian way of life."

"So, is it similar to a magic wand?" Jerry asked, still fascinated with the thought of possessing magic.

"No, no. You will understand more once you have absorbed its energy. That is why you must remain alert as you travel. I can't say any more at this time."

"Does this mean you will be escorting and helping me through these chambers?" Jerry's dimples creased his cheeks as he grinned.

"Not as I am now. I will be with you, though you may not see me." She placed her hand on his shoulder, and he marveled at her beauty. "You will discover specific power-up stations enabling you to learn the aether's ability. Seek them out. Trust in your heart and don't always believe what you see." Then she vanished.

Light continued to beam into the cavern from an unknown source. He stood there, one foot perched in front of the other, staring at the strange twisted shaft. He still didn't understand its implications, let alone the power she said it possessed.

He glanced around. Who was this Andromeda? What sort of person wanders the halls of a crazy, mixed-up world such as this? Like a dream, none of it seemed real. It was as if he were asleep in a world of fantasies, lost in a realm of the unknown, rich with possibilities but also fraught with danger.

His journey, while it terrified him, brought a sense of curiosity. Could he really become all that was told to him? And what about his former life? What would become of that? He would think about that later. For now, Jerry turned to Mr. G. "It looks like you're about to receive a new and improved body." He removed the vines that bound the geode to his walking stick and positioned Mr. G on the yoke of the aether and secured him. Jerry sighed. "If this is what it takes to escape this place and return to my life, then it is what it is. At least she makes this place less gloomy, someone to talk to, something to look forward to."

CHAPTER SEVEN

THE ART OF DECEPTION

With little resolve, Jerry knew he had to press forward. He had no choice but to follow the path before him.

He marveled at the unusual rock formations that regularly changed. *These certainly don't fit any of the specimens I ever studied.* A large cave pool rested by the trail. He'd never seen a body of water so completely motionless, so calm and clear that it was as if the water were invisible. He bent down and touched the still surface, dipping his hand into the glass-like calm. Ripples staggered across the lifeless pool. It was like he'd stepped into another world, a world of unbelief and wonder.

"How can the subterranean cavern's design and terrain vary so much, Mr. G?" Radiant red overhangs streaked with vibrant violet auras emanated a warmth in the cool cavern. Outrageous orange and yellow stalagmites lined the trail as though he were on his way to the Wizard of Oz. But where was the Wicked Witch of the West? "I wonder how much time we have left in our hourglass."

Jerry paused in awe at the surrounding beauty until he caught sight of a small group of geometric pillars bordering the multicolored path. A strong aura radiated from one in particular. Taller than the rest, it beckoned to him and pulled him close. *What a strange structure to find so far down.* He stood there for a few moments, silent and unmoving. *It reminds me of Parthenon columns found in Greece, but how could it be?*

Strange symbols wrapped around it. He ran his fingers over them, his heart pounding. Moments later, several small openings materialized.

Okay, what do we have here?

Jerry studied the slots and the symbols associated with them. *I sense something powerful ... but what, I don't know.* The anuns on his aether began to glow. Then it dawned on him. *Of course—this must be the power-up station Andromeda told me to seek out. But what do I do now?* Jerry looked at the column and then his aether. *Maybe...*

He cautiously inserted the aether into the awaiting slot but was surprised when it ejected back into his hands. "Okay, Mr. G, what did I do wrong?" Jerry reviewed the structure's details more carefully. Once again, he placed the aether in a small opening, but this time he paired its symbols with the column's emblems. A bluish hue glowed and pulsated from the anuns, triggered by the pillar's energy. Within seconds, a beacon of light surged from the glowing staff to the cavern's roof. Jerry jumped backward, his face pale. Mr. G's eyes burned as though they were on fire.

Panic took hold, paralyzing him. He tried to ignore the terror that had seized him, but how? What was he to do? Then he zeroed in on his inner voice, telling himself to stay calm, to breathe, and to trust in the words of Andromeda.

Sweat dripped from his forehead, his breath slowing. The cavern's brilliance faded, and the ambient light returned. More emblems had seared into the aether. He stared at the glowing anuns. They seemed to breathe with him, pulsing with each heartbeat, calming his fear.

Curious, Jerry extended his trembling arm and gripped the radiant shaft. A warm tingle infused his body. *Whew! I feel kind of numb all over.*

"You did it!" Andromeda appeared next to him.

"Agh, you scared the rocks out of me."

"I'm sorry." Her emerald eyes rested on his. "I didn't mean to frighten you, but I need to explain what just happened." Andromeda sought to soothe his tension. "You have just received one of many powers ... a specific power useful for a specific threat. You need to learn when and how to engage this force. But I should warn you: it has limited functions. Since a symbiotic relationship exists between you and your aether, it will take time to master your ability and control." Andromeda pointed to the symbols. "You must learn to merge your mind with the aether, allowing your thoughts to regulate its effects. But most of all, be patient!"

His eyes fixated on her; warm tingles passed through his body. "Can you show me how my wand works?"

"It's not a wand!" She took Jerry's hand in hers and repositioned his fingers on the aether's golden symbols, lightly gripping his hand. "First, you must learn to free your mind and remove all distractions." Her eyes shifted to his, her touch warm. "Now, focus on the aether's energy as though it's a part of your body." She released his hand, slowly. "Once connected, it will do the rest until you have mastered its power."

"What power?" Jerry asked, his voice shaky.

"This energy of which I speak is the essence that drives all of nature. It's the air you breathe ... the forces that surround you. It is you, and you are it." It was as if she could hear his worried thoughts. She spoke, her voice gentle. "Patience. You will understand more as you progress. Practice until it becomes an extension of your consciousness. Listen to your heart—it will tell you what to do. You'll be given more instructions the next time you see Julean."

Julean? Yeah, right.

"Can you stay with me for a while? I won't be a pest." Jerry shifted his weight. "It's so lonely down here, and Mr. G isn't much for conversation. I'd love to have your company, even for a short time."

"Sorry, but I'm not permitted to travel with you during this period." Andromeda looked up and nodded. "Maybe later." No sooner had she apologized than she vanished, leaving him with more questions without answers.

"No offense, Mr. G, but Andromeda is the only thing that makes this place tolerable." Jerry scanned the chamber and then fixated on his aether. "At least I think she's real, but I still don't know how to use this carved stick or even what it does."

Recalling Andromeda's words, he purged his mind of confusion and focused on the aether's symbols. His fingers molded instinctively around its shaft with a strange familiarity. A warmth embraced him like an old friend. Suddenly, the anuns glowed, sending a burst of energy throughout his body.

"Wow! What a rush."

Jerry closed his eyes and tried to envision the aether as an extension of his body. Energy surged through his frame, unlike anything he'd ever experienced before. The air swirled and crackled around him. A sudden burst of light force exploded from his aether, shooting upward. His eyes shot open. It was as if a symphony of flames had immersed the chamber in a theatrical show of brilliance but vanished when Jerry lost his concentration.

"Whoa! Did I do that?" Fatigued, Jerry stared at Mr. G. "It worked ... I think. But I still don't know how to use it." Jerry ran his fingers over the glowing anuns, drawing strength from their power. He was unfamiliar with his current ability and recognized the need to learn its function. Time was shifting, changing around him—he was changing, and this new power intrigued him.

Jerry had run out of food and water after hiking several hours deep into the bowels of the earth, avoiding scattered sinkholes and loose debris. His stomach rumbled with hunger, and waves of fatigue rippled through him. How long had it been since he had a real meal? Would there be sufficient food in a place so removed from reality? If he hadn't been so desperate to prove himself, so intent on taking Mark's bet, he'd be feasting with Mandy right now. If only, if only. Who was the fool now?

Jerry stopped.

"Mr. G, what's that smell?" The sudden fresh scent of strawberries tickled his nose. He lifted his head and scanned the trail ahead of him. A secluded orchard had materialized in a clearing just off the central pathway. *Is it real or is it just another illusion?* Jerry hurried toward the sanctuary, his nose twitching. *Could it be ...*

At the orchard, a small gurgling stream magically appeared from within the cavern's wall, and as in the previous chamber, it mysteriously disappeared back into the ground. A raucous noise echoed in his stomach, reminding him that he hadn't eaten in hours. Jerry's gaze shot to the trees.

Smooth gray bark that flaked off the trunks revealed a mottled, irregular patchwork of oranges and reds. Shaggy-gray convoluted branches culminated in a magnificent display of pink flowers with yellow throats, yielding a candelabra effect.

"Mr. G, I'm so hungry I could eat a—" Jerry paused. The tree's fruit had the form of a strawberry but emitted a bluish-white hue. "Okay, are these radioactive or what?"

He wavered until the pangs of hunger overcame his fear. *Surely, Andromeda wouldn't allow me to eat something that would prove fatal.* He plucked a fruit from the tree, cut it into two pieces with his knife, and placed a plump, juicy slice between his teeth.

"Mmm ... Mr. G ... this is even more amazing than the other." After devouring the mouth-watering delicacy, Jerry had an insatiable desire to indulge in more. "The flavor reminds me of a sweet, succulent strawberry, only with more of a sugary zing."

Once again, his mind expanded with a surge of enlightenment, but this time without side effects. He now recognized and understood a galactic knowledge he'd never known existed, including how the Milky Way had evolved. *So, it is true. Our universe was born from vast clouds of gas and dust, matter organized into celestial creations. It seems so simple yet so complex.*

His body's regenerative properties went into overdrive, healing the injuries he'd sustained from his fall within a matter of minutes. "Mr. G, this is incredible! My scrapes and scratches are disappearing as I speak." Jerry rubbed his eyes. "It's like watching a time-lapse video."

A dry, pasty throat reminded him of his thirst, prompting him to seek relief. Jerry worked his way through the flowering trees, oohing and ahhing at the sanctuary's beauty. Then he caught a glimpse of movement near the sparkling stream and his pulse quickened. Andromeda was kneeling by its edge, pouring something into the water.

Her silky black hair shimmered in the cavern's ubiquitous light, gently moving as though it had a life of its own. She had changed into a stunning red and yellow gown, matching the colorful petals fluttering down from the surrounding trees, her long draping sleeves swaying with every move.

Their eyes met and she rose quickly, slipping the empty vial into her bodice. She spoke before Jerry could ask her what she was doing. "Oh, I didn't know you were here, but I'm glad you are. I just checked the water to make sure it remained clean and pure."

Andromeda had suffused the flowing water with a powerful amnesiac, a slow-acting ambrosia that cleansed the memories of past loves, bewitching an individual into embracing the one they're with.

"Please stay," he implored. "I'm so happy to see you, and I have so many questions."

"First, you must drink." She shot a smile at him. "Then we can talk."

Jerry bent down to satisfy his thirst. He cupped his hands, dipped them into the crystal clear liquid, and lifted them to his lips. Jerry felt the cold spring water slide down his throat and splash in his stomach. Suddenly, his head swirled, his vision blurred, and his thoughts shifted toward Andromeda.

Jerry sank to the ground. "Whoa, is this going to happen every time I eat or drink?"

"No, but there may be times that your body reacts, depending on the circumstances."

"That's exactly why we need to talk." Jerry held his head in his hands as he stood. "What's happening to me? I know my body is changing, but how and into what?"

"You are evolving, undergoing a process that will change your life." She knelt at his side, resting her hand on his shoulder. "You'll heal faster, become stronger, and develop abilities that I'm unable to explain at this time. When you meet Julean, he will tell you more." She stood and smiled. "Please trust me. You won't be disappointed. And make sure you take enough water for your journey." Then she vanished.

"What journey? I have more questions." Jerry plopped back onto the ground, expelling a groan of frustration. Seeing

Andromeda sparked an emotional wave of desire for Mandy. He lay there staring at the stars above, thinking about the girl he'd left behind, wondering if he would ever see her again.

The absence of sound created a strange stillness, not just silence, but a feeling of emptiness, a sense of loneliness. Regret and remorse ravaged his soul for not telling Mandy how much he loved her before leaving, and it weighed upon him. He recalled the first time they met. It was at a school dance. He fell in love at first sight.

A potpourri of fragrances hung in the air, wafting through the gym, but one scent stood out, an exquisitely delicious scent, that of Mandy. Motley Faction was the band. Strobes flashed in the darkened ballroom. Magic electrified the air when she walked into the room. All eyes were on her. Her charm and beauty seduced me the instant I saw her. The music quickly faded into the background, and I just stared. I pushed my way through the crowd and asked her to dance. When I held her in my arms, her body merged with mine. Her every move captivated me.

That night, she captured my heart. I'd never fallen so hard for anyone. Deep inside, I knew I would never let her get away. I had vowed never to become involved in a serious relationship—that was until I met Mandy! Now, here I am ... all alone ... wishing she was here.

Tears pooled in his eyes. He yearned to hold her close, her soft lips pressed against his, telling her how much he loved her. Several days had passed since he'd last seen Mandy. Who could've known life was so fragile, so innocent. In a heartbeat, it felt like a part of his life was vanishing, losing memories and dreams that could have been. Would he ever see her again?

Jerry grabbed a clump of dirt and crushed it in his hand. It was he who'd chosen to enter the caverns alone. He alone! It seemed incomprehensible what was taking place. If someone were to tell him about these experiences, he wouldn't have believed them. Now more than ever, Jerry wanted to complete his journey and return to the one he loved. He pushed himself up and reloaded with food and water, stuffing his backpack with as many bluish-white strawberries as he could.

CHAPTER EIGHT

LYRA'S MUSIC

Night and day were concealed, wrapped within the confines of the cavern. His need for sleep and rest diminished while his energy increased. Days morphed into minutes, and the reflections of time were rapidly fading.

After traveling for the space of half an hour, a soft hiss whispered in the air, ushering in dampness and, with it, a faint tinkling. Out of nowhere, the pattering of rain mingled with the cavern's lifeblood, dripping and echoing throughout. Rays of light emanated from each raindrop, splashing the rainbow's colors throughout the misty chamber. Flashes of greens, yellows, and blues created a visual wonderland.

Jerry quickened his pace as the rainfall became heavier. *How is this possible? I'm inside a cave.* The wind, now whipped into a frenzy, sent stinging drops of rain, like tiny needles pricking his face. Sloshing along the soggy trail, he squinted through the harsh rain, slowly scanning the chamber in search of shelter. Dirt and debris crusted his boots.

He caught sight of a towering stalagmite with a small wooden door and made his way toward it. Musical notes had been carved into it. *I don't know who lives here, but I've got to get out of this weather.* When he pushed open the door, it chimed. "Hello, is anyone home?" Jerry peeked inside.

"Mr. G ... can you believe this?" A spacious, hollow room was filled with all the amenities of home. Pictures hung on its walls. They resembled gnomes. Doll-size chairs surrounded a clef-shaped table. The floor was polished white marble with a streak of green. White and black stairs that resembled the keys of a piano spiraled up to another level. *What is this place, and who lives here?*

Jerry shook the rain from his body, stamped his feet, and stepped inside. The scent of lavender splashed the room and matched the overall tone. New Age flute music filled the air, soothing his senses. Warm orange walls created an eclectic, Bohemian appearance. On the table rested a leather-bound book titled *How to Intertwine Harmony into the Most Ardent Soul.*

Moments later, a small agitated person descended the stairway and confronted Jerry. He had a round body with spindly legs and arms. A pointed yellow hat sat atop his head. Dressed in a multicolored coat, he had long dark braided hair, and it swirled around his neck to the ground. He stood about three feet in height, and his long nose quivered when he spoke.

"Why have you invaded my home?" he asked, tapping his foot on the shiny floor.

"My name is Jerry, and I'm seeking shelter from the storm. I mean you no harm. I'll be on my way as soon as it stops raining."

"Where did you come from?"

"My memory is a bit hazy, but it's usually my overexuberance and rash decisions that get me into trouble." Jerry sighed. "Right now, I'm trying to find a way out of here. But who are you?"

"I'm Lyra, one of the overseers of music." His voice came out tenor with a sweet, musical quality. "You know music can calm the most savage beast."

"Were you the one who saved me from those vicious rock creatures?" Jerry asked, his eyes open wide.

"Yes. Wasn't my tune awesome?" Lyra beamed with pride. "And I can do more with my compositions, given the opportunity. You know, perfect harmony supports perfect melody."

"I'll be forever in your debt for saving my life, but I need more help. I want to go home and would appreciate any assistance you could offer."

"Once you have engaged in the transition, you cannot go back." Lyra's smile drooped. "If you tried, there would be severe consequences, including death. Your only hope is to complete your journey."

"Is there anything you can do to help with my quest? I have no idea what lies ahead of me."

"I'm sorry, all I have to offer is my music, but there may be others along the way that can provide aid."

The pattering of rain had stopped, and Jerry stepped outside. The air was cooler, and for the moment he stood observing the surrounding area.

"Why isn't the ground wet, and what are all these weird flowers?" Jerry bent down. "They weren't here when I first arrived."

"Oh, these." Lyra reached down, plucked a single petal, and placed it in Jerry's hand. "They're apus flowers, which can make one invisible. The effect only lasts for a short time, but it can come in handy."

"How do they work?" Jerry inspected the strange blossom.

"It's simple. Remove the petals and eat them."

"Will it make Mr. G invisible, too?" Jerry held out his aether.

"Anything that touches you will become invisible."

"Wow! How cool is that?" Jerry tilted his head. "Do you mind if I take a few?"

"You can have as many as you want." Lyra picked several. "The amazing thing about the flowers is they last a long time."

"They look like violets but have a strange glow." Jerry leaned over and sniffed the blossoms. "And they smell like sweet lavender."

"Go on, take as many as you want." Lyra nodded. "When the water falls, more just pop up."

After rummaging through his pack, he found several small plastic bags rolled up and held together by a rubber band. He stripped one from the roll, stuffed a handful of apus flowers into it, and placed it in his backpack. Jerry thanked Lyra for his hospitality and left.

He paused in contemplation. Jerry glanced back the way he had come and then at the path that urged him forward, wondering if he would ever find a way out. In the stillness, distant dripping sounds reminded Jerry that the cavern was still evolving ... just like him.

CHAPTER NINE

THE CONFRONTATION

Behind him, it felt as though a lifetime had already passed and before him stretched a trail so long it seemed to disappear into a veil of darkness. Sometimes the cavern felt relaxed, with an open expanse, other times claustrophobic, dark and coffin-like. Clutching his aether and keeping his breath steady, he crept along an ever-changing pathway.

A cold draft licked his face; gooseflesh rippled across his arms. Jerry spun in awe at the emerging chamber. Rose-colored quartz wrapped in gold and silver ingots dripped from the ceiling. Blue sapphires draped the walls along with fire opals and rubies.

Were these real or were they fleeting like those in the house of illusions, deceptions that would crumble and disintegrate after a while? And what good were they if he couldn't find a way out? But just in case, he chiseled a few samples from the walls and placed them in his pack.

A short distance farther on, the colorful array of rock formations faded into a traditional cavern bordered with stalagmites and stalactites. Dark recesses with shallow cave pools bubbled a foul sulfur odor. *Ugh, there's that wonderful smell again.* He pulled a tissue from his pants pocket and held it over his nose. A sudden flash of light shot down from the ceiling to a glass-like surface a stone's throw from where he stood.

Julean!

Jerry was anxious to see him and wasted no time, kicking up dust from the fine silt that coated the trail as he hurried toward the shining beam. Once there, he glanced around and then passed his hand through the band of light, his brain boiling with questions.

Julean appeared. "How may I help you?"

"I have a bone to pick with you!"

"A bone?"

"I'm upset!" Jerry's face was tightening, his lips pressing together, rolling into a thin line. "So far, all I've encountered have been traps and beasts that have tried to kill me! If this is a prelude to what will come, then I want out—now!"

"Let me ask you a few questions." Julean's gleaming white continence gave way to an icy stare, and his voice was etched with annoyance. "Is your time on Earth not borrowed?"

"What are you talking about?"

"None are that far away from death! Wouldn't you like to live longer without pain and suffering?"

"Only a fool would say no."

"You have many forces that struggle inside of you." Julean leaned in. "Eventually, one will prevail."

Jerry shook his head. "I have no idea what you're talking about."

"These forces have to be challenged, fought, and conquered if you are to succeed on your journey."

Jerry shrugged. "I still don't know what you mean."

"What you consider threats may be opportunities to improve your life."

Jerry stood confused. "You mean if I don't find my way to the grave first!"

"Let me ask you"—Julean stroked his chin—"has your ability to reason problems improved?"

"Well, sort of, I guess." Jerry stepped back, rubbing the back of his neck.

"What about your perception of danger?"

"Yeah, maybe some."

"What did you feel as you ran through the collapsing tunnel?"

"I don't know ... Manipulated."

"Manipulated?" Julean's eyes narrowed.

"You know, as though someone seized control of my mind ... like I was on autopilot."

"And what about the staff Andromeda gave you? You have no idea of the force you hold in your hand. This power is not a thing to be taken lightly. Your problem: patience!"

"Will I get to see more of her?" He let his anger slowly subside and allowed the thrill of seeing Andromeda to invigorate him.

"She will be assisting as you develop and progress toward your destiny. I can tell you—"

"What destiny? I need to know what's happening to me and why I'm here."

"The process you are going through is a complex transformation of body and mind." Julean leaned toward Jerry, his stare ardent. "Only the most valiant can complete the journey. Your physical composition will have changed. Sickness and pain ... gone." Julean's eyes twinkled, his voice softened. "You will have the opportunity to become like the ancients, living thousands of years. You will never want again!"

Silence engulfed Jerry as Julean circled him.

"You will develop powers and abilities beyond your imagination, things incomprehensible to you now."

Jerry's facial muscles went limp, his voice weak. "This all sounds fascinating, but what if I can't reach the seventh seal?"

"That is why I will be working with you to perfect your abilities as you progress." Julean's voice strengthened. "My purpose is to make sure you have the necessary training to reach your goals. Each chamber provides the essential food and water to assist in your transformation, and there will be those along the way who can help with your journey, giving you the opportunity to gain from their wisdom."

"This is a lot to take in." So many thoughts were running through his head. "What about the life I left behind. Will I be able to go back?"

"Your life will have changed. Your desires will be different."

Jerry remained tied to his past, but with his memories of Mandy quickly fading, the prospect of living hundreds of years was becoming attractive. Was he ready to give up his life in Tucson and pursue a life that promised a paradisiacal world free from pain and suffering but held hidden dangers?

"I definitely don't want to be trapped down here forever." Jerry sighed. "So what do I need to do?"

"Don't believe everything you see or hear," Julean said. "You are changing as we speak. Trust your senses and skills. Your challenges are going to become more difficult as you progress. One must stumble and fall before he gains experience, but with each obstacle conquered, you will gain wisdom and power. Together, we will have the opportunity to work on improving your capacity to master these trials."

"I still feel uneasy about all this." Jerry's mind squirmed with doubt.

"Give me a chance to win your trust." Julean held his hand out. "Today, we begin your training."

Jerry paused before taking his hand. "What choice do I really have?" That was it then—he would leave the world he knew and all those who were linked to him. There was no turning back. But what now? What really awaited him? If he made it to the seventh seal, perhaps he could figure things out from there, but he dreaded the journey.

A smile popped up on Julean's face. He warned of concealments, deceptions, and decoys that plagued the pathway to the seventh seal. After spending the better part of an hour explaining and reviewing the actions of Jerry's aether, he said, "Learn and perfect your skills. You will need them. Remember, the most worn trail may be the easiest but not necessarily the best." Then he vanished.

Jerry still felt a woeful weight on his heart. He stood torn between wanting to return home to his friends in Tucson and wanting to pursue a utopian life, existing for thousands of years in a place he knew nothing about. The thought of living without needs or wants touched a sensitive nerve in his heart. Did a great destiny await him, or was this just some foolish dream?

He was overwhelmed by his experience with Julean and felt like he was drowning in his thoughts. *How many people have walked these same trails, leaving their life behind them? What happened to them? How many made it? What if I don't?*

From the moment Andromeda had tainted the spring's drinking water with a powerful amnesiac, his memories of Mandy had been fading, like stars running out of hydrogen, collapsing and dying, swallowed up by the immensity of space. He began to accept his evolution, enamored with the thought of living longer, and vowed to reach the seventh seal.

CHAPTER TEN

MANDY, THE DISTANT MEMORY

The stars beamed overhead, casting the cavern in silver. The trails splintered off the central path like tunnels in an anthill. Jerry stopped frequently and studied the routes on the map he'd drawn, trying to visualize the pathways in his head. He was developing the capacity to connect with his conscience and sense what he wasn't seeing. In his mind, Julean's words echoed: "Trust in your innate ability."

In spite of his newfound skills, he was lonely. Things seemed foreign. The want of closeness, the need of a warm heart weighed him down. "Why me? Why indeed?" Jerry stared at Mr. G. "Hey, don't give me that look! You're no help."

"Would you like some company?" Andromeda asked as she appeared next to him.

"Yes!" He spoke so fast he could hardly get his words out. "I'd love your company. I feel lost, and I still don't know what I'm doing. Isn't there anything you can do to help?"

"Whoa! Slow down." Andromeda flashed a daring smile. "I'm here to assist with your journey to the seventh seal." She touched his hand. A spark of emotional energy shot between them. "You have embarked on a mission that is going to change your life. I'm sure Julean has mentioned some of the things that await you."

"Only that I will live longer without wants or needs." His pulse quickened as he gazed upon her sweet face, her long black hair glistening under the cavern's ubiquitous light.

"Imagine a life full of freedom." Andromeda took his hand in hers. "Freedom to do things you never dreamed of."

"So ... are you going to be there? You know—" Jerry's heart hummed. "I feel relaxed when I'm with you." For a brief instant, they were lost in each other's eyes.

"I, too, feel a connection, but you must not lose focus on your goal." She blushed as she caressed his hand. "I'm excited to help with your transition and look forward to our time together."

"Can you tell me more about what is happening to me?" Jerry asked as he moved closer to her side.

"I'm limited on what I can say, but the fact you are here speaks volumes about you. Fear prevents most from entering the cave. Only the most daring and intrepid take a chance." Her eyes penetrated his. "But you ... you have qualities I have seldom seen."

"What qualities?" His face drew close.

"You have an innate gift that cannot be taught. Your knowledge, your physical conditioning, and your ability to adapt are remarkable." *Plus, you're really cute.* "Your potential will take you beyond anything you ever dreamed."

"You know, I keep hearing about my future possibilities, but honestly, I don't understand what that means. What's going to happen once I reach the seventh chamber?"

"I can only review the things you've gone through thus far, but you must believe me when I say you will not be disappointed." She tilted her head and smiled. "Patience. I have a feeling you and I are going to become good friends."

She had other plans now that Mandy had become a distant memory—oh yes. It would take time for him to fall in love, but like the slow grains of sand filtering through an hourglass, time was on her side, and no one could stop her.

CHAPTER ELEVEN

OPHIUCHUS

Jerry resumed his trek toward the third seal with his thoughts drifting toward Andromeda. More than once, he recalled her soft touch against his skin, her charming smile, her glistening black hair resting on her slender shoulders. Everything felt new, and he wanted to soak up every sweet moment of it. Nothing he did removed her from his thoughts until he came to an abrupt halt, nearly falling into a massive chasm.

"Whoa, Mr. G." He lurched backward. "I guess we need to pay more attention to where we're going."

Jerry inched his way to its edge and stared down into an immense blackness. The clacking of rock debris tumbling into the enormous gulf echoed a warning of death. A ghostly breeze shivered across his cheeks as he explored the surrounding area. No way could he pass over this huge hole. He sat down near its fragile lip and stared into the nothingness, mesmerized by the caverns echoing sounds.

Trust in your heart.

Perched on the edge of the chasm, he slipped into a trance, his eyes closed, oblivious to the passage of time, gripping each thought like studs on an ice cleat biting into a slippery glacier.

Suddenly, his eyes popped open. Just feet from him an obscure translucent bridge became visible, spanning the expanse. Was this real or another attempt at deception? Jerry stood and placed one foot on the lucent crossing, causing it to illuminate.

"Okay, Mr. G, this seems real, but how stable is it?" Jerry took a single unsettling step onto the first segment. His weight caused the bridge to sway as though it were on a rope. Clammy hands held tight to Mr. G. "I hope you're not afraid of heights."

He exhaled a slow breath and began walking across the wobbly bridge feeling like he could fall at any time. Like a high-wire artist, he used his aether as a balancing rod. The links seemed to hold his weight, so he continued to cross the dubious overpass. With each step, more sections became illuminated until he reached the end. "Phew, I guess we bridged that gap, but now what?"

The instant he stepped off the last segment, the connection vanished behind him and the cavern dimmed. A bitter odor permeated the chamber while a mossy slime plagued its interior. Stalagmites resembling venomous rattlesnakes bordered a narrow, convoluted trail. Jerry bit his lip, and his eyes darted about. *Do more snakes await?* Then he spotted the next entry. It was less than a hundred yards away, and he hurried to it, slipping and sliding on the slimy surface.

He scanned the sealed wall, hoping to find the symbols that would open the next chamber. Stretching his left arm above his head, he brushed off the moss that covered the rock face. *They must be here somewhere under all this grunge.*

Gradually, several markings materialized, but he didn't recognize any of the engraved images. His heart tumbled. *Great. Now what do I do?* Jerry stood helpless, wiping his hand on his pants. Somehow, he'd missed the signs along the way and had to backtrack to find them.

He slapped a ruddy limestone stalagmite in frustration, wishing Andromeda were there to help. *She did stress the importance of staying vigilant. I can't become lazy in this place. If I do, it could cost me my life.*

A faint hiss wheezed through the cavern as he turned and started back, making short stops, poking in and around the stalagmites, seeking clues. An unsettling silence followed him, sending a tremor through his body. Jerry tried to swallow, but his throat was too dry.

He stopped at a broken boulder, reached into his pack, and pulled out his canteen. When he tilted his head back to take a long gulp, he caught sight of a strange spiral column hiding behind the huge stone. A spark of courage pushed him forward, and he placed his canteen back in his pack and crept toward the unusual form, his heart racing.

The coiled structure was a little shorter than Jerry, and its opaque surface distorted strange symbols that hid inside it. Several slithering snake motifs animated its exterior, poised to strike. He warily circled the artifact, eager to find a way to unmask its secret. Then he paused. *What else are you hiding? Something inside is—*

A powerful feeling interrupted his thoughts. Without thinking further, his hand shot out and tapped the spiral pedestal. The hissing serpents scattered and disappeared inside. The stand quivered.

"Oh great!" Jerry's legs went weak, his eyes wide. "Now what?"

Slowly, the configuration molted its outer covering like a snake. The convoluted form slinked toward him, morphing into a strange creature with a snake-like body. Jerry slipped and fell backward.

"I am Ophiuchus," the creature announced with a chilling low rasp. "What do you seek?"

Shocked that the creature could speak, Jerry stood and replied, "I'm seeking the symbols to the third seal."

"No one shall pass through without an offering." Ophiuchus rose up hissing, flashing a dark diamondback pattern that ran the length of its shiny, smooth olive skin. Its vertical black eyes stared unflinchingly at Jerry. Two yellow crescents at the corners of its mouth oozed lethal venom.

Jerry's face paled and he swallowed hard. "I ... I don't have an offering."

"Then you will be the offering!" Ophiuchus lunged forward, fangs protruding, hissing and striking.

Jerry's bewilderment and disbelief quickly turned to terror. He turned to run, but where? Behind him remained the dark chasm, which would mean certain death if he tried to cross it. A knot that had formed in Jerry's stomach suddenly moved to his throat, tying his voice into silence. He spotted a large boulder and ran to it, his legs wobbling. Crouched behind the protective stone, his breathing became shallow and erratic. He struggled to remember Julean's counsel. *How can I unite my mind to my aether with this thing trying to kill me?*

Ophiuchus coiled around a jagged stone and hurled the deadly object toward him. The rock shattered against the boulder. Jerry rose. Sweaty hands cleaved to his aether as he envisioned a force surging from it, striking the creature dead.

Nothing!

"Once I embrace you with my death grip, it will be your last breath." Ophiuchus aggressively snaked toward him, closing off any escape. Its eyes burned with an intense rage. Its teeth clenched, yellowed with age.

Trust in your heart.

The slimy creature was about to strike again when a powerful surge erupted from Jerry's aether, enveloping Ophiuchus in an incendiary wave of pure energy.

Naïve to the power he held, Jerry gasped in shock. "Incredible!" His body shook. Sweat poured from his face. "Mr. G ... that was unbelievable!" Every fiber of his being felt alive as if an explosion of energy had shot through him.

Wrapped in an array of sizzling energy, Ophiuchus was decomposing like acid on metal, leaving behind a sparkling crystalline column.

His heart pounded. *I'm tingling as though my blood is rushing back into my veins.* He exhaled a deep breath and looked at his aether. *This power—just what is it?*

A trembling finger reached out and touched the column to make sure it was harmless. Yes, it was dormant. He groaned and covered his eyes with his left hand. He had to learn to use and control this power, whatever it was. Only then could his questions be answered.

Jerry watched as new symbols were unmasked, similar to what he'd seen at the sealed entry. He now had the keys to open the next gateway and scrambled toward it, slipping and sliding on the mossy ground.

Once there, he lifted a shaky hand and began touching the inscriptions one by one. As he touched the last one, he let out a heavy sigh. Suddenly, the wall morphed into a misty blue veil.

Despite his inexperience, he'd killed Ophiuchus. But what danger lurked in the next chamber. Would Julean's training see him through?

With his eyes closed, he drew a long breath and stepped through the shimmering curtain, fearful of what might lie ahead.

CHAPTER TWELVE

ANTILA AND THE AQUARIANS

A sense of danger descended over Jerry when he peered into the next passage. The air was thick with a nasty putrid odor. His eyes burned. A strange glow emanated from the limestone formations. He stood motionless, facing a gallery crowded with sharp stalagmites and stalactites that looked like voracious jaws of teeth just waiting to devour him. Glistening water spiraled down the threatening spikes like drool on a lion's fangs. A pernicious gurgle rumbled deep within the cavern's throat.

Great! Am I to be eaten before I even get started?

He eased his way through a chamber that quickly narrowed into a tunnel-like passageway not more than eight feet tall. The rocky interior was changing. The stalagmites and stalactites were disappearing, leaving a corridor of mucus-like secretions oozing from its lining.

Jerry lowered his aether and pressed Mr. G against its gooey surface. A clear fluid trickled through its protective sheath, bubbling and emitting yellow smoke. Not far from him, several fizzling rodents were decomposing, their flesh liquefying. *I may have avoided death by Ophiuchus only to have been swallowed and eaten by a living gastric pit.*

He watched as a thick, serous liquid dripped throughout the passage. A few caustic drops fell and splattered on his neck. "Ouch!" He winced. "My skin is on fire." He rubbed the back of his neck, trying to wipe the acid-like substance off. "Mr. G, this really stings and burns."

Time was running out. His clothing was breaking down from the dripping acid, and it wouldn't be long before he joined the other victims. Sweat trickled down his face; his pulse throbbed in his throat.

No way could he get through the passage before the enzymatic emulsion consumed him. He was trapped. Somehow, there had to be an answer, but what? He blinked and shook his head, recalling the words of Julean. *Relax your mind. Allow your thoughts to guide you.*

He closed his eyes and fixated on his dilemma. A chill met his face as his vision opened to a different view. The slender hallway had taken on an altered appearance.

"Holy geode, Mr. G. Do you see what I see?"

The digestive juices were rolling back, offering a clear path. Too often did Jerry's emotions guide his steps when his eyes could not see, but not this time. This time liberated eyes led the way.

He shifted his feet frequently, avoiding the acidic hazard, listening to the thoughts of his mind as though an invisible force were forging a path through the tunnel of death. He wished he could sprint through the corridor but knew that would be reckless. Each juicy step was like a suction cup that sank deep into the soft lining. He neither paused nor looked back as he made his way through the mushy trap, his heart racing, his palms sweating.

Moments later, a light appeared not far from him and his spirits lifted. With the end in sight, he hustled to the exit, his thoughts focused on survival. Finally, he stepped out of the gastric chamber, free from its lethal acid.

The tunnel opened to a large room filled with limestone columns, flowstone, stalactites, stalagmites, and mirrored pools. Copious amounts of light continued to penetrate the cavern, reflecting off the glistening forms.

Jerry sighed in relief, grabbed his pack and sat down. He inspected his clothes and found only minor damage. Scratching his head, he marveled at the aether's resilience to the acid.

"Mr. G, that was incredible." He stared into the geode's tiny slits. "My head felt flushed as though a calming storm took over, enabling me to see past the debris that cluttered my thoughts. My body acted on its own...like I was the passenger." Yawning, he set Mr. G down by his pack. "I wish I had a bed where I could get a good night's sleep."

Jerry lay down on his stomach with his chin clasped in his hands, the past events swirling in his mind. He closed his eyes, thinking he would rest for only a few minutes, but fell asleep.

Hours later, Jerry woke to sprays of cool water splashing against his face. The air was alive, fresh and pure. He lifted his face from the cold, hard ground and forced his eyes open. Where was he? Tiny winged creatures were orchestrating the most amazing aerial display of air and water he'd ever seen. He sat up and rubbed his eyes. *Have I awakened to a dream?*

Magical fantasies of characters came to life in a veil of mist. Just like the images seen at Disneyland's *Fantasmic!*, the fanciful shapes ranged from exploding clouds to winged serpents bursting into fountains of yellows, blues, and greens.

These small entities resembled tiny fairies, each one dressed in multicolored apparel. One little sprite darted toward him and asked, "Who are you?"

"My name is Jerry, but who are you?" He rose and looked around. A multitude of tiny persons hovered above him.

"Antila is my name, and we are Aquarians." The little pixie buzzed above him. "We control the water and air in our world." Antila appeared to be perplexed. "Are you proficient in all the ways of an Enifian? You're not arrayed in the usual dress of an Enifian."

"Who are these Enifians and what do they dress like?"

"Surely, you have met Andromeda." Antila threw his head back and boasted, "She is the overseer of illusions."

"What can you tell me about her?" Jerry's eyes grew wide. "You know, the two of us have become quite friendly."

"If you are so close, you know more than I. If not, you will learn more in due time." After offering his adieu, Antila addressed the Aquarians, and they faded away deep into the chamber.

"Well, Mr. G, I didn't get a chance to introduce you, but at least he didn't want to eat us."

Before Jerry resumed his journey to the next seal, he turned and looked back from whence he'd come. The tunnel's mouth had become dark and cold. He shuddered at the thought that he could've been killed. Jerry had suffered through many misfortunes and indignities in life, and he wondered if his luck was about to change.

CHAPTER THIRTEEN

THE KISS

A bioluminescent chamber of various plants, stalagmites, and stalactites created a strange wonderland of blinking and twinkling forms. A golden mesh of mucus threads and spider webs netted the structures together in a glowing display of color. It was as if he'd become immersed in a living fairy tale.

Out of the corner of his eye, he caught sight of a translucent column pulsing a soft blue light. Its calming energy stood out among the other luminous stalagmites that lined the trail. The fluted shaft was similar to what he had found in the previous chamber, except smaller. *Another power-up!* His fear eased, allowing the thrill of the quest to excite him. *Just think what I could do with all this power. All those years that I felt like I had a target painted on my back ... those years that I felt alone and helpless. What would they think of me now?*

Jerry explored the crystalline pedestal and detected several symbols that matched the anuns on his aether. *Aha, this slender structure has the ciphers so close together. It's a bit confusing.* He tried to place his aether in the opening, aligning it with the column's symbols. But try as he might, the heavily adorned shaft wouldn't fit into the matching slot. After wasting the better part of an hour tromping around looking for a way to access the column's power, he kicked at the dirt and sighed. *Why must everything be so hard?* Just as he was ready to leave, sweet orchids scented the air, and then Andromeda appeared.

"Giving up so fast?"

"Oh, I'm so glad you're here." Jerry's countenance brightened, and his dimples deepened as he flashed a wide smile. "You know, I've studied the symbols on the pillar, but when I tried to place my scepter into the matching slot, it wouldn't fit."

"Things may not always be what they appear." Her eyes rested on his; her voice was gentle. "Did you first activate the symbols in the appropriate order on your aether?"

Jerry examined the anuns and then touched the images in the sequence shown on the pillar. Instantly, the aether shrank. He quickly inserted the smaller shaft into the appropriate aperture, and within seconds it started to glow, filling the cavern with an iridescent yellow.

Rays of light erupted from Mr. G's eyes, shooting a laser-like beam into the chamber. Jerry watched in awe as more images formed on his aether. It was as if an invisible finger were burning the enchanted anuns deep into its shaft.

Jerry drew an anxious breath and pulled it from the pillar, holding it tightly in his hands. The aether, reduced in size, came to his shoulder, but the convoluted curves still had a DNA appearance. Its smooth texture emanated a warm glow and molded to his hand as though it were becoming a part of his very essence. He stared at it, riveted by its beauty.

"What now?" No sooner had he asked the question than he became lightheaded. "Whoa, everything is spinning. I feel like I'm going to pass out." Jerry released the aether and abruptly sat down with his head between his legs. "Phew, was that supposed to happen?" Jerry shook his head. "I almost blacked out!"

"No. You're okay," Andromeda said as she rushed to his side.

"Man, I feel like I just got smacked," Jerry said, rubbing his head.

"Relax. I'm here to help."

"You forgot to tell me to buckle up."

"You're fine."

"If this is going to happen every time, you can keep your power." Jerry stood, still rubbing his head.

"Relax. You're past the hard part." She giggled.

"What's so funny?"

"You are."

"I'm not laughing."

"You're so dramatic." She continued to giggle. "Was it really that bad?"

"I guess not." Jerry realized how much he had missed that sound. He calmed. Her dazzling smile and cheery voice made his heart race. "I'm sorry. It's just that things are moving so fast, and I still don't know what's happening to me."

Andromeda was quick to explain the acquired properties and effects now available to him. "As you progress, your body will change with each power-up. Your innermost essence will experience modifications. The column will transfer its power to you each time you place the scepter in one of its slots." She took his aether. "You must allow your mind to coalesce with your aether if you are to master control of its full potential. Once you can do this, you will be able to do things only imagined in your dreams."

"I don't know. I have pretty crazy dreams," Jerry said, stroking his face.

"Your transformation will progress until you experience the same powers, emotions, and abilities as mine." Andromeda was intense. "Your response may vary depending on the station. You need to understand—each power-up yields a different capability, so you must be prepared to accept its transference."

They spent the next hour talking about what life would be like and the amazing adventures he would encounter. Andromeda began to fill his void of loneliness. Jerry was falling in love with her, his memories of Mandy having faded, locked away in the deepest recesses of his mind.

"Can you stay with me as I journey to the next seal?"

"Unfortunately, I can't. As the overseer of illusions, I am strictly governed, and our rules limit my interference. I will suffer severe consequences if I try to intervene more than permitted. But I'm confident in your ability to succeed and will help when able. Remember, seek out Julean and follow his advice."

Once again, Andromeda vanished, but before leaving, she flashed a flirtatious smile and winked.

Jerry no longer needed to consult the map he'd drawn, having memorized its details. Focused on finding the fourth seal, he was back on track, wary of the paths that lay ahead. *It's obvious my journey is becoming more treacherous, longer, and more fatiguing with each chamber, but what about Andromeda? How much can she help? What did she mean when she said—*

A rumbling belly interrupted his thoughts. *Ugh, my stomach has been growling in protest for the past hour. I'll need to ration my supplies if I don't come across something soon.*

Then his ears perked up. *Is that ... water?* He scanned the chamber. In the distance, another multicolored oasis came into view, flaunting magenta bushes, a small orchard, and a soft, bubbling spring.

"Yes! I'm so hungry I could eat a rock. No offense intended, Mr. G." Jerry grunted and rushed toward the secluded orchard, his mouth dry.

Each tree brandished a rich, shiny mahogany-colored bark that drooped with contorted branches. Clouds of pure white blooms smothered the limbs, and jasmine scented the air. But where was the fruit? Jerry lifted the floral cover and unveiled its offerings.

"Aha, there you are." He plucked one from the low-hanging branch and inspected it. "Interesting, I've never seen a star-shaped fruit before." He turned to Mr. G. "I wish you could taste it first." He hesitated but then bit into the bright yellow produce, hoping for no side effects. "Wow!" A thick fleshy outer layer covered a sweet, delicious inner core that had a hint of jasmine. "The flavors just keep getting better and better."

Jerry feasted on the succulent fruits, devouring them with a voracious appetite. An immediate surge of power and physical strength rushed in and engulfed his lifeblood. *My skin feels really tight, like it's going to explode.* Jerry flexed his arm. "Mr. G, I feel pumped up, as though I just worked out."

Each time he bit into the cavern's unique produce, he sensed changes in his body and mind, as if he'd consumed a magic elixir. His perception of life was changing. His hopes and desires now rested on his transition, one that included Andromeda. It was as though Jerry were surfing the wave of time, sometimes on its crest, sometimes on its face, leaving his past behind him in its wake.

"So, Mr. G, whaddya think of my secret garden?" Jerry turned, admiring the scenery. "My thoughts exactly."

He bent over and drank from the spring, quenching his thirst. *Even the water tastes sweeter, and it has a minty fragrance to it.* After taking another long swallow, he filled his canteen, stood up, and looked around.

An infusion of emotion began to fill his body, an emotion that was changing, becoming more intense, more passionate. He found himself thinking of Andromeda more and more. It was like he'd been sucked into a black hole of amnesia, his memories of Mandy erased. Now more than ever, Jerry wished Andromeda were there in person.

"Andromeda, are you here?"

"Yes, I'm here!" Flaunting a playful smile, she appeared next to him, close enough for their lips to touch—if he dared.

He studied her face, his eyes gazing into hers, allowing them into his heart. It was as if he were trapped inside of a breathless moment, unable to resist her charm and beauty.

Jerry gently touched her face. He watched the flutter of her eyelids, the movement of her chest, her smooth, silky skin. His heart thumped like he was a kid on his first date. Reacting to each tender stroke, her face flushed as she allowed herself to be pulled close. Their eyes locked, and with a passionate craving, Jerry clutched her in his arms. His chest pressed against hers. Her pounding heart reverberated, merging with his, beating in unison, becoming one. His warm breath caressed her neck. She lifted her head with a submissive stare. A tender breeze exhaled throughout the cavern. The air was supercharged. Then, their lips touched.

The expanse erupted into an aurora borealis. Gentle crackling mingled with a soft hiss. The cavern was like a shifting waterfall, immersing them in a fiery swirl of emotion. Jerry had fallen in love with Andromeda. As their lips intertwined, he hoped the moment would last forever. Their passion seemed like an eternity. Enveloped in a euphoric aura, they held each other in complete bliss.

"I've wanted to do that for a long time," Jerry said, feeling somewhat embarrassed. "I hope you aren't upset. I mean ... I—"

"I didn't think you were ever going to kiss me. I've been waiting for you to decide if you were interested or not," Andromeda gushed, her emerald eyes bright.

Jerry was surprised at her forwardness but breathed a sigh of relief, having been afraid she might reject him. "I don't know much about you or where I'm going, but I'd love to get to know you better."

"I only have a limited time that I can spend with you but will give you what I can."

Jerry felt like he'd just found a missing puzzle piece of his life, someone he could share his thoughts with, someone he could trust. He wanted to be part of her life but wasn't sure if he could.

"I know my physical and mental prowess have become stronger, but how will they help me ... us? I mean, can you tell me more about my abilities and powers?"

"I'm sorry. I thought you wanted to know more about me."

"I do, but—" His face reddened.

"I'm teasing. You have much to learn." Embraced in a warm glow, she sighed. "I'm forbidden to say any more at this time, but when you meet Julean, take advantage of what he has to offer. He can elevate your training to the next level if you let him."

Andromeda wanted to spend more time with Jerry, but the primary overseers beckoned to her. "I wish I could travel with you," Andromeda moaned, "but we will meet again, soon." She released his hand and then vanished.

Watching her leave was difficult, but Jerry moved forward, eager to finish his journey as quickly as possible. Replenished with food, water, and energy, he headed off in search of the fourth seal.

CHAPTER FOURTEEN

PROMETHION

It seemed like ages since Jerry had begun his quest. No longer requiring eight hours of sleep, he needed only an occasional nap. He trudged forward, trying not to think about Andromeda—how her touch sent a wave of desire through him so strong he couldn't think of anything else. The sensation of their kiss lingered on his lips. His palms grew sweaty. It took all his self-control to steady his breath. He reminded himself that he mustn't lose focus. To do so could mean death.

Hours later, the cavern's path narrowed, and the air blistered against his face as though he'd opened a hot oven door. Crackling and popping echoed throughout the cavern. *Why is it so hot in here?* Solidified magma in mid-drip and lava icicles draped the interior. Jerry wiped the drizzling sweat from his forehead with the back of his hand. *Have I ventured into an active molten flow?*

Then he stopped.

A roaring inferno blocked his way. Loose volcanic gravel skated under his feet as he tried to find a way past the conflagration. Jerry swallowed hard. "Mr. G, how are we going to get around this mess?"

He stumbled to get away from the blaze, but the ravenous flames shifted toward him. Suddenly, it was as if the gates of hell had burst open and a frightening creature rose up, taking the form of a fiery beast. Like a human torch, it emanated an intense heat, consuming everything in its path.

Jerry staggered backward, his heart racing. Wait a minute. Hadn't he just defeated Ophiuchus? With his newly acquired power, how hard could it be to eliminate this minor inconvenience?

The skulking figure stood in front of him, turned in such a way as to shield itself from an attack. Fiery blotches dripped, igniting the ground around it. Its eyes burned like red-hot embers, shifting from side to side as though it were trying to discern Jerry's power. Then, without warning, the flaming creature hurled a massive heat wave toward Jerry.

Jerry dived sideways, the red-hot surge scorching his left hand. Pain shot through his blistered fingers as he struggled to clear his thoughts. He jumped up, shaking. Jerry forced a breath and tried to merge his mind with his aether, but nothing happened. He tried again. Still, nothing. Reality sunk in. He was about to be cooked to death in his own skin. With the beast almost upon him, he turned and ran.

"Holy geode!" Grasping his aether, Jerry leaped over fallen stalactites and chunks of stone, barely keeping his footing as he slipped on the loose gravel. The creature barreled toward him, hurling flames of fire.

The air was stifling. Sweat flew off his forehead and spilled down his temples. His heart felt like it was going to explode, pumping a nervous blood through his neck and to his head. Then he spotted a large crevice next to a sharp, jagged ledge and fled to it.

Crouched inside the fissure, behind the ridge of rock, he tried to connect with his aether, but still nothing. *Ugh, why isn't this working?* He was trapped. A wave of nausea rippled through his gut as though he'd fallen from a plummeting roller coaster. Why couldn't he connect to his aether? Was this to be his end? Where was Andromeda?

The air ruptured into a massive blaze; sparks flew everywhere. Jerry cringed. Fireballs exploded, shooting flames in all directions. A suffocating heat engulfed him. Just when he felt like he was going to combust, the anuns glowed, and a surge of energy erupted from his aether, wrapping him in a protective barrier.

He flinched as another flaming inferno shot toward him. The aether's shielding deflected the massive firestorm, but how long would it last? His courage was failing him.

"Andromeda...anybody...I need help. Now! Come on! Somebody."

Jerry was lost in a tangle of confusion and nightmares, ready to give up hope, but then a soft hiss penetrated the cavern. A gentle mist infused the expanse. Huddled in his protected buffer, he looked up, his eyes wide. *What in the geode?*

The same delightful array of air and water he had seen earlier from the Aquarians now hovered above him. Hope filled his heart as Antila appeared and unleashed a bombardment of aerial raids, inundating the blazing fiend with an array of aqueous arrows and winged serpents. Water burst and splashed the area with an immense percussion.

The enraged beast spun away from Jerry and hurled incendiary flames toward the quick little sprites. Fiery explosions ignited the sky in a blaze of flashing lights. Hydrothermal cracks erupted from the floor, spewing forth plumes of steam. Waves of thundering blasts shook the air.

Formations of two or three tiny warriors zigzagged about, easily dodging the endless volleys of fire, striking the infuriated creature at will.

The heat soared. Although Jerry's protective shield kept him from bursting into flames, he felt like that could happen at any moment. Soaked in sweat, he became dizzy but held tight to his aether.

Antila and his airborne combatants remained undaunted, flooding the raging monster with water cannons and unusual cloud manifestations. Jerry stared in awe, his eyes transfixed on the battle. Then, with an all-out assault, the spirited sprites released a massive assortment of aqueous weapons. Winged gargoyles, gigantic serpents, and volcanic explosions erupted, extinguishing the beast in a steamy downpour.

After one last gasp, the smoldering creature lay dead.

Antila flew over to Jerry. "Are you all right?"

"I think so." He held his throbbing hand open to examine the burn. The blisters had disappeared, and the injured epidermis was sloughing off, healing without scarring. He marveled at how fast he was recovering. "What was that thing?" Jerry asked, still shaking.

"That thing was Promethion, who stole the frong of fire we hold dear."

"The frong of fire?" Jerry asked with a vacant stare.

"The frong is a vessel that protects us from fiery beasts." Antila buzzed above him. "We must guard its power to keep creatures like Promethion from existing. That menace has been a pest way too long, and now that we have the frong back in our possession, we're more than happy it's gone."

"Your arsenal of weapons was incredible. I mean ... I've never seen anything so amazing." Jerry waved his injured hand in the air. "How is it done?"

"We have a device called a Varanastra." Antila held a crystal object that looked like a winged fish. Images flashed inside its translucent matrix, revealing strange and unusual forms similar to the weapons used to attack Promethion. "The Varanastra is unique. It gives us the ability to create any shape as long as it's composed of water. It has helped us with many confrontations. Most do not realize its power."

Jerry gazed in awe, gripping his aether close. The strange patterns worming inside the crystal fascinated him.

"You should know your abilities before confronting something you can't handle." Antila fluttered close to Jerry. "Next time, we may not be able to help."

"I am indeed lucky." His voice strained, his shoulders slumped forward. "I still have much to learn."

Antila nodded, then turned and flew away with the Aquarians.

Left alone, Jerry's head teemed with uncertainty. *Why wasn't I able to eradicate the flaming beast? I could've been killed. Where's Andromeda, and why didn't she help?*

CHAPTER FIFTEEN

THE THREADS OF DOUBT

Jerry's thoughts were hazy, his mind whirling with doubts, unsure of his abilities. Hesitantly, he found his way back to the central path. Stars lit the chamber with a shining elegance. The cavern opened into a gallery of rock forms that included limestone totem poles, flowstone, sandstone shelves, cave pools, and, of course, stalagmites. He was still trying to clear his head and piece together what had happened. "Andromeda, are you here?"

"Yes, I'm here." She sighed, appearing next to him. She placed her hand on his shoulder. "Are you all right?"

"Did you see what happened?" Jerry turned, wiping the sweat dripping from his nose. "I guess I'm still confused about my abilities."

"Yes, I saw it ... and I—"

"Why couldn't I eliminate the beast?" Jerry clasped her soft hand and peered into her watery eyes.

"Promethion was different." She squeezed his hand to give him strength, but her eyes spoke more than her words. "You need to take greater thought and study it out as your challenges get harder."

"But I don't understand. It was so easy with Ophiuchus." His voice choked. "Why didn't you rescue me?"

"What you experienced was real." Tears trickled down her cheeks. "Promethion was an actual physical entity, not a deception. Our laws restrict me from helping. Remember, I'm the overseer of illusions, and as such, I cannot help with real circumstances without suffering severe consequences. You must defeat and overcome these challenges set before you without my help. But those who you befriend along the way may be an excellent resource for you in your travels."

"Will you walk with me for a while?" Jerry sighed. "I'm still a little dazed and could use your company right now."

Andromeda embraced Jerry. "It hurts me to see you like this," she whispered, "but I promise ... I'll do everything I can to help, but you must use caution."

Grasping each other's hands, they strolled toward the fourth seal. The longer they walked, the stronger his emotions became, filling his heart with desire. Then he stopped and pulled her close. Jerry cupped her face with his hands. "We've only known each other for a short time," he whispered, "but I'm afraid I've fallen in love with you."

Andromeda touched his face. "Is it true?"

"It's true." His eyes rested on hers as he caressed her face. "This feeling I have ... it's madly insane. I don't understand your world or your situation, but I need to know, is it possible for us ... you know ... to be together forever?"

"Oh, Jerry. I fell in love with you the first time we met." She looked wide-eyed at Jerry, blinking. "Nothing would make me happier than to spend my life with you. Our union is possible, but you must complete your journey to the seventh seal. I can't say any more at this time, only that we can be together."

Andromeda's plan had been hatched and was growing. With each breath, their passion blossomed. They craved constant companionship. At that moment, they embraced with such hunger that even the stars above them blushed, causing the cavern to dim.

Once again, the overseers summoned Andromeda, but she reassured Jerry his goal was attainable and reinforced the need to trust in his heart. Then she touched his cheek and vanished.

Amid the subdued agony of defeat, Jerry searched for Julean. A cushion of soft silt absorbed the sound of his footsteps. After what felt like an hour, he spotted a glass-like surface; Julean was near.

The terrain was similar to a mirror's reflection except that it was moving, flowing, rippling into different images, constantly changing as Jerry strolled across its mantle of disguise. One moment he was walking silently across a calm, open sea, and the next he was passing through the flurry of a raging snowstorm. *Okay, I don't get it. What does this portend?*

Off in the distance, a dim light emanated from the cavern's roof. As he drew near the unfamiliar illumination, it was as if he stood in an abalone shell, exposing iridescent hues of colorful layers beneath his feet. No doubt, this was Julean's hangout, but this one was different from his previous encounters.

Suddenly, the light became brighter; the beacon pulsed with an irregular pattern. Jerry instinctively passed his hand through the beam, but nothing happened.

"Okay, Mr. G, what's going on? Hmm, I wonder ..."

Jerry placed his hand in the pulsing ray, holding it steady. At once, a brilliant exhibition of blue light appeared, and with it Julean.

Surprised at his appearance, Jerry spouted, "You've changed."

His skin radiated a bluish hue, and his apparel had transformed into an elegant white robe that illuminated a colorful array of symbols. "As have you," Julean said in a deep tone.

"Wow, even your voice has changed."

"How may I help?" Julean gave a courteous bow.

"Well ..." Jerry shifted his feet and then boldly declared, "Promethion almost killed me. If Antila hadn't rescued me, I'd be dead."

"And yet here you are." With a magical spark in his eyes, Julean took Jerry's aether and pointed to its engravings. "Do you see the various anuns?"

"But of course. Every time I power up, different inscriptions appear."

"These are coded symbols that you need to master." Julean walked around him in contemplation. "As your mind connects with them, you will be able to generate the power you have assimilated. But ... it takes patience and much work to command this sort of control. Most of all, you must believe. That's why we will be spending more time together."

Jerry let out a long exhale and reached for his canteen. The lengthy swallow quenched his thirst but did little to relieve his impatience. Tempered from his trials but also from a corporeal renewal, he had become more competent in his abilities but lacked discipline.

"Before you connect to your aether, you must cleanse your mind of all distractions, and then you must be certain ... absolutely clear ... about what you wish to accomplish before engaging it." Julean's gaze was piercing, as though he could see right through Jerry. "It must become an extension of your being, an involuntary reflex, just like breathing—that is, if you want to make it to the portal. But"—Julean held up his finger—"you need to know when to back away from a confrontation when you are not able to connect."

"Wait a minute!" Jerry waved his hand. "What do you mean ... *portal*?"

"Marvelous things await you there." Julean's eyes twinkled.

"And what is your definition of *marvelous*?" Jerry's mind wandered, wondering what lay in wait for him.

"Once you obtain access to the last chamber, I will give you more information that will help transport you to your next destination."

"What destination? You mean Enif?"

"That is all I can say. It is time we begin your training."

Even after extensive preparation with Julean, threads of doubt remained. *What if I can't connect to my aether? Will I know when to back away? What if I can't succeed?*

CHAPTER SIXTEEN

LYRO THE LYRE

Once again, Jerry turned and set his sights on the next seal, feeling less anxious but still concerned about his abilities. The air sparked with energy as he reflected on how far he had come and what he'd left behind. *It seems so long ago since I first stepped into these crazy caverns. Sometimes I have to stop and think, Who am I, really? Out there life was different, but in here I feel empowered. Still, something is missing, like I'm not complete. I just wish I knew what it was.*

In spite of his yearnings, Jerry continued to focus on his training while he traveled. *Julean's right. The more I use my aether, the more my power increases. My instincts are maturing into a consciousness far beyond that of any human capacity, but—*

His thoughts were interrupted when a hint of salt pinched his nose. The chamber had opened into a cathedral-type room with luminous stalactites hanging from the vaulted ceiling like glowing icicles. Large cube-shaped columns dotted the area among the stalagmites and flowstone.

"Mr. G, this looks like pink halite. There must've been a lake here at one time, but this far down?" Jerry broke off a sample and placed it against his tongue. "Yup, it's salt. Wanna taste?" Jerry extended his hand to Mr. G. "Oh, that's right, you don't like rock salt."

Subtle sounds whispered through the cavern like a sighing wind. Jerry glanced around, taking in the ambience of the natural lighting and luminous minerals. Then he caught sight of another pillar. It began to hum, drawing him close. His heart pounded as though he had just discovered a gold mine, the only difference being that this wasn't fool's gold.

The rose-colored column blended in with the surrounding structures, radiating a peaceful hue of red. Its form was symmetrical and cube-shaped like a Rubik's cube, and it had multiple openings that rotated as if on a synchronized timer. He tried to match the anuns from his aether to the pillar's symbols but couldn't because of their constant motion. He released a frustrated breath, shaking his head. *This is impossible.* Then Julean's counsel seeped into his mind. *Too many times do your emotions guide your eyes. Remove the veneer that blinds you. Open your mind and see things the way they really are.*

With his aether in hand, he fixated on the revolving symbols and relaxed. Like a snake shedding its skin, a veil lifted from his eyes, and the synchronized cubed-segments halted their movement, revealing a series of ciphers.

He inhaled a quick breath and inserted his aether into the matching slot. Before he could exhale, his staff ignited the cavern in fiery trails of fuchsia, bathing it in a surreal color. It was as if the entire chamber had exploded into a thousand shooting sparks, hissing and popping. Mr. G's tiny eyes burned orange and widened as though he had awakened. Jerry's pulse raced.

Once the spectacle had calmed, he removed the aether, his eyes sparkling in awe. An immediate transfer of energy engulfed him, causing a restless shiver to cut through him like cold steel. His soul quiet, his mind emptied of everything— everything except a sense of peace and tranquility. "Mr. G, this feeling is incredible." Jerry inspected the anuns closely. "I'm not quite sure what just happened, but maybe Julean will know."

Jerry grabbed a star-shaped fruit from his pack and ate it, washing it down with a long gulp of water. Then he pulled his lightweight vest tighter about him and started back to the main trail. In the quiet solitude of the cavern, his mind shifted to his friends back home. *So much has happened. I don't think Mark or Joe would ever believe my story.* Who in their right mind would? Even now, he questioned his sanity. Was this real or a dream waiting for him to wake up?

His eyes swung to his aether. *And you ... just how powerful are you?* In a life where hope had been lost, for a moment he felt important.

The intoxicating sense of adventure lulled him into an altered state of security. Cool moisture rode on a brisk air current, bringing a musty odor with it. His footsteps echoed sharp and hollow as he strolled into the unknown, haunted by the sound of dripping water, pulsing throughout the cavern as if it had a heartbeat.

In less than an hour, the voluminous chamber of pink halite yielded to a smaller but colorful gallery. Hundreds of twinkling stars lit up the cavern, emitting a spectrum of color as though he were looking through a prism. A multitude of rock formations ruled the corridor, including gigantic stalagmites that looked like huge pawns from a chessboard. Blue-green fungi, red mosses, and yellow ferns proliferated, promoting a sense of stillness.

Jerry suppressed a yawn and shook his head, trying to stay awake. He had tired from his journey and sought a place to rest. *Man, I sure could use a nap, but where?* Then he spotted an entrance to a towering stalagmite just off the trail. His pulse quickened. He paused when a familiar feeling filled his soul. *I wonder ... Could it be?* He hurried over and knocked on a door no more than three feet tall, expecting to see a friendly face. When no one answered, he eased the wooden entry open, hoping to find Lyra.

A hint of carnations filled the air as he crossed the threshold. Charms and pendants adorned the walls. Framed pictures of gnomes added a splash of color to the room, giving it a unique personal touch. The walls, dressed in an array of hues, represented the colors of the rainbow. Small chairs and the same clef-shaped table huddled next to a cozy fireplace. A hole in the floor led to a dark basement. The serenity of silence spilled into the room. Within moments of lying down, Jerry fell fast asleep.

After napping for a few hours, he awoke to a soothing melody. In front of him stood a small man who looked like Lyra's twin. Jerry rubbed his eyes. "Who are you?"

"I'm Lyro, the brother of Lyra. We are from the Lyre clan and are overseers of music." A pointed red hat jiggled as it sat atop his head. He had the same round body and spindly legs and arms as Lyra. In the same multicolored outfit as Lyra, he wore his dark braided hair on the opposite side, and his pointed ears fluttered when he spoke.

"My name is Jerry, and I've met your brother, Lyra," Jerry said, yawning. "It was he who rescued me from the terrible rock beasts. His music was so enchanting that its melody caused a deep slumber to overcome them."

"Well, you know, he's not as good as I am." With his hands behind his back, Lyro rocked on his heels. "I have the ability to harmonize music so well even the aquilas can't harm you."

"Who are the aquilas?" Jerry sat up and flashed a suspicious glare.

"They live near the Eridanus River." Lyro narrowed his eyes. "They are birds of prey who can rip a person to shreds in a matter of minutes. Only my music can see you safely through."

"Where is this Eridanus River?" Jerry asked, now wide awake.

"Oh, you'll know when you have found that treacherous waterway. The aquilas' shrieks will cause you to tremble, or should I say, when they begin to devour your flesh, you'll wish you had never ventured to the Eridanus."

Jerry's pulse throbbed in his ears. Beads of perspiration dotted his forehead. Stilled, he stood silent.

"Are you okay?" Lyro said.

Jerry's mouth opened. A frightened lisp entered his voice. "Scuse me, but—"

"Squeeze you?" Lyro looked puzzled.

"No, I mean—can you ..." Jerry paused to gather his thoughts. *Andromeda did say I should seek those who could aid me in my journey.* "Will you be able to help if I encounter these ... aquilas?"

"All you need to do is call. I take great pride in my ability."

Jerry sagged against Lyro's doorway, cloaked in relief and silent humility. After his encounter with Promethion, he worried. He had become proficient in many of his abilities, with the notable exception of one: that of judgment, a vital quality needed in his quest.

"I suppose I should be on my way and only hope I never need your services."

"If you do, I'm just a shout away."

Jerry wondered about the aquilas as he thanked Lyro for his hospitality and stepped outside refreshed and ready to resume his odyssey. Just as the door clicked shut behind him, something shiny caught his attention. Next to a bright red fern, a gold emblem flashed on a bean-shaped container. Jerry picked up the unusual case, wondering what it stored. A single clasp held it shut, and blazoned on one side was a gilded image that resembled a pair of glasses.

He released the latch and it popped open. A set of ordinary spectacles rested within the strange case, or so it seemed. On inspection, the lenses were thick and opaque. He took them out and placed them on his face.

"Well, Mr. G, what do you think?" Jerry waved his arms in front of him as though he were blind. "I can't see a thing, but maybe you can." Jerry took them off and tried to position them over the tiny eyes of Mr. G, but they were too large and didn't fit. "They don't do a thing for you."

He replaced them into the bean-shaped container and closed the latch, hoping they possessed an essential element that could help him with his journey. Jerry turned to Mr. G. "They must be good for something, but what, I don't know. For now, let's try to stay as far away from the aquilas as possible." With that, he stowed them in his pack and resumed his trek.

CHAPTER SEVENTEEN

VIRGA, THE GODDESS OF JUSTICE

An hour later, the gallery of blue-green fungi, red mosses, and yellow ferns disappeared into a twisting pathway of cobblestone surrounded by vast mineral deposits rising from the floor. Stout stalagmites and limestone tapestries of reds and yellows made from iron oxide deposits proliferated, along with deadly sinkholes that could swallow him in an instant. Jerry stopped. *I sense something, but I'm not sure what.*

A stellar aberration of light made it look as if the cavern's stars were moving, shining their brightness into the chamber. Shadows skulked everywhere. A musty blast of warm, moist air flushed his face and ruffled his hair. *Okay, that was weird.* A nervous chill rattled through him, his stomach churning in angst. "Mr. G, I suppose it's time to move on."

Jerry's heels clunked on the dusty old cobbled highway, breaking the silence, until he came upon a woman with long flaming hair. She wore a bright yellow gown adorned with hypnotic symbols. Her amber face was mesmerizing, but it was her eyes that seized Jerry's attention. Nothing human had eyes like that. In fact, no living thing he'd ever seen had eyes like that. Each bulging eye had two blood-red pupils, pulsing and glowing as though they were on fire. Next to her, restrained with chains of silver, snarled two black panthers. Jerry's gaze shot past her, fixating on the next sealed entry, not more than fifty yards behind her.

"I mean you no harm, but I must—"

"Silence!" She threw up her hands. "How dare you show disrespect! I am Virga, Goddess of Justice." Her voice was dull and raspy, as if she had shouted once too often.

Jerry winced at the hardness of her tone. Her panthers snorted and pawed the ground as though they were starved, waiting for him to make one mistake.

At one time, Virga was revered by those who lived in the neighboring constellations near Alpha Virginis. Born as a mortal, she became the Goddess of Justice before wickedness spread throughout Spica. She absconded to the sky, where she no longer had to tolerate what she loathed. The whole region lived in terror and chaos—something that gave her pleasure, as she so despised them all. As punishment, her angel-like wings had been clipped, and she was exiled to serve an indefinite term in the caverns on Earth. Now she tormented those who sought to pass.

"Do we really need to do this?" Jerry raised his aether in preparation for battle.

Virga chuckled.

Okay, what's so funny? He scowled and rubbed his neck. Was she so powerful that he needed to back off, or was she bluffing? The thought of losing again felt like a spike being driven into his heart. He regretted his weak encounter with Promethion, but that couldn't happen again, could it?

"I don't think you understand." Jerry stood defiant. "I don't want to hurt you, but I will if I must."

Virga threw her head back and rolled her eyes. "Do your worst."

Jerry advanced slowly toward her panthers; energy surged to his aether. Abruptly, her head dropped and her stare turned cold and lifeless. Then, without warning, she seized control of his mind. Jerry tried to fight back, but as hard as he sought to wrest his gaze from her, he could not. He struggled as the tendrils of her psyche wrapped around his consciousness, squeezing his thoughts, making them hers. Virga had taken complete control of his mental and physical capacities.

"I told you to leave." She smiled and blinked in pleasure. "Now, let's see if you can fly!"

Jerry, now a helpless puppet, spun around and shuffled toward a bottomless sinkhole. He exerted all the strength he had, but her domination forced him to continue his death march toward the endless pit.

Step by step, he inched closer to his demise, hoping his aether would do something, anything. Just as he was about to fall into the bottomless abyss, Andromeda appeared, instantly generating an illusion of a gigantic winged viper. Virga, frightened at the creature's ferocity, lost her telekinetic lock on Jerry, allowing him to escape.

The two rushed back beyond the reach of Virga's powers and huddled behind a group of flowstone draperies. Jerry rubbed his head in embarrassment. "I thought you weren't permitted to assist me in elements of reality," he said, his mind still foggy.

"I couldn't let you fall to your death." The worried expression on her face spoke volumes. "I will face the consequences of helping you, but I just couldn't let you die." Jerking her head to the side, she nodded. "I'm being summoned, but remember I am always with you."

She vanished, leaving him alone to challenge Virga once again. He had to find a way past that vain witch, but how? He was defenseless against her power to control his mind. And he still had to contend with her panthers. Jerry trembled at the danger he was about to put himself in but knew of no other way.

As energy poured into his aether, he flashed back to his encounter with Lyra. He had picked several of the apus flowers reputed to grant invisibility. *Maybe I can sneak past Virga and her four-legged cohorts if she can't see me. But how long can I stay hidden? Lyra did say the effects were temporary.* His shaky fingers reached into his pack and pulled a few petals out, and he ingested them.

Within seconds, Jerry became invisible. *Whoa! This is incredible. Hope it works.* He held his breath and tried to creep past Virga and her guardians, but his light footsteps prompted her panthers to snarl as though they detected his presence.

Virga snapped at her pets. "What do you see, abooksigun?" which meant "wildcats." "Is someone there?" She reached out to feel the air but felt nothing. Turning to her pets, she rubbed their ears. "It's all right. Calm down."

Once past her, he eased his way forward, striving to avoid even the slightest noise. Each soft step advanced faster until he reached the sealed gate. Gradually, several symbols materialized, but where was the key?

Time was running out. The invisibility was wearing off; his heart pounded. He would need to consume more apus flowers or make his escape. Just as he turned to leave, a hidden cavity opened next to the sealed door. He reached into the receptacle and grabbed a small stone stelae. Numerous vague markings were embossed on the stone slab. *Great! These don't make any sense at all.* With his fingers now visible, he tried to activate the gate's symbols but was unsuccessful.

He had failed again. Panic filled his heart. Then he remembered the opaque glasses he had found. *If these don't work, I'm dead!* He quickly pulled them from his pack and put them on. Instantly, the stone's symbols sharpened and became clear. With his body materializing, he raced to activate the ciphers in the order shown, touching them one at a time.

Infuriated, Virga turned and released her pets. Jerry glanced over his shoulder. *Must hurry.* With no time to spare, the enigmatic door morphed into a misty blue curtain. Jerry dashed through, sealing the entry and barring the panthers behind him.

CHAPTER EIGHTEEN

THE ENCHANTED BOOK

A single torch dimly lit a drab, small alcove. Jerry glanced around, squinting. Hard-baked dirt crumbled beneath his footsteps. A slow drip echoed within the room as though it were bleeding its life essence. Decay and weathering had occurred, producing a dense humid stuffiness. Rock formations had broken down, and heat had stretched the outcroppings of metamorphic rocks, layering them with black streaks of manganese oxide and white dolomite, like stripes on a zebra.

His heart was still pumping hard when he wiped the sweat from his forehead. "Mr. G, that was too close, but what have I done?" Thoughts of Andromeda pressed in on him, hammering him with guilt. He worried that he had damaged their relationship and didn't want to lose her. Poor judgment had led to negligence, and even now he felt his face burn with humiliation.

Jerry's eyes had adjusted enough to spot a narrow passageway no more than twenty feet ahead. But after his encounter with Virga, he was reluctant to move through the narrow hallway. His trials were far from over, and doubt clouded his thoughts. He stood on the hard stony ground, his aether in hand, and let out a long-held breath.

He didn't want to go on, but he knew he had to. Everything seemed to be in slow motion, dreamlike. He tried to probe for potential dangers ahead, but something troubled his vision. A presence in the passage blocked his ability to engage his senses.

Intuitively, he put on the opaque glasses he had been holding. To his surprise, the lens opacity revealed a network of thorns and thistles, moving and writhing as though they were alive. *This is amazing. It's like looking through infrared lenses.*

Thick crowded vines with tiger-claw barbs covered the entire corridor. A flash of white caught his eye. It wasn't until he crept closer that he realized they were the bones of a previous victim. It was obvious that the creeping plants were predatory, and with razor-sharp points, the slightest scratch could prove lethal.

Jerry glanced around. He wondered what other lost soul might find their way into this dungeon of nightmares and discover the remnants of a half-eaten set of decaying bones—his!

A vine's tendril crept against his leg, and Jerry jerked backward, narrowly averting its attempt to poison him. His poise was unraveling. His confidence languished and his relationship with Andromeda stood in question. A burning throb formed in his stomach. Had the remorse of failure clouded his judgment? Jerry closed his eyes and sighed. "Mr. G, one more mistake ... may be my last."

After pacing the alcove for over an hour, he lost patience. Resolve settled in his heart, bringing stillness and certainty. Where else could he go? Jerry knew there was no turning back. *If there ever was a God, please help me now.*

He gulped a deep breath and readied himself. *I guess it's do or die.* With the glasses as his guide, he would have to manage only a few steps at a time, tiptoeing around the barbed threats, hoping to avoid certain death. Jerry inched his way past the vine's tentacles, sidestepping and dodging their lethal reach. A small mouse darted under his feet only to meet its doom from the vine's sharp, toxic teeth. Doubt caused him to hesitate after seeing more bodies ravaged to the bone. *Can't stop now. Got to keep going.*

Multiple tendrils labored to weave and position themselves to ensnare him as he bobbed up and down, slinking through the carnivorous passage. Several near misses were met with waves of anxiety and cold nausea. He pushed numerous poisonous barbs out of his way with his aether. Finally, after what seemed like an eternity, his heart lifted when the end came into view. Seconds later, he stood outside the tunnel, drenched with perspiration but unscathed.

"Mr. G, I can't believe we made it through that tangled mess, but now what?"

The channel had opened to a large room filled with limestone columns, stalactites, and stalagmites encrusted with growths of brown algae, red lichens, and green moss. A faint fish-tank odor stuck in his nose while ambient light showered the chamber with a peaceful shade of soft yellow.

With his heart still thumping, he removed the glasses and placed them in his pack. Before advancing any further, Jerry took the time to collect his thoughts. *How many ways must I screw up? What's going to happen to Andromeda? No way can I survive this ordeal without her help.* So many things shot through his mind as he cleared his throat, trying to control the quiver in his voice. "Are you still with me?"

"Yes, I am here." Andromeda appeared next to him, her face melancholy.

Jerry lifted his weary eyes, heavy with grief, and sighed. "I'm so sorry you had to intervene to save my life. I'm almost afraid to ask, but what—"

"The General Council held a court, and I was granted a reprieve since my father is the chief overseer." Andromeda turned and stared past Jerry, her face heavy with thought. "My dad knew how much I loved you and gave me a stern warning. He said I cannot take our laws lightly, and the next time I broke one of our statutes, I would face the full consequences of my actions."

He could tell she was trying to remain composed, but there was no doubt she was worried. "I feel terrible." His shoulders slumped; his grip fumbled on his aether. "I don't know what I'd do if I lost you."

"If it wasn't for Virga's fear of vipers, you would be dead!" Andromeda stopped his fidgeting with her hand. "You must take heed in every situation. Your challenges are going to get more difficult, which means you need to put more thought into your actions. Another wrong decision may cost you your life, and with it ... me. I have requested more time together so I may assist you in your travels. Reluctantly, they have given me permission to help you on your quest to the seventh seal, but my help will be limited."

"I love you so much." His voice broke.

"Do you?"

"What must I do to prove myself?" Jerry squeezed her hand.

"Stop and think! You're too predictable."

"This is killing me." Jerry lowered his head.

"It should."

"I promise. I'll never let this happen again," Jerry said with his hand over his heart.

"Desires influence our choices, and choices shape our priorities, which in the end determine our actions."

"But I'm still learning."

With a wistful expression, she took his hand and placed it against her face. Her touch was reassuring. Jerry's heart warmed, his gazed fixed on her. "You need to take my feelings into consideration," she said softly. "What if I'd lost you?"

The instant the words left her mouth, Mandy's image flashed across Jerry's mind. His face stiffened, mask-like.

"What's wrong? You look like you just lost your best friend."

"I think I did." He shook his head. "What you just said ... Like déjà vu ... I've heard those same words before ... from someone very close, but I ..." Jerry strained to recall that moment. "I can't—"

"Oh!" Andromeda brought her left hand to her mouth. "Was it me?"

When he tried to visualize the face he'd seen, it blurred into Andromeda's delicate features. "No, the face was different, but I just can't—"

"Jerry, please!" Her shoulders dropped and her eyes searched his. "You've been through a lot. You need to let it go."

"I know." He pulled her close, his face full of remorse. "I know." He didn't want to cause her further pain, but there had been something powerful about the impression he'd just had. For now, though, he wanted Andromeda by his side, in his arms, feeling her love. He yearned for the time they would be together forever, away from the cavern's trials.

Because their relationship was becoming more intimate, she was quick to remind him that before their union could take place, he had to finish his transformation. After spending more than an hour together, she said, "It is within the confines of reflection we are able to become conscious of the insights that can lead us to awareness, but one must use caution." She touched his face and gazed into his eyes. "You must learn to discern what your capabilities are and when to engage them. If you let your heart lead, it will not fail you. My time has lapsed, and I must leave, but I will always be close."

She released Jerry's hand and vanished, buoying him in hope. Once again, he grabbed his pack and set his sights on the next seal, wondering about the tender impression he had received. *Why was it so strong? Something was still missing, but what?*

Within a few hours, the mugginess had given way to a light, airy atmosphere. The fish-tank odor had been swept away, allowing Jerry to inhale a fresh breath of air. Drops of water rolled down the solemn walls and dripped into the surrounding cave pools. Reflections from the twinkling stars above rippled across their surface, flashing their light throughout the chamber. A yellow hue imbued the trail with warmth, while glowing crystal mounds and scattered stalagmites offered a peaceful setting.

From time to time, Jerry would stop, take his dirty, torn clothes off, and bathe in one of the sparkling cave pools. Then he would replace his clothes, wishing he had a clean set to put on.

It had been only a week since he had entered the caverns, and his impatience had gotten him into trouble. But now more than ever, he was determined to reach the portal. Jerry recalled how he loved to fish for trout. How he would scour the creek, patiently waiting, searching for the next opportunity. It was time for him to start fishing, to reel in his impatience, using the skills he had learned to guide his decisions.

The thoughts about trout caused his stomach to grumble, reminding him he was running low on food and water. Tossing his pack aside, he pulled out his canteen and gulped down the last of its contents, letting it spill down his chin. After wiping his mouth with the back of his hand, he caught sight of something shimmering about a hundred yards off the trail.

Rocks skittered under his feet as he grabbed his pack and hurried to an area that had the same unusual vegetation he had seen in other chambers.

A sweet blend of buttery maple and vanilla splashed the air with its scent. Ornamental trees flaunted a gray exfoliating bark that revealed a yellow inner lining. Pendulous trusses of yellow pea-like blossoms and copious amounts of bird-shaped fruit filled their branches.

Jerry closed his eyes in contemplation while a spring gurgled soothingly, rushing to feed the secluded sanctuary. A tranquil breeze touched his soul. With his spirits lifted and hope renewed, he looked forward to feasting.

"Ah, Mr. G, I can't wait!" Just then, a funny little man dressed in a red tunic popped up from behind a group of magenta bushes, holding a luminous blue flower.

"Whoa!" Jerry jumped backward. "You startled me."

"Sorry 'bout that." The gray-haired man peered through his tiny spectacles. "I'm Oden, overseer of the cavern's jinans."

"Jinans?"

"Yes, *jinan* is the name given to the cavern's paradise gardens."

Jerry threw a glance at the garden's beauty. "They do have a certain celestial nature to them. I'm Jerry, pleased to meet you."

Oden nodded. "Like a beta cephei?" He extended a luminous purple flower to Jerry. "Their fragrance is out of this world. They come from the blue star Albireo."

"Does it have any special powers?"

"No. It just smells good."

"What do you think, Mr. G?" Jerry turned to a set of eyes that were still glowing from the last power-up. "I've never seen a flower so breathtaking. Last time I was in the garden with Andromeda, I had nothing to offer."

"What was she doing there?" Oden's eyes narrowed.

"I believe it was in the second chamber. She was checking the water's purity."

"That's my responsibility!" Oden's face reddened. His eyes turned dark.

"Uh-oh, did I just get her into trouble?" Jerry looked down, rubbing the back of his neck.

"Not to worry. Her father sits on Enif's ruling council. She gets pretty much anything she wants." He blinked and his face twitched. "But I may have already said too much."

"Relax. I won't say a word. But if you're the caretaker, who were the androids I saw in the first chamber?"

"They're part of the management system I oversee. They help preserve and maintain the jinans."

"So, what can you tell me about these?" Jerry pointed to the bird-shaped fruit.

"Oh, they're called avians, a favorite food of the pavo bird."

"The pavo bird?" Jerry's eyes widened. "Are they related to the aquilas?"

"No, they're quite harmless, but they like to pick at the fruit." Oden turned and glanced around. "I'm finished here, that is if it's okay with Andromeda," he said in a huffy voice, and then he vanished.

"Interesting." Jerry stroked his chin. "It sounds like Earth isn't the only place that espouses nepotism."

Jerry spun back to the tree and raised a cluster of yellow pea-like blossoms, plucking one of the bird-shaped fruit from its branch. Unspotted brown upperparts and snowy-white crescents along the wing gave the appearance of a dove. After examining the fruit, he peeled off the dry outer skin and sank his teeth into its sweet, juicy pulp.

"Incredible! Mr. G, it reminds me of a chocolate truffle. Too bad it's not on your diet."

Suddenly, Jerry's face twitched, and his body tingled. "What's happening?" In the next breath, he rose like an eagle, as if he'd sprouted wings, the barriers of nature lifted. His body felt like it was occupying empty space, freeing him from the chains of gravity.

"Holy geode!" Jerry fought back terror as he glanced down. He'd never cared much for heights. Even when his profession required him to ascend lofty trails, there was always dirt under his feet.

"Mr. G, I always dreamed of flying but never thought it possible." His heart raced as he dangled fifty feet from the ceiling, hovering next to a stalactite like a balloon. "So, how do I get down?" His gaze darted about, looking for a way to descend. Then he calmed and closed his eyes, pushing his fears aside. *Okay, I need to relax and let my mind take control.*

Thoughts of himself sinking, swimming downward in the air, seized his consciousness. His breathing slowed. He felt like he was walking underwater, sluggish and delayed. When his feet touched the ground, he opened his eyes. *Incredible. Never in a million years did I think this was possible.*

Jerry's heart pounded with excitement. An insatiable hunger pulsed with every beat. For the first time, he was beginning to understand what was happening. *Julean wasn't kidding when he said I would have powers beyond my belief.* Abilities never imagined were becoming a reality. Jerry smiled and looked at his aether. No doubt, great things awaited him on Enif. With Andromeda at his side, he would never want again. But for now, he needed to quench his thirst.

He strolled over to the gurgling spring, bent down, and filled his canteen. Raising it to his lips, he felt the cold water rush down his throat, savoring its sweet taste. With each gulp, his mind expanded, opening his eyes to a new realm. Jerry lifted his head and froze in amazement. The sublime beauty of the cavern emanated a peaceful sense of hope.

Subterranean cave formations simmered with a spectrum of color and majesty. Amber stalactites glimmered as they dripped their lifeblood into glistening aquamarine pools. Cave crystals emanated bright greens. Lemon-yellow droplets spiraled down soda straws. Limestone draperies flashed sapphire blues and translucent turquoises.

Jerry was about to turn away when a white stone altar not far from the babbling spring caught his eye. *Odd, that wasn't here before.* He rushed over and found a book lying in its center. He glanced around before picking it up. The volume was sealed, and holographic symbols embellished the binding. He rotated the text around, searching for a way to unlock its contents but couldn't solve the mystery.

"Okay, Mr. G, how do I get this thing open?" He took off his backpack and set it next to his aether. "It was placed here for a reason." When Jerry unzipped his pack, the opaque glasses fell out. *Okay, is this a fortuitous moment?*

With the lenses on his face, he stared sightlessly at the book. Within moments, his vision cleared as though a fog had been wiped from his eyes. The symbols faded but then reappeared. "Yes!" Jerry shook his fist in the air. "It's the constellation Pegasus. I get it. Mr. G, this is similar to what I had to face at the cave's entrance. All I need to do is to activate each star based on their alignment in Pegasus."

Jerry's knowledge had expanded dramatically, enabling him to recognize each star and its placement in the universe. After he had touched the twenty-third star, Rho, the protective cover vaporized into a fine mist.

With the seal broken, he pulled back a brown leather cover, inhaling odd scents, each one unique. The first page exploded with animations of creatures he'd never seen before. His breath caught. Strange flying beasts, serpent-shaped shrubs, and bizarre flora suddenly came alive. Weird-looking creatures darted about as he flipped through the pages. *Incredible! But what am I supposed to do with this?*

He tried touching the images, but nothing happened except that a few faint grunts and strange squawks could be heard. He probed, shook, and even turned the book on end, but again nothing happened. "Mr. G, this must be important. Otherwise, why would it have been placed here? Got any suggestions?" Jerry stared at the book. "Of course, maybe Julean can help."

Unable to understand what he was viewing, he placed the enchanted book in his pack and left the sanctuary, passing through dense swirls of mist. *Great. Is it going to rain again?*

He pulled his vest tightly around him and headed down a long tortuous tunnel, wiping the moisture from his face with his hand, wondering what secrets the book held.

CHAPTER NINETEEN

CETI'S LAKE

Several days had passed since Jerry had last slept. The strands of time were being woven tightly together into the fabric of the universe. It was as if nature's clock had surrendered to the magic of the cavern. Days were but hours as his physical needs for sleep diminished.

After pushing a steady pace over a rocky footpath, Jerry took a short break to gulp down some water and munch a stored avian. Once his hunger was satisfied, he resumed his trek, scrambling down a narrow lava trail.

It wasn't long before he came to a wide channel that dropped down into a vast chamber. The hard rocky trail had become sandy. The air was thick with humidity and a hint of salt.

"Mr. G, it smells like we're on a beach in Southern California."

In the distance, a large body of water emerged. A milky veil of fog had rolled in, blanketing the lake. The waves lapped against the shore, and a blast of cold air caused a chill in Jerry's bones.

"Unbelievable, a lake! Huh, too bad we don't have any fishing gear." Jerry's gaze shifted to Mr. G. "But then again, we'd probably catch a fish that would try to eat us."

Each grainy step brought him closer to the beach. He listened to the rolling waves slapping against the lake's foamy edge. Then he caught sight of a small wooden rowboat resting near the shore. He glanced around. "Is anyone here?" he shouted.

Silence filled the salty air as he shuffled over to the abandoned craft. It was in dire need of varnishing, and bird droppings decorated its warped plank seats. Painted across its bobbing stern was the word *Hope*.

Hope? That doesn't sound promising. But I wonder, is the vessel seaworthy? He looked around for a set of oars but found only a hefty rope attached to the bow. *How can one cross this vast body of water without a means to propel this tired craft? Maybe there's another way.*

A creature that looked like a dolphin poked its head out of the water, and Jerry jumped back. "You were inspecting the Lake of Ceti. Searching for something?"

"Whoa! I've never heard a dolphin speak." Jerry knelt. "I'm seeking passage to the next seal, and it appears the only way to cross this lake is in this small boat."

"Delphinius here, from the Delphini clan." Delphinius resembled a dolphin but was larger and had a beefy nose that looked like it could be used as a weapon. "What you seek is dangerous. Ceti does not permit travelers on his water."

"Who is this Ceti, and how can I cross this massive reservoir without confronting him?"

"Ceti is a most dangerous creature, a sea monster who rules the lake. He frowns on travelers who invade his water. But one weakness he has. Find the pods from the carina tree and you may be able to sedate him long enough to cross."

"Okay, so where can I find these ... carina pods?"

"Scorpi protects them. They are tough to obtain, they are. He is the yew spinney guardian, and his quick and powerful stinger can paralyze you with a single strike. He lives in the hills of Corona, which hold dangers of their own."

"Whoa, wait." Jerry rubbed the back of his neck. "The hills of what?"

"Go back from whence you came and you will see a V-shaped tunnel on your right. Follow the path, and the hills of Corona you will find. Remember, Scorpi is devious and quick to place his stinger in you."

"Tell me more about this ... Scorpi."

"Seen him I haven't. Rumor has it his stinger can kill."

"Well, can you describe what the carina pods look like?"

"The carina you can't miss. A thin bark covers its trunk. Into the branches, flaming red veins run upward. Dangerous limbs protect the pods inside. Razor-sharp leaves have deadly thorns and emanate a red iridescence." He smiled and nodded his head. "They can be broken or cut easily. Once inside, the pods are white with small black spots."

"What about—"

"Shhh." Delphinius dipped his head. "Leave. We've awakened Ceti." With that, he slid back into the water and disappeared.

Jerry gathered his gear together and rushed off to find the speckled white pods. *Ceti ... Scorpi ... hills of Corona. Where's Julean when you need him?*

A pervasive light infused the cavern, like sunlight piercing through a foggy day. The salty air dissipated, and the trail became hard and rocky. After twenty minutes on a path that curved and then curved again, he spotted the small V-shaped tunnel.

Bat droppings plastered the passage's floor, and stale, musty slime reeked from within its walls. Jerry worked his way through the awkward corridor, guano crunching beneath his feet. His stride was slow and deliberate, and he used his aether to help maintain balance. Finally, an opening appeared, exposing an entirely different world with a series of large colorful peaks.

"Mr. G, these must be the hills of Corona." His mouth gaped. "They're gorgeous."

The alpine hills featured a scenic backdrop that projected striking red and golden cave flora. Clouds of mist offered shades of mystic pink and lavender to the already majestic ambience. A cool breeze brushed his nostrils with the scent of wild lilacs dipped in honey. *No way! This is like a world within a world. How can something so incredible survive in the depths of the Earth?*

He spotted a small path going straight up the largest knoll and rushed to the trailhead. The trail was steep and narrow, and a fall could prove fatal. Jerry lingered for a moment, staring at a route full of decaying rock with sharp, ragged corners. "Mr. G, this makes the Finger Rock Canyon trail in Tucson look like a piece of cake."

Jerry placed his right foot on the first ledge and pushed off, but the brittle shelf was unable to support his weight and collapsed, sending him flying backward. He landed hard on his butt and grunted. "Well, that didn't work. You okay?" Jerry got to his feet and brushed the dirt off his pants. *All right, just how am I going to make it up this fragile sandstone?*

Then, he remembered that at the last jinan, he had defied gravity. His pulse soared with the thought of becoming airborne, and beads of sweat popped from his forehead. He hesitated as his brain rushed with the options he had available. *Maybe there's another route?* Jerry scoured the area but found that this was the only trail that led to the top. He sighed. *What if I lose concentration and fall? I could die.* He hadn't mastered the ability to levitate and trembled at the thought of flying. After trying to talk himself out of it, resolve settled in his mind. What else could he do? He had to trust his heart and let it lead him.

Jerry blew out a nervous breath, closed his eyes, and focused his thoughts on levitating. Within moments, he was floating above the ground as if he had been pumped full of helium. Queasiness filled his stomach, but he pushed past the nausea, puffing short bursts of air through his pursed lips. When Jerry opened his eyes, his despair eased, allowing him to ascend the path without the fear of its collapsing. For the first time, he was having a little fun with his capabilities. His confidence was improving, but he still didn't like heights.

With the ability to avoid a forceful pressure on the crumbling sandstone, he moved up the hill with ease. It wasn't long before the terrain flattened, becoming firm and granite-like. "Mr. G, this looks stable enough to walk on. What do you think?" Jerry nodded. "Me too. Let's give it a go."

After touching down, he began to ascend the mount on foot, relieved to be back on solid ground. About a mile up, the topography changed again. Strange concentric cylindrical rocks plagued the path. Skeletal remains of unfortunate victims lay scattered farther down the trail.

"Mr. G, something's not right here." Jerry leaned forward and pushed one of the stones away from the path with his aether. Long crystalline spikes shot out from its core like quills of a porcupine. He jumped back. "Whoa, not so fast." His muscles twitching, he was weak-kneed and a little frenzied. "I think we just missed becoming part of the field of corpses." An icy shiver of relief pierced his gut, as though someone had just poured freezing water down his back. *I mustn't be so impetuous. I'm a dead man if I rush through this place.*

Jerry paused and glanced around. He considered floating across the precarious terrain but wasn't sure if he could maintain the altitude without more practice. Interminable stretches of the scattered stones posed extreme danger. One scratch could prove deadly.

He sucked in a deep breath, trying to calm himself down. One step at a time, he probed and pushed the lethal stones out of his way as if he were in a minefield. His tentative feet slipped on loose debris, one foot barely touching a threatening rock, and he froze. Sweat drizzling down his face, his heart hammered. Exhaling a slow breath, he lifted his leg, careful to avoid any further contact, and stepped backward onto safe ground. "Mr. G, that's as close to becoming a shish kebab as I ever want to get."

At the trail's end, he could make out an open area of colorful flowers near the hill's crest. Jerry hurried to the field and stopped at its edge, where he set his pack down. He wiped the sweat from his forehead with the back of his hand, pulled out his canteen, and downed a long gulp. He looked around and wondered. *Surely, these couldn't be a threat, something so peaceful and serene.*

But his heart said something else. Tall leafless stems with sharp thorns displayed bright crimson and orange petals that emanated a warm glow. They came to his waist and stood straight as if reaching for the sky. Their delicious scent enticed him, and he tapped the blossoms with his aether. The stimulation caused a fine mist to erupt, infusing the area with a sticky sap. Jerry bent down and watched the subtle haze drift downward, immersing the accumulation of dead organic debris in its goo, causing it to sizzle and dissolve.

He got to his feet and rubbed the back of his neck. *Great! How am I going to get past these carnivorous plants?* Jerry tried to connect to his aether but couldn't. *Well, I'm certainly not going to just stroll through this field of dreams.* His mind strayed, seeking a safe passage. Then a thought whispered silently to his heart. *Float across.*

Jerry dreaded becoming airborne again, but with the threat of being liquefied, he grabbed his pack and threw it around his shoulders. "They say practice makes perfect." He turned and stared at Mr. G. "If I can't maintain my altitude, we're both toast."

Once again, Jerry blew out a tense breath, closed his eyes, and focused his thoughts on levitating. His body responded, rising above the vibrant crimson and orange blossoms. He exhaled a sigh of relief. *The second time feels easier. Maybe practice does make perfect.* Then, just as his confidence was peaking, his dangling vest snagged on a sharp thorn, triggering the flower to emit a caustic mist. Jerry quickly yanked on his jacket, breaking off the flower's stem, and he went into a downward spin. But this time he didn't panic. Using his aether, he slowed his descent by pushing upward from the ground, enabling him to regain altitude.

"Whew. Mr. G, that was close." Jerry looked down. "Never a break here. In the future, I'll keep my vest zipped." Upon reaching the summit, he touched down, exhausted. Jerry took off his backpack and sat on a cold, hard rock. He stretched and then pulled an avian out of his pack and ate it.

With a soft blue light streaming around him, he drew a deep breath and inhaled an intoxicating fragrance he'd never smelled before. His eyes roamed, taking in the panorama of the vast woodland that surrounded him. Species he'd never seen before captivated his senses.

Trees with rainbow bark flashed several color changes from green to blue to purple to orange and, finally, to yellow, giving it a kaleidoscopic effect. Macabre trees with curled, twisted branches stripped bare like bony fingers shifted in the cavern's sudden breeze as though they were reaching for him. Other trees had barren trunks and limbs that ended in sharp spiky leaves and oozed a bright red sap.

Grasping his aether closer, he peered around to see if Scorpi was in the vicinity. A breeze shot past him, making the branches of the trees moan and creek, sending a chill up his neck. Then he saw the carina tree, standing alone, like bait for the naïve. *Hmm, this could prove interesting.*

Jerry crept through the wooded landscape, trying to stay quiet, his eyes glued to the carina tree. Staying hidden behind the larger trees, he methodically worked his way to the sequestered tree. As Jerry neared the carina, he spotted the thin translucent covering Delphinius had described. *Yes, this is it!* The lucent layer revealed a vascular system of nourishment from the xylem and phloem. Like a pulsing heartbeat, flaming red veins surged to the extended limbs.

Jerry eased over and set his pack on the ground, placing his aether against its trunk. He looked up and stared at the tree's protective branches. *Great, I'll need to grow another ten feet before I am able to reach the pods.* Once more, a thought whispered in his mind. *Rise above your ability.* Jerry sighed. *Here we go again.* He closed his eyes and felt weightless energy flow through him, pulling him upward. When he opened them, he was hovering next to the tree's thorny extremities. The ascent had proved easy enough but strained his nerves.

He labored as quietly as possible to remove the defensive barbs. However, the procedure was more complicated than he'd been led to believe. Jerry pulled his knife from its sheath and began to hack out a section sufficient for him to enter, but he worried about the excessive noise he was making. *The limbs snap easily enough but are a pain to cut through.*

Once he was inside the heart of the tree, removing the polka-dotted pods was a simple task, and after picking several, he placed them inside his vest and headed back down. Before becoming weightless, he popped his head out from the branches and took a peek to see if it was clear. Scorpi was waiting, circling the tree. His heart sank. *Holy geode! This must be the jaws of scorpions.* The predatory arachnid was at least ten feet long and half that tall.

With a hard, loud thud, Scorpi struck the ground with his stinger and snapped his claws, challenging him. Jerry looked around for his aether. "Oh, no! I can't believe I left it on the ground." He clung to a limb, feeling helpless, squeezing his eyes shut. "Mr. G! Ugh, I can't believe I left you behind."

A prickle crawled up his neck as Scorpi circled the tree, clicking his pincers. How could he have erred again? He should've brought his gear with him. But no, he was in too much of a hurry to get back to the lake. He'd had it with his poor decision-making, and right now thinking made his head ache.

Jerry shuddered, trying to control the panic that throbbed within him. He knew full well he didn't stand a chance without his aether. He steadied himself with his left hand, clutching tightly to a sturdy branch. Then a thought whispered to his heart. *Open your mind and believe.* Jerry rubbed the back of his neck. *Believe what?* His gaze shifted to his gear. *Can it be that easy?*

He sucked in a breath of courage, closed his eyes, and summoned his aether to him. Silent thoughts took control. He tingled as his aether slowly lifted from the ground and floated into his hands. "Mr. G, I'll never let you go again." Jerry hugged him like a long-lost friend. "But now what? We're an easy target if we try to float down."

A touch of attitude flowed through Jerry like a rushing river, forging a strength within. He knew what he had to do. His pulse quickened and powerful energy surged through his body that he had not felt before. Jerry swallowed the knot in his throat, jumped down, and rolled away from Scorpi. Venom oozed from the scorpion's potent stinger as he sped toward Jerry, flinging his tail and striking the earth next to him. Jerry sprang up ready to fight.

With lightning-quick speed, Scorpi attacked again. Jerry leaped away from the deadly stinger but tripped on an exposed root, falling hard to the ground. He quickly rolled over and released a mighty blast from his scepter, striking the lethal menace. The massive scorpion froze in its steps, his assault cut short, the potent stinger stopping inches from Jerry's head. He lay on his back, the air knocked out of him, cringing at the sight.

Jerry had harnessed Scorpi's power, paralyzing the predatory arthropod. "Mr. G, that was way too close!" He rose up and leaned against the carina, his legs heavy. He stared at the motionless scorpion. "I think it's time we leave."

On the way down from the long winding slope, he replayed the moment with Scorpi over and over in his mind. Had his reaction come a split-second later, he'd be dead. He had learned a valuable lesson, a lesson of refining and purging. Adversity was a severe instructor, one that led to increased enlightenment and sharpening of skills. With the pods stowed within his vest, Jerry hastened his descent back to the lake, unsure how long Scorpi would remain incapacitated.

At the field of flowers, Jerry stopped and tapped the crimson and orange blossoms with his aether again. But this time, they released not only a caustic mist but also spewed upward a yellow noxious gas. "You've got to be kidding!" Jerry slumped. "So, Mr. G, what do we do now?" He paced, kicking at the loose rocks, watching them tumble into the toxic plants. Jerry looked around, unsure of his next move. "Okay, we need to downshift and slow up." His thoughts rippled over his options. Then an impression emerged. *Abandon your eyes and open your mind.* He paused to reflect. *What led me past the poisonous vines?*

Jerry unzipped his backpack, pulled out the opaque glasses, and placed them on his face. Now when he viewed the field, an area of white petals paved a path through the crimson flowers. Bees with huge mandibles and horned tails buzzed above them. *Why aren't they dying from the deadly vapor?* Jerry strolled over to the white blossoms and tapped them. "It's clear." He stared at Mr. G. "Don't give me that look. I didn't know." Jerry sighed. "I need to open my thoughts more to the things that can assist with my journey."

With the aid of his optics, he snaked his way down the hill until he came to the trail he had made earlier among the strange cylindrical rocks. He removed his glasses and scanned the area. *The way looks clear, but I can't take anything for granted.* Once again, he tested his way, probing the ground one step at a time as he ventured forward. After he had reached the region of sandstone, he became weightless and drifted to safety, touching down on solid ground.

"Mr. G, it seems there are no shortcuts in this place. Instead, opposition confronts us at every turn." Jerry sighed. "Mom always said life was full of battles, but it'd be nice to get an occasional break."

With his pack on his back, he was off. In little time, he had found his way through the small V-shaped tunnel and proceeded to reunite with Delphinius.

At the path's convergence, he detected a pillar he had missed earlier. It had blended in with the strange forms shaped by the drippings from the limestone. A haunting breeze prickled his skin, while an unpleasant odor assaulted his olfactory senses. Something different emanated from this structure, something foreboding.

When Jerry approached the column, the cavern's natural radiance became depressed and muted as if someone had reined in the light, pouring darkness into the damp, moldy chamber, filling it with despair and gloom. An unsettling silence met his ears. "Mr. G, I feel like I just entered the inner sanctum."

He moved a little closer, wary of the pillar. The twisted stone was decomposing, and the symbols were old and difficult to see. The ground surrounding the column was black and hard-baked. Scraped across the column's surface were streaks of red, as though blood had been spilled. *What happened here?* He scratched his head. *Did someone or something die? What secrets lie within its heart?*

The support seemed functional and intact, but did he dare obtain its power? As Jerry searched for a placement for the aether, a plaque came into view at the pillar's decaying base. Inscribed was a warning: "The seed once planted cannot be removed."

What seed? What does it mean? Jerry paced, rubbing his neck. *I wish Julean were here to help.* What consequences would come if he were to obtain its power? He'd yet to place boundaries on his actions, so why start now? Jerry hesitated but then placed his aether in the only slot available and stepped back. *I hope I'm doing the right thing.*

The pillar ignited with an eerie glow. Mr. G's eyes flickered with a dim blue light. The ground shook and rumbled, and Jerry struggled to maintain his balance. Then a beacon of shadows shot up into the cavern's roof and an energy pulse knocked him to the ground. He gasped as the cavern exploded into a dark, dismal display of macabre images. The column spewed out nauseous, black clouds of gloom. He lay there, groggy from the aftereffect.

Jerry rose, his chest tightening. Scattered thoughts filled his mind as though he were going crazy. He staggered and fell. Gradually, things calmed. "Never have I experienced anything so depressing." He exhaled a fuzzy breath. "Mr. G, are you all right?"

He rose and seized his aether from the pillar. Once again, a surge of energy erupted, but this time it was different. Jerry felt something cold entering his body, and within moments he felt tired and lethargic as if he had, been drugged. The chill spread through him, sucking him down into blackness, into an unimaginable expanse of nothingness. Numbness began to overtake him. The prickling tension mounted with every passing second until he was completely numb, buried beneath an icy cold state of misery.

He pulled a stored fruit out of his pack, ate it, and washed it down with a gulp of fresh spring water. Within seconds, his vitality was restored, the intense emotion of despair stripped from him as though he had just stepped out of a warm soothing bath, washed clean of the dirt of hopelessness. Jerry stood there for a few moments and then poured some water into his hand and splashed it on his face and along the back of his neck. He worried about what had just taken place and anxiously awaited his meeting with Julean. But for now, it was off to find Delphinius to discuss Ceti.

At Ceti's lake, Jerry jogged to the place where he had met Delphinius. A salty humidity hung in the air, and the soothing sounds of waves lapping against a frothy shore eased his angst.

"Delphinius, are you here?" Jerry whispered, wanting to avoid arousing Ceti. "I have returned." For the next several minutes, he stood at the edge of the lake quietly trying to summon Delphinius.

Finally, Delphinius popped his head out of the lake. "Back so soon? Collected the pods, have you?"

"Yes, it was quite the journey."

"Shhh, please. Ceti is upset with our clan."

"How can your family live, or for that matter survive, in the same body of water with a sea monster?" Jerry asked with a puzzled stare.

"We are an enormous and resilient clan, we are!" Delphinius whispered. "We have had our conflicts with him and have come out victors. Since our numbers are great, we are able to defend ourselves against his brutality. He minds his business, we mind ours. But when we help our friends cross the lake, he becomes furious."

"Is that why he's upset now?"

"Yes. We helped a Fafnir cross, and he is outraged now. But his anger will pass. It always does."

"What's a Fafnir?"

"An indigenous native, they are. From time to time, they come out seeking help to pass by Ceti."

"I don't mean to trouble you, but how do we get Ceti to eat the pods?"

"This time every day, he leaves the water to eat the local vegetation. Place them in his path, yes, his path, and they will be too tempting for him to pass up."

After rushing to the shoreline, Jerry laid out the spotted treats so he wouldn't miss them and then hurried to an outcropping of rocks that hung over the lake and hid.

"Hey, what happened to the fog?" Jerry asked.

"Oh, it comes and goes. Today is clear, so crossing is easier. When the fog is present, it is hard to guide, but we should be all right."

It wasn't long before Ceti exited the lake to consume his usual meal from the native foliage. Jerry's face froze in shock.

"Holy geode!" Jerry gulped past a lump stuck in his throat. "He must be over a hundred feet long and almost as tall. In all my life, I've never—"

"Shhh."

"He's massive," Jerry mouthed.

With four legs and a scaly green body, the intimidating form rose from the water, grunted, and stomped his way onto shore. His dark green head looked like a giant horned lizard, trimmed with glistening yellow streaks. Sharp piercing fangs flashed with several rows of teeth. His eyes, black as tar, seared right through you.

Jerry held his breath as Ceti drew close to the pods. The creature abruptly stopped and looked around as though something were amiss. Jerry remained riveted as the beast lowered his head and sniffed the pods and then, in an instant, gobbled them down. In just a few short minutes, he yawned and retreated to his domain, disappearing beneath its surface.

Jerry glanced at the lake and watched the water settle. Nervous thoughts oscillated within his mind. *What if Ceti wakes before I reach the other side? What if I have to fight this massive creature?* After his experience with Virga, he worried.

"Now we cross the lake," Delphinius said, nodding his head.

"Are you sure?" Jerry fidgeted uneasily, his eyes darting to the sides, as if wishing he could just forget the whole thing.

"Of course he sleeps. We must go now!"

Once Jerry was in the small boat, Delphinius asked him to throw him the rope connected to the bow. With Delphinius controlling the navigation, the small craft sped across the lake, plowing through the choppy waves. Spray showered Jerry's face as the hull slapped the swells. Salt water stung his eyes and coated his throat. It was a vast body of water, and crossing the bumpy swells felt like an eternity.

"How much longer before we're there?" Jerry's eyes shifted about, searching for any suspicious activity.

"I am not sure, but close we should be by the time his sedation wears off."

After several minutes of scanning the water, Jerry began to relax as he focused on the rippling waves, glistening with a twinkling light as though glitter had been tossed into the lake. Finally, the beach came into sight, and a bright hope flashed inside of him. *Yes! We're going to make it.*

Suddenly, a disturbance in the water caused it to boil as if something had awakened beneath the surface. The air quivered, and Ceti emerged. Terror seized Jerry's mind. The fierce gigantic beast rose up from the lake, sending a massive wall of water toward him.

Ceti was livid! Jerry's heart plunged like a person in a freefall. How could he defeat something so powerful, so overwhelming? Infuriated with the Delphinian clan, Ceti sent another massive wave that lifted the small boat on its crest and tossed it like a toy to the shore.

Delirious with rage, the sea monster thundered toward Jerry. The Delphinians, dancing among the waves, leaped high above the water and pounded Ceti with extreme force. The strength of their strike was staggering, causing him to leave the water. The mighty clan barked and slapped the water with their flippers, creating loud, raucous splashes.

Jerry's feet froze. He couldn't wrest his gaze from Ceti. Was this an illusion? How could any creature be so vast, so menacing? The air was heavy with anticipation and uncertainty.

Now, facing Ceti all alone, Jerry clasped his aether and merged his mind with its essence. Intense energy surged through him. He sucked in a restless breath, knowing he hadn't mastered the aether's full potential. *If I fail, I may die.* A sudden urge to run came over him, but run where?

Jerry stumbled in the sand just as the giant beast sent a blazing stream of fire toward him. He dived away from the fiery mass, his hair singed. The air popped and crackled. Jerry grunted, jumped up, and unleashed a barrage of force, striking the sea monster's head with a thunderous explosion. He felt the energy roll, electrify, and course through his body like the blood surging through his veins.

The vicious creature took a few dizzying steps, shook his head, and raged toward him, releasing a wild storm of fireballs. Jerry's heart pounded as though it were going to beat out of his chest. Desperation and hopelessness engulfed him. But then, just when he thought all was lost, a shield of white light encircled him. As Jerry clung to his aether, a feeling like he had never felt swept over him, protecting him from the massive conflagration. A flicker of hope sparked within his soul. *Incredible! But now what do I do?*

Ceti's rage strengthened with each assault. Jerry struggled to avoid the onslaught as the colossal beast lashed out with gnashing teeth and a tail that snapped like a whip. He was knocked back against a huge boulder, and pain shot through his back and leg. Every muscle in his body ached as he lay there, gasping for air. Jerry tried to get up but hesitated a bit too long. Ceti's tail smacked him again, throwing him backward in a burst of pain. His back slammed against a jagged stalagmite, shattering the column into pieces.

Jerry's mouth went dry. Knowing he had to win this battle without any help, he shuddered. But something powerful burned inside him when he held his aether close, sending a wave of comfort through his heart. It felt alive, as though its force pulsed through him, merging with him. His breathing slowed and his nerves stilled. He quickly grabbed an avian fruit and bit into it.

Instantly, his body responded with a surge of strength. He managed to release an energy blast that lacerated an exposed area under Ceti's neck, sending him tumbling backward. The creature rose, shaking his head, clearly dazed by the force of the blast. He threw his head back and roared, letting out a thunderous howl. The sound was horrific, louder than anything Jerry had ever heard.

Jerry grimaced, scrambling to get out of the creature's way, and then released a powerful blast that caused the monstrous sea creature to stumble and fall. Several penetrating lacerations opened down to the bone. He watched as they bled and oozed.

The beast stood disoriented.

Jerry seized the moment and sent a flurry of massive detonations that tore and battered the sea monster's flesh.

Ceti struggled. His eyes became distant, his breathing irregular. Jerry sensed the beast was tiring and hammered him with explosive shockwaves. With slow steps, Ceti retreated to the water and limped backward into its depths. Finally beaten, he submerged into the lake while all the Delphinians cheered.

Jerry slumped onto the cold ground, the stillness of the water reflecting in his eyes. He let out a long-held breath and wiped the sweat from his face. Then he turned to Delphinius. "Is it over?"

"It is indeed!" he exclaimed. "You have beaten Ceti. You have embarrassed him and put him to shame. He will never bother you again."

"I ... I hope you're right." His words were jittery. "I never want to face that demon again." Staring down, he shook his head in disbelief. "Thanks for assisting me against this dreadful creature."

Delphinius nodded and leaped into the air, somersaulted, and splashed back into the lake, disappearing beneath its surface.

With his wounds healing quickly, Jerry sat trying to absorb all that had occurred. So much had happened so fast. He glanced around. A warm breeze wrapped him in a blanket of humidity. It'd been just over a week since the start of his journey, but during that time his sojourn in the caverns had changed him. He reached into his pocket and rolled the iron pyrite nugget between his fingers, letting out a woeful breath as he recalled the last night he had spent with his friends. It seemed so distant now, and he wondered if he'd ever see them again. Even though a tender and loving bond with Andromeda was growing, something in his life was still missing.

CHAPTER TWENTY

LEO'S RING

Jerry grunted and pushed off the cold ground, setting his sights on the next seal. His nerves were still on edge as he walked down the sandy path, hearing nothing but the sound of his own soft footsteps. He marveled at the changing scenery; the earthen walls distilled a tropical scent that mixed with a fresh organic perfume from the flowering plants that flourished along the cavern's floor. The mood mellowed, and his thoughts turned to Andromeda.

"Did you see my battle with Ceti?"

"Yes," Andromeda gushed as she appeared next to him, "My stomach twisted and churned during your conflict with him. You need to understand—Ceti is a formidable enemy not easily defeated. You've proven yourself worthy!"

His gaze drifted wistfully toward Andromeda. "I long for the time we'll be together ... away from the chaos that reigns here."

She smiled and touched his face. "Remember to let your heart guide. It will not fail you."

"I thought I was going to die," Jerry said, rubbing the back of his neck. "It was like I was trapped inside of hell. It was all so crazy."

"But you won."

"Won what?"

"You beat Ceti."

"Yeah, but I almost died."

"You don't understand. Each time you use your abilities, your life force increases."

"Did you bring flowers?"

"Flowers?" Andromeda scrunched her eyebrows together.

"Yeah, just in case I died." Jerry's dimples deepened as he winked at her.

"Oh ..." Andromeda splashed a wide smile. "You have no idea how much your power just grew."

"My aether was incredible, but I'm still confused. Can you help me understand more about its use?"

"Indeed I can!" Andromeda's eyes sparkled like fire. "The aether will adapt to each situation, depending on your need or the confrontation. As you progress with your knowledge and training, you will reach a point when you'll have complete control. Right now, it will react to your circumstances, but at some point you will command its performance." Andromeda moved closer. "Each time you receive a transfer of energy from the power-up stations, you'll be infused with additional abilities. Your power will increase as you use it. Think of a battery charger—the longer you use it, the more it will charge."

"So now I'm a human battery."

"No, that's just an example." Andromeda rolled her eyes. "Only when you connect with your aether will your mind direct its power. You may come across some situations where you can't connect, such as your encounter with Promethion. These conditions require outside help or developing your mind control. The more experience you have, the more power you will generate."

"How will I know?" His eyes rested on hers. "I don't want another Virga or Promethion."

"If you're unable to merge your mind with the aether, you'll know not to engage."

"What if I don't have a choice? What do I do?"

"Your protective shield affords a simple but powerful and efficient means of protection against all adverse situations."

"You still didn't answer my question."

"Fear and doubt can cause unrest." She spoke with hesitancy. "The forces that are attacking you both inside and out have to be challenged, fought, and conquered. You must believe and trust in your heart."

Jerry felt a warmth radiate into his soul, as if he were standing next to a blazing fire. He was determined to become more disciplined. *Why is this so hard? When will I learn to let my heart guide?* After an hour together, Jerry said, "You've seen me in action. You've also saved my life. Thus far, based on what you've observed, do I have the ability to ... you know ... make it?"

"I empathize with your apprehension. You still have much to learn, but as your trials become more complicated, you'll grow in your ability to meet those challenges. Every encounter, every confrontation will give you experience. I will be with you, but ultimately it is you who must prevail."

Jerry brought his right hand to his temple. "I know. I'm trying."

"I must caution you, though. Some trails may alter your fate." She grasped his hand and squeezed it. "One in particular. If you enter the pathway of memories, it may distort your past and present recollections, destroying any hope and dreams we may have had for real happiness. The effect may appear harmless but can be devastating. Please, heed my warnings." After embracing him one last time, she vanished.

Jerry had heard the worry in her voice. *What is this memory path? I've never seen Andromeda so nervous. For her sake, I will try to avoid the trail if possible.*

Cool temperatures and a slight breeze ushered Jerry along the earthen path. The vast chamber narrowed to a corridor filled with dense vegetation sandwiched between and around various rock forms. Woody plants and shrubs bordered the trail, exhibiting lush yellow-green leaves and reddish-black stems. Calcite drips from the ceiling echoed throughout the cavern as they deposited their precipitates onto smaller limestone stalagmites. A pervasive white light beamed down optimism, reflecting a change in Jerry's countenance. Then the familiar smell of smoke permeated the damp unfiltered air. His heart quickened.

"Uh-oh, Mr. G." His grip tightened on his aether. "I hope this isn't another situation like Promethion."

He crept along the path until a wooden hut came into view. A lazy curl of gray smoke rose from a convoluted stovepipe, dissipating into the air above the tiny cottage. Jerry breathed a sigh of relief. *Well, that explains the smoke, but what lies inside?*

The little shack was nestled against a backdrop of red flowering trees and exuded warmth. Dilapidated tin-can shingles draped on its roof complemented the rustic panels nailed to its sides. Jerry strolled over to the small cottage but didn't see anyone around. He stood on a rickety porch that squeaked and stared at a weathered gray door. *I don't sense anything, but still ...*

Next to the entrance hung a little copper bell attached to a braided rope. He tried to connect to his aether but couldn't. "Well, Mr. G, whaddya say we give it a go?" Jerry stared into his still-glowing eyes. "Me, too!" When he gave the rope a tug, an odd clunking noise erupted. "It sounds like an old cowbell." He couldn't help but smile. "Huh, the way things are going, I wouldn't be surprised if a cow answered."

After waiting a few seconds, the door creaked open. "How may I assist you?" an old man said.

"Well, to be honest"—Jerry cleared his throat—"your place was so close to the trail, I thought I would stop and see if anyone was home. I'm not sure if you can assist me with anything, but I thought I would ask."

Dressed in overalls and boots, the elderly man had seen the shades of time. Etched into his face were the signs of wear. His expressive eyes drooped with the years but still had a twinkle of youth. His wispy gray hair straggled across balding spots on his head, and he hunched over a cane and moved slowly. "My name is Leo from the constellation Leonis. Many years ago, I trained exotic animals, but now I offer advice to travelers."

Leo had been known as the "Little King" when he lived on the royal star Regulus. His reputation as an exotic animal trainer had preceded him throughout the sector.

"Please, come in and have a seat," Leo motioned to him.

"You know, I think I'll take you up on that."

"Take me where?" Leo said, pointing to his ear. "I'm a bit hard of hearing."

"No, I mean, I ... I'll take you up on your offer."

"Oh, uh, okay," Leo muttered.

Once inside, Jerry noticed several pictures hung on the walls. It was obvious most were from Leo's younger days. It reminded him of big-game hunters posing after the kill. Some displayed creatures he had never seen.

Tarnished browns covered the walls. Trinkets and old glass bottles filled several wooden shelves held up with deer antler brackets. Candles and kerosene lamps emanated a soft magnetic aura that created solemnity and warmth. Jerry felt right at home and slid into a rustic cedar chair, sniffing the air. An exquisite aroma of something freshly baked permeated the hut.

Leo turned up the wick in his oil lamp. "Would you like a lion's breath? I just made them.

"A lion's breath?"

"Sure, they're made from the lion bush found on the regal star. Try one. They look a little like a ginger snap but have more of a bite to them." Jerry reached for one but hesitated. Leo waved his hand. "I'm joking. They don't bite. I promise."

"Sorry, I don't mean to unnerve you, but I have learned anything is possible down here. What and where is the regal star?" Jerry asked as he munched on the tasty treat.

"Oh, I believe you call it Jupiter. Avela controls that particular sector."

"Who is Avela, and are you talking about the planet Jupiter in our solar system?"

"Whoops, I've already said too much. All these years have taken a toll on my memory." Leo pointed to his head.

"I don't mean to impose, but how old are you?"

"Last count, I was almost twelve hundred of your years."

"Seriously?" Astounded, Jerry sat there with his mouth gaping.

"Oh, yes. You know, people used to live hundreds of years on Earth before its orbit changed. In fact, I recall training several dangerous animals on its moon."

"Did you ever work with lions and tigers?"

"Oh, yes. They were the simple ones."

"Were you ever in danger?"

"Of course." Leo scratched his head with the battered fingers of a man who had spent a life training ferocious predators, truly dangerous creatures that demanded respect. "That reminds me of the time I trained an arato."

"An arato?"

"I had just learned my trade and been given the assignment to go the Algol star system. I had never seen an arato, but when he scowled at me, it seemed like he had a vendetta from the start. This particular neamid was a clever one. He was a warthog-crocodile hybrid and stood about three feet in height." Leo shook his head. "Because I was still naïve, I almost lost my life that day."

"Sounds hazardous."

"Well, it certainly wasn't for the squeamish."

"So, what happened?" Jerry leaned back and stretched his arms wide.

"I was getting ready to teach this ornery critter to follow my command when he lunged at me and tore into my side. If I hadn't had my ring, I would have been his lunch that day."

"What ring?"

"Heh, much to the devious fiend's surprise, I transformed into a certium and proceeded to kick his butt. After that, I never had another problem."

Just as Jerry was getting into his story, a loud thud shook the tiny hut. He shot out of his chair, rushed to the door, and swung it open. His breath caught and his face paled. "What in the geode is that?" A winged creature with a lion's body and a serpent's head stood outside, pawing at the ground.

"That, my friend, is a grackal," Leo said, his voice shaky. "This devious beast has a poisonous venom which can be lethal. It's been hanging around my cottage waiting for me to make a mistake."

"What does it want with you?"

"They're scavengers seeking to prey on the old and weak." Leo groaned in frustration. "They usually travel in pairs, which makes them hard to kill, but I only see the one today."

Before reacting, Jerry recalled the words of Andromeda: "You need to avoid those situations where you can't engage your mind. Learn to trust in your heart."

With confidence, he grasped his aether. Its energy surged with power, and he knew he had the capacity to confront the grackal. "This will be the last time he harasses you."

Jerry stepped outside and lowered his aether. The beast snorted and lunged at him. A mighty blast exploded from his staff, striking the creature square in the chest, ending the battle before it had even started. In disbelief, he viewed the venomous creature lying dead.

"Incredible!" Jerry stood stunned. For the first time, he'd felt his mind take control, seizing the moment and discharging the power he'd begun to master.

The old man hurried outside and saw the grackal lying on the ground lifeless. "You did it!" Leo dabbed his forehead with a wrinkled cloth he'd pulled from his shirt pocket. "I can't believe it's dead!" He fidgeted about and fished a small clear box from his pocket. "I have something for you." The crystalline case revealed a ring with an octagonal stone that frequently changed colors. "Take this with you. This little rascal has powers only a man of your skill can harness."

"What does the ring do?"

"This little beauty can change your appearance when in trouble. It saved my life many times." Leo rubbed his chin. "It has been too long since I've engaged the ring's power. I don't remember how to activate it, but I'm sure you can find a way."

"No, Leo." Jerry held his hand up. "I couldn't take something that has meant so much to you."

"You must." He grabbed Jerry's hand and placed the ring in it. "I have no need of it, but you … It may be the one thing that saves your life."

Jerry's face warmed while he gazed upon it. "You have lived a life most people dream of. I feel as though I've known you forever. Maybe someday we can meet again." Jerry lowered his head respectfully, and after offering his good-byes, resumed his trek toward the next seal.

He was fascinated with the unusual gift but thought it best to wait before recklessly trying to see how the ring worked. If he transformed into another creature, he wanted to make sure the spell was reversible.

CHAPTER TWENTY-ONE

THE AQUILAS

ı

Back on the main trail, he caught sight of a small tributary flowing next to Leo's cottage and parallel to the central pathway. It's low ebbing hum echoed throughout the cavern, bringing a sense of serenity. A warmth cascaded down from the cavern's ever-present brightness, splattering flashes of light across the rippling water, filling him with peace and contentment.

Within the hour, the cavern opened to a much larger area with a river coursing through it. The air was so thick he could taste the rich, earthy quality of the native habitat. The aquamarine flow splashed against the glistening rocks. Magenta leaves draped over the shimmering ripples of water, and intense algal blooms of blue-green algae covered the banks. Strange insects were sucked down eddies of swirling water as though someone had just unplugged a bathtub drain. With the meandering current exposing such visual displays of color, he wondered if it had a dark side.

After he'd hiked but a short distance, the trail became faint, disappearing at the water's edge. *Great. Am I going to have to swim across this wide channel?* Jerry rubbed the back of his neck as he scanned the area. Hope flashed inside him when a narrow wooden bridge came into view. "Yes!" His face brightened. "Mr. G, we aren't getting wet today." He rushed to the structure, but just before crossing the overpass, he caught sight of a small sign posted next to the entrance: "The Eridanus River."

Jerry had a bad feeling about this. Recalling Lyro's warning, he hesitated. Was this the nesting area of the aquilas? Sweat beaded on his forehead. Maybe there was another way around it, but where? Several small trails led away from the main path, but he was afraid he would get lost if he strayed. Sucking in an anxious breath, he crept forward, moving without a sound.

Once he was across the Eridanus River, a grove of colorful trees came into sight. They were similar to blue hydrangeas, with showy mopped-head blooms, only bigger. A familiar scent filled his nose: slightly sulfury, with a pinch of seaweed and a briny quality. *It smells like I'm near the ocean again.*

A sense of danger flashed through his mind, and he abruptly halted his steps. There was a sudden dryness in his throat, his tongue sticking to the roof of his mouth. Jerry lifted his canteen from his belt and gulped a long drink, staring straight ahead. He wiped his mouth with the back of his hand, focusing on several subtle movements in the dense flowering trees. But what was he seeing? *Were these the aquilas Lyro spoke of?*

Jerry crept along, hugging the tree line, trying to stay out of sight. A single tan feather floated down and landed at his feet, and he glanced up into the branches. *Oh, my ... They're huge.* His eyes grew wide. Looking like gigantic eagles, the aquilas flapped wildly, shedding tufts of brown as they beat their wings against their chests. Jerry sensed agitation by the way they fluttered their feathers. How would he get past them now?

Mammoth, angry birds with beaks like serrated knives stared him down with dark opaque eyes. Fear besieged him as if he were a lamb in a slaughterhouse. Was he to be their next meal? He quickly opened his pack and removed the bag of apus flowers. With his supply running low, he gulped down a few, hoping it would be enough. In seconds, he became invisible and eased his way forward.

Unaware of his imprints in the soft sand, he was caught off guard by the aquilas' keen senses. At once, they swarmed above him, littering the sky and filling the cavern with high-pitched screeches. His knees buckled and he collapsed to the ground, trying to connect with his aether. Sweat poured from his forehead as he closed his eyes and formed a mental image of pure light encasing him in its protection. Instantly, an energy shield encircled him.

The aquilas swooped down and bombarded him with powerful talons and bloodthirsty beaks. He gasped at their speed and their ability to veer and turn so fast. His heart pounded as his cold, clammy hands squeezed his aether, hoping the defensive buffer would hold. He tried to produce an offensive assault but couldn't. His thoughts quickly shifted to Lyro.

"Lyro, I need assistance, right now!" Tension shot up his neck and his lips quivered. "If you can hear me, please help."

The aquilas continued their ferocious attack, pounding him without pause. Jerry became desperate. Where was Lyro? Would he—*could* he—come to his rescue?

Then a sudden melody met his ears. Harmonically tuned notes floated through the air, sweeping through the cavern like a soft lullaby, calming and pacifying the frenzied creatures. Seconds later, the aquilas were fast asleep. Not a single bird stirred. Even the trees drooped in reverence. Jerry breathed a sigh of relief just as Lyro became visible.

"See, I told you!" Lyro boasted. "My music is so powerful even the aquilas can't resist its magical charm."

"You came!" Jerry stood, clinging to his aether. "You saved my life! I'll be forever in debt to you and your brother."

"Oh, yes. My brother and I are always competing against each other, but he'll never be able to best me! The harmony I weave into my music can entice the most ardent of souls."

"Oh, I understand competition," Jerry said, nodding his head. "My life has been filled with people who doubted my abilities. It always seemed I was never quite good enough ... like I was in a race I couldn't win."

"Is that why you're here now?"

"Well, it started with a bet." Jerry's face reddened. "I mean ... I was struggling financially ... I had to—"

"You don't have to explain yourself to me."

"No, I mean—"

"It's okay." Lyro held his hand up. "Just remember, if you doubt yourself, you add fuel to your doubt."

Jerry stood stiffly, not knowing what to say.

"It's been fun. If you're ever in need, just call my name." With a flick of his wrist, Lyro disappeared.

The grimace on Jerry's face revealed his true inner feelings. Even now he doubted. What if he couldn't complete his quest? What if his abilities lacked? Every time he felt like he was making progress, something was there to knock him down. Despite his ambivalence, Jerry was gaining significant wisdom, but for now he was off to the next chamber.

CHAPTER TWENTY-TWO

CANYON OF FEARS

Jerry plodded along for the better part of an hour before the narrow corridor opened to a massive chamber filled with glistening crystals. A white light emanated from above as though a visible aura had engulfed the cavern. Clear crystalline quartz stalagmites and stalactites reflected slivers of rainbow light that bounced off the walls, giving rise to a psychedelic effect. Jerry's breath caught. "Mr. G, I've never seen anything so beautiful."

The soft sound of water dripping into aquamarine pools added a serene tinkling to the cavern, filling him with a quiet stillness. He no longer felt the cavern's cold breath; rather, warmth embraced his body in a relaxed glow. Fear and worry left him. Bliss enveloped his soul with a feeling of euphoria like nothing he'd ever experienced. Was this a prelude to what life would be like on Enif? Is so, he couldn't wait. He would do anything to see it happen. Anything!

A spinning orb came into view. *What's this?* Jerry hustled to investigate. The air sparked with energy, and he instinctively knew Julean was near, but where was the beam of light?

The orb hovered in one spot about five feet off the ground, like a balloon without strings. When a series of bright lights erupted from it, Jerry jerked backward. A surge of kaleidoscopic brilliance projected throughout the cavern, adding a spectrum of geometric color. He paused in contemplation. *So how do I activate this thing? Hmm, I wonder ...*

No sooner had Jerry passed his hand through the colorful bands than a brilliant white light erupted, and with it appeared Julean.

"How may I help you?" Julean asked, his hands splayed across his chest.

"It's good to see you again. I have so many questions since we last met." His eyes shifted to Julean's vesture. "Why do the symbols on your robe continue to change?"

"As you progress through each chamber, the knowledge you acquire is reflected in my vestments." Julean pointed to his robe. "With each progression, I have the opportunity to instruct and help you improve the abilities you receive. And—"

"Speaking of instruction, what do you know about this ring? Leo gave it to me as a gift and said the stone had the capability to alter my shape, but he didn't remember how it worked. Can you help?"

"This indeed is a special gift." With a lifted eyebrow, Julean peered at the ring. "It is a ring of transfiguration!

The bearer of this stone wields power to transform their physical form at will, morphing into anything they wish, but only when in trouble. If you examine the gem closely, the colors constantly change." Julean rotated it in his hand. "Its variation symbolizes your capacity to alter your form just as the coloration varies. If in trouble, place it on your finger and meditate on what form you want to take. If you can't decide, the stone will make the best choice available."

Jerry slipped the ring onto his finger, but nothing happened. "Now, how does this work?"

"You must envision the form you desire." Annoyed, Julean pursed his lips as though he'd just sucked a lemon. "As you focus on the image, your body will morph into that shape, but only if you are in trouble. I must emphasize, only when you are in need!"

"Sorry." Jerry felt blood rush to his face. "I guess I need to pay more attention, but I've been obsessed with the ring's capability." He took the ring off and placed it in a secure pocket. "If you don't mind, I have a few more questions."

"Of course, that is why I am here."

"At the last jinan, I met Oden."

"Oh, yes, he is the caretaker of the jinans."

"He called this an avian." Jerry opened his pack and pulled out a bird-shaped fruit. "After eating it ... well ... I panicked when I saw myself floating almost fifty feet in the air. Since then, I've calmed down, but I still don't feel like I have complete control." Jerry scratched his head. "What can you tell me?"

"The avian's power is still maturing inside you. Once it reaches its maturation point, the constraints that hold you back will be broken, freeing your spirit. Like an eagle, you will glide on currents of wind, soaring to unimaginable heights."

"Right now, I prefer the earth under my feet." Jerry gave a half smile. "But what about—"

"You need to understand." Julean waved his hands in the air as though he were about to conjure something up. "These powers ... these abilities ... they are maturing in you as we speak. It takes time to develop their full potential. Your capacity to grow is directly proportionate to their use. Each time you engage them, whether it be in actual need or practice, your proficiency improves."

"Got it." Jerry relaxed and shifted his hip to the side. "I have another question. At my last power-up, I came across what seemed to be a broken-down pillar that was still intact. A plaque at its base said something about a seed once planted can't be removed."

"Stop there!" Julean's expression suddenly became grim. "You have acquired a malicious power many try to avoid. The power of dissolution is extremely dangerous. It is imperative that you shun this function while still in the caverns. To negate this warning would mean the end of your travel and the end of you. Since all matter is created, our laws dictate it be destroyed or evolve at some point. This ability can terminate any creation. The power of dissolution commands the utmost respect and is dangerous to the untrained."

"Can I get rid of it?" Jerry's face turned pale.

"Unfortunately, no. But you need not worry about it now. It has no application in the caverns, and its potential requires time to mature. Right now, we must focus on getting to the next entry."

Rattled about the disconcerting power, Jerry acquiesced to Julean's demands, allowing him to continue his instruction. The lessons were taking longer and longer, and with each exercise, Jerry's power was becoming stronger, creating an extremely potent force. After several hours of training, Jerry asked, "What do you think? Am I making sufficient strides that will enable me to get to the portal?"

Julean placed his hand on Jerry's shoulder. "Your life is a reflection of your thoughts and actions. Like a puzzle, it takes time for all the pieces to come together before you can see the complete picture." He smiled. "Your puzzle is coming together, but you're still missing a few pieces. Once you become more adroit in your decision-making, you will have mastered the biggest part. Remember, trust in your heart." Then he vanished.

"Wait! What about this ... book?" Jerry's voice faded. "Oh, well. Next time." He turned, placed the book back in his pack, and left.

As the light dimmed and the cavern shifted into a shadowy canyon, Jerry picked up his pace, a cool, dry breeze creasing his cheeks. Each step grated against a pebbled surface. The canyon's walls rose several stories high, and their length extended far into a dark expanse. Erosion had sculpted the layers of sandstone into strange and colorful shapes. *Reminds me of the rainbow fluorite I found back home, only more vibrant.*

At first glance, he didn't notice the inscription near the entrance, but with a second look, he read "Canyon of Fears"

"Mr. G, what do you think it's trying to tell us?" In light of his experience with Ceti, Jerry hesitated, scanning the chamber for more traps. "I once read fear was a natural response to moving closer to the truth, but I wonder." Unaware of what the caption alluded to, he launched his journey into the canyon, holding fast to his aether. *Will this be another test of my abilities, or will I encounter more illusions?*

A tremor of trepidation and uncertainty prevailed as his footsteps faded deep into the bowels of the canyon. Phosphorescent rocks skittered down the steep walls, sending his nerves jumping. Then, without warning, four solid transparent barriers shot up around him, encasing him in a sealed chamber. *What in the geode ...*

The oppressive atmosphere made the container feel tomblike, as if he were trapped in a glass coffin—a coffin with little air. Panic seized Jerry when water gushed into the closed structure.

"Oh, no, no, no!"

As the liquid horror rose, he pounded on the thick walls. Jerry desperately tried to connect to his aether but couldn't. He tried again.

Nothing happened.

A death quiver caused his heart to plunge. He felt alone and powerless with no escape. His breathing was shallow, coming in short jerks and spasms. In desperation, he tried to suck in more air but failed. If he was to live, it was up to him. With the water almost to his shoulders, he was running out of time.

There must be a way out. I need to calm down.

Jerry floundered within the sealed cage, his hands trembling. Then he realized that the vessel had no bottom. He grabbed his knife, bent down, and wildly dug into the hard ground at the chamber's base. With the waterline rising quickly, coming up for air was becoming daunting. He shuddered. *One of my worst fears might be coming true: drowning!*

The water, now inches from the top, splashed into his nose as he inhaled his last breath. *Got to hurry!* He dropped down and frantically jabbed his knife into the dirt until, finally, the ground gave way, allowing his hands to slip under the booth's thick edge. With all his strength, he lifted. Water seeped between his fingers, slowly at first and then a little faster. Adrenaline surged to his arms; the container wobbled.

His chest burned and he became lightheaded. Water entered his nose and mouth and began to leak into his lungs. Jerry's muscles writhed with incredible body tension, his legs and arms shaking as though he were going into a seizure. *No time. Got to do it now!* A sudden surge of energy erupted in his muscles, and with one last heave he lifted the sepulcher of doom and released the water.

Jerry lay choking and gasping for air. When he sat up, he coughed and spit up the water that had seeped into his lungs.

"Holy geode!" he turned to Mr. G. "A lot of help you were. We could've drowned!"

Numerous concerns coursed through his mind. Jerry shuddered at the thought of going deeper into the canyon. He stared at the shadows along the towering walls.

"Mr. G, no wonder it's called the Canyon of Fears. It focuses on your worst nightmares and subjects you to them."

Jerry had a phobia about drowning and now brooded over his trek into the canyon of terror. He unzipped his pack to make sure everything was dry and intact. Then he rose up, chilled by the wetness, and resumed his quest. He tried to still his nerves, remembering Lyro's words, but deep inside doubt remained, for it was he who had to conquer his fears.

Weary and anxious, he stumbled down the unnerving corridor, accompanied by a strange presence. A shiver rippled through him. He tried to close off his thoughts to the feeling, but he couldn't push it away. Jerry shuddered and drew a deep breath. What horror did the canyon still possess? Would it be an illusion or would it be the thing that claimed his life?

Erosive carvings on the canyon's smooth interior evoked images of sinister creatures. Eerie eyes followed his every move. Ghostly teeth etched into the limestone structures sneered as he hustled past. A gusty wind whipped through the narrowed gap as though exhaling a mighty breath. Jerry scratched his head. "Mr. G, I feel like we're in a haunted house, except this is real!"

A sudden earthy aroma filled his nose as a low buzzing vibrated the air. *That scent—I've smelled it before.* His grip tightened on his aether.

Minutes passed, but nothing happened. The farther he went on the canyon floor, the softer the buzzing became. He released a slow breath, hoping he was safe, at least for the moment. But relief gave way to misery when a massive swarm of killer bees burst forth from the shadowy walls.

"Not bees!"

His heart plummeted to his feet as he flashed back to his youth. When he was eight years old, a swarm of bees stung his face numerous times. His eyes swelled shut, and his breathing became sporadic. He suffered severe pain and almost died. Now he cringed at the sight of them.

As a loud buzzing vibrated against his ears, the fear of death wedged deep within his throat. Heavy feet paralyzed Jerry as he focused on the terrifying insects. Then a surge of mettle shot through his veins. Energy rushed into his aether as fear began to feed his courage.

A soft hiss sounded in the air when an effervescence erupted from the ground. Thousands of tiny bubbles burst forth, engulfing the toxic pests. Jerry watched the swarm fall helplessly to the ground, unable to fly.

"We did it!" Jerry jumped in the air. "Where is your mighty sting now?"

Jerry celebrated while the stranded bees floundered on the ground. He trudged through the crunchy critters, hoping his nightmares were over, but the fear of making bad decisions lingered in his mind.

At the canyon's end, Jerry caught sight of a small crossbow hanging on a sparkling-clear stalagmite. A quiver filled with crystal arrows hung next to it. He crept over to the glistening column and slowly lifted the bow. *So, is a dark knight going to appear next?* Jerry glanced around, expecting trouble. His eyes shot to an engraving that suddenly materialized on its barrel: "The greatest weapon one has is the ability to choose one correctly over another."

"Mr. G, it makes sense to me, but things still hinge on my decision-making." Jerry sighed. "But then, where's the challenge if there is perfection?"

Although he didn't understand how to exploit their value, he placed the two in his pack and continued his travels.

CHAPTER TWENTY-THREE

AURIGA, THE CHARIOTEER

Over the next few hours, an ambient light shone throughout the cavern as though the sun were shining. The topography quickly changed into an arid desert paved with cholla and saguaro cacti. *Saguaro ... really? I feel like I'm back in Tucson.* His hair whipped about in a warm gust, and fragrant cactus blossoms added freshness to the air while his feet pounded against a dusty hard-baked floor.

Jerry was just starting to relax when another pillar emerged from between two hefty, identical saguaros. Their towering limbs swayed, flailing their barbed arms and making it impossible for him to reach the next power-up. Stumbling back, Jerry regained his balance as he ducked under their attack. Each time he approached, they swung toward him. He ran his hand through his hair and looked at Mr. G. "So how are we going to get past these thorny guardians?"

Instantly, a burst of energy surged through his body. *Oh, yeah.* Letting out a slow breath, he gripped his aether and discharged a booming shockwave, shattering the massive saguaros into tiny pieces.

"Mr. G, that was so easy." Jerry raised the end of his aether to his mouth and blew on it as if it were a smoking gun. "Andromeda was right—my power is getting stronger."

With the way clear, he made his way to a square tapered column with multiple compartments. Each one held a precious stone. The pillar was carved from white marble and glistened as though it were wet. Jerry rubbed the back of his neck. *I know this is a power-up station, but I have no idea what I'm supposed to do.* He circled the structure looking for an answer. A perceived aura radiated from the fire opal and jade, but when he tried to connect to them, he became confused. With the need for further enlightenment, he called for Andromeda.

"I need your help. None of this makes any sense."

"Are you focusing on the gems' beauty or their power?" Andromeda asked, appearing next to him.

"They are gorgeous, but not as gorgeous as you." His eyes widened in delight.

"Stop. You need to concentrate," she said, blushing.

"Oh, I am." Jerry locked on to her sparkling green eyes and just stared.

"You can place your scepter in any compartment, and you will receive power, but"—Andromeda touched the gleaming stones as she circled the column—"only one can harvest all that is available from the pillar. Sooo, which shall it be?"

"What will we eat once we're on Enif?"

"Jerry! Your not paying attention."

"Oh yes I am."

She pointed to the column. "Do you want my help?"

"Of course. It's just that I don't get to see you that often."

"Well, then ..."

Jerry shifted his gaze to the glistening column and tried to connect with each precious gem. A subtle change occurred when he passed his aether over the fire opal. Its transparent opulence flashed every color of the spectrum like lightning in a rainbow. "It must be the opal!"

"Are you sure?"

"I think so. Its energy feels stronger."

He promptly placed his aether into the fire opal's slot and stood back, waiting for a response. A sudden array of dazzling colors shot out from the anuns. "Wow! This is powerful."

Iridescent greens, scarlet reds, and bright yellows flashed through the cavern as if they'd been drawn from the depths of a luminous prism. Moments later, its gleaming radiance morphed into a ruddy black opalescence with a multitude of symbols, glowing and pulsing like a heartbeat.

Jerry traded glances with Andromeda and grabbed the radiant staff. Mr. G's eyes twinkled with warmth. This time it was different when he assimilated its power. His aether had become an extension of his body, one that interwove with his mind, one that infused his very soul.

"Incredible!" Jerry stood stunned. It was as if a veil had been lifted from his mind, allowing him the power to read the thoughts of others. "This is so surreal. It feels as though ... as though I'm connected to the universe." Jerry's eyes darted about like he'd just been given sight. After his encounter with Virga, he craved the ability to read minds, but even more so, he wanted the capacity to dominate thoughts.

"For now, you have power over the simpleminded. Later, you will command a far greater influence." She tipped her head and stared at him. "Developing your telepathic power is like exercising in a gym. You can't perform one exercise and expect instant results. Likewise, it takes time to cultivate an ability to forge your thoughts with someone and even more patience to control their actions. Before you can subject another to your command, you will need to devote many hours if you are to master the capacity of telepathy. Even then, to exert dominion over someone or something may be impossible if they have a strong will."

"When will I be able to have you with me constantly?" Jerry said, changing subjects. "You know what I mean. How much longer must I go through this ordeal before we can spend our lives together?" As he studied her eyes, he sensed a concern, almost fear. He tried to invade her thoughts, but she blocked his intrusion.

She lunged forward and embraced him with passion. "Ever since your encounter with Virga, I've known you've had a strong desire to acquire the power of mind dominance. But you need to understand that mastering telepathy takes time, sometimes years." She leaned back and looked at him with worry swarming in her eyes. "Prying into my thoughts could prove dangerous. Certain things could terminate your quest that can only be divulged at the portal."

Jerry craved to hold and caress her. He traced every inch of her face until locking onto her glistening emerald eyes. Her soft touch against his lips made his heart race. "I can't stop thinking about you," he whispered as he stroked her face. "You're the most fascinating woman I have ever met. Time can't pass too quickly."

Their lips passionately fused together. Temperatures rose. Embracing as if they were never going to see each other again, Andromeda pulled away. "Before our union can take place, you must finish your transformation. It remains imperative that you stay focused on the challenges you still need to conquer."

"So, tell me more about this Enif."

"The heavens are always blue, and peace abounds. No one wants. Pain and illness are nonexistent. We live much longer than the typical human. Not everything is bliss—we have our responsibilities—but we are able to enjoy life in a deeper way than most. We do have to abide by our natural laws, but accepting them is something we all do."

"What do you mean ... *natural laws?*"

"Certain laws have always existed in the universe. They have always been and will always be. The force and power of nature give life to all matter. Our regulations do not change, and as such, we all enjoy peace and tranquility."

"Will we be able to enjoy life together ... you know ... forever?"

"Oh, yes!" Her eyes sparkled with excitement. "Once you have made the full transformation, our union will be consummated in the Tower of Enif."

"The Tower of Enif?"

"I can't say any more at this time. I am forbidden to give you more information until you open the seventh chamber."

They spent the next few hours reviewing the skills he had learned, except that of telepathy. Her time had expired, and she embraced him. "You must move on and continue your quest. I know you're excited about the ability to read minds, but it's imperative that you focus on the skills that will see you through. They will be required as you progress through each chamber."

Before Jerry could question her further, she said, "I have something for you." Andromeda removed a scarab necklace from around her neck. "This amulet was given to me by my father. It's fashioned from the same fire opal you just received." She placed it around his neck and clasped it shut. "In the presence of fire, its energy will protect you, allowing you to free up your aether's power for something other than defensive maneuvers."

Jerry brought the crystal close to his eye, and a flame flickered within it. "It's like an eternal flame."

"Yes, so you'll never forget me."

He stared at the scarab pendant dangling at the end of the golden chain. "How does it work? I mean ... how do I activate it?"

"It's active as we speak." Turning her head to the side, she nodded. "I'm being summoned, but remember I am always with you." Then she vanished.

With his pack on his back, he set his sights on the next seal, wondering why Andromeda seemed so reluctant to help him with his mind-reading. He'd never seen her so worried and anxious. Was something amiss or was she just trying to protect him? And what about this amulet? Was it a diversion or did he really need it? No matter. He would practice his telepathy whenever possible until it became his strength. Then he would make his discovery.

The pathway broadened and a stale, musty odor prevailed. Jagged rocks and boulders lined a soft clay trail layered with hematite-stained sandstone. Chalky dust settled in his mouth. *This looks a lot like the red rocks of Sedona.* Stalactites hung from the ceiling like stilettos waiting to plunge into the unsuspecting. Strewn about were large cat-like tracks. Chewed bones lay scattered across the cavern's floor, having been gnawed on by wild animals or perhaps the stone creatures in the first chamber.

Fear mounted amid a shuddering warm breeze. A faint glow radiated from the scarab amulet—a glow that warmed his soul. An instant later, the red light grew brighter. Jerry held it in his hand, waiting, wondering what it meant.

A sharp turn emerged ahead and he slowed his pace. The path turned and then turned again. Jerry crept close, hugging the walls and peeking around the corners. He sensed something—a presence.

His breath caught when he saw a man in a flaming chariot guarding the next entry. He was stout, like a bodybuilder. Slashed across his bulging biceps, grotesque scars rippled as though they were alive. Adorned in defensive armor, he looked like a gladiator. Bronze shielding surrounded his forearms, and shimmering golden plates protected his thighs. Fastened to his chest was a glistening silver breastplate.

Jerry studied his cold black eyes, noting the rigidity of his jaw muscles, the hardness of his face. He held a whip of flames that crackled and popped like burning juniper. Harnessed next to him were two blazing teams of anxious lions, tearing a mangled body apart with their teeth and snapping at each other in a tussle of gluttony. Jerry lost his breath. *That explains the tracks and gnawed bones, but who in the geode is this guy?*

He fought the urge to run and sucked in a deep breath. *How am I going to contend with this titan, let alone his crazed pets?* His eyes locked on to the flaming lions and his mind went numb. Jerry was beside himself and found he was slipping into the familiar maelstrom of doubt and indecision. After a long moment, his thoughts cleared and he eased around the corner, his fingers firmly grasping his aether.

"Who goes there?" The warrior snapped his whip and the lions lunged forward, jerking the chariot.

Startled, Jerry jumped back. "I seek passage to the seventh seal." He tilted his head as if thinking. *Maybe I can get into his mind.*

"I am Auriga the charioteer and the fifth seal guardian." He glared at him and then turned his head and spit. "No one shall pass!"

Jerry tapped into his consciousness and learned that Auriga was the son of Vulcan from Capella. He'd been born with deformed legs that led him to invent the four-lion chariot. This invention earned him a place of honor in the sky. He trained chariot lions that were ostensibly faster than any horse. Later in life, he met an enchantress who restored his legs with a strength beyond that of any mortal. After receiving his renewed vigor, he often challenged those who had taken advantage of him in his younger years, and they raced their chariots in duels to the death.

He dared his rival, Pelops, the son of King Melisseus to a race. Auriga killed him after winning the event on the star Capella. He was cursed and sent to guard the caverns of Earth. Incensed with his banishment, he took out his frustration on the unfortunate travelers who traversed the subterranean channels.

Now that I know a little bit about you, let's see how strong your will is. Jerry tried to take control of Auriga's mind, but he was blocked. Aware of his prowess, he turned and retreated, feeling the man's glare as he rounded the corner he had just come from.

A heaviness spilled into the air. Dingy water seeping from crevices echoed throughout the chamber. Jerry stared at his fidgeting hands. *I wish Julean were here to give me advice.* He looked at Mr. G. "What say you? Are you up for the task?" Jerry pulled his canteen from his waist and took a quick swallow. He recalled Julean's words. *Let your heart lead. It will not let you down.* Jerry replaced his canteen and decided on a plan.

The apus flowers wouldn't be sufficient this time, with Auriga camped close to the entry, but he had the scarab amulet and Leo's ring, although neither had been tested. Jerry's hands shook as he reached for his aether, but the moment his fingers closed around it, a surge of energy flowed through him. Gulping a breath of confidence, he stepped around the corner and confronted the charioteer, his heart racing. "Step aside. I wish to avoid conflict, but I will pass!"

Auriga's face darkened, his voice gushed bitterness. "Better men than you have tried, only to have their throats crushed and insides ripped out!" Suddenly, a whip of flames shot through the air, snapping fiery lashes of death toward Jerry.

With the scarab amulet placed against his heart, the searing flogs glanced off his chest. Auriga gave a contemptuous scowl and unleashed his blazing lions.

Please, don't let me down this time! Jerry held fast to his aether and discharged a barrage of explosive energy at the ferocious beasts. The flaming felines were repelled for the moment, but then they surrounded him and unleashed a storm of terror, blasting him with lethal waves of fire.

Engaged in a blazing inferno, Jerry eliminated each lion with a show of tremendous force. Moving with ease, he fought off their attacks, discharging sonic blasts of pure energy. Within moments, he stopped and glanced around. Only ashes remained.

Breathing heavily and flaring his nostrils, Auriga was livid. "I'm not finished with you yet!" Anger flowed through him like a tsunami, and he jumped from his chariot and rushed Jerry.

Without much thought, Jerry snatched Leo's ring from his pocket and slipped it onto his finger. A strange feeling engulfed him as if every cell in his body were vibrating, and in an instant he morphed into a creature from the constellation Centaurus.

Auriga hesitated, but then like an angry bull he charged straight at him.

Now as a centaur, half man and half horse, Jerry's first instinct was to punch and kick as he reared up against the guardian. In his frenzy, he struck Auriga's jaw, knocking it out of joint.

Dazed, the charioteer snarled out a curse and double-fisted the centaur's back with such force that Jerry staggered backward, moaning and gasping for air. Before he could recover, Auriga was on him again, slamming his head into the rocky ground.

Letting out a breath of shock, Jerry grunted and shook his head in frustration. Then, gritting his teeth through the throbbing pain, he leaped up and kicked Auriga across the cavern floor. He slammed into a giant stalagmite.

"Argh!" Screaming profanities, Auriga roared toward him and punched the gallant steed repetitively, knocking the breath out of him.

A wave of pain shot through Jerry's body. Outraged, he turned and kicked with powerful thrusts, tearing into the gladiator's flesh.

Auriga fell backward, shaking his head. He got to his feet and seized a boulder. The massive rock shot out from his brawny hands like a rocket. With a dull thud, it struck the centaur hard.

A stab of pain shot through Jerry's body, sharp and deep. He slumped to the damp ground, the cavern's pale light reflecting in his eyes. He reeled in agony, and he wondered if he would survive Auriga's vicious attack.

Desperation and hopelessness engulfed him. Then he thought of Andromeda, and her sweet touch on his face buoyed his spirits. *Can't give up now.*

Auriga ripped a stalagmite from the ground and hurled it like a javelin.

Jerry jerked and twisted his head to the side, exposing his face to the oncoming projectile. With a whoosh, the lethal spear shattered against a nearby boulder, just missing him. The next several moments were lost in a mayhem of crashes and roars as waves of rubble smashed into the worried centaur.

Blood running from his nose and into his throat, Jerry choked and spit it on the ground. *Enough! This ends now.* Wiping the red ooze from his mouth, he gritted his teeth and hammered Auriga with massive kicks. The force of the attack was so powerful it split Auriga's skull in half, sending a thunderous crack echoing through the chamber. Auriga lay there, his eyes staring with a vacant darkness glazed by death.

Weakened and battered, Jerry removed the ring and assumed his usual form. He rolled onto his back and lay there a moment, breathing heavily despite the pain. *Things don't get any easier, do they?* After exhaling a deep breath, he pushed himself up, pulled an avian out of his pack and ate it. Within seconds, he stood rejuvenated. A change rippled across Jerry's countenance that reflected confidence. For the first time, he realized his limitations but also understood how to choose the right weapon and when to exploit it.

"Mr. G, that was incredible." Jerry took a victory breath. "Finally, I feel like I'm getting this stuff down." He watched as bright rainbow colors swirled inside the ring's stone. "Too bad

I didn't have this when I was back in high school. Things might have been different."

Jerry placed the ring in his pocket, zipped it shut, and ran his fingers over the etchings on the stone barrier. He searched for the keys that would unlock the fifth seal but came up empty, and his heart sank. Without those symbols, he would be lost in the fourth chamber forever. *They've got to be here somewhere.* Jerry stood silently and relaxed his mind. In the corner of his eye, symbols flashed from the chariot's gilded wheels. He rushed over to the glinting figures. "Mr. G, this is it!" The codes had been inscribed onto the golden rims.

After a quick glance, he returned to the sealed entrance and touched the symbols one at a time. The stone door slowly morphed into a misty blue veil. Jerry stared at the shimmering curtain and felt a chill. His chest aching, he closed his eyes. *How much more of this must I go through?* The cavern seemed to breathe, whispering life into his soul and hope for tomorrow. He opened his eyes and looked back before slipping through.

CHAPTER TWENTY-FOUR

WITHOUT DARK, THERE IS NO LIGHT

The musty odor of straw instilled his first, slow breath. Jerry now resided in a small confined room that resembled a crumbling old stone barn. Gray mortared stones added to the rustic aesthetic. The ground had worn thin, and fine sediment dusted the area, making his nose twitch. Bales of hay, rusty buckets, and other items from years gone by were scattered about. *It's a little weird being in a place that resembles my grandfather's old barn where I used to work as a youth. While other boys were enjoying their summer vacation, I was cleaning up chicken poop and all the other crappy jobs.* He shivered with anxiety. *Even now, it feels stuffy and claustrophobic.*

Eerie shadows wiggled on the walls, cast by a quivering firelight. The dim flame of a torch anchored in the wall wavered with indecision near three open entrances. An uneasy silence filled the room. His dilemma: choosing the correct one.

Jerry moved closer to the flickering yellow light, its faint flame fluttering in the musty draft. Everything dwindled away into the shadows except for the strange symbols next to each entry. *These images look like parts of a face, but I have no idea what they mean. Maybe ...*

He deliberated over which access to take, but something blocked his thoughts, making what rested ahead of him impossible to visualize. "Well, Mr. G, what do you think?" Unclear on what to do, he chose the middle passage.

Torches attached to the walls lit the interior with an unnerving flickering. White quartzite salted gray and charcoal stones, reflecting the dimness of the flames. A gentle breeze brushed against his face as he maneuvered through a series of twists and turns. *This appears to be a massive underground labyrinth, but where is it taking me?*

Within the limestone wall, a winding underworld took Jerry deep within its grasp. Like an ant in an anthill, he crawled around in the underground tunnels of chaos, searching for something, anything that could help him find a way out. Despite the slight breeze, the corridor was warm, his shuffling steps the only sound.

The nightmarish spiral of unnerving channels led him into blind alleys and wrong turns. Ugh, this is insane. Fraught with desperation, he decided to mark his route, hoping to retrace his steps. Like a rat on a wheel, working furiously yet going nowhere, he felt imprisoned in a cage of futility.

He wasted the better part of an hour tromping around looking in vain for an exit. *Another dead end. Now what?* He kicked at the dirt and blinked hard in frustration. "Mr. G, I don't know if we're ever going to get out of this cursed place." Mr. G's eyes just glowed. "Hey, it's not my fault, and you're no help."

He stopped to take a drink but panicked when he shook his canteen. *Great! I'm almost out of water.* Then his eyes caught sight of several faint symbols hidden within the passageway's shadowy dimness. "Wait a minute." He leaned close, wiped the dust off the engravings, and ran his fingers slowly over them. Jerry paused for a quiet moment of reflection. *According to these, if I stay to the right, I should end up back at the entrance.*

Over the next hour, Jerry wandered the corridors until finally exiting the labyrinth back where he'd started. He sighed. "Well, Mr. G, what do we do now?" Once again, he shook his canteen. *If I don't find water soon, I won't have to worry about finding a way out.*

Jerry methodically devised a way to mark the trail and plot a map. But which entry was the right one? He approached each entrance, double-checking the images he had inspected earlier. Then it dawned on him: the third figure looked like a nose. *Could it be that easy? Enif does represent the nose of Pegasus.* "Well, Mr. G, let's hope the second time is a charm."

Inside the labyrinth, Jerry tagged the walls with his knife and took notes associated with the symbols in each passage. He created a chart that provided guidance as he worked his way through the complicated channels. After backtracking and monitoring each corridor, a distinct pattern of codes emerged that led to another channel. Counting the intersections allowed him to move deeper into the maze without revisiting the same route.

Jerry halted when the corridor vanished into a void that had opened less than a foot from him. He fumbled around, unsure of its reality. *Okay, is this real or just another illusion?* He inched his way to the massive crater, pausing at its mouth, staring into an ever-widening scar as though human hands had cut and shaped it.

He stood with one hand in a pocket of his Levi's, the other on his aether. Jerry looked down at the lifeless dark hole, the edges crumbling and debris falling, echoing into the endless abyss. A presence, something powerful, compelled him to sit and meditate. He sat, keeping one hand on his aether and the other on the ground.

Suddenly, voices echoed through the maze of his mind. A jumble of screams and macabre groans haunted his thoughts, and terror gnawed and twisted at his insides. Sweat coated his skin as though he had just showered. It was like he was walking a tight wire and losing his balance.

Within seconds, his mind teemed with love, hatred, happiness, and sadness. He felt trapped and then liberated. A combination of shame, guilt, and inadequacy replaced that of elation and power. A tremendous pressure filled his soul. His body shook so hard he thought it would shake to pieces. Nauseated and dizzy, he felt like he was going to vomit.

His emotions continued to escalate, causing him to feel confused and at times horrified. His head throbbed as though he had been tasered, his thinking distorted and impaired. Drool dripped from the corners of his lips. At a heightened level of awareness, Jerry's passions reached their zenith. Then, without warning, they disappeared, leaving him in a realm of profound darkness.

Emptiness greeted his mind, a shell without emotions, void of thought. Within a few moments, his mental process activated as though someone had flipped a switch. By walking the labyrinth of his mind, Jerry was able to discover and put into perspective some of the most important aspects of his journey. *Holy geode, that was powerful, but I understand now. Without the dark, one cannot see the light.* He gazed upward as if he could see past the cavern's barrier, deep into the firmament above. *This power I have ... I mustn't take it for granted or let it go to my head. To do so could shut out my heart and with it the potential to see because of shortsighted wisdom.*

An instant later, the abyss vanished and a dark passage loomed before him. While he might have been used to the darkness, he had learned not to trust his eyes but to focus on what he couldn't see. Striding into the corridor, he found it to be cold but dry. He tensed as he crept through the passage, waiting for any movement that would spring him into action, Mr. G's glowing eyes lighting the way. It was unnerving— dead of sound. From the darkness, the end of the maze came into view, allowing access to the next chamber. Once he was through the passage, it sealed.

Jerry reflected on what had transpired. "Mr. G, I feel like I just had my mind purged, an emotional cleansing of sorts— something you wouldn't understand. This whole process has been fatiguing, but I wonder—"

A sudden golden light permeated the chamber. Thirst-stricken and hungry, he turned and stared at Mr. G. "Right now, I wish you were a divining rod." Jerry had drunk all his water, and worry nagged him with every step.

Hours later, a lemony scent met his nose. *Another jinan?* He caught a glimpse of several trees in the distance. *Yes!* His stomach growled eagerly and he sprinted toward the grove.

Each tree exposed a white trunk that peeled in thin horizontal strips, revealing a reddish inner bark. Pendulous branches drooped to the ground. The jinan exuded a serenity, immersing him in a warm glow, but disappointment filled his heart when he lifted the sagging limbs.

"An apple?" He shot a stare of contempt. "Really ... an apple?" Jerry took a quick glance around. "Mr. G, I hope looks are deceiving."

A cool breeze brushed against his face as he plucked several of the fruits from the slumping branches. Jerry nibbled and then bit into the succulent round treat. The taste exploded in his mouth.

"Yes!" Shaking his fist, he rejoiced. "The flavor—it's like ... it's like a lemony sweet tart." He smacked his lips. "Mr. G, all is good!"

A sudden tingling engulfed his body. "Whoa, now what?" Jerry's body's regenerative properties sprang into overdrive. Cellular turnover happened more quickly than before. His outward appearance had changed, and his countenance radiated a visible glow.

"Wow! Mr. G, all of my blemishes have disappeared!" he said, gazing at his reflection in a cave pool. "My hair is thicker, and my skin is like a newborn's." He paused for a moment and glanced around. No one was there to share his good news, and he reflected on his friends back home. *What would Mark and Joe think of me now? Would they even recognize me? Hopefully, when this is all over, I'll be able to return and celebrate my victory.*

Jerry was still basking in his recent renovation when a secluded tree came into sight. Elation swept over him and he sprinted to the unusual find, his taste buds tingling in anticipation.

The lone tree flaunted an exfoliated tan bark with cinnamon patches. It had a delightful fragrance similar to a rose's, and the distinctive branches displayed multi-petaled flowers in a dark maroon presentation. Jerry plucked one of the pyramid-shaped fruits from a low-hanging branch and examined it. *Oh, this is interesting. Each side has a different color similar to a Rubik's pyramid.* His stomach twitched with excitement as he sank his teeth into the unusual fruit, but it turned out to be tasteless, like cardboard.

"Something's not right. I feel absolutely nothing."

Jerry ate another, hoping for further changes. Nothing happened. "Uh-oh. Mr. G, did I screw up again?" Jerry's countenance dropped. "Maybe I should wait and consult Julean before eating more."

A parched throat reminded him of his thirst, and he hurried to the small stream that supported the area's vegetation. The low hum of water rushed and splashed along its course as though it were late to an appointment. After filling his canteen, he put the container to his lips, closed his eyes, and felt the cool, refreshing liquid slide down his throat. "Ahh!" He wiped his mouth with the back of his hand. "Mr. G, never did a beverage taste so sweet."

Suddenly, he was seized by a surge of strength he had not sensed before. The tone of his muscles tightened. Blood rushed to every part of his body. His heart pumped stronger, and his lung capacity increased like that of a marathon runner.

"I can't believe what's happening to me." Jerry held his arm out and looked at this hand. "I feel like I'm being molded into something I don't yet comprehend." He turned to Mr. G. "Sometimes I wonder if it's just a dream and at any time I'll wake up."

After evaluating the area for different vegetation, he decided to pick more fruit and be on his way. Though he didn't perceive any change from the pyramid produce, he wisely chose to gather a few extra for his journey.

CHAPTER TWENTY-FIVE

ZETA'S POWDER

It wasn't long after he had left the jinan that he came upon a sanctuary of beauty, and his eyes widened at the sight of a real garden of paradise. Poised at its center was a massive multi-tiered fountain with a dazzling spray of water that cascaded into a shimmering lagoon of changing color. *Incredible!*

The air was crisp, and a sweet exotic aroma filled the cavern. Marble columns with floral motifs supported a canopy of vines that encased the botanical garden. Lemon-yellow blossoms blended with the brightest greens. Sparkling orange leaves and lavender stems adorned the refuge in a fascinating array that tantalized the senses.

He glanced around and wandered to the fountain, where he knelt and sipped its delicious liquid. Within moments, he became tired and fell asleep against a marble colonnade.

An hour later, he awoke, startled by the soft clip-clop of hooves. Jerry peered over the rim of the fountain and saw a unicorn sipping the water. *Could it be?* He rubbed his eyes. *I've never seen anything so ... so beautiful and elegant.*

Taller than an average horse, she was pure white with sky-blue eyes. She sported a magnificent mane and tail that shone like moonlit silver. A spiral horn protruded from her forehead.

The unicorn caught sight of Jerry and said, "Are you a friend or a foe?"

"I would hope that I'm a friend," he responded. "But I must confess I've never seen a unicorn before."

"I am Zeta and I come from the constellation Monoceros. Since I am one of the few that remain, I must use caution."

"I mean you no harm, but why so cautious?"

"Some would kill for my bane of evil."

"Bane of evil?"

"Yes, a unicorn's horn has mystical healing powers."

"Really?" Jerry's interest was piqued. "What's so powerful about your horn that you have to guard against death?"

"Evil poisons exist that even your powers cannot help." She shook her head and neck and trotted over. "The powder from a unicorn's horn can neutralize the most potent poison. Even the touch of a unicorn's horn can offer a cure."

Jerry's eyes narrowed, his head tilted. "So how can a person obtain this ... this mystical powder?" *I'm not sure what awaits me, but this may be the one thing that saves my life.*

"Only from the horn of a willing purebred unicorn. Of course, that is me."

"So then, what do I need to do ... I mean ... I have no money?"

"How do I know you are worthy of my horn?" Zeta leaned in close and locked her eyes on Jerry's. "I know nothing of you."

"Do you know Andromeda? She will vouch for me."

"Before I offer my services to you, I require your help." Zeta lifted her head and gave a closed smile. "Garwin has stolen my magic talisman, and I need you to find his dwelling and retrieve the charm."

"Who in the geode is Garwin?" Jerry stared, the creases at the side of his eyes deepening. "And just how dangerous is this person?"

"Garwin is a scavenger who will steal anything. He belongs to the Chamelius clan and can be difficult to find. His residence is not far. Go to the fountain's north side." Zeta pointed with her horn. "There you will see a rocky trail. Follow it till you come to a hill that looks like a camel. His dwelling is at the top. But be careful—Garwin likes to place traps around his lodging."

"What does the talisman look like?"

"It is a small crystalline ring that gives me the ability to camouflage myself when in danger." Zeta used her hoof to draw a circle in the dirt. "My name is inscribed on it."

"Camouflage?"

"When I wear the ring on my horn, I blend in with the scenery. Since it has been inside his dwelling, the amulet will need recharging before I can use its power."

Jerry waited for a moment and smiled. "Okay, you've got a deal." *Sounds similar to the apus flowers.* Sweat slid down his face, prickling his skin. *I hope this trip is worth the risk.* Jerry left in a hurry, wanting to resume his journey to the sixth seal as quickly as possible.

At the fountain's north side, he picked up the rocky trail and began his mission to find Garwin's residence. Time ticked quickly before multiple hills came into view. Casting his eyes about, he located the peak that looked like a camel. A dome-shaped dwelling had been built into the earth, blending in with its natural environment. *Amazing! I don't know if I would've ever found this place without Zeta's help.* Jerry remembered her warning and exercised caution as he approached Garwin's habitat, sidestepping the simple traps set on the path to his residence.

Once he was inside, a voice demanded, "What right do you have entering my home without invitation?"

Jerry snooped around but couldn't discern where the voice was coming from. The humidity had elevated, and a variety of ficus plants and dwarf umbrella trees dotted the interior. "I'm here to retrieve the talisman you have stolen from Zeta," he said boldly.

"How dare you accuse me of such a petty theft?"

"Only a thief would hide from his accuser." Jerry sought the voice's source, but it remained elusive. "Show yourself or I will begin my search without your consent."

Jerry caught a faint glimpse of a shadow that thickened and drifted. Stepping away from a well-decorated wall, a lizard-shaped creature had camouflaged himself, blending in with his background.

"I don't know who you are, but I demand you leave my home at once!"

"My name is Jerry and I'm on a mission to help Zeta find her stolen talisman." Jerry's grip tightened on his aether and his energy surged. "It is imperative you turn the charm over before I cause damage that you don't want!"

"I didn't steal his talisman but only borrowed it," Garwin said, sobbing. "You see, my son has been poisoned and I needed the amulet to bargain for a cure. Without the unicorn's magic powder, my son will die."

"Why didn't you just ask? Zeta seems fair-minded, and I'm sure she would have been more than happy to help your son. Give me the talisman and let's return to explain your situation."

Garwin consented and tagged along to plead his case on behalf of his son.

At the lagoon, Zeta was nowhere in sight. Jerry called out, "I've returned with Garwin and your talisman."

"Thanks, but why did you bring him here?" Zeta stepped out from behind an enormous boulder. "I have no wish to talk to a thief!"

"Garwin is here to ask for your forgiveness, but also for your help. Garwin's son was poisoned, and without your assistance he may die. The only way he thought you would help was to create a bargaining chip with your talisman."

"Stealing something as a negotiating chip does not endear you to me." Zeta's facial muscles tightened. "The cure from my horn is not something easily bargained for, and if you want my help, there must be restitution!"

"I was in dire need of your magic," Garwin said, sobbing again. "I'll do whatever it takes to save the life of my son."

Compassion triumphed as Zeta drew a pouch from her cache with her mouth. "Take the powder from my horn, but I require something from the Chamelius clan to assist me in getting past Ceti. It's a device allowing me to control his actions as I pass over the lake."

"Ceti attacked me, but I defeated him with the help of Delphinius." Jerry's eyes grew wide. "That's one beast I never want to face again."

Garwin's gaze shifted to Zeta. "I know the instrument you speak of, and it's within my ability to secure it for you." Assuring Zeta he would return with the device, Garwin left, agreeing to meet back at the fountain.

With the ring back in Zeta's possession, Jerry asked, "What about our agreement? I've lived up to my end of the bargain."

"I am sincerely indebted to you." Zeta smiled and reached into her satchel with her mouth. "This pouch contains the powder of my horn. Take it as a token of my appreciation. Maybe someday we will meet again, but until then, I must be off."

After placing the small bag in his pack, Jerry was back on track to the sixth seal. Having become an ambassador of healing between the two, he left with a warm feeling.

CHAPTER TWENTY-SIX

CIRCINUS AND THE ENCHANTED FEATHERS

A blast of cool, moist air flushed Jerry's face and ruffled his hair. He cinched his vest tight and hastened his gait toward the sixth seal. An abundance of lush vegetation flourished between and around tall columns and clear sheets of dripstone, and a fruity fragrance similar to that of apricots spilled into the air. Spears of limestone stalactites formed a maw of teeth dripping with water.

Jerry bent down to tighten the laces of his boots and glanced ahead. Several small trails splintered away from the central path. "Okay, Mr. G, which should I take?" He sighed and rubbed the back of his neck. "I'm not connecting with any of them. What about you?" Mr. G's eyes flickered with indecision. Jerry nodded, "I agree, let's not wander unless prompted."

Dampness spilling into the cavern, he felt a sudden urge. Something unusual caught his roaming eye. Farther down the path, a multicolored stone pathway shimmered. Perhaps it was a trick of the cavern's ever-present light, but it glistened like glass. *Talk about a yellow brick road! I feel like I'm in Candyland.*

The scenery was a delightful change from what he had been seeing. Fairy-tale mushrooms, blushing red ferns, and various fungal organisms flourished along the route. He felt like Alice in Wonderland when he spied huge pink mushrooms that sparkled like a series of open umbrellas prepared for rain. Mingled among them were luminous mushrooms that looked like exotic jellyfish, undulating and pulsing with life.

Just as Jerry was about to turn back, he spotted a spiral staircase encircling a giant purple mushroom. *Oh, this looks interesting.* He eased his way to the steps and cautiously ascended the stairway.

At the top of the stairs, a small gong with a wooden mallet was attached to the door. Auspicious Buddhist symbols embossed the unusual cymbal. "Mr. G, these images remind me of a Tibetan prayer gong found in the sacred mountains of Tibet." *Just one of the geological sites where I wanted to go but could never afford.*

Jerry lifted the mallet with his thumb and finger and gently tapped the chime twice. Much to his surprise, a deep tone reverberated from it with each strike, though the second was much louder. He waited a few minutes.

Should I leave, or should I try to enter?

The moment he reached for the handle, the door opened. Inside the mushroom-shaped dwelling was a man wearing a straw hat with three feathers attached. He seemed a bit overweight at five-foot-six, and his red face showed the wear of time, leathery and wrinkled. However, he had the countenance of a bright star, and his clothes, bright and colorful, resembled those of a peasant of old. He offering a weathered, beaten handshake. "What can I do for you?"

"I'm Jerry," he said, shaking his hand. Not sure what to say, he blurted out, "I've been exposed to more danger than I ever dreamed. As I am yet vulnerable, I seek assistance in securing my destiny." His face flushed. *Ugh, I can't believe I just said that.*

"I am Circinus from the Circini clan." Amused, the man chuckled. "Just what is your destiny?"

"My hope is to complete my transformation and to live my life with Andromeda." Jerry's face reddened still more and he grinned. "Other than that, I haven't a clue."

"That is a noble intention indeed. How can I be of assistance?"

It was as if Jerry had stubbed his toe and wasn't sure what to say. Fumbling for words, he finally said, "Well ... uh ... it was by chance that I found you." He paused. "I don't know what other dangers or challenges I may face, but I'd appreciate anything you can do to assist with my journey."

"Since I'm so far off the main trail, I don't get a lot of visitors. Won't you come in?"

Inside, glowing lavender mushrooms pulsed with life, and mushroom-shaped lamps ignited the room in a bright shade of yellow. A web of threadlike mycelium branched out against the walls, looking like static electricity on an underexposed photo. Wood stump stools surrounded a mushroom-shaped counter.

Circular designs, including pictures of odd fungi, adorned the room. *Holy geode, I feel like I just stepped into the Mushroom World in a Super Mario game.*

"As you travel toward the portal, you will encounter an enchanted wall. Only with the feather from the columba bird can the mystic wall be animated."

"Enchanted wall?" Jerry's left eyebrow lifted.

"Only at this discerning wall can you see what your destiny holds." Circinus leaned in. "Countless shy away from knowing what lies ahead of them. They fear their future."

Jerry's face twitched. "My future?"

"Your reality reflects what you see and what you believe. Only at the wall can you burst the veil that blinds your eyes."

"What's a columba bird, and where can I find them?"

"The birds you seek are from the Columbae clan and can be found on top of Mount Columb." Circinus paused. "The trek can prove treacherous. You must exercise caution."

"How do I find this ... Mount Columb?"

"You're in luck," Circinus said. "If you stay on the same trail that led to me, it will take you to the mountain. There you will see a narrow path. Follow it and you will find their nesting site. Once there, you should find plenty of feathers just lying around."

I have no way of knowing which direction a particular choice will take me. It might turn out right or it might turn out wrong. Maybe this could help with my fear of making bad decisions.

Jerry thanked the man and departed to find the columba bird's nesting site, optimistic about his future.

On the journey to Mount Columb, a fresh breeze and a pale light led the way. The trail became uneven and rocky, ornamented by colorful fungi and ferns. Spying a low-hanging charm from an odd-looking mushroom, Jerry reached up and collected the trinket. The thought of holding more power in his hand sent a thrill through his body. He could taste the power; he hungered for it.

But his excitement switched to panic when the ground rumbled and shook violently as if it were alive. Jerry steadied himself several times, his legs shaking with every step. Then the earth suddenly ripped open, large crevasses dividing the landscape.

It was a trap!

Before he could return the alluring charm, the rocky floor collapsed under him and his heart plummeted with it. Instinctively, he became weightless and ascended above the ground as the earth continued to break up and fragment. In a desperate attempt, he stretched upward and replaced the amulet. Within moments, the quaking calmed and the chasms settled, sealing shut. Desire had consumed Jerry. In his rush for more power, he had placed his life in jeopardy.

Bad luck continues to plague me. Jerry let out a frustrated breath, his body trembling. *Why do things continue to be so hard?* Then he recalled his experience at the maze. *My lust for power shut out my heart and my ability to see because of shortsighted wisdom. I guess I still have much to learn.*

At the foot of Mount Columb, Jerry breathed a sigh of relief and began his ascent. *At least the trail isn't as steep as the hills of Corona.* Just as he cleared the first ledge, the same poisonous flowers he'd encountered before sprayed a toxic mist in his face. He choked and coughed, and sweat flowed down his cheeks. His muscles became rigid as though he were going into a seizure. *Got to get Zeta's powder.*

Jerry fumbled his way into his pack and with spastic fingers opened Zeta's pouch and forced a pinch of its powder into his mouth. Within seconds, his body relaxed. He flipped onto his back and lay there a moment, breathing heavily. The powder had cured him, but in retrospect, he realized that if he hadn't helped Zeta, he'd be dead. He pulled his canteen from his waist and gulped down half its contents. "Mr. G," Jerry said, staring into his glowing eyes, "I sure wish this was over." Jerry grabbed his aether, forced himself up and continued his mission, but now with a dampened pace.

Halfway up the trail, he came across a den of sleeping foxes nestled in a hollow cavity of the mountain. He froze. *Got to be quiet.* When he tried to tiptoe past them, one frisky little pup popped out and asked, "What are you doing here?"

"I'm seeking feathers from the columba bird." Jerry tightened his grip on his aether.

"I'm Julius." He jumped up and down. "Let me help. Let me help."

"Shhh, okay, okay, but what about your family?"

"Aww, they're no fun." His eyes drooped. "All they wanna do is sleep."

"I don't know. This could be risky—"

"Not for me." He continued to jump and shout. "I wanna help. I wanna help."

"Okay, but please be careful." *Dare I put my trust in someone so young?*

As Julius bounded up the mountain, Jerry tried to keep up. He seemed to know the way, bypassing the endless traps and pitfalls. But what then? What kind of reception waited for him? Were the columba birds bloodthirsty like the aquilas, or were they passive—maybe even helpful?

"Slow up. You're losing me," Jerry shouted.

"We're almost there!"

"Right ... okay."

Julius moved with fluid, snake-like ease along the tortuous route while Jerry grunted his way after him like an awkward novice. Finally, he crested the ledge that overlooked the columba's roosting habitat. Scattered in the middle of a semi-open rocky terrain were several bowl-shaped structures. Interwoven sticks formed large nests, and a grass-like material provided a soft center.

"See, I told you so." Julius bounced around as though it were his personal playground while Jerry paused to catch his breath.

It was quiet. Jerry warily crept into the area, turning his head in all directions. "Where are all the birds?"

"Oh, they've left to feed."

Feathers littered the ground. Jerry picked one up and shook his head. "These look like ordinary pigeon feathers."

"Naw, they're columba." Julius continued to run and jump around like a kid in a schoolyard.

"I hope you're right." After picking up several, Jerry placed them in his pack, and with Julius as his guide, he hastened down the mountain and thanked him for his service.

Jerry stopped by to let Circinus know he had obtained the feathers, and upon entering his residence, he stared at the same pigeon-like quills protruding from Circinus's hat.

"Wait a minute." Jerry's eyes narrowed. "Why did you send me on a treacherous journey when you had them here the whole time?"

"I have found those who receive something for nothing have a tendency to take it for granted." He looked at Jerry solemnly. "When you reach the enchanted wall, you will receive what you are worthy of."

Jerry didn't quite understand what he meant but thanked him and turned to leave.

"Wait. Look around you." Circinus held his hand up. "What do you see?"

"Mushroom-shaped chairs, tables, even a mushroom-shaped piano." Jerry gave a confused look.

"Okay, but what else do you see?"

"Uh, glowing lavender mushrooms?"

"Ask yourself this question." The lines on his face deepened. "What do most people seek in life?"

"I'm not sure ... Power ... wealth ... fame?"

"You've already noticed that everything here has a circular form." Circinus held a mushroom-shaped ring in his heavily veined hand. "Can you show me where the starting point of a circle begins or ends?"

Jerry shrugged and shook his head.

"People spend a lifetime searching for happiness, only to end up back where they started." Then he said something that struck a chord with Jerry. "It's the fulfillment of the experience that gives enjoyment to all things. The remarkable thing about a circle is that you can never get lost. Your starting point is also your ending point. If you don't have a start or end point, you'll never reach your goal or, in your case, your destiny. But wait—I have something that might just help you." He rummaged around in his pocket. "Ah, here it is." Opening his hand, he revealed a bronze-shaped medallion. "If you get lost or need help in finding the safest path, this little device can assist."

"You know, I have the cavern's entire map memorized." Intrigued, Jerry inspected the device. "How does it work?"

"It's similar to a compass, except it will show the best direction for your journey. If you leave the trail, your map may not show your position." Circinus insisted he take the unique gadget. "If you seek something specifically, ask and the needle will display the best course."

Jerry slipped it into his pants pocket and muttered his thanks, unsure how much it would really help, and once again set off to find the central pathway.

While he traveled, smaller lanes shot out in various directions, leading away from the main route. Each time he passed by one, he tried to connect with its energy, but nothing sparked his interest until he chanced upon the pathway of memories.

CHAPTER TWENTY-SEVEN

THE PATHWAY OF MEMORIES

A soft ubiquitous light infused the cavern like sunlight piercing through a cloudy day. Paving this particular promenade were snowy-white bricks adorned with symbols unknown to Jerry. The scented air stirred memories of a lavender fragrance his mother often sprayed to freshen their home when he was a youth. Rows of animated castle towers surrounded by a sparkling array of stalagmites and stalactites draped in flowstone dotted the path. He recalled Andromeda's warning and wrestled with indecision. Powerful emotions swelled deep within, and a silent duel raged. Like a wild animal clawing to get out, his curiosity tore at his gut until finally he relinquished the battle and gave in to the urge. *I'm not sure what I feel, but there's something ... something familiar ...*

Like a moth drawn to fire, he couldn't wait to see what was inside the towers. *I'll only take a peek and then be on my way.* Moments after he had stepped onto the snowy-white walkway, music erupted. "Love Story," by Taylor Swift, spilled into the air.

Jerry stopped. His heart pounded. Once again, powerful feelings overwhelmed him. *What's happening? Why do I feel so ... so emotional?*

Jerry approached the first ivory tower, slowing his step. Video inducements projected onto its exterior wall enticed him to draw close. Visions of his youth revealed special times with his parents. Jerry stared at his father. He missed him terribly. Even though his dad had been stern and disciplined, he loved Jerry and participated in as many activities as he could. Jerry wished they had had more time together.

He warily strolled around the entrance, viewing the allurements. Two solid oak doors stood guard. Crafted in the wood were images that morphed and changed as if they were able to pierce the veil of Jerry's forgotten memories.

"Mr. G, that's me!" Jerry twisted and turned to view the shifting scenes. "And those kids ... they were my friends."

Moments of his youth flashed in his mind in swirls and glimpses, exposing loose displaced details. Jerry struggled to reclaim the footsteps of his past but was unable to reignite those old flames. Confusion had trapped his thoughts while only a few threads of his memory united him with his childhood.

He pushed open the wooden doors and stepped inside, trying to calm himself. Jerry turned slowly, his breath quickening. It was like entering an imaginary realm. *This is incredible!* A carved rosewood staircase soared to the tower's peak, displaying animated dragons spewing flames and mythical phoenixes flaunting brilliant scarlet and gold plumage. Panoramic videos surrounded him, projecting forgotten times of his youth. He watched with eagerness, his emotions strangely stirred, his past surfacing like an island rising from the sea.

He saw himself hitting the ball and running to first base in his first T-ball game. "Hey, I wasn't too bad as a little guy." His parents fussed over him, cheering him on. After the event, they went out for ice cream like they always had. "Look at that! My favorite ice-cream parlor, Baskin-Robbins. They had the best. I always ordered chocolate chip."

Mysteries of his life were being pulled from the deepest recesses of his mind. As with a person with Alzheimer's, the lost and forgotten memories were rising, reigniting a past filled with passions, desires, and hopes. Jerry found himself experiencing these precious moments vicariously through the holograms, his emotions interlaced with each event as it unfolded before him. He spun to see his family camping at Oak Creek Canyon.

"Ahhh, Mr. G, the creek's gurgling whirr ... the wind rustling through the giant pines ... Those were sweet times." Nostalgia filled his heart, and he yearned for yesterday's treasures. "I'd wake up at sunrise, unzip the tent's faded-green flap, and step outside. The brisk air, the crackling and snapping of a roaring fire were pure bliss. My dad always had a stack of freshly cut pine. I loved the wood that oozed a sticky sap. It burned hot and fast." Then Jerry caught sight of his mother cooking their breakfast.

"Oh, Mr. G, the smell of bacon and eggs sizzling on a hot Coleman stove—life was so sublime."

He recalled how many things his parents had done for him and how much they'd loved him. Jerry missed the early days of his youth, creating a strong desire to see more. His heart raced as he scrambled up the carved rosewood stairway. After reaching the second level, the staircase disappeared, leaving him near a veiled door. Once he was through the shrouded cloak, it dissipated as the room morphed into another memory.

Surging around him were holograms that reviewed flashbacks of his younger years. Jerry's thoughts started to interweave with the events as they unfolded. He remembered his first day of school—he was so scared that he had laid his head down on his desk until his mother came to take him home. *I was terrified. The other children just stared. Mrs. Gaffney was gentle and tried to help me, but I wouldn't budge, not an inch. All I wanted was my mom.*

He turned and saw his neighbor Joe. *We both shopped at the same thrift store and wore the same mismatched clothes, but he never complained. When others put me down, he was there defending me. Joe was like the brother I never had, always kind and caring.*

He spun again to see his first kiss with Marilyn Brooks as a freshman in high school. She was his first true love. *I felt awkward, tentative at first. Then it was passionate, romantic, and it seemed to last forever.*

Like dreams blowing in the wind, the faces flashed before him. Reflections of tender moments touched his heart, causing him to tingle with excitement.

"Mr. G ..." Jerry stood staring at the events as they unfolded before him. "Sometimes we forget about the good parts of life because we're so wrapped up in trying to forget about the bad parts. I didn't always see the wonderful people who accepted me for who I was. I only saw the people who didn't. I know Andromeda has encouraged me to trust in my heart." Jerry sighed. "But how can I let my heart lead if it remains imprisoned in my past, behind years of doubt? How do I break the chains of distrust and suspicion?"

Jerry paused and glanced around. *Ah, youth. I was so sure of myself, sure that I understood things that, in truth, I didn't. Life wasn't filled with black-and-white absolutes but shades of grays that affected every situation. My life was hard. I always felt justified in my actions, but how many treasures did I miss because of my blindness?*

His thoughts weren't broken, just twisted. He'd been living a lie, measuring his self-worth in all the wrong ways. *I never felt I was good enough, no matter what I did. I was always trying to prove my worth. I feared judgment from others because I constantly judged myself. My past chained me to my actions. It wasn't about what I did or didn't do, or even who I tried to be. But now I'm free. I alone am enough, with nothing more to prove.*

At that moment, Jerry's heart opened wide, as though the tectonic plates of his tragic childhood had just shifted, breaking down the thick layers of bitter sediment that had built up over the years and letting in love and appreciation he had forgotten. Jerry made a vow: He would complete his odyssey and return home, wherever that may be.

Lost in his childhood memories, Jerry remained captivated by his past. A palpable nostalgia warmed his soul. Multiple scents wafted in the air. Starved for more, he continued his search.

Another stairway materialized and Jerry quickly ascended to the next level, eager to view more holograms of past events. He watched as he explored the Superstition Mountains, digging for buried treasure, including the Lost Dutchman's gold mine. Jerry recalled the feelings he'd had the day he found a vast deposit of iron pyrite. *Wow, I can't believe how naïve I was. I thought I was rich. Too bad it wasn't real gold. But then I wouldn't have met Andromeda.*

He reached into his pocket and squeezed the chunk of pyrite. *How ironic. This was to keep me centered on becoming rich, to prove myself. Oh, how things have changed!*

The shock of so many memories invading his mind had stirred up strong emotions, making him shut down. Jerry left the edifice to collect his thoughts, vowing to be a different man. It was as if a weight had been lifted. But inside, something was still missing.

Outside, the scent of orchids saturated the air, and the song "Love Story" echoed from a small, pristine white tower not more than fifty feet from him. A holographic scene flashed across its surface, replaying the same snippet over and over. Like a blinking billboard, it showed Jerry getting out of his old Chevy truck near a gray condominium. There it was again ... that feeling ... like déjà vu. A familiar thrill sparked the embers of his heart, stirring strong emotions. A powerful urge to discover what hid inside burned within him. *It's my truck, but I don't recognize—*

"Jerry, wait!" Andromeda appeared next to him, her eyes wide.

"Oh, I'm so glad you're here." Jerry smiled. "You wouldn't believe what I just went through."

"That's why I'm here."

"What do you mean?"

"You mustn't go any further." Andromeda's face betrayed panic.

"Why?" He looked perplexed.

"Do you want to relive those early years of pain, seeing your father die a slow, agonizing death from a body riddled with cancer, or watch your mother crushed and disfigured in a horrifying car accident?"

Instantly, guilt pummeled him with memories of his mother's tragedy. He felt like he was fighting a hailstorm from the past, struggling to remain composed. He shook the thought away and gazed at Andromeda's long flowing hair, waving in the cavern's cool breeze. Then his eyes narrowed. "How do you know these things?"

"You forget, I can read your mind." She touched his face and stared deep into his eyes. "Trust me. Pain and despair await you if you continue ... and ... I can't bear to see you go through it again."

"They can't be all bad." Jerry pointed to the tower he had just visited. "What I experienced inside that one awakened me to the lie I'd been living."

"You were fortunate. There are a few with precious moments, but most are designed to inflict memories of heartbreak."

"I don't understand. Why?"

"This place is a testing ground, a place of trials and temptations, but it's not necessary that you subject yourself to all of them. That's why I'm here to help guide you."

Jerry sat in silence, staring at the tower that called to him, urging him to enter. A sudden wave of nostalgia swept over him, but he couldn't make out its source. Something seemed lost ... something powerful.

Leaning forward, she kissed him. "Do you love me?"

"Why would you even ask such a silly question?" He was lifted by her consoling smile, but she was hiding something. Of that he was sure. But what? Jerry embraced her. "I'm just curious."

"Then I plead with you—leave now before your past distorts your future."

He brushed away the silky strands of hair that had fallen into her face. "You know, it was like I was dreaming, except the scenes were so real."

"Jerry, please!"

He looked into her eyes. Something was wrong, but he couldn't discern what it was. Still, he knew she loved him. He tried to probe her mind, but she blocked his invasion and questioned his motive. Naturally, he said it was to find out if she still loved him as much as he loved her. Jerry tried to erase the emotion from his face, but he could tell she sensed concern. Should he confront her about his feelings? No, he had to keep it a secret, at least until the time was right. But now wasn't the time. If he didn't stay focused on his journey, the opportunity might never arrive.

For the moment, they embraced each other tightly and gave aid and comfort. While he cuddled with Andromeda, he peeked back over his shoulder. *It's not worth losing her due to my negligence. Maybe there will be a time I can revisit this chamber, but now I need to move on.*

Jerry took a slow breath. "I've missed you so much." His eyes became lost in hers as he pulled her close. "Can't we just elope to Enif? It'd be so much easier."

"Oh, stop." Andromeda slapped his arm playfully. "Do you really want me?"

"Do I need to answer that?"

"Well, sometimes I feel like you just don't understand."

"Quite honestly, sometimes I don't." Jerry ached for her constant companionship as he touched her face. "I would sacrifice my soul for you. It's just ... it's just ... well, sometimes things can be a little overwhelming."

"I know. I don't mean to come off so hard."

Her breath caressed his face as he gazed into her eyes, and their lips met. A current of passion shot through his body as she embraced him. With each touch, their hunger for each other grew.

"So now what?" Jerry said.

"You've made tremendous progress and you're nearing your goal. There is no other way! After you go through the sixth seal, you will be tested more aggressively, experiencing hostile conditions and complex conflicts. You must remain resolute if you are to make it through. This much I can tell you: once you pass through the seventh seal, you still have to obtain the power to transport to our world." Andromeda held him close. "Once there, you will experience happiness like none other. The things you'll be able to do will astound you. Opportunities to travel the universe and to create wondrous marvels await you."

"I hear you, but I can't grasp what you're saying." Jerry took Andromeda's hands in his; they felt warm and soft. "The flame of my desire burns hot, but my wick is getting low. Are you sure there is no other way?"

"Jerry, all my dreams are with you, but I can only do so much." Embracing him tighter, she sighed. "I'm teaching you everything I can and giving instruction when possible. I'm bound by the laws governing my people, but remember this ... I will always be with you."

After spending two hours together during which Jerry practiced and received further instruction, Andromeda gave him explicit warnings. "Your skills ... your knowledge ... your very heart will be tested to its core. I have said this before, but it is imperative that you trust in your heart and learn our ways. If you get in trouble, I may not be able to help. Please, be careful and remember what you have learned."

After they embraced one last time, she vanished, leaving Jerry to continue his trek. The air in the cavern was fresh and invigorating. A sense of contentment seeped into his soul, filling him with gratitude. Yet something stirred in his heart—a sadness for the life he'd left behind. He wasn't sure if he would ever go back. Now more than ever, he yearned to be united with Andromeda and to live in her world, one filled with peace and happiness.

CHAPTER TWENTY-EIGHT

TAURI'S RING

The erosion of time continued to slow, lessening Jerry's requirement for sleep. Short naps were all he needed. He sat on the hard stony ground, his aether in hand, and let out a long-held breath. He leaned forward and looked into a cave pool, gazing at his reflection on its surface as though it were a mirror. *Who are you?* Jerry tossed a stone into the unwavering water, shattering the face that stared at him. *That kind of sums up my life, but for the first time, I feel like I have real hope.* Deep inside, he still doubted. Was he enough? What really awaited him?

Jerry grunted, pushed himself off the ground and slung his pack over his shoulders, determined to complete his quest. After he'd walked for the better part of an hour on a winding dirt trail, the passageway narrowed and the ceiling lowered. The smell of dank, musty air surrounded him. Jerry knelt and then crawled over and between damp rock formations until he came to a vast chamber that resembled the Midwest. *No way!* He blinked in disbelief.

Rolling plains and barren grasslands dominated the landscape. Jerry plunged headlong through an opening in the wall out of the dimness and into a chamber hued in red. *I feel like I'm wearing tinted glasses.* A strange reddish glow illuminated the cavern as he continued his journey, trying to take everything in. Then he spotted something unusual. Across the open expanse stood an object that looked like a statue, not of a man but of a bull.

Jerry tugged his vest tighter around his body and bounded over a series of dusty berms until he reached the figure. *This reminds me of a minotaur.* Warm wisps of air brushed against his face as he stood there immobile, his eyes darting about. Then an inscription appeared at its base venerating Tauri, the Cretan bull's brother, the lord of war. *Who is this Tauri? What does it mean, "lord of war?"* With the head of a bull and the body of a man, he had to represent something powerful. Didn't he?

The life-size bronze tribute stood on a square metallic pedestal. The chamber's reddish hue reflected in the statue's eyes, making them seem alive. Suddenly, a powerful force engulfed Jerry and energy swirled around him. His eyes widened as the air crackled and sparked and then slowly subsided.

His nerves now calmed, he was swallowed by a serene awareness, and his eyes were directed to an obscure alcove in the bull's ear. He reached in and felt a toggle switch. Intuitively, he flipped it.

Startled, Jerry jerked his hand back when a hidden compartment on the left horn popped open. Isolated in the cubicle was the ring of Tauri. He took the ring out and examined it. The face detailed an engraving of the king and his warriors. Inscribed on its band was a warning: "Whosoever wears the ring shall wield its power, if worthy."

"Okay, Mr. G, what in the geode does that mean?" Jerry hesitated in taking it. Once again, he doubted. *Have I proven myself worthy? Is this another trap?* His inner critic continued to plague him. Then he recalled Andromeda's advice. *Trust in your heart and learn our ways.*

Jerry closed his eyes, seeking to tap into his innate power, and no sooner had he started to meditate than something stirred inside him. Like a quiet wind, a soft whisper touched his heart, compelling him to take the venerated band. After a moment, he snatched the ring and tucked it in his pocket, zipping it shut. Turning to Mr. G, he sighed. "How does one free himself from a past of negative thoughts?"

A warm, harsh wind met Jerry's face as dust devils swirled. From the corner of his eye, he caught sight of a square tapered pillar not more than a hundred yards from where he stood. He recognized it as another power-up station and quickened his steps, eager to examine the column.

This pillar contains compartments similar to the last chamber but with different stones. Jerry circled the structure, examining each gem. Fascinated with their sparkling radiance, he passed his aether over each opening, linking his mind to their energy. "Mr. G, I stand confused. I sense two distinct auras, the sapphire and the emerald. What do you think?" Jerry stared at the silent eyes. "You're no help."

Jerry rubbed the back of his neck, unable to determine which compartment would be best-suited to place his aether. *Both stones have a high refractive index, but I can't discern which essence is stronger.* His anxiety grew the longer he waited until, finally, he exhaled a long breath and placed his aether in the sapphire's slot.

The anuns pulsed and shimmered with a variation of color. Vivid blues, starburst yellows, and streaming purples electrified the air around them. "Mr. G ... your eyes ... they're blue!"

Jerry grabbed his aether to assimilate its energy. The moment his fingers closed around it, a brilliant surge of light shot out, illuminating the cavern in a spectrum of color. Jerry gasped in astonishment. "Holy geode, I feel like I'm at a Fourth of July fireworks!"

His heart and mind were aglow. It was as though a power had cleared his mind of a misty fog. Now he thought with almost flawless clarity, though incompletion lingered. The emerald's energy continued to call out to him. *Is it possible two distinct offerings exist?* Jerry hesitated. *I don't want to lose what I have gained. Maybe I should ask for help. No, I need to do this myself.*

Too many times he had depended on Andromeda for help. It was time for him to take control and demonstrate his abilities. The elegant lines of the emerald flashed a vivid shade of intense green; its luster pulsed as though alive, harmonizing with his essence. Confident in his decision, he set his aether into the open slot and waited.

Like a bolt of lightning, his scepter ignited the expanse, spraying the cavern with brilliant hues of green.

"Mr. G ... your eyes ... now they're green!"

This time when Jerry grasped his aether, a powerful surge of energy dropped him to his knees and his body began to burn like fire. He felt a supernatural power he'd never before experienced. But relief soon flooded him with a soothing sensation of freshness and vitality. *I'm not sure what just happened, but I feel as though something has awakened within me. I'm in need of answers.*

At the prompting of a rumbling stomach, he unzipped his pack and pulled out an apple from the last jinan and ate it. With each altering bite, his conversion became more apparent. He was like an infant maturing a little at a time, gaining qualities and abilities he hadn't known were attainable.

With his strength restored, he circled the pillar to make sure no further offerings were available and then resumed his journey to the sixth seal. Before he left, Jerry condemned his actions. *I must open up my mind to all possibilities and not restrict my options. I wonder how many opportunities I've missed. Had I not focused more on this last column, I may have lost a crucial part of my transformation.*

The gentle hills gave way to a landscape of limestone, dolomite, and gypsum rocks. Like an underground plumbing network, water percolated down from the ceiling's cracks and crevasses, creating fanciful forms. Mushroom-like stalagmites flanked either side of the trail, waterfalls of flowstone covered the walls, and soda straws hung like icicles. *These remind me of Karchner caverns near Tucson, which I frequented as a youth.* While his friends ran about town, going to movies and hanging out at the thrift store, Jerry would disappear into the depths of the Earth, embracing the marvels that touched his heart.

His thoughts were cut short when the cavern's light brightened. In the distance, a spinning sphere radiated a luminous light, and hurried footsteps brought him to the site. Was it the activation portal for Julean, or was it something more ominous?

Jerry took a quick glance around and then touched the rotating orb, hoping to see Julean. Nothing happened. *This must be the triggering mechanism, but how do I initiate a response?* After analyzing the sphere, he became frustrated.

Once again, he recalled Andromeda's words. *Remember to let your heart lead.* He pressed his eyes shut, clearing his mind of all thoughts. Jerry stood motionless and waited.

And he waited longer.

Finally, a subtle ripple of air caressed his face and he opened his eyes. Another orb had materialized. *Wow, a clandestine globe hiding in the open.* His hand shot out and touched it, triggering a beacon of light to descend, and with it Julean. *Andromeda was right. I need to trust more in my heart.*

Julean wore his usual vestment, but this time his robe was not only illuminated but also three-dimensional. New symbols and planets now adorned his garment, and it was animated!

"Wow, your ensemble is amazing!" Jerry examined his robe. "But what does all this mean?"

"The time has come to expand your awareness." Julean's eyes twinkled like stars. "Your story is one of many that extend beyond time, beyond the very essence of the universe, even before the dawn of creation. It has always been and will always be. You must learn to allow your mind to become more pervasive, penetrating the portals of time and space."

"Whoa, that's way over my head." Jerry stared with a vacant look.

"Time does not exist as you think of it." Julean's eyes drifted upward as if he could see past the cavern's barrier and deep into space. "It is expressed in waves of potentials. Time is relevant and can be changed or altered, depending on where you are in the universe. Time's quantum effects can influence future and past events, but"—he hesitated, his stare shifting back to Jerry—"only those in authority can determine the necessity."

"That's really deep." Jerry stared blankly. "I'm not sure if I can grasp the total concept."

"No need. There will come a time when you will." Julean placed his hand on Jerry's shoulder. "We are going to be spending a lot of time together, but first, do you have any questions?"

"Well"—Jerry paused for a moment—"I came across the Shrine of Tauri and discovered its secret ... a ring." He unzipped his pocket and removed the coveted band. "It came with a warning, but I felt compelled to take it anyway. I thought it prudent to consult you before trying it on. So, what say you?"

"You made a wise choice in waiting." Julean gave a look of surprise. "The ring of Tauri commands a formidable force! Tauri is the lord of war, and only the most worthy can call upon the warlord's warriors to help in a time of crisis."

Jerry turned his head and cocked it. "Just how powerful is it, and do I stand worthy to use it?"

"Slow down!" Julean held his hand up. "To call down his legion of warriors, you must first place it on your finger and then align the emblem with the constellation of Taurus. Once you have connected with the constellation, you will control the mightiest throng of warriors ever assembled for battle. But I must warn you—this command can only be used once, and the decision should not be made lightly. You will know when to activate Tauri's legion. Until then, place the ring in a protective area and do not lose it."

Jerry secured his prize in an inside pocket and zipped it shut. "I have another question. I came across a pillar that allowed access to two slots. After securing the sapphire's energy, I hesitated but then chose to acquire the emerald's power. The instant I grasped the aether, my body burned, and I felt something I had never experienced before." Jerry paused in contemplation. "Did I make the correct choice, and if so, what did I gain from the jewel?"

"Yes indeed!" Julean raised both hands high in the air, celebrating Jerry's decision. "The more you assimilate, the better and faster you can progress. The emerald bestows the gift of wisdom and enlightenment and is the symbol of eternal life. Without it, your days would be shortened on Enif. Its essence confers a wonderful rejuvenating quality. It combats aging and aids in healing."

"If I may ask one more question." Jerry brought his hand to his head. "I know I've acquired the clairvoyant capability, but I'm having trouble accessing this power. Not only do I need help with my proficiency, but I want to learn how to influence the thoughts of others."

"Learning to control thoughts can be a dangerous and provocative process." Julean leaned toward Jerry, his stare daunting. "Just as a child must crawl before he walks, certain rules are necessary to understand if you are to implement telepathy correctly. Without standards, the lines are often blurred between good and evil. You will have the ability to confound and obscure the thoughts of those near you, making things appear as they are not. But ... these things are not to be trifled with. Capacity and competence are the rewards of patience and practice."

Jerry's exuberance about perfecting his mental prowess yielded to Julean's counsel. "I understand. Sometimes I get too impatient, but I am grateful for your help."

After several hours of training, Julean waved him off. "Enough for now. Refresh yourself with the fruit harvested in your last area. Your meal will continue to assist in your transformation."

"Oh, I almost forgot," Jerry said, opening his pack. "At the last jinan, I found a tree with strange-looking fruit. They're shaped like a pyramid, each side with a different color." He handed the fruit to Julean. "I ate a few but became concerned when nothing happened. I mean ... I didn't feel anything, but I picked a few just in case. So, are these good, bad or whatever?"

"You have found a precious gift that appears at random." Julean's eyes widened, reflecting surprise. "This is called an illumid. After ingesting several, you will develop another ability that will help in your quest and beyond. Its maturation process takes time, but when realized, you will be rewarded." Julean placed his hand on Jerry's shoulder. "Patience, my friend. Train as you go forward and don't look back. I can't say more at this time."

Julean vanished, leaving Jerry to contemplate his instructions and warnings. Thoughts bounced around in his head like a pinballs. *If I understood him right, I'll eventually experience the illumid's effect but not until it matures. But what are its effects, and why was he reluctant to tell me? Just how long am I going to live? And what about Tauri and his warriors?* Jerry gathered his things together and set off to find the sixth seal, pondering his future.

CHAPTER TWENTY-NINE

SERPENTIUS

Jerry explored several trails that led to dead ends. *Like so many things in my life, the paths I chose ended up empty.* He paused to rest, his thoughts drifting to his home back in Tucson. Deep inside, he still longed to see his friends and missed the camaraderie they often enjoyed. Would life on Enif really be as impressive as he was led to believe? How happy could he really be if he never saw his friends again? He sighed, kicking small rocks into the shadows. He continued to doubt, wondering if he would survive the challenges ahead of him.

A sultry draft interrupted his thoughts, filling his nose with a nauseating stench. *What's that smell?* An eerie silence permeated the chamber. The trail had faded into a rugged terrain, dominated by large boulders and small cliffs. Potholes were strewn all about, making it difficult to traverse without twisting an ankle.

Farther down the pathway, he caught sight of a large opening on the side of a limestone outcropping. Maybe it was his imagination, but he sensed something. *What in the geode could live in such a place? And that foul odor, it reeks of something that has been dead for a while.*

Nearing the opening, Jerry froze when a menacing snake-like creature emerged. The giant cobra displayed human features and had slick, shiny green scales that shimmered as he moved. His opalescent black eyes were protected by a clear veil, and a forked tongue flicked in and out of his mouth. From the corner of his eye, Jerry saw previous victims lying in the creature's den, motionless.

The serpent bared a set of fangs that looked like daggers and hissed. "Why are you infringing on my territory?"

Stumbling back, Jerry regained his balance. "I didn't mean to infringe on you … I only seek passage."

"I am Sssserpentius." He slithered around Jerry, his upper body standing erect, as if he were looking for the right moment to strike. "Do you think me sssstupid?"

Jerry quickly tapped into the serpent's consciousness and learned that he came from the Eagle Nebula, which was part of the Pillars of Creation in that star-forming system. He once lived in a paradisiacal garden without anything to detract from his enjoyment. That was until he became jealous and killed his brother, Glaucus. Once the prime minister discovered his secret act, he exiled Serpentius to the caverns on Earth.

"I mean you no harm," Jerry said as he tried to take control of his mind. "I just want to pass."

Suddenly, the hood around the serpent's head flared, and Jerry jerked backward, stumbling and almost falling.

Serpentius lunged toward him and pulled him into his constrictive coils.

Jerry wiggled free, rolled and jumped to his feet but lost his aether in the process. "Oh, no! Mr. G!" His heart sank.

The serpent struck in rapid thrusts but missed as Jerry hastened his steps, scrambling away from the predator. He tried to recover his aether but became trapped between two boulders, unable to escape.

Serpentius rose up. His lower jaw separated from the upper, and his fangs oozed venom oozed like a pair of hypodermic needles.

A cold chill slithered down Jerry's spine. Time for ingesting the apus flowers had run out, and without his aether he was as good as dead. Then he recalled his encounter with Auriga. He quickly pulled Leo's ring from his vest and slipped it onto his finger. Within moments, he had transformed into a large Indian mongoose.

Serpentius watched the transmutation and backed off. The pair warily circled each other, exchanging tense looks, waiting for the right moment. Serpentius lunged forward and struck over and over into a coat of thick fur, wild and furious.

With the agility of a mongoose, Jerry leaped and danced away from the fatal daggers. Serpentius struck relentlessly only to come away with a mouthful of fuzz. The slithering snake became furious and spit venom to try to slow Jerry down. His frustration grew as he failed to sink his long poisonous fangs into the mongoose.

Jerry watched the black eyes, the flickering tongue, the fangs extended. Moving with ease, he seized the moment and flipped Serpentius over, sinking his teeth deeply into the cobra's head. Each bite became more lethal, sinking deeper and deeper. The mongoose's quick reactions took their toll on Serpentius until, finally, he inflicted the mortal wound.

Triumphant, Jerry removed the ring with his mouth and returned to his usual form. Amazed at his transformation, he backed away, giving space to the serpent's death. A foul stench remained. His heart thumped as if he had just finished a marathon. With a deep sigh of relief, he leaned down and picked up his aether, reflecting on what had transpired.

"Mr. G, that was incredible. But I wonder how you would've fared against this piece of slime." He tilted his head and relaxed. The tension in his jaw loosened. "I can't believe how good I feel ... and the power I gained." Jerry stared at the ring's stone, mesmerized by its constantly changing colors. *Now I understand what Leo meant when he said it saved his life many times. This is a treasure more valuable than all the gold in the world.*

A faint groan inside Serpentius's den interrupted his thoughts. He secured the ring in his pocket and crept toward the unnerving sound, grasping his aether tightly. Inside, he found himself unprepared for what he'd stumbled upon. It was Lyra! He lay on his back, motionless, his eyes glazed over. Jerry rushed to his side.

Lyra lifted a strained stare.

"Lyra!" Jerry stood frozen, unsure what to do. No doubt he had succumbed to the serpent's poison, but what could Jerry do? He glanced around and saw two decaying, lifeless bodies, their stench filling his nose. *There's got to be something ...*

He flashed to his experience with the poison flowers. "Yes!" Jerry snapped his fingers. "Lyra, hang on." He quickly retrieved the pouch Zeta had given him and, kneeling, lifted Lyra's head and administered the unicorn powder, hoping it would prove successful against such a potent poison.

Within moments, Lyra's eyes opened and his muscles quivered. "Jerry," he said in a faint whisper. "What are you doing here?"

"Better question is how did you end up here?"

"I got caught up in my arrogance trying to outdo my brother." Slowly responding to the powder's magical effect, Lyra sat up. "I thought my music was so powerful that even Serpentius would succumb to its soothing harmony. Obviously, I have my limitations." Lyra sighed as he shook his head sheepishly, his eyes trying to focus. "If you hadn't come along I would've been his next meal."

"Do you think you'll be okay?"

"I think so," Lyra said as he stood up and rubbed his head.

"If I hadn't met Zeta, both of us would be dead." Jerry held out the pouch Zeta had given him. "This contains the mystical healing power of the unicorn."

"I heard tell of its powerful effect against poisons but never thought I'd need it." Lyra shifted his gaze to the pouch. "Who is Zeta?"

"She's the unicorn I met in the last chamber. Even Serpentius's venom was no match for the horn's magic."

"Did I ever learn a lesson," Lyra said, still groggy. "Don't ever let your successes make you so arrogant you lose your life over them."

Jerry pointed to his head and tapped on it. "My skull is a little thick, but I think I'm finally getting it." He paused to place his hand on Lyra's shoulder. "You know, we make a good team. We've been able to save each other's life. When this is all over, maybe we can meet up and spend some time together."

"I would love to! Maybe we can include my brother, too, but—" Lyra's face turned pale.

"Is something wrong?"

"No ... Well, yes." Lyra hung his head. "Please don't tell Lyro about my stupidity. He would never let me live it down."

"Lyra, your secret is safe with me." Jerry patted him on his back. "The next time we meet, you can teach me the magic of your music and I can share some of the things I've learned."

Jerry dawdled while he attended to Lyra's well-being, and then gathered his gear and resumed his journey to the sixth seal. Time had passed fast, and up to this point he'd felt fortunate, but uncertainty still lingered in his mind. After following a winding trail studded with loose rocks, he stopped for a moment, pulled his canteen from his waist, and gulped down a few quick swigs. Jerry wiped the dribble from his mouth and glanced up at a canopy of twinkling stars, marveling at the bright shade of blue they projected throughout the chamber. *Sometimes, I still feel like I'm dreaming. No one back home would ever believe this.*

A weariness filled his mind, and he lay down to rest on a sandy patch of ground, playing the past event with Serpentius over and over in his mind, giving rise to a feeling of accomplishment, of having made the right decision. He fought to keep his eyes open, but they had grown so heavy that sleep overcame him.

CHAPTER THIRTY

CASSIOPEIA, THE SITTING QUEEN

Jerry awoke with a sense of urgency. After his encounter with Serpentius, he'd fallen asleep exhausted, but now he felt rejuvenated and ready to continue his quest. He stood and looked around. It hadn't been much more than a few weeks since he entered the cavern, but it felt as though years had passed.

It was cold and damp. The chamber's constant humidity leached away the warmth, chilling Jerry at times. He cinched his vest tighter to his body and continued his descent, marveling at the surrounding artwork.

Flat shelfstone tables glistened with water. Hanging helictites looked like strands of spaghetti that curled and twisted in every direction. Totem-pole stalagmites towered over him like giant redwoods. It was like discovering a hidden wonder tucked deep within the bowels of the Earth, a world like none other!

Several hours later, the passage opened to a huge cavity that had a cathedral-like appearance. A brightness shone down from the ceiling, illuminating the interior. After stepping inside, he looked up and listened to the silence. *How many centuries did it take to sculpt such a chamber?* Water wept from the fern-draped cavern. Clusters of pink blossoms provided a delicious fragrance. Then his keen eyes caught sight of a structure down the trail.

He followed the passageway until it terminated at a massive articulated stone wall that seamlessly fused into the surrounding cut rock. Each brick had been chiseled from the whitest marble with streaks of ebony flashing through it. An impressive citadel resembling an old English castle loomed behind two heavy cedar doors in which were carved serpents and dragons. His mouth fell open and his thoughts scrambled for answers. *No way! What is a medieval castle doing way down here? How is this possible ... and who lives here?*

He shook his head and walked closer, running his hand over the detailed engravings. "Mr. G, what do you think? Dare we enter?" His eyes darted about, looking for a way past the foreboding barriers, but no other way existed except through the two huge gates. He turned and looked at his aether. Mr. G's eyes glared green. "I guess we really don't have much choice, do we?"

Jerry leaned his shoulder into the hefty wooden doors. They gave a little. Grunting, he pushed again and they creaked open. He peeked inside. *Wow! Incredible.* His eyes widened at an impressive stone stairway that led from the inner courtyard to the castle's threshold.

Two huge gargoyle statues adorned the palace's entrance on each side. Part dragon and part lion, the grotesquely carved legends sent chills down his spine. It was as if they were in a deep slumber, silent guardians resting on granite pedestals, waiting ...

He stepped into the courtyard, wondering who or what he would encounter next. No sooner had he started up the steps than the castle door opened and a woman of royalty confronted him.

Startled, Jerry froze.

Arrayed in a sumptuous red silk gown embroidered with queenly motifs, she moved with an eloquent glide. A thick wave of sweet perfume clung to his nose. Her rosy-red attire was stunning and complemented her silky crimson hair. She flashed a plastic smile and spoke in a smooth voice as she demanded, "Who dares enter the castle of Queen Cassiopeia?"

"My name is Jerry." He tightened his grip on his aether. "I'm on a quest to the seventh seal and seek passage through your castle."

"Come closer so I may see your face." Her unblinking stare rushed to his eyes. "For me to allow passage, you must feast at my table tonight. Come and I will give you rest from your travels."

"How do I know this isn't a trap?" Energy surged to his aether as his eyes fixated on hers.

"Look around. I have no army, nor do I have traps to harm you." She opened her arms. "I am but a lonely queen who seeks your company."

Jerry stood in silence as he surveyed the area.

"Feast with me tonight and then be on your way." Her smile widened, exposing her glistening white teeth. "You won't regret it."

"If I suspect—" Jerry tried to connect with her mind but couldn't.

"You have nothing to worry about. Come, you'll see. I—"

"Your highness." A servant had emerged from a doorway. "We are having trouble hanging—"

"Don't interrupt!" Cassiopeia gave her a harsh stare. "Can't you see we have a guest?"

"Excuse me, your highness. I am so sorry." She gave an awkward bow and slipped back into a dark corner. "It won't happen again."

"Where were we?" The queen turned and gave a forced smile. "Oh, yes, I was about to invite you inside."

"Just what are you having difficulty ... hanging?" Not a muscle of his face twitched, nor did he blink.

"Oh, one of my paintings. Maybe I'll have the opportunity to paint your portrait. But please, come." Her request was royal, absolute—uttered with an inflection that was irresistible. "Let me entertain you. Come and rest."

Placated for the time, Jerry offered a lopsided smile. *How long has it been since I've sat down at a table, feasting on real food? Who knows, perhaps she can assist with my travels.*

"It'll be my pleasure to dine with such a charming and beautiful queen."

Though he still doubted her sincerity, she was stunning and captivating. Charmed by her alluring eyes and charismatic smile, Jerry wasn't at all anxious to leave. *Why didn't*

Andromeda tell me about Queen Cassiopeia? Is there a jealousy thing going on?

"This way," she said, turning and expecting Jerry to follow her, which he did with some reservation.

Inside the palace, oil lamps scented the air with fresh exotic bergamot blended with a hint of calla lily and white jasmine. An updraft caused the flames to flutter and their light to flicker. The high vaulted ceilings emanated a dark, damp but warm magnificence to the cool old chambers.

He was taken to a room that included a fireplace and a cozy bed with heavy blankets. Decorative woodwork and tapestries adorned the walls. A cartouche representing the constellation Cassiopeia caught his attention. It dawned on him that she was the sitting queen from that star system. *Oh, my. She must command great power. Maybe she can offer a way to bypass some of my trials.* He sat and bounced on the bed a few times before stretching out with a yawn. *Still ... something here is strange, but I can't tell ...*

Jerry nodded off to sleep but became startled when he heard a loud rap. He jumped up and opened the iron-studded door, holding his aether close. He recognized the servant as the one whom Cassiopeia had scolded earlier. Clearing her throat, she bowed politely and invited him to follow her.

Oil lamps lit the way to the banquet, casting a yellow glow onto glistening paintings of men that hung in the castle. There was something odd about the artwork. The images seemed almost real, as though the subjects had been caught off guard. Their desperate eyes and parted lips revealed something dreadful, but what?

Upon entering the dining chamber, Jerry's breath quickened. A huge table filled the banquet hall, and food was piled high on fine china. Overhead hung an elegant eight-candle crystal chandelier that looked like an exotic octopus with curving outstretched arms. Beneath the flickering light rested a centerpiece of ruffled sweet-pea blossoms tucked into a bouquet of gardenias. Silver glasses filled with an exquisite herbal infusion squared off before ornately carved wooden chairs. The rousing aromas of freshly baked bread and a variety of exotic foods seemed to soothe his soul.

Queen Cassiopeia smiled. "Did you have a quiet rest ... by yourself?"

"Indeed I did," Jerry said, his eyes darting about in disbelief. "I can't thank you enough for your generosity. By the way, who are all those men in the portraits?"

"Oh, just some pictures I've collected over the years. But I'm excited and I have prepared a special meal for you. Please, sit and indulge yourself."

After once again thanking her for her kindness, he pulled out a chair and sat behind a plate of delicious-smelling vegetables. Jerry took a bite of warm buttered potatoes and closed his eyes in delight. "I haven't eaten this good—this well—in almost a month." Between mouthfuls, he tried to get Cassiopeia to tell him more about herself, hoping she could help with his quest, but she seemed reluctant.

A smile spread across her face as she nibbled at her food and dabbed the corners of her mouth. "We have plenty more, so don't be shy." She seemed impatient and urged him to eat more. With each bite, his hunger grew. Her servants kept bringing platters of roasted meats, vegetables, and herbal drinks that tasted so sweet that it was as if he were consuming nectar from the gods.

After he had filled his stomach with the delights of his hostess, he wiped his face with a napkin and pushed his plate away. Cassiopeia sat there with a silly grin on her face as though she were waiting for something to happen.

"Is everything okay?" Jerry's eyes narrowed as he yawned.

"Of course. It does my heart good to see a man enjoy his food."

He suddenly became tired and pushed his chair from the table. "I'm exhausted. Do you mind if I rest before I leave?"

"But of course. You've had a long and treacherous journey. Come and rest." The queen had added *Laurus nobilis* to his food, a magical herb used to seduce the strongest of men. She searched his eyes. "After you have refreshed, you can be on your way." As if she had anticipated his weariness, she snatched his hand and escorted him down a dimly lit hall. "I have prepared a special room just for you. You'll have plenty of time to complete your journey, but for now relax. We will talk later."

Jerry woke a few hours later feeling complacent, without any urgency to leave. Upon seeing Cassiopeia, his heart raced. "Oh, my ... You're ... you're gorgeous!" Her beauty hypnotized him.

"You flatter me." Feigning embarrassment, she drew close to Jerry. "You know, life as a queen can get very lonely, and I could use a man of your stature." She looked down. "But, no ..."

"Go on. Tell me what you were thinking." Now under her spell, he had no desire to abandon her.

"Well ..." her eyes shifted to his. "How would you like to spend the rest of your life here ... with me?"

"Are you serious?"

"Yes. I will make you my king."

"Me!" Jerry brought his hand to his chest. "Your king!"

"Yes, my king."

"Where do I sign?" Jerry grinned, his dimples deepening. Under the influence of the magical herbs, he had forgotten his love for Andromeda and embraced Cassiopeia with passion.

"Come, and I will show you your room." She grabbed his hand. "You have no idea how happy your life is about to become."

With each passing day, Jerry grew more complacent, having no desire to leave Cassiopeia's side. He found himself falling into a daily routine of waking up in a bed that swallowed him in soft sheets of satin, sipping sweet nectar, and eating heavenly foods that differed every day. Cassiopeia was right—what was the hurry? As far as he was concerned, the portal could wait. Try as he might, he couldn't remember why he needed to leave so soon. Not only had he lost his perception of reality, but he'd begun to plan his life with Cassiopeia, having forgotten about Andromeda. As long as he remained under the control of her powerful spell, he was helpless.

It had been almost two weeks since his enslavement, and every day was pretty much the same until one fortuitous morning. In her haste to inspect the herbs in her garden, she had forgotten to place the magical potion in his breakfast. The darkness that clouded his mind began to dissipate like a misty breath on a cold morning. Slowly, he recalled his mission and his love for Andromeda. Jerry shuddered. How long had he been under the queen's spell? What about Andromeda? Why hadn't she intervened? A sense of urgency filled his heart. He felt naked without his aether and pack and wondered where Cassiopeia had hidden them. When she returned from the garden, he acted as though nothing were wrong and embraced her.

"You know, I've never seen the entire castle." Jerry ran his fingers through her hair, lifted it, and watched the strands softly fall around her face. "Would you mind giving me a tour?"

She clasped his hand and smiled. "I can't now, but one of my servants will show you around. Afterward, we will have lunch."

"I don't know if I can stand being away from you, but I will try," Jerry said, feigning disappointment.

"I need to prepare our day. Later, we will spend time together." She released his hand and hurried off, disappearing into the castle's hallway.

Jerry quickly dismissed the servant and directed his mental prowess to locate his possessions. He stalked through the numerous chambers, half expecting to run into Cassiopeia, until his mind led him to a hidden closet cloaked behind a bookcase that held his aether captive.

Moments later, he wrapped his fingers around the glowing anuns, feeling the familiar warmth as though he had found a long-lost friend. "Mr. G, it's so good to see you again, but for now we need to hurry." Jerry sprinted to the rear exit, but before he could leave, Cassiopeia confronted him. She had a puzzled glare on her face when he emerged with his aether.

"Where are you going, my love, and what are you doing with that staff?"

"Uh ..." Jerry bit his lip. "I found this in ... uh ... a room upstairs, and, uh ... I thought I'd go for a walk."

"Oh, no!" Her face fell as if he had slapped her. Cassiopeia realized she had forgotten to place the magical herbs in his breakfast that morning and was stunned. As she studied him, her lips formed a hard, thin line. "I insist you return and have lunch with me now!"

"I'm leaving to continue my trek to the seventh seal." Jerry had had it, and he knew dining with the queen would place him under her spell again. "I don't want to harm you, so please, stay out of my way!"

The chamber was soft with twilight, the air thick and humid. Cassiopeia closed her eyes and started chanting. *"Surge lapidi tutores, ut eum interficerent."* Suddenly, the two-winged gargoyles that guarded her castle flew high above them. Their appearance was daunting as they hovered overhead. Donning huge bat-like wings and spewing a blistering fire from their ferocious jaws, they poised for an attack.

"One scratch from my loyal pets will transform you into one of my paintings. Only yours will hang over my bed." She snickered in delight. "A real tribute to my consummate conquests of weak and pathetic men."

An ominous vibrating tension sprang from him. Jerry stood stiffly, not knowing what to do. He took a quick glance around, unable to find shelter among the diminutive speleothems. *Great, here we go again.* He immediately coalesced with his aether and immersed himself in a protective shield.

The vicious demons released a thunderous shriek and swooped down, spewing fireballs from their mouths. The assassins clawed and snapped as they dived, trying to knock him down and pin him to the ground. Jerry struggled against their speed and ferocity but remained alert and mobile.

A sudden rush of power surged through his veins. "Okay Mr. G, time for action." He raised his aether and released a blistering explosion, igniting the air around them. The sky boomed in a pyrotechnic flash that stunned the winged demons. The infuriated beasts shook off the attack and countered with another round of fiery blasts.

Jerry dropped, rolled, and released a massive sonic discharge that shredded the wings of one malevolent gargoyle. It fell from the sky, floundering helplessly and screeching in pain. He followed with an incendiary burst of energy that swallowed the wingless demon in a storm of fire as it slammed to the ground. Ravaged by flames, it lay there comatose.

Its partner retaliated with a fiery deluge that engulfed Jerry in a living inferno. Protected by the scarab amulet, he retaliated with a blistering storm that echoed throughout the chamber.

The grotesque creature spun, twisted, and rose high above him, evading the blazing tempest. With lightning speed, it lashed out, scratching and biting, trying to invoke its curse.

Jerry lunged backward as its razor-sharp talons ripped into the collar of his shirt. He had avoided becoming part of Cassiopeia's prized collection that hung on her wall but was getting tired. He puffed out a short breath and whirled, striking the creature with a sonic blast. It screamed—screamed like nothing he'd ever heard—as it fell from the sky before crashing to the hard ground. Before the terror could regain its balance, he bludgeoned it with a massive shockwave, causing it to rupture into a heap of rubble.

With Cassiopeia's guardians slain, Jerry stared at her for a moment, his eyes lost, bloodshot, weary. "Release my pack if you don't want to end up a mangled casualty." His words were hard and callused.

Stunned at his immense power, she consented to his demand and relinquished his gear. "Please go and leave me to my ..." She pointed to the trail as her voice trailed off.

Jerry could see the panicky look in her eyes. Anger filled his heart, but he didn't want to think anymore. He just wanted to leave, to get away—anywhere. He hesitated but then lifted his pack, shifted it onto his shoulders, and was off.

He felt like he'd just eaten a poisoned apple, sick and nauseated. A chill shook Jerry as his thoughts shifted to Andromeda. Would she ever speak to him again? He surely couldn't forgive himself. Indecision plagued him; he felt deserted and depressed. What lay ahead of him? More adversity? His thoughts smoldered in his mind, consuming his soul. What was he to do now?

Once again, doubt crept into his mind. Jerry stopped and stared vacantly into the dimness of the cavern, letting numbness curb his ambition. He poked at the ground with his aether, trying to muster the strength to move on.

After chiding himself for what seemed like an eternity, Jerry sighed. "Andromeda...are you still with me?" he said, his voice breaking.

"Jerry, I will always be with you," her voice responded in an agonized tenor.

"Can ... can I see you?"

"Oh, Jerry." Andromeda appeared next to him, sobbing, her words choked. "I ... I wanted to warn you, but I was forbidden. My emotions are usually under control, but in this case, my father had to restrain me. I am so sorry I wasn't able to rescue you from that sleazy witch!"

"I didn't have control of my senses." Relieved, Jerry pulled her close. "Can you ever forgive me? The pain of being apart from you is more than I can bear. Everything I ever dreamed of ... I found in you. You are my heart and soul. I long to have you in my arms ... to be one. I will love you until my dying breath!"

"It wasn't your fault." Andromeda threw her arms around him, still weeping. "She subjected you to the potent herb *Laurus nobilis*. The strongest of men cannot resist its powerful effect. No one can escape its bewitching magic. You have no idea how much I wanted to destroy her! If my father had not intervened, she would be dead ... and I ... I would be constrained and our relationship ... terminated. But I'm proud of you. You prevailed against a powerful entity when countless have failed."

"I didn't know what I was doing," He hung his head in shame. "I didn't mean to hurt you. I tried ... I ... ugh, I hate myself."

She lifted his chin. "It's all behind you now."

"I don't understand. Why would such a beautiful woman resort to deceit to force someone to love her?"

"Indeed, why?" Andromeda dropped her gaze to her feet.

"Did I say something wrong?"

"No ... I suppose love can make a person do things they wouldn't otherwise do." Tears splashed on her cheeks as she turned her head.

"Are you sure you're okay?"

"I'll be fine." Andromeda lifted her gaze. "It's been hard seeing you with her, but it's behind us now."

"I'm sorry, but I just can't stop thinking about my time with Cassiopeia. It was so—"

"Jerry! Stop! It's over." Andromeda gently touched his face. Her eyes pierced his. "Bury that which is buried."

"Huh?" Jerry's eyes moistened with remorse. "What do you mean?"

"I have forgiven you. You need to let that memory go and focus on your future and not your past. What we have, and what we will have, awaits us, but only if you attain your goal. You need to stay focused."

"I guess I'm still struggling to understand the Enifian way of life."

"You're so tense." Andromeda ran her soft hands across Jerry's neck and shoulders, pressing and stretching away the tension. Within moments, the muscles relaxed like ice melting into water. "I've been given permission to travel with you for a while." Andromeda's warm hand rested against his face. "But please, forget the past, and let's enjoy the short time we have together."

For the moment, they sat and cuddled, discussing their life as Enifians. His eyes drifted into hers, excited that Andromeda would be at his side even if it were only for a little while.

"Are you able to eat any of the fruit I've picked?" Jerry asked as he pulled an apple from his pack.

"I appreciate the offer, but I'm not able to share in your diet. Once you've completed your transformation, you'll be unable to consume any altering provisions due to their detrimental effect on your well-being. But for now, they are essential for your continued progress."

"Oh, you know, I found a weird-shaped fruit that Julean told me was special. However, he didn't say why, only that I must be patient."

"What does it look like?"

"It's similar to a pyramid and has a different color on each side." He opened his pack and pulled an illumid out of his pack and placed it in her hand. "Is there anything you can tell me about it?"

"Just that its effect matures in phases." Andromeda turned the fruit around, observing the different colors. "Once its essence has reached its saturation point, you'll realize the final result. Other than that, I can't say much more."

Satisfied with her answer, Jerry was grateful to have her next to him, away from the clutches of Cassiopeia. For the first time since his captivity, they were together hand in hand and so in love. As they journeyed, Jerry continued to probe for more information regarding her world.

"What are the people like on Enif, and how many braved the same transformation I'm going through?"

"I'm only allowed to share certain things." She seemed nervous, not wanting to reveal too much. "Our culture has eradicated hunger and greed, and there are no material wants. We are free to do things you could never dream of doing on Earth. The opportunities are endless, and we live hundreds of years, slowly aging." She placed her hand on his face. "I don't know how many were like you, but I do know of some that were successful."

"What do you do for money?"

"It has no place on Enif."

"Sooo, everything is free?"

She nodded. "Yes, it's been like that for eons."

"I can have anything I want without working?"

"We all have assignments, but it's something we all do, kind of like a beehive. We all work to support the good of all."

"I still don't get it."

"You need not worry. When that time comes, I will help you understand."

She flipped her shiny black hair around her shoulder and tilted her head. "You need to concentrate on completing your goal and stop dreaming about the next world until it becomes a reality."

In his excitement, he almost missed another opportunity to increase his knowledge and power by bypassing a lucent cylinder stationed between two towering stalagmites. Since his encounter with Queen Cassiopeia, Jerry had been struggling to concentrate on his mission. Afflicted with self-doubt, he couldn't take his mind off of Andromeda. *I really need her by my side, but I'm having trouble concentrating on my quest. Got to stay focused if she's going to remain.*

"I know I'm a distraction, but it's just for a short time." She frowned. "I'll only be able to travel with you a little farther before I have to leave."

"No!" Jerry's faced reddened. He had opened his thoughts, forgetting she could read his mind. "You can't leave. Please!"

"Relax. I'm not going anywhere."

They approached the tube-shaped pillar, their hands clutching tightly. Flashes of light emanated from the crystal-like structure, reflecting the cavern's scintillating brightness. A continuation of precious stones adorned the round translucent unit, each one placed in a separate compartment. Jerry passed his aether over the openings, assessing each one.

"The essence of the malachite and poppy jasper are both strong. Jerry stroked his chin. "In fact, both are very strong. Does it really matter which I choose first?"

"If you do not select correctly, you will experience diminished power." She urged him on with her eyes. "If one is even the slightest bit stronger, you should access it first."

As soon as Jerry cleared his mind, the malachite's energy connected to him. Its circular bands of green radiated a soothing awareness that seemed to unlock his psyche and calm his tension. He glanced at Andromeda and then placed his aether into its aperture.

A brilliant light shot out from the anuns, illuminating the cavern with various shades of green. Mr. G's eyes were still glowing when he seized the aether in his hands. Intense energy surged through his body. His breath caught, and he dropped to his knees.

"Are you okay?" Andromeda ran to his side and grabbed his arm.

"Whew, I'm all right, but this one packed a punch. The strength given from the malachite is incredible. I feel like the holes in my aura have just been filled." Jerry looked up. A warmth cascaded down from the cavern's beaming stars, flickering their brightness across the cavern. "Strange. Somehow I feel more connected to the stars than ever before."

Jerry bounced to his feet and reviewed the precious gems for the last time. He hesitated before inserting his aether into the poppy jasper's slot. Within moments, bright yellow and red energy rings flooded the cavern. The anuns glowed reddish-orange, and the aether vibrated and twisted, becoming more convoluted. Etched into it were new auspicious symbols. When Jerry grasped the glowing staff, a tingling sensation shot throughout his body as though he had placed his finger into an electric socket.

"Wow, what a rush!" Jerry shook his head. His pupils were huge. "That was pure energy, but ... what just happened?"

"The jasper's essence is slow and constant." Static electricity sparked when she touched his hand. "It aligns your innate ability with the electromagnetic energies within the universe. Since each planet has its own frequency, you will need to fine-tune yours accordingly."

Jerry brushed the hair from his vacant eyes. "Just how many planets am I going to live on?"

Andromeda drew close to Jerry and lowered her voice. "Only Enif, but you'll need this ability to create."

"Create?"

Her eyes pleaded. "Please, I can't say any more. Once we're on Enif, you'll understand."

Jerry acquiesced and examined the tube-shaped pillar to make sure he didn't miss any other offerings. Satisfied with his experience, he grasped Andromeda's hand and pulled her close. His eyes traced the softness of her face. He sighed. "How much more must I go through?"

"If I could switch places with you, I would. What you will be facing, you need to do alone. Trust in your heart, my love, for it will see you through. My time is up. I'm being summoned."

He gently touched her lips, and with a loving breath he exhaled. "I know you have to go, but I feel an emptiness each time you depart. Our time is always limited, and I—"

Like two comets rushing to collide, they smothered each other in a blaze of passion, a passion that could not be quenched. Then she vanished.

A smile crept up on his face as he thought about her words. *She did say "create." But did she mean other worlds? I always knew minerals had various frequencies, but planets?* Then something stirred in his heart, a feeling of relief that she had forgiven him. Jerry whistled as he threw his pack around his shoulders, grabbed his aether, and resumed his quest, dreaming about Andromeda—and creating worlds!

CHAPTER THIRTY-ONE

THE ENCHANTED WALL

A potent energy vortex emerged over a huge vertical monolith. A soft hum began to resonate in the air like a high-tension power line. Jerry eased his way toward the structure, his heart hammering. *What in the geode is this thing?* He sensed something, something powerful. A heaviness spilled into the air as he ran his fingers over a flawlessly smooth wall that had been fashioned on the side of a cliff.

There was something significant about the strange edifice, but he wasn't sure just what. A perceived aura radiated from within it, beckoning to his mind, pulling him close like steel to a magnet. Its pulsed essence seemed to invade his inner soul. When he fixated on the vertical surface, several indiscernible images materialized. Then it dawned on him. *This must be the enchanted wall Circinus told me about.*

Blurred images rippled beneath its surface, waiting to merge with his mind. He unzipped his pack and removed the columba bird's feather and placed it against the wall, but nothing happened. Jerry shook his head. *Okay, Circinus said this would activate the wall, but how? Maybe it needs to be attached to me.* Jerry took a piece of string from his pack, tied the plume around his neck, and crouched with his palms against the sheer face.

Within moments, his thoughts disappeared into the façade and his mind opened to a dream, a vision of wonder, a place of fertile ground. It was as if he'd been transported to another world. Like the Garden of Eden, it overflowed with lush and prismatic vegetation. He marveled at the delicate, ornate flowers, seeing buds of light burst into vibrant blue and pink petals. Luminous black and yellow butterflies hovered above the succulent blossoms that dotted the landscape. From the limbs of graceful magenta trees, bright yellow leaves glowed, sharing their light with the natural creations around them. A warmth embraced him when he realized he'd had dreams of this place long before entering the caverns. Maybe it was a coincidence, but the feelings he felt yanked at his heart as though it were his true home.

Everywhere he looked, he was mesmerized by the pristine beauty generated by the landscape. Breathtaking and awe-inspiring mountains soared high above him, making him feel vulnerable and fragile but at the same time instilling a desire to strive for new heights. Rainbows formed in the mist of stunning waterfalls. Mountain streams plummeted into turquoise pools of sparkling water. Nature seemed to be in perfect balance.

Then a voice echoed through his mind. "Behold!" His eyes opened to a scene where people interacted with this paradisiacal land. He saw them eating fruit that imparted immortal nectar, allowing some to live for thousands of years without suffering illness or disease. Happiness prevailed, and there were no needs or wants. Never had he felt such peace.

Jerry's mind raced. His blood surged with a passion to go to this Shangri-La—this mythical utopia, free from the earthly travails of man. His underlying desires resurfaced, giving a thrill to the adventure that lay ahead. *I'll have everything I ever wanted and never want again. But what about Andromeda?*

The voice came again. "Behold!" His heart dropped when he witnessed life without her. *How can this be? Do I mess up? Does something happen to her?* Shocked, he looked away, but when he gazed back into his destiny, he saw life with her. Confusion flooded his mind, and then it stilled, giving way to the wisdom of the wall.

"Can one divide the flame of love? Can a heart be split in half? Only one true love can be woven into the fabric of your soul. Seek that golden thread of love that will bind your tapestry of happiness."

Only one true love? Is there another love I don't know about? Now I'm really confused. A shimmering blue aura engulfed his essence. His body burned and trembled as words kept coming.

"Peel the veneer that holds you back. Seek the potential you suppress. A thousand thoughts may blur the way, and indecision may prove fatal. Obstacles may fill the crossroads of life, but tomorrow's passions depend on the choices made today."

Like a whisper in the wind, the voice of the wall sounded again. "Behold!" Jerry's eyes opened to a man high on a mountain, sitting next to a roaring campfire. A mass of curly brown hair spilled out from under an old cowboy hat, and his beady little eyes pierced the darkness like glowing embers. He was holding a book, but Jerry couldn't see what was in it.

Then a foreboding voice spoke to his mind, "Seek out the man on the mountain to learn more of your destiny."

Peeling his hands off the wall caused a thick barrier to form, sealing the images deep within the cliff. Jerry reflected on all that had happened.

How do I discover the power that's inside of me? My mind seems clear, but my thoughts do wander at times. Is Andromeda the flame of love? Who is this mountain man?

Jerry left the enchanted wall with more questions than answers. He had seen the future, hadn't he? Yet he doubted. Was it real or just a foolish hope to dream of a life without adversity? Perhaps the vision he had seen at the wall had not been complete. Maybe he should have tried to penetrate its barrier once again. No matter, he had seen Enif in its glory. Resolve had settled in his heart, and he was determined. Now more than ever, a passionate desire to escape these caverns burned inside him. Either he would finish his journey and fulfill his destiny or he would simply fade away like a mild sunburn.

With so many thoughts bouncing around in his brain, Jerry resumed his trek, his boots pounding a less-trodden path, practicing and training as he marched toward his goal. An awakening was occurring like a wave of energy infusing him with a breath of fresh air, and telepathy was becoming a significant part of his repertoire. He frequently tried to tap into his telepathic powers, delving deep into his psyche but lacking the ability to control thoughts. Sometimes he received flashes of insight, as if he were dreaming and unable to seize the power he wished for. In spite of all he had learned, he realized that one minor mistake could forfeit his life, and with it Andromeda.

CHAPTER THIRTY-TWO

GEMINID

Jerry relaxed and released a deep sigh. He romanticized the scenes of Enif he had seen at the enchanted wall, the sublime landscape filling his mind with thoughts of peace and tranquility. He could almost smell the flowers' fragrances, the air's purity. Then his senses awakened to loose rocks dashing and rattling down narrow, barren walls.

Mounds of fallen rubble lay piled along the trail, and the ground had become hard and compact. Ahead of him, the cavern tapered into a corridor strewn with jagged stones that crumbled under his footsteps. A warm breeze fluttered through the air, bringing with it a strong odor that forced Jerry to catch his breath.

Just as he paused to hydrate, the ground lurched beneath his feet. Boulders and loose debris ricocheted overhead, crashing down around him. Fear caught in his throat. *What now? Am I to be buried in an avalanche?* Jerry recoiled and ducked as a deafening rock slide abruptly blocked his path, causing dust to whip around, filling his nose and scratching at his eyes. He blinked and coughed as dirt spilled into the cavern. Waving the clouds of dust out of his face, he stumbled back, waiting for the murky haze to disperse.

"Mr. G, you all right?" Jerry brushed the dirt away from the still-glowing eyes. "This is one huge pile of rocks. How are we going to—wait, maybe we can float over it."

Jerry exhaled a deep breath and lifted his eyes upward, allowing weightless energy to flow through him. But before he could lift off, the mountain of boulders quaked and wobbled. He stopped and watched the rubble merge together, stone by stone, into a massive rock-like creature. Gigantic rocks formed each extremity, and its core resembled molten magma.

A sudden wave of dread overtook him. He tried to swallow but had no spit. How could he ever hope to fight such an opponent? Jerry fought to rein in his fear and stumbled backward.

The creature eyed him curiously. "Who dares wake Geminid?" it said in a raspy voice. The mammoth beast lumbered toward him, each slow step pounding the ground hard. "What is this, my snack for the day? Your bones may be just what I need to rock my world."

Jerry shook off his stupor and tried to merge with the creature's mind but was unable to connect. As he glanced around, looking for a place of safety, molten lava suddenly spewed from Geminid's core, blistering everything in its path. Before Jerry could leap out of the way, a blob of slag seared his leg. He grabbed his calf, trying to blot out an excruciating pain that shot through every nerve in his body.

"What's wrong?" The rock giant lumbered toward him. "Can't take the heat?"

Suddenly, Jerry's pain turned to power; a strength coursed inside like a roaring fire. Energy surged to his aether, but before he could react, the creature stomped its feet violently, causing him to lose balance. *I feel like I'm on a bus traveling on a street filled with huge potholes.*

Stalactites broke loose from the cavern's ceiling. Like torpedoes, they peppered the ground all around him. Instinctively, Jerry formed a shield of protection that enveloped his body. The projectiles bounced off the defensive barrier, but the molten assaults became difficult to dodge with the earth shaking under his feet.

The boisterous creature continued to bruise and batter the ground, causing massive fissures and gaps to form. Stumbling backward, Jerry regained his balance and sent a fiery blast toward Geminid, striking the beast in the head.

Outraged, Geminid shook its head and began launching rock shards from its arms like a cannon, pummeling Jerry with small nuggets and knocking him to the ground. He grunted and pushed himself up. A sharp pain shot through his chest from the deep bruising. Their eyes met, and in an instant Jerry unleashed a powerful sonic blast that echoed into the heart of the creature, fracturing part of its core. Then, with a pulsed attack, he sliced through the rock demon like butter, causing it to shatter.

The battle was over. All that remained were small rocks that littered the trail and lingering fumes from liquefied lava. "Holy geode!" Jerry turned and looked at his aether. "Mr. G ...

the power … it was amazing." This was the first time he had experienced a force of such immense magnitude. He stood in awe, holding his aether tight. *Just how powerful are you? Each conflict has been different. Each response has been precise.*

His power was becoming more lethal—and he wanted more! Jerry searched deep within himself, seeking the truth. Then an image appeared in his mind. *The thought becomes more intense until its intensity is such that the idea becomes a credible weapon.* So many things rambled through his brain that he didn't quite understand, but for now it was time to refocus himself on his quest.

He picked up a few shattered remains to examine their matrix. *The shards are a form of cooled lava, but how in the world can something made of an inorganic mineral demonstrate organic properties.* Jerry shook his head and tossed the small fragments over his shoulder. The stones exploded on impact, sending him to his knees. "Whoa! Mr. G, these act like hand grenades."

Jerry stood in silence. *Even though I have my aether, these could come in handy.* He turned to Mr. G. "Hey, if we get bored, we can always fling a few around for fun."

After placing several small explosive shards in his pack, he turned and stepped carefully through the jumble of rock and resumed his journey.

CHAPTER THIRTY-THREE

THE SECRET OF THE FLOATING VAULT

Ever since his encounter at the enchanted wall, Jerry couldn't stop wondering about the other love. He wanted to ask Andromeda what she knew but felt awkward, and he certainly didn't want to offend her. He'd have to wait for the right time. For now, he would focus his efforts on reaching the next seal.

The hours faded as he ambled along an old dried-up streambed, the ground crackling and crunching under his boots. A soft blue light emanated from within the cavern's walls, illuminating the area just enough to see. The passage led to a small antechamber crowded with various speleothems. The ceiling was so low he had to duck and waddle through the corridor. *Sure glad I'm not claustrophobic.*

A faint flapping of wings gave Jerry a start, causing him to hit his head against a low-hanging stalactite. "Ow!" He moaned and rubbed his forehead. "Mr. G, that really smarted, but what was that sound?"

Moments later, the corridor emptied into a large cavernous chamber, but something seemed odd. Jerry stopped and looked around. The air was still and thick. His skin prickled and his pulse quickened.

The scenery had changed from a dusty, barren landscape to an area dense in vegetation. Big burly trees resembling the mighty oak abounded, and the ground was rough and rocky. About twenty feet above him loomed a magnificent building flashing a sign that read "Treasure of the Sixth Seal"

What treasure? Is it the key to the next seal, or am I looking at another illusion, attempting to lure me in with its riches? His mind reeled. What was this strange building doing hovering in the middle of this vast chamber? Why was it isolated so high off the ground?

The structure was fashioned from the finest gold he had ever seen. Trimmed with a stone called hematite, a type of iron oxide, the edifice exhibited an alphabet of radiant colors. For the time being, he fixated on the air-bound treasure, unsure what to do. "Mr. G, if this holds the answer to the sixth seal, then we need to find a way in, but how?"

A light breeze rustled leaves against the rocky surface while an earthy odor permeated the air. Jerry scanned the area. His best chance to enter the hovering safe was to float to its entrance.

He closed his eyes and exhaled a nervous breath, hoping this would be a simple process. Just as he became weightless, the treasury's guardian swooped down and confronted him. It was a griffin.

Startled, Jerry retreated to the ground. His eyes stared vacantly; words fled. With the body of a lion and the head and wings of an eagle, he posed a formidable threat. Jerry had read that such a creature could tear a man to pieces in a matter of minutes, but he had his aether to protect him, didn't he?

"What is it you seek?" The griffin flapped his wings fiercely, sending a torrent of air over him.

Jerry shielded his face from the dirt and debris blown into the air by the powerful downdraft. "I know you are noble and wise and wish to avoid any—"

"I am the guardian of the vault," the griffin declared. "No one shall enter!"

Jerry sucked in a breath and gritted his teeth. *Maybe I can breach his mind and take control.* He quickly cleared his head of all distractions and visualized a channel of energy to the griffin. *Your thoughts are my thoughts. Your actions are my actions.*

Within moments, he had seized control of the beast. The winged terror was drifting from the vault when, suddenly, he fought back, breaking Jerry's telekinetic lock.

Jerry groaned. *Now what do I do?* His thoughts flashed to Leo's ring, but before he could unzip his pocket, his aether surged with energy. He stood immobile with narrowed eyes. The fear of making bad decisions still haunted him, but after dispatching Geminid with relative ease, he was sure this skirmish would be short-lived. Jerry raised his aether, but before he could engage its power, the griffin was on him.

The ominous creature attacked with his mighty talons, its claws sharper than any Damascus sword. For all his training,

Jerry wasn't fast enough to avoid its attack and was thrown, slamming his head face-first into a large brawny oak. In a daze, he pushed up from the ground and tried to form a defensive shield but was flung into another burly tree. The griffin lashed out with lightning speed, slashing and tearing with every approach.

A dull thud echoed when Jerry's body collided with the ground. He's *fast—too fast. Got to get away.* His eyes darted, seeking a place of refuge. He struggled to maintain the protective shield of his aether as the vicious beast bashed him against another jagged boulder, straining and twisting his neck. He tried to focus, but even when he did get a shot off, the griffin easily evaded the attack, zipping about like a speedy hummingbird.

"You're making this way too easy," the griffin said.

Before Jerry could recover, the beast launched into flight, smashing him into the gritty ground and sending dull slashes of pain across his head. The rocky surface scraped and tore into his arms. Pain rippled through him, but he suppressed the groan. *Ugh, I'm losing my focus, unable to maintain my shield.*

He scanned the area, searching, searching for safety. There! A massive boulder just feet away. Jerry gritted his teeth and lunged toward it, but the beast struck again before he could reach it. His head throbbed mercilessly, his body, too. If he could just get a break. *I've been smashed so many times I feel like a piñata.*

A bolt of panic shot through him. His heart pounded as though it would beat out of his chest. Then he recalled

Andromeda's words. *Trust in your heart. It will not let you down.*

"Leave now if you want to survive!" the griffin roared.

Jerry's eyes flashed. "Yes, I may die here, but I'm going to put up one hellacious fight, and you ... well ... you may wish I hadn't." His words were slow and deliberate. He staggered to his feet and forced a breath. He wouldn't be thwarted. Somehow, he would claim victory. Jerry raised his aether and released a surge of sonic energy that knocked the elusive threat from the sky.

The griffin crumpled to the earth but was up in an instant, his eyes ravenous. He initiated a ground assault, lashing out with his deadly talons. The beast blitzed and snapped relentlessly. *This guy is like the Energizer bunny—he keeps on going and going. He's got to tire soon ... I hope.*

Sweat dripped down his face, stinging his eyes. His body throbbed in pain from the constant drubbing, but he stayed focused, his energy shield holding up against the vicious battering.

Finally, the demon paused his attack. *Must act now!* Jerry quickly unleashed an explosive charge, striking the creature in the chest. The griffin fell but swiftly rose, staggering.

He sensed the guardian was wearing down. *Now is my chance to take control.* "Now, my friend, let's see what you have," Jerry shouted with renewed vigor

The griffin ruffled his feathers and then charged forward, grunting.

A warm breeze shot past him. Stillness filled the area. Jerry relaxed, his actions becoming automatic. With lightning-quick reflexes, he rolled, leaped, and fired a sonic blast, rendering the creature dazed and confused. The cavern thundered with explosive energy. He hammered the tired guardian with tremendous force, each strike taking its toll.

The weary griffin labored to evade the deadly assaults. Blast after blast, the legend suffered severe wounds, burns, and paralysis. Ulcerated gashes oozed blood. Lacerated wings and body punctures inflicted the weakened beast. Ravaged and exhausted, the creature let out a shrill cry as it stumbled and fell to the earth. The spark in its eyes faded and then disappeared.

Motionless, the griffin lay dead.

Jerry stole a breath. "Mr. G, we did it!" He turned to his aether. "That's as close to death as I ever want to experience. Don't you think?" He stretched his neck to each side, popping his bones. "Me, too."

A gentle mist crawled throughout the chamber, bringing a cool breeze. He stopped and drank from his canteen and then wiped the condensation from his face. Jerry had sustained extensive injuries and watched his body repair the damaged tissue.

Incredible! He was bathed in a warm glow, soothing and comforting in a way he had never experienced. *I'm beginning to understand what Andromeda meant when she spoke of a world without disease.*

Quiet fell. Leaves rustled. Jerry swallowed once, twice. He raised his eyes to the hovering vault. What still waited for him? With the griffin defeated, he had no choice but to gain access to the floating treasury.

Like Superman, he leaped upward and took flight, swimming through the air. It didn't take him long to reach the suspended stronghold, but now what? Fatigued and battle-weary, he stood at its entrance for what seemed like an hour, waiting and wondering. *What lies beyond this barrier? Is it a trap or another creature like the griffin? No matter, I've got to be ready.*

Jerry touched the unguarded door, and it popped open with a loud metallic click. Inside the entry, there were no twisting hallways but rather one straight corridor that seemed to go on forever. Paper lanterns splashed an icy shade of blue into the long arched, windowless passageway; the floor glistened with a silvery-blue sheen. Once past the threshold, he was alone, at least for the moment.

He drew his aether close, his grip tightening as he entered the long passage, silent save for his footsteps. After walking only a short distance, it became apparent—the corridor was getting longer and longer. He recalled falling into a pit, unable to ascend the stairway. *If my memory serves me right, the harder I climbed, the farther the exit moved away.* "Mr. G, I feel like a hamster on a wheel, going nowhere fast."

Jerry fished around in his pack and found the opaque glasses he had stowed away. Once they were on his face, the hall shortened and another entrance appeared. *Holy geode, I've got to remember that this place is not as it seems.* Jerry crept toward a pale blue metal door. Icy fingers of frost streaked across it. Chills raced down his arms when he touched the frigid handle. *Why so cold?* He eased the door open just enough to peek inside.

Away from the door, a sentry stood guard. His eyes were cold and pale as if made from ice. He was large in stature and girded in a uniform that reminded Jerry of a Roman centurion. His armor included engraved gold greaves that covered his arms and sported leather protection for his back and shoulders, primed for any attack. He held a spear like none Jerry had ever seen. The lance beamed an iridescent blue glow. The room was airtight and without windows, and the only way in or out was past the silent sentinel.

His gaze shot to an elaborate security device with a neon-combination mechanism situated next to a small round door on a steel-armored wall toward the rear of the room. Odd clicking noises in repeated patterns, echoed in the enclosed chamber, along with a quiet hum. *That must be the vault's treasure, but how am I going to get past this brawny lookout?* His stomach churned with anxiety and his muscles tightened. Then his mind opened. *Of course—the apus flowers should do the trick.*

He took a few from his pack and ingested them. Cloaked in invisibility, Jerry slipped around the guard, who now had his back to him. Inside, the temperature was zero, and he drew in a deep breath of brittle air and eased his way to the vault, his footsteps soft and silent. *Brrr, I feel like I just opened a freezer. I just hope I'm not the frozen dessert.*

His eyes were drawn to a blue neon light that flashed on and off. But what did it mean? Writing gradually appeared on it. He leaned forward, staring at a single phrase: "What has eyes and can't see and a tongue and can't speak?"

Jerry rolled his eyes. *You've got to be kidding! A riddle?* His eyes burned and watered, and his face ached from the severe cold. He glanced around, seeking anything that could help, his mind whirling in confusion. *What in the geode does this mean?* He sighed. *If I can't figure this out before my invisibility wears off, I may not make it out alive.*

He fidgeted about, pressing his mind for an answer. He shivered with a biting chill. Every breath seared his lungs with a burning cold. His fingers ached and patches of frost formed on his face. *Never in my life have I been so cold.* Jerry rubbed his hands to ease the chill. *I have no idea what the answer is, but I do know it's time to exit this place.*

His toes were numb and his feet throbbed. As he turned to leave, one of his bootlaces loosened. As he bent down to retie the lace, it hit him. *My shoes! The shoelaces go through the eyes, and every shoe has a tongue as part of its anatomy.* He was wearing the answer.

Jerry glanced back at the guard and then turned and whispered, "A shoe," his voice barely perceptible.

The blue neon light flashed, the humming stopped, and the vault popped open, revealing a single object: a clear sphere that exhibited a curious beauty like none he had ever seen before. He snatched the small ball and stuffed it in his pants pocket. But when he tried to leave, the centurion confronted him. Though the brawny guard couldn't see Jerry, he blocked the exit, trapping him inside. With his lance lowered, the centurion scattered the room with a stream of frosty crystals, turning everything it hit into solid ice. He remained stationary and did not speak.

Jerry's quick reflexes allowed him to dodge the barrage of ice charges without incident other than the formation of a few icicles in his hair. *No wonder it's freezing in here, but how do I get past Mr. Freeze?*

His teeth chattered, and he shivered as he slipped Leo's ring onto his finger, but nothing happened. Dread filled his lungs and his breath quickened. *Great, now isn't the time for a wardrobe malfunction.* His eyes shifted to his aether. Instantly, a powerful force engulfed his frame. *I can do this!* Jerry forced a deep breath and calmed, but his muscles remained tense and rigid. Still invisible, he lowered his aether and blasted the silent sentinel with a massive firestorm.

The centurion shook it off and sprayed the room with another freezing stream of ice. Jerry dropped to the floor and lay flat. A deadly stillness infused the chamber. A glare of death emanated from the tense, menacing fiend, but still, he remained silent.

The aether's power surged, strengthening Jerry. He leaped up, turned, and unleashed a barrage of energy missiles at the fearless guard, knocking him down. The blasts shook the walls so hard Jerry almost fell. He was surprised at the warmth the aether emitted and began to exploit its devastating power.

The centurion staggered to his feet, trying to avoid the onslaught of explosives. Unable to retaliate against Jerry's continual attacks, he tired fast from relentless waves of detonations. The stumbling guard looked barely conscious, his head hung low and his legs wobbling beneath him. Then, with a timely hit, the formidable foe fell to the floor, unable to continue his assault.

Now visible, Jerry sprinted around him, shutting the door with a loud click, hurrying to the exit before the centurion could regain consciousness.

Moments later, a garbled sound followed him, whether from pain or rage Jerry couldn't tell. He didn't care. He bolted through the long hallway and out the door. Outside the vault, he became weightless, floated to the ground, and rushed away from the treasury.

He stopped and took the translucent ball out of his pocket and inspected its curious workmanship. It was the size of a golf ball, and inside was a series of symbols suspended in a strange blue solution. They seemed to float around in no apparent order. When he shook the small sphere, it was like stirring up the tiny particles of a snow globe, sending the symbols darting about in their little world. *I'm not sure how this small device is going to open the sixth seal, but I hope to understand its secret once I reach the next gate.*

After so many encounters, Jerry tired. He lowered his pack to the ground and scanned the area, checking for trouble. For all he knew, evils lurked around every rock and stone, just waiting to kill him. He couldn't afford to let his guard down. To do so could mean his life.

Jerry sat on a granite shelf and sighed as he reflected on his past. Things had changed so much that his life back home felt foreign. He thought about the city where he grew up. The long hot summers, the dusty monsoons, the late-night bantering with his friends at Joe's house—it all seemed so distant.

He yawned. *I need to catch a few z's.* Jerry scouted the area and found a spot of soft ground just off the trail next to an outcropping of limestone. He adjusted his pack for a pillow and laid his head on it, wishing that when he awoke his quest would be over. He tossed about until he found a comfortable position. *Sometimes I still wonder if I'm dreaming.* Thoughts of his past life continued to flash across his mind until his eyes grew weary and closed.

CHAPTER THIRTY-FOUR

THE ELASTIC PRISONS

After a short nap, Jerry woke with a jerk. He raised his head and glanced around, wondering if it had all been a dream. But no, he was still trapped, nowhere to go but forward. He threw his pack around his shoulders, grabbed his aether, and resumed his trek.

It wasn't long before he caught sight of another spinning orb off the path. A faint whooshing sound echoed against his ear as though he resided in a huge seashell. The cavern had dimmed, and a cluster of barnacles and shells from an old, dried-up lake bed covered the ground. Like a string of Christmas lights, roots dangled from the ceiling, glistening with water that had collected on them.

Jerry sprinted toward the shiny sphere, the cavern's floor crunching under his feet. Not unlike in the last chamber, the suspended ball radiated white light, but when he touched its brightness, nothing happened. He recalled his last encounter and shut his eyes, meditating and waiting. Once again, a subtle ripple of air caressed his face, and when he opened his eyes, a second orb had materialized. The instant he tapped the shiny unit, a beacon of white light poured down, and with it Julean.

Jerry surveyed his robe, his eyes darting about. "Julean, nothing has changed since we last met. You still have the same three-dimensional vesture with the same symbols and planets."

"Ah, you have missed a few notable celestial bodies," Said Julean, always the mentor.

"Oh, yes, I see them. They look like small planets, or are they asteroids?"

"That they are. Since asteroids are harder to see, you need a keen eye to find them. It's clear that you are becoming more astute in your observations."

"Every time we've met, your apparel has changed." Jerry scratched his head. "I still don't understand all this ... I mean the reason for the variation."

Julean smiled. "I tried to inform you when we last met, but you weren't ready. Consider your circumstances for a moment. From the beginning, your knowledge and power have increased exponentially, and your conversion has been continuous and progressive. During your transition, there has been a parallel consequence. Every phase of growth and accomplishment has been recorded, and the universe has been preparing a place to receive you. Things are changing in space as you evolve. Once your transformation is complete, your adventure will continue. A sector is morphing and organizing as we speak."

Jerry was like a sponge, hanging on his every word. "Whew, it sounds amazing, but I still don't understand everything that's happened. Maybe in time it'll sink in."

Julean nodded. "All will be known in due course."

"I found an enchanted wall, but I'm not sure if this is something I should review with you." Feeling awkward, he hesitated.

"It is okay to share your thoughts with me. What we discuss, no one knows."

"Well"—Jerry fidgeted with his aether—"when my mind merged with the wall's heart, I beheld a land of indescribable beauty, which I presumed was a foreshadowing of my life on Enif, but then it mentioned another love, asking if a heart can be divided. Can you shed any light on their meanings?"

"I believe you to be correct in the first, but matters of a personal nature I am not privy to. Those you must search out for yourself."

"I was afraid you were going to say that." Jerry looked away as though distracted by the glistening speleothems. "Sooo, how well do you know Andromeda?"

"She is the overseer of illusions and daughter of Avela, the chief overseer of Enif." Julean raised his eyebrow. "Young Jerry, I know what you are trying to do, and if you continue, your focus will be lost, and with it your ability to finish your quest."

"Well, I had to try, didn't I?"

"Anything else before we proceed?"

"Strong statements or declarations appeared, regarding my ability to make choices, but I'm not quite sure what they meant."

"Well, you already know making a wrong decision could prove fatal." Julean squared his shoulders. "As you continue to progress, things will become more difficult and more dangerous. Which power or ability to implement may mean the difference between life and death. Distractions can cripple your ability to focus. Your mission is to complete your quest. However, to do so, you must remain vigilant. Do not rest on your laurels. Continue to practice, and most of all trust in your heart."

Jerry paused to ponder his words. "I also saw a man wearing a cowboy hat. He was sitting next to a campfire holding a book. I was told to seek him out to learn more about my destiny, but I have no idea how to find him."

"When you see smoke rising from a mountain, you will know."

"What about the book he held?" Jerry removed the leather-bound volume from his pack. "Is this it? I found it a while back and meant to quiz you about it but forgot."

"This book you found is powerful. It is essential for your success both here and on Enif, but I can't say more at this time."

Jerry had more questions but thought it best to wait. The future depended on his ability to conquer the remaining few chambers, and he certainly didn't want to lose focus.

After an intense training session that lasted for hours, Jerry asked, "How much more are we going to do?"

"We are finished until we meet again." Julean advised him to stay attentive and then vanished.

Jerry's heart lifted, and with a sigh he gathered his gear and started off. He stopped and sat on a rock next to a cave pool, its surface glass-like, reflecting the shimmering brilliance of a canopy of stars overhead. He shook his head. *I still can't believe this is real.* How long had he been traveling within the depths of the caverns? There was no accounting for time. Minutes, days—they were all the same, cloaked in the confines of a place where day and night ceased to exist. How much longer did he have before he reached the portal? How much more adversity awaited him? He drank from his canteen and wiped his forehead, his thoughts drifting toward Andromeda.

A lofty gust flicked his hair to and fro, trying to make up its mind which way to go. His nose twitched at the scent of sweet orchids suddenly saturating the air.

"Andromeda, are you here?" he called out.

"Oh, yes! Yes, I am." She appeared. "You are doing so well. The sixth seal is within your grasp, but please, you must continue your vigilance."

"It's good to see you again." With a warm embrace, he gazed into her gleaming eyes. "Do you mind if we hang out for a while?"

Andromeda sighed. "I only have a short window but will stay as long as possible."

Jerry scooted closer and wrapped his arms around her, leaning his forehead against hers. "You know, Julean said the universe was changing—preparing a place that would allow for my continued journey. But I still don't quite understand what that means."

"Once you have completed your transition, you will have the opportunity to create things of your own." Trying to moderate his questions, Andromeda leaned back and lifted his chin. "The astronomical implications are innumerable. Have you ever stared into space and wondered if you were alone?"

"I've always questioned what was out there. Never did I believe we were the only creatures in this infinite universe."

"You have no idea what awaits you, but it will be worth it."

"You keep telling me how great things are going to be, but other than what I saw at the enchanted wall, I don't have a clue. Why can't you share more information?"

"Do you know what happens to a computer when it overloads and crashes?"

"Yeah, kinda."

"Please, trust me."

"Are you saying I'm a computer?"

"No, it's just that you shouldn't plan your success before it arrives."

"Huh?" Jerry cocked his head. "What do you mean?"

"The power in that book can cause you to lose focus ... lose your concentration, which can lead to disastrous results."

Jerry's eyes widened. "This book!" He pulled the special edition from his pack. "Julean said its power is essential for my success both here and on Enif."

It was obvious she had said too much, and with her finger over his mouth, she shushed him.

"Please, don't ask me for more. Can't we just relax and enjoy our time together?"

Jerry calmed, and for the next hour they talked and dreamed about their life together. Afterward, the overseers summoned Andromeda. With one last passionate embrace, she vanished, leaving him to contemplate his quest. *What's so powerful in that book that's going to help me here and when I'm on Enif? Does it possess some kind of magic? No matter, it sounds like I'll be creating things in the universe—but I still don't know what and how.*

Bright strands of starlight drifted downward, lighting the way. Jerry looked around as he ventured through winding corridors of glistening limestone walls, down a hard granite path, and across an open expanse filled with giant crystalline stalagmites that sparkled like polished silver.

He had traveled for almost an hour when a sudden humidity thickened the air. Sweat trickled down his forehead. A smooth narrow pathway, void of speleothems, led to the next sealed chamber. Jerry sniffed the air and a strange vinyl-like odor filled his lungs. He glanced around and grunted. "Mr. G, something's not right. What do you think?" An eerie wind moaned as it raced past him. "I agree, but we can't stay here."

While he wrestled with indecision, his attention was drawn to something in the distance. The pathway shimmered and reflected an unusual aura. *Okay, this is weird.* Jerry's soft footsteps eased forward, breaking the silence. Suddenly, a translucent sphere engulfed him. *What in the geode?* His heartbeat quickened.

A massive bubble had enveloped him. Panic struck when it slowly lifted him off the ground. *Oh, no ... This is really bad!* The transparent membrane stretched and expanded as he struggled to escape. The elastic barrier absorbed his forceful attempts to kick and punch his way out as though it were made of latex. In desperation, he opened his pack and rummaged through it only to come up empty. *Ugh, Julean never prepared me for this.* His aether could prove dangerous with him inside, and Leo's ring didn't make sense. A thought flashed through his mind.

My knife!

Jerry grabbed his blade and punctured the lining. *This has to work.* He sliced through the membrane and cut his way out before floating too far off the ground. Then, after dropping to the surface, he retreated back where he had started, his heart racing.

He wiped the sweat from his forehead and tried to connect to his aether but came up empty. "Mr. G, how are we going to get past these plastic prisons?" He tried running, jumping, even floating across, but in each attempt a giant bubble swallowed him, forcing him to use his knife.

Frustrated, Jerry stopped and pondered his situation. *There's got to be a way to get past these elastic nightmares, but how? Wait! Maybe ...* He pulled the crossbow from his pack and reread the engraving. "The greatest weapon one has is the ability to choose one correctly over another." *Is now the time to use the bow?*

Jerry secured his aether to his pack and loaded a crystal arrow onto the crossbow. Inside the crystalline shaft, a light flashed and flickered as though it were alive, trying to escape.

Whoa, whoa, whoa. Something just woke up.

He positioned himself in an athletic stance, one foot behind the other, ready to sprint to the sealed door. "Mr. G, if this doesn't work, I don't know what we'll do." He exhaled a deep breath. "Three, two, one!"

Twang!

The arrow jumped off the bow, and Jerry sprinted into the narrow corridor. In an amazing feat, the magic dart pierced the menacing bubbles, bursting them before they could form around him. The enchanted shaft circled back after each hit, popping each elastic sphere until he stood at the secured entry.

"Yes! We did it!" he shouted, shaking his fist. He loosened his aether from his pack and looked into Mr. G's glowing eyes. "We good?" Jerry brushed the hair from his eyes and sighed. "It's scary to think what would have happened if we hadn't found the bow. Right now, we'd be in serious trouble."

Jerry ran his hand over the engravings inscribed next to the sixth seal. *Okay, let's see if I can open this thing.* He removed the small orb from his pocket and twirled it between his fingers, looking for a way to activate it. The blue solution had turned red, and the strange symbols drifted about in no particular order or pattern. When he shook it, nothing happened. The glasses didn't help either. He groaned in frustration. *Maybe I can randomly match its images to the characters on the door.* Still nothing. Then he reflected on the words of Andromeda. *I need to trust in my heart and believe.*

Perhaps if I focus intently on the small orb, my eyes will be opened.

Jerry held the device in his hands and meditated on it, hoping to reveal its code. Little by little, the red solution faded, becoming clear. The symbols zipped around and formed a four-character sequence, matching the wall's engravings. Jerry raised an anxious finger and touched the encryptions, each one emitting an ominous blue hue. After he had activated the last symbol, the rock barrier fizzed into a misty blue veil, allowing access.

Before he stepped through the sixth seal, he stopped and drank from his canteen, clearing his throat of dirt and dryness. Jerry knew his journey was about to get harder—of that he had no doubt. His heart told him so. With almost no water left, he replaced his canteen, hoisted his pack onto his back, and slipped through the glimmering entrance.

CHAPTER THIRTY-FIVE

THE SHIELD'S TRIAD

Jerry entered a small, cozy odd-shaped room with a low ceiling. A sharp pine smell imparted familiarity. Medieval bricks adorned its walls, and dusty, messy strands of silk that spiders used to trap their prey filled the cracks and corners. A large stone hearth gave warmth and flickered images of peace into the room. The open blaze crackled and popped, casting flashes of orange light across his face. Reflections of an open campfire from his youth brought a deep-rooted attraction to the fire's force, a soothing tonic for his nerves. His mind tingled with an acute awareness as he viewed four primitive doors, each one intricately engraved with various motifs that hung on old wrought iron strap hinges.

He approached the first entry and froze. A fiery scene carved into the wood came to life. It was as if the door had been set ablaze, burning but not consuming. He hesitantly placed his hand into the flames. *Strange. They tickle and feel cool to the touch.* He stepped back and looked around. *Is this another illusion, or will it be a test by fire?*

Jerry opened the door and eased himself over the threshold, nearly tripping. He tried to merge with his aether but couldn't. A chill went through him. *Great. I hope the scarab amulet doesn't let me down.*

Step by step, Jerry crept down a dark and gloomy corridor so long it disappeared into a veil of obscurity. He strained to see but couldn't penetrate the blackness that engulfed him.

Suddenly, screaming waves of heat shot up, immersing him in a blazing inferno. *Whoa! Where'd that come from?* The atmosphere was thick, and sweat poured down his face. His left hand pressed the amulet close to his chest, hoping its magic would hold up through the fiery blazes.

Jerry shuffled through the hallway, the flames crackling and popping as though he were inside a raging furnace. His head throbbed, his temples pounding in time with his heartbeat.

Moments later, the corridor ended at a tapered pedestal that burned, but like the entrance, it wasn't being consumed. Blue and yellow flames whipped around the podium, producing an immense heat. A single gold token rested on it. Jerry grunted. "Mr. G, I have no idea what this thing is." He looked around. *Is this another trap?* Forcing himself to relax, he inhaled through his nose, exhaled, and snatched the medallion from the pedestal. He stepped back and waited.

Slowly, the thick and oppressive flames disappeared, and the corridor brightened as though someone had just turned on the lights. *Interesting, but there must be more to it than that.* What was this strange token? He flipped it around and recognized the coin's image as the same fiery motif he'd seen at the entrance. Unaware of its purpose, he placed the medallion in his pants pocket and exited the hallway.

Back in the foyer, he drew the gold token from his pocket and examined it. *I still don't know what to do with this. Maybe Julean can—*

An audible click interrupted his thoughts, prompting him to turn just in time to see the second entry pop open. A two-headed serpent had been carved into the thick wooden door, and it hissed on his approach. "Mr. G, after our encounter with Serpentius, confrontation with another reptile could prove lethal. You up for this?" Mr. G's eyes had turned light blue, almost white, after Jerry's conflict with the centurion. "Don't you dare look at me that way! I didn't lose you on purpose. If it weren't for Leo's ring, neither one of us would be here. I need to know if you're with me."

Energy surged to his aether. "Okay! Let's do this." He stepped across the threshold, his pulse quickening. Beeswax candles emitted a sickly sweet aroma and flickered a muted yellow into the corridor. His muscles were tense and his body buzzed.

Jerry navigated through a passageway that moved in a slow slithering motion as though it were alive. The walls rippled and waved when he touched the smooth interior. He recalled Julean's warning: "To lose focus could mean death." Anxiety grew as he traveled deeper into the hallway.

Suddenly, a two-headed snake emerged inches from his face. A poisonous smile touched its lips, its dark eyes glinting with deceit. Petulance hissed in its voice. "They say two heads are better than one."

"If I had two heads, one would conflict with the other, leading to indecision," Jerry said.

Without giving the serpent time to distract or harm him, Jerry discharged a violent display of force at the slithering menace. Enveloped in a tangled display of crackling energy, the reptile shrieked in agony and crumpled to the ground. The devious serpent lay there dead.

Jerry eased forward and glanced around the corner. "What in the geode?" He was stunned to see an array of lethal arrows the fiend had prepared to use on him. Once again, the words of Julean came to him: "Indecision may prove fatal."

He cautiously followed the passage until the channel terminated at a rippling serpentine altar that displayed another token. "Mr. G, it seems safe enough, but just in case, I hope you're ready." He snatched the medallion and stepped back, waiting for a response. Suddenly, the corridor straightened, granting quick access to the exit. Jerry inspected the coin's image and once again found it to have the same motif as the entrance. He rubbed the back of his neck and stuck the medallion in his pocket. *I still don't know the meaning of these tokens or the image they possess, but I hope something will come to light soon.*

Back in the foyer, firelight flickered on the walls, bringing a moment of relief. His eyes closed and his mind relaxed. Jerry knew he had to press forward but was weary of the constant challenges. *Andromeda said it was going to get harder, but a little respite every once in a while would be nice.*

A growling stomach prompted him to unzip his pack and pull out his last apple. After swallowing the last bite, he washed it down with the remaining bit of water from his canteen and headed toward the next entry.

A loud clunk signaled the opening of the third door, where an animated scene had been carved into the wooden entry depicting a frenzied flock of birds, tearing and ripping at each other. Jerry flashed to his experiences with the aquilas. *If they're related, I'm in trouble.* His heart hammered in his ears. *I'm buried so deep within these walls I'm not even sure if Lyro could help.*

Jerry lingered at the entrance before opening his pack and taking out the bag of apus flowers. Invisibility was his lone chance of sneaking by the deadly fowl. He was running low on the magical petals and ate only a few, hoping the effect would last until he obtained the altar's token.

After inhaling a breath of courage, he pushed the door open and looked around. In the distance, he heard screeching. Bird droppings stained the interior and a foul odor clogged his nose. He eased forward, his heart thumping. The farther he tiptoed into the corridor, the louder the shrieks echoed. He stopped and his gaze shot upward. Nesting burrows littered the walls, and a flock of birds was perched on a ledge, their beaks serrated like a knife. His legs weak, a shiver shook his body. *There must be more than a dozen.*

Feeling faint, he stepped back and pressed himself against the wall, trying to remain silent over the screeching squawks above him. Razor-sharp beaks scraped and grated against each other like two knives being sharpened.

Overhead, two birds fought over a freshly killed rodent, slicing and tearing through it like butter. Then he spotted the altar. *Got to get to the pedestal.* Jerry sprinted forward, but in his haste he carelessly kicked up some dirt, alerting the birds to his presence.

Within seconds, they launched toward him. Jerry lunged forward and tried to grab the medallion, but before he had it in his grasp, one predatory fiend ripped into his leg. He groaned as a wave of pain shot through him. His stomach burned and he retched, but nothing came out. Then the birds of prey vanished, leaving him with a racing heart and another souvenir.

"Holy geode!" Jerry slipped his pack off and set it on the ground. "Mr. G, that was really stupid!" He lifted his left pant leg and watched the wound heal, the skin regenerating without scarring. "We almost became lunch for a bunch of shredding machines." He stood and sighed. "Now is not the time to become careless."

Jerry dusted himself off, threw his pack around his back and exited the passageway. He walked to the fireplace and stared down, its warmth soothing his soul. Jerry sat for a time by the hearth, cross-legged, watching the flames frolic about as if they had no cares. The crackling and popping brought comfort while he concentrated on the last entry.

This animation was different. A stunning display of water tumbling down a multi-tiered fountain presented a serene feeling, yet he wondered, *What threat does this fount present?* "Mr. G, what do you think?" Jerry stared silently at the dynamic image. *I'm not sensing anything, but...*

His pulse quickened with the thought of another near-death ordeal like the one he experienced in the Canyon of Fears. He wiped his sweaty hands on his pants, walked over, and opened the creaking door, holding one hand over his heart as if to calm it. Jerry slid past the threshold and crept down a corridor layered in gold and silver. The ceiling emanated a bright phosphorescence that brushed the walls with a soft glow. *This is gorgeous, but I feel like I'm back in the house of illusions.*

Minutes later, the passageway emptied into a large cavity. Jerry found himself standing in front of an elegant quatrefoil-shaped fountain delicately sculpted in earth-toned stone, its pool reflecting a warm radiance from the surrounding phosphorescence.

Muscles tensed, his eyes scanning the chamber for trouble, he edged closer. Confused, he rested his hands on the fountain's lip and leaned over. His face, just inches from the glass-like pool, betrayed a look of doubt. Nothing seemed real anymore. Time had become meaningless in a world separated from everything he thought to be true. Feeling removed from reality, Jerry stood there not knowing what to do. Then an image rippled into view, showing the medallions being tossed into the water.

In the midst of a deep breath, Jerry stepped back and began pitching the coins in, one at a time. Once the last had been tossed in, he eased his way forward and peered into the quivering liquid. The water stirred and bubbled as if boiling, and then it calmed. Something shiny glistened beneath its surface. He ran his hand through his hair. *This must've been some kind of chemical reaction, but for what purpose?*

Jerry placed his finger in the pool, testing its temperature. *Strange. It's cool to the touch.* He reached in and withdrew a shield-shaped pendant attached to a silver chain, water dripping from it. Three platinum inlays flashed in a setting of pure gold. He turned the pendant over and read the engraving: "Together, we shall be one."

Who's we? Jerry squinted. *And what does it mean one?* He paused for a moment. "Mr. G, got any clues to what this means?"

Jerry draped it around the geode's binding. "I didn't think so, but maybe the water is potable." He cupped his hands, dipped them into the fountain, and brought them to his lips. He sipped the water, but before he could even swallow, a wave of nausea hit his gut hard. He gagged and spit onto the ground. *This tastes awful.*

The water in his canteen had run out long ago, and now he worried about his survival. Not only was water necessary for his continued transformation, but without a sufficient supply, he would surely die. Jerry harrumphed and stared at the end of the rocky, jagged passage. *Okay, where do I go now? Maybe I missed something in the foyer.*

After gathering his things, he removed the pendant from his aether and placed it around his neck. A euphoric rush shot through his frame. "Whew, Mr. G, that was weird." Suddenly, the ground trembled and a breach in the wall appeared. His muscles tensed and he clutched his aether tightly. "Great. Is this another trap?"

A slight breeze stirred the thick air and Jerry stood in silence, his mind seeming to devour his thoughts. Then a spark of courage flashed inside him as though a hidden power deep inside had taken control. "Mr. G, it's time we move on." He stripped his pack off his back and held it in his arms. Then he squeezed through the vertical fissure, clinging to his aether. Once he was through, the gap crackled shut.

A muted light infused the cavern, like the first morning rays. The air was alive with a potpourri of scents. Besieged by the beauty of the mineral kingdom, colorful crystals sparkled, showering their brilliance on him. Suspended vines festooned the ceiling, while a patchwork of yellow ferns covered the cavern's floor.

Finally, I'm in the sixth chamber, and it's beautiful. Now is the time I need to bare my teeth and dominate my weakness with courage. Jerry held the pendant in his hand and stared. *There's got to be more to this than just providing an outlet, but right now I need to find water.*

Fatigued and thirsty, he lifted his canteen to his mouth, turned it upside down, and watched the last drop of water trickle onto his dry tongue. He had hoped to have found the next jinan before he had run out of food and water, but with nothing in sight, he worried. Jerry shouldered his pack and marched forward, firm and resolute, focused on reaching the portal.

Hours passed and he began to languish from thirst, his muscles cramping. "Mr. G, if we don't find water soon, we won't have to worry about reaching the next chamber, let alone the portal." His gait slowing, he was about to collapse. Then a soft gurgling met his ears. *Could it be?* In his weakened state, he forced his trembling legs to carry him off the trail and down a flowstone slide to the hopeful sound.

His heart lifted when the next jinan came into view, which included the usual babbling spring. Jerry limped to the water's edge, dunked his head into the cool liquid, and shook his hair like a dog. He pushed his hair back, filled his canteen, and drank furiously, draining and refilling it over and over. His body tingled and his ears popped. It was as if something had breathed a new life into him. *Is it possible? I feel like my chest became lighter and my oxygen demands lessened.*

Jerry lay back a moment, resting against a rock, the cavern's starlight wrapping him in a warm blanket of peace. He thought about the life he had left behind, the day-to-day struggles of earthly existence. How could he ever go back to a normal life again, having evolved into an almost immortal state of being? Any desire to return to the place where he grew up was dwindling like a flickering flame. His thoughts were interrupted when Oden emerged from behind a large red flowering bush.

"Oh, it's you." Jerry stood up, surprised.

"Tis a pleasure to see you again." Oden wore a robe of dazzling colors with botanical designs woven into the fabric, showcasing plants Jerry had never seen before. "Your trek is going well?"

"Other than getting thrashed around like a rag doll and almost dying from a lack of water, not too bad."

"Are you not carrying a nix with you?"

"A nix?"

"Yes. They grow wild." Oden bent down and plucked something that looked like a gourd with a long slender neck from a leafy red bush. "They're hollow, and when filled they never run dry."

"But each jinan is different."

"No problem. Just submerge the nix into the spring and it will adapt to the water's chemistry."

Jerry took the nix, pulled his knife out, and lopped off the narrowed end. Then, kneeling at the water's edge, he filled the container and capped it with a piece of cork he found in his pack. "Why didn't Andromeda tell me about this?"

"Just because she's Avela's daughter doesn't mean she knows everything."

A smile crept onto Jerry's face as he placed the nix in his pack. "You've been so helpful, but I was wondering, how well do you know her?"

"I know enough to mind my own business." Oden's brow furrowed, and he resumed his pruning.

"I don't mean to intrude, but—"

"Then don't." Oden turned to Jerry. "I pretty much stay to myself. My job is to make sure our creations provide the correct balance so travelers can assimilate properly." With that, he raised his arms and vanished.

Well, okay. Jerry shrugged. *Why is he so evasive whenever I quiz him about Andromeda? No matter, at least I won't have to worry about water again.*

The refreshing scent of citrus drew his attention to the well-manicured garden of trees. Each one exhibited shaggy brown bark with multiple trunks. Unusual, ghostly white and gray patches marked its appearance. Crowned with magenta leaves, they shimmered with an eerie glow.

Jerry lifted one of the iridescent branches, exposing a bright yellow fruit. *How interesting. It looks like a tennis ball.* He sniffed the perfectly round fruit, plucked it from the limb, and took a small bite. His eyes opened wide. "Mr. G, it's so sweet." He bit off a larger bite and chewed heartily. "Mmm, it reminds me of the lemon truffles Mom used to make."

After eating several, Jerry became dizzy. Startled, he grabbed his head. It felt like a vice grip had just been clamped to his skull, crushing it. Jerry snorted in despair, but then his tension eased and a soft glow imbued his soul. He blinked and shook his head. There, under the cavern's twinkling stars, he beheld a divine order to the constellations he had never detected before.

Amazing! Things counterintuitive and difficult to understand now seemed simple. *Even with complex mathematics, I would've never been able to grasp the physics associated with the stellar patterns and alignment.*

For the first time, he understood that a regulatory method existed. *Each star system generates specific energies that provide proper motion within their boundaries designed to govern the universe's activities. Distant nebulae and galaxies also form part of the constellation's authority, but I'm not sure how that affects me.*

After a short rest, he was ready to move on, but before he left, he caught sight of an isolated tree. *Is that another illumid?* Jerry rushed to the lone tree, his heart pumping hard. He recalled Andromeda's words: "Whenever possible, eat the fruit of that tree. Its effect takes time to mature, but when it does, you'll not be disappointed."

Still unaware of what the effect would be, he chose to gather as many as possible before leaving. With a full stomach, a head spinning with questions, and a renewed vigor, he resumed his quest.

CHAPTER THIRTY-SIX

THE OLD SHAMAN

The jinan's sounds dwindled as the splashing and gurgling hushed behind him. Jerry followed a winding trail filled with long stretches of solitude. Instead of a well-manicured paradise garden, dwarf trees, dried up and withered, blended into a landscape of giant calcite columns. Strange animals crossed his path: rodents with glowing green eyes and huge spiders with long fangs.

Like tiny grains of sand falling through an hourglass, stacking up, one after another, time was ever lengthening, becoming irrelevant. Jerry walked with a steady gait, passing through a massive chamber studded with spiky plants and a diversity of glistening formations, some several stories tall, others petite and fragile.

A cloud of tiny flashes materialized not more than ten feet from him, halting his steps. *What in the geode is this?* Luminous fireflies danced along a path like brilliant sparks of light. *They're lining up as though they are rolling out the red carpet. It's obvious they want me to follow, but why?*

Dampness settled over him with no breeze to stir the thick air. Jerry paused to sip water from his nix. *Maybe this is the way to the mountain man I saw at the enchanted wall. No matter. I will be prepared.* After a quick glance around, he stepped onto the shimmering pathway and walked carefully, wary of what may lie ahead of him.

The trail was a rugged route filled with all sorts of devious threats. He dodged flying insects that thought he was a blood bank, along with jumping cactus that attacked him relentlessly. After what seemed like an hour of constant annoyance, the path ended at a clearing where a single tepee stood.

For several moments, Jerry stood in silence, clenching his aether so tightly his knuckles whitened. A cool, moist breeze fluttered beneath his nose, and the brilliance of twilight beamed down from a constellation he didn't recognize. Sagebrush, mingled with an occasional stalagmite, surrounded the open area. He looked troubled and bewildered, not knowing what to do. Why had he been led here? Who could live in such a place?

The air vibrated in his ear with a sudden drumming, beating a rhythm that seemed to sync with his heart, its melody touching his soul in a sweet and soothing way. Peace pierced his mind as his noiseless footsteps found their way to the tepee's entrance. The buffalo-skin tent exhibited scenes of crows hopping and flying about. *Something powerful is in the air, something magical. I feel like I just entered an enchanted place ... maybe even sacred.*

A sudden flapping from above startled him, and Jerry jumped back as a large black crow flew into the tepee. A chill crept up his neck, strangling his throat. He swallowed, trying to loosen his breath. "Is—is—anyone here?"

Jerry stood listening to the rustling of clothing inside, waiting for an answer. Gently, the tent's flap was pulled back, exposing a man with long black stringy hair. Dressed in the trimmings of a shaman, he extended an invitation.

"I am Night Blackbird, but call me Chogan. Please, come." He motioned to Jerry. "Come into my humble dwelling."

Inside, a blue and black rug lay on the ground, detailing the constellation Corvus. The mat's eleven stars pulsed as if alive. In the center was an incense burner in the shape of a blackbird, emitting a faint fragrance of sagebrush. A dim blue light added to the ambience, but Jerry was unaware of its source.

"Please, sit." His eyes were dark as night, and his skin was bronzed and heavily lined. Chogan sat cross-legged on the rug across from Jerry and bowed his head. He was clothed in brown leather, and a yellow braided sash wrapped around his waist was etched with symbols and writing. A colorful band that held various types of feathers adorned his head. He lifted his head and their eyes met. "What is it you seek?"

"I've been on a mission to find the last seal containing the portal. I don't mean to impose, but I'm seeking help from those who may be able to assist me in my journey."

"The fact you have made it this far tells me much about your character." His eyes seemed to pierce the veil that shielded Jerry's soul. "Only the bravest of persons could have endured such a dangerous trek."

He gently took hold of Jerry's hands and began meditating. The old shaman fell into a trance, chanting in his native tongue. Jerry sat still, unblinking, letting his breath slow and his heart calm.

Hazy tendrils of smoke rose from the burning incense, lifting high into the air, morphing into the form of an eagle. Each majestic cloud of vapor soared upward and then dissipated.

Chogan recited his mantra, filling the tepee with energy. It was as though he could see into an unseen realm, communicating with entities no one else could see. *I don't know what he's chanting, but it feels like I'm in an electrical storm.*

Thunder crashed down all around them. Lightning lit up the area, and flashes of brilliance cast ominous shadows around the tent. *What on Earth is happening?* Jerry didn't budge. He'd never experienced anything like this before. *This is incredible! I have no idea what he is doing, but his magic must be powerful.*

Several minutes later, Chogan released Jerry's hands, static sparking between their fingertips. His leathered old face appeared composed in the tent's dimness. "I have received a vision from the spirits that have passed on." A smile emerged on his dark-stained lips. "Your courage precedes you, and they have taken an interest in helping you on your journey."

Chogan opened his hands. "Take these and place one on each wrist. They will assist you in your journey." Crumpled together were two bands of purple beads. "These are pearls of wisdom."

"Pearls of wisdom?"

"Making wrong choices may prove fatal. They are imbued with magical energy that will harmonize with your essence, imparting their wisdom to your mind."

Jerry took the bands and placed them on his wrists. "How do they—"

"I also have special magic to give you." Chogan opened a small engraved box, reached in, and transferred a crystallized powder to a leather pouch. Then, after sealing it shut, he gave the precious contents to Jerry. "This powder halts time." His eyes widened, reflecting concern. "The concentrate only works for a few seconds, but it may offer enough time to flee, or perhaps it may mean the difference between life and death."

Jerry offered gratitude but was a little confused. "If needed, how do I use this ... this time powder?"

The old shaman leaned over and whispered in his ear. "Just take a pinch of the dust and cast it into the air. It will do the rest, but remember, the effect will only stop time for a few seconds."

Jerry thanked him and pushed himself up, slinging his pack over his shoulders. Exhaling a relaxed breath, he stepped outside, where he paused to listen to the whisper of rustling within the small tent. Seconds later, a large black crow flew out and disappeared into the expanse. He pulled the flap open. Inside, the incense was still burning, but Chogan had vanished.

Goose bumps rippled down his arms. Never had he felt so calm. Jerry knew he lacked wisdom and discernment and wondered if he had just been handed the tools necessary to fight the evils that lurked around every corner. Could these beads of wisdom truly help discern truth from deception? He looked at his aether. "Mr. G, I'm too attached to my thoughts. I need to get out of my head and into my heart, but sometimes it's hard to give up old habits."

Hope rising, he headed back to the main path eager to learn more about his charming accessories. "Mr. G, I heard what he said, but I'm not sure if I entirely understand how to fully implement them. Maybe Julean can offer further guidance."

Jerry traveled through a dusty corridor for hours, trudging along a path plagued by tangled weeds and thorny bushes. The cavern's light had dimmed and the humidity had thickened. He mulled over the event that would necessitate the use of his new acquisitions. What covert situations still awaited him? The possibilities were beyond reckoning—and worrisome. But now wasn't the time to ponder their implications. As he shook the thoughts from his head, his golden pendant started to pulse. *Strange. It feels like my entire body is vibrating.*

Jerry stopped and lifted the throbbing charm from his chest. Its intensity changed as he turned and rotated it, trying to understand what was happening. He looked up, sweat dripping off the tip of his nose, his eyes darting around.

Like a magnet, the pendant pulled him toward a group of sandstone columns ranging from a few feet to more than twenty feet tall. *Movement of carbonic acid must have fractured and etched the bedrock, leaving a series of limestone blocks as isolated spires, but I've never seen so many.*

Jerry stood next to a polished white pillar that looked like a church steeple reaching high into the cavern. His body shook—but not from fear. No, there was a force surging through him, something powerful, something merging with his soul. *What is this thing?*

A sudden wave of energy shot out from the pendant and burned an image of a shield onto the glistening column. Jerry stiffened in response. A tremor shot through him, and his eyes beamed with excitement. *Could this be the next power-up?*

Pausing for a moment, he recognized the icon. "Mr. G, this has the same shape as the golden shield." The charm continued to pulse, drawing him closer to the glowing image. *Hmm, I wonder ...*

Jerry removed the pendant from the chain and coupled it to the gleaming symbol. The charm surged with a blinding light, which then softened. *Whoa, I feel like I just looked into the sun.* He rubbed his eyes. *What's this?* Several slots had opened on the steeple-shaped column, and its matrix had transformed into an ebony marble. Angelic wind chimes flowed softly past his ears, and animated fairies wove in and out of the openings like bees buzzing around a hive. Jerry stood hypnotized by the mood of the animation, one that took his breath away. *Amazing! What kind of magic is this?* He reached out, but his fingers passed through the intangible ghostly figures as if there were nothing there.

The golden shield ceased to pulsate, and the fire symbol had changed, taking on a reddish hue. He uncoupled the pendant from the column and placed it back on his chain, unsure why the fire emblem had altered its appearance. *Strange, it doesn't feel hot, but I feel something, something different.*

Jerry was confident this was the next power-up and circled the pillar several times, looking to access its power. *Just how do I get into this thing?* He stopped and passed his aether over the openings. Abruptly, the animated fairies disappeared, unveiling several precious stones next to the apertures. *Aha, I knew this was the next power-up, but which one?*

A warm, soft glow radiated from the amber crystal. Its energy was intense and pulled him close. "Mr. G, this is it!" Jerry took a deep breath, placed his aether into its slot, and stepped back.

Suddenly, a beacon of pure light surged from the glowing rod to the cavern's roof. A visual animation exploded in the heavens, producing an aerial illustration of creatures he had never seen.

"Mr. G, this is incredible!" Satyrs, mermaids, elves, and imps filled the cavern, along with other folklore beings that had never been verified as real. "It makes one wonder if these things really existed or if they were a figment of our imagination?" Jerry stroked his face. "At least I understand why the pedestal was animated."

He grabbed his aether, excited about the power he would receive. A bizarre feeling surged through his body. *Great! Now what?* A bluish hue distorted his vision and he gazed around as if in a stupor. "Mr. G, this is crazy." He squeezed his eyes shut and then opened them. "Even you look foggy." Within a few seconds, his vision normalized but left him fatigued. Jerry shook his head. "I have no idea what just happened, but—"

A sudden wave of energy drew his attention to the diamond. Its reflection sparkled and flashed an intense brilliancy. *Wow! This stone is powerful.* He inserted his aether into its slot and waited. The air crackled and grew heavy. An unpleasant metallic taste filled his mouth as if he were sucking on a bunch of old pennies. Then, without warning, lightning bolts crashed down, striking the earth around him.

Jerry dropped to the ground. *Holy geode!* Every muscle quivered as though he were freezing. Sparks hissed and crackled, filling the air with bright blue flashes of light. He gasped at the ominous sight, wondering if this would be his last breath. Breathing in and out, he forced oxygen into his lungs to calm his racing pulse.

Gradually, the air stilled and all became quiet. Jerry exhaled a nervous breath, rose up, and grasped his aether. An electrical surge shot through his frame, making him glow. *Whew, I've never felt anything so powerful and so scary. It feels as though a thousand spiders are crawling over my entire body.*

Static electricity sparked from Mr. G's eyes, causing the air to flicker. "Oh, yeah! The force is with us now!" Jerry tore his focus from Mr. G and fixated on an inscription flashing next to the diamond: "A teardrop from the gods."

A teardrop from the gods? What could be so powerful that it would come from a god? I have so many questions. I can't wait to see what Julean has to say.

Hours later, after leaving the barren landscape and withered foliage behind, Jerry grew weary of his travels and needed a break. He couldn't keep his eyes open. A soft breeze hushed by, gently caressing his face. Dripping water echoed throughout the chamber.

He moseyed over to a large stalagmite and slumped down, his back against its smooth surface, and rested his pack on the ground. Jerry tried to doze, but he felt nervous whenever he closed his eyes, fearful of what dreadful creature awaited him upon awakening. From time to time he opened his eyes, glanced around, and dropped back into a guarded sleep, dreaming of a place called Enif.

CHAPTER THIRTY-SEVEN

THE POWER OF ILLUSIONS

A few hours later, Jerry awoke, refreshed and ready to resume his quest. He gathered his things together and started down a trail that had become less rugged. A gentle breeze grazed his face, a freshness pervaded the cavern, and cave popcorn seemed to pop up all around. Cave crystals dripped their life essence into glistening pools of turquoise water. Then he spotted another spinning orb isolated in a small clearing just off the central pathway.

Jerry tightened his pack and slid down a steep slippery slope of flowstone and landed next to the rotating sphere. *This unit is entirely different from the previous chambers.* The orb reminded him of a kaleidoscopic globe found in the old discos, its colorful light diverging in all directions.

Jerry stepped forward, looking for a way to activate the orb. *Things keep changing, but there's got to be a way to contact Julean.* He passed his hand through the multicolored beams, but nothing happened. Why didn't it work? What was he doing wrong? Jerry stared at the orb, relaxing his grip on his aether. *Of course, need to focus.* He closed his eyes and reached deep into his psyche. Then exhaling a deep breath, he eased them open.

Several orbs now spun around him, flashing a blinding brilliance. *Agh, too bright.* Jerry grabbed the opaque glasses from his pack and placed them on his face, blocking out the extreme brightness.

A single orb flashed a radiant splendor, quenching his soul with serenity. *Yes! Found it.* His hand shot out and touched the shining sphere, sending a torrent of white light streaming to the ground, and with it Julean.

Jerry quickly inspected his robe, reviewing it for new and different symbols. He pointed. "Are these ... planets?"

"I am glad you have noticed. These indeed are planets, but not in your solar system. These are worlds where opportunities await. They have not yet been identified. You will have the responsibility for naming the planetary creations after you achieve full transformation. Once on Enif, you will learn more, but for now, do you have any questions?"

Jerry's eyes were wide with excitement. "In the sixth chamber, I obtained a necklace with a golden charm shaped like a shield." He lifted the pendant from his chest to show Julean. "On my way to the seventh seal, it began to pulsate—sending vibrations throughout my body—leading me to my next power-up. After coupling it to the column, the pulsing stopped." Jerry placed the pendant in Julean's hand. "That's when the fire symbol changed, taking on this reddish hue, but I don't know ..." Jerry's voice trailed off, his eyes seeking answers.

Julean's eyebrows raised. "Ah, the golden shield is essential for your progress. The farther you penetrate the depths of the Earth, the harder it will become to find the columns. This pendant is like a homing beacon, providing direction to help locate your next power-up."

"But what about the changes? I mean ... check out the fire icon."

"If you look closely, three insignias are embellished on the shield. Each one represents a distinct danger to you. Fire, stone, and certain types of magic. Once you have matched the shield to the last pillar, you will have discovered another weapon—a weapon of defense."

"A weapon of defense?" Jerry gave a puzzled stare. "Each time you couple the pendant to the pillar's matching icon, one of the insignias will charge. Once all three have been activated, the amulet will provide another form of protection."

"Okay, but I still don't quite understand," Jerry asked, his forehead wrinkling.

"For example, if attacked by fire, the charm will emit a reddish tone, repelling the assault. A grayish glow guards against stone attacks, and if the pendant radiates a bluish hue, you will be protected against magic."

"What do you mean ... magic?" Jerry asked, stroking his chin.

"The charm defends against weak magic." Julean returned the pendant to Jerry. "Do not suppose the shield will provide protection against every magic. You will need all the wisdom you can gather to help decide."

"That reminds me. I met an old shaman off the main trail who gave me a set of beaded wristbands. Jerry extended his arms and turned his wrist. "I'm not sure if I fully understand how to use them. He also gave me this packet of powder to freeze time." Jerry reached into his vest and pulled out a small leather pouch.

"The beads are one thing, but it's rare that the old sage would give up his time powder." Julean smiled. "You are indeed fortunate. Just cast the concentrate into the air and it will freeze time for three to five seconds, giving you the opportunity to run or attack. But the powder should only be utilized in a situation of dire need. You need to consider your options before using this precious gift, as there is only a small amount."

Jerry stood in silence, hanging on his every word.

Julean's gaze shifted to Jerry's wrist. "And the beaded bands ... they offer wisdom to the bearer, but only if they are touching." He pressed the wristbands together. "If indecision fills your thoughts, concentrate and focus on the beads. Your mind will open to your circumstance, offering a better chance to make the right choice. But remember—always trust in your heart."

"If there's one thing I need, it's more wisdom." Jerry fidgeted a little. "I have a few other questions if you don't mind."

Julean nodded. "But of course."

Jerry recounted his experience with the amber stone. "What in the geode were all those bizarre creatures? They seemed so real yet so elusive."

"Well done!" Julean's eyes widened. "You now have the power to create illusions of your own. But beware, it takes much discipline to master this ability."

"Really!" Excitement sparkled in Jerry's eyes. "Illusions?"

"Yes. This gift is not only necessary as you proceed through the caverns but is essential once you have passed through the portal." Sensing impatience in Jerry, he held out his hand. "Slow down. It takes effort and real vision to generate an illusion, but once mastered, you will have command of things never imagined."

"Oh, I almost forgot." Jerry waved his hand. "I received another power-up, one that scared the rocks out of me. At the diamond slot, lightning flashed all around and the air groaned with thunderous crashes. Just as I was about to be consumed, it subsided." Jerry paused. "When I gripped my aether, I received a shock—my body glowed. Even now, I feel a bit charged."

"You have been given the gift of the gods!" Julean's eyes grew wider. "The diamond's energy originates from pure light rained to Earth from God. Its strength offers both offensive and defensive abilities. If threatened with a severe electrical force, your scepter will absorb the voltage. But you also possess a primal force that affords omnipotent authority." Julean's eyes narrowed. "Only when its essence fully matures within you will you be able to destroy all evil. Its strength will increase as you wield it until, by and by, it becomes in you a force so strong that the powers of the universe will be at your command."

"Whew! That's a little over my head." Jerry's head rocked with questions. He wanted to know more, to hear how powerful he was to become, but Julean held a hand up.

"It is time. We must train. Your questions will be answered as you progress, but for now ... be patient and focus on your quest."

Jerry blew out a breath. "All right, but you will teach me how to create illusions, won't you?"

"But of course." Julean coached Jerry more intensely than he had up to this point, and after several hours of preparation they rested.

"Do you think I'm ready?" Jerry's mood turned serious. "I need an honest opinion. How close am I to becoming an Enifian?"

"We do not live in the same dimension of time as those on Earth, nor are we hampered by its finiteness. In ways that are not clear to you, we see beyond the obvious, something you will not understand until you have experienced a full transition."

"Okay." He shifted his feet, sighed, and looked Julean in the eyes. "Be straight. What chance do I have to make it to the portal?"

"You have made more progress than most at this point. Having said that, I must caution you to exercise what you have acquired expeditiously. You have the abilities and the weaponry, but you must work on your decision-making. Trust no one but your heart!" Julean's smile creased his face, and then he vanished.

Jerry stood there for a moment longer, reflecting on Julean's words, eager to try his hand at creating illusions. A stiff wind stirred around him, rippling his dark brown hair. He was aware of every fiber in his body, and for the first time he felt a power developing within him that he hadn't felt before. His heart pounded with excitement at the thought of creating, shaping, and manipulating things, even if they weren't real. But how could these illusions help him on his journey, and why would they be essential once he resided on Enif? He could only imagine what the possibilities were—to allow the wings of his imagination to soar, to bring his dreams to life. The prospects were indeed endless!

CHAPTER THIRTY-EIGHT

GRUS

Jerry had lost count of the number of days that had passed since he'd started his journey. It didn't matter, though, nor did he care. He gaped at the ground. Sharp reddish-brown rocks crunched beneath his feet, stretching as far as he could see, rising into jagged outcroppings that looked like monsters waiting to come alive. Amid the fanciful surroundings, the shapes and forms nature had created fueled his imagination.

Jerry traversed the open trail for hours, and from time to time he would stop and try to conjure something up. Without much thought, he would produce distorted images of mutated creatures that were difficult to maintain. Even though he was having fun trying to create different illusions, they were generating more problems than they were worth. *Julean was right. This is going to take some time before I'm able to transfer the animation of my thoughts into real-time illusions.*

His inability to master the illusions caused him to become annoyed, and so he stopped. Instead, he focused on the visual exercises Julean had given him, trying to access the essence of his mind. Maybe with enough practice, he would be able to extend his thoughts into a sustainable form. Jerry continued the mental aerobics until he caught a glimpse of movement farther down the trail, something strange, a shapeless figure that shifted between gnarled boulders and stalagmites.

From a distance, a large long-legged bird resembling a crane, with a red head and a gray body, materialized. He eased toward the unusual entity. Then, like a puff of smoke, the mysterious creature slipped into the shadows and disappeared. Jerry shook his head as if to clear out the cobwebs. "Mr. G, did you see that?" But there was nothing. Nothing there. Did he imagine it or was it another illusion?

Jerry inched his way through the chamber, his fingers caressing the anuns, waiting for something to happen. *Something is going on. I can feel it.* Sweat drizzled down his cheeks and his heart sparked with worry. He gazed upward to an endless expanse filled with the twinkling stars of Pegasus, seeking strength.

Suddenly, a tall, thin man stepped out from behind a sheet of flowstone. "My name is Grus, and I help weary travelers!" Dressed in a red suit and plenty of flashy jewelry, the lanky man stood grinning from ear to ear.

"And just how can you help me?" Jerry's jaw clenched tight, his eyes narrowed.

"I can offer you powerful magic. If you follow me, I can introduce you to the residents who will give you potent charms and pendants. Now, I'm not talking about any potion. These powerful brews will allow you to avoid even the most dangerous encounters, but only if you take advantage of it now."

His eyes emotionless, he spoke quickly. Jerry tried to intrude into his mind but was shut out. He waited a moment for him to quiet. "Few do things without reason." He tilted his head and glared. "Just what is your motivation?"

"I am but a humble person, a person who tries to assist the weary traveler as well as those who live here." He ran his hand through his greased black hair and smiled. "It is a symbiotic relationship for all."

Jerry could barely stand to hear him speak. His words grated on his ears like a used car salesman's. "I don't know ..." He vacillated, unsure of what to do. Something inside him didn't seem right, but what if it were true?

"It's but a short distance to the shelters of those you seek. We must hurry if we're to find them home."

Though he viewed him with skepticism, Jerry agreed to go. "Just get on with it, but if you speak to deceive, you will suffer the consequences."

Grus snapped his fingers. "You have my word."

Jerry left the trail and followed the lanky man through and around low-hanging stalactites, both silent the entire journey.

Clouds of mosquitoes and gnats buzzed as the two swatted their way through a path of sage and dust. Jerry slapped his neck and face. *Too bad my powers don't include insect repellent.* He swatted at more bugs. *I wonder if they have mosquitoes on Enif.*

Thirty minutes later, they stopped at a small stone hut covered with a thatched roof. Grass-like shrubs lined a pebbled walkway that led to a wicker door. A fetid armpit odor saturated the air.

"Wait here and I will see if they are home," Grus said and disappeared through the rattan door.

Jerry was getting excited. "I wonder who lives here and if they really do have something that can assist in my quest."

An old, gray-haired woman stepped out, holding a bottle of clear liquid, rubbing her gnarled fingers over it. Brown, wrinkled skin signaled her age. Her eyes were dull and cloudy. She had a beaklike nose with crusty warts hanging from it. She stooped over a cane for support, and when she spoke, her voice quivered.

"This is a magic potion that will make even the most dangerous creature vanish." She gave a sweet twisted smile. "Since I don't request money, I wish to trade my magic elixir for the golden charm around your neck."

He leaned in close enough to see what was in her hand but far enough to avoid her stench. She smelled terrible, like rotten eggs. What was in that container? Poison? How was he to know whether she spoke the truth? Jerry gave a vacant stare. "I don't think so." He knew he wouldn't be able to progress without the charm. "I can't give this up. No way!"

The old woman turned and slipped back inside the hut, and a homely boy dressed in rags stepped out.

"Hey, mister." The lad appeared sickly, with sunken eyes and messy hair. "I'll trade you this magic potion for your cool necklace." He coughed several times, spitting up green mucus. "This will help you get past all the bad monsters."

The small scruffy boy pleaded with Jerry, tempting him. *If this potion propelled me past all the dangers and threats that await me, I wouldn't need the golden shield.*

"How do I know this will work?"

The child sobbed. "I'm sick, and I have scary dreams," he said weakly.

"What kind of scary dreams?"

"Without your pretty necklace, I'll die."

Surely, a little child wouldn't deceive me. But then he recalled the advice from Julean. *Wait—I can engage the beads of wisdom to help with this decision.*

After asking for a moment, Jerry placed his wrists together and meditated on the small boy. With his mind unblocked, death and tragedy riddled his conscience. *Ugh, no way!* He glanced back at the hut—the child had disappeared. In his place was a charming young girl with a pointy little nose and hazel eyes. Her straight, shiny blond hair lifted in the breeze.

"I'm the young boy's sister. He's very ill and wasn't able to stay. If you would only give us your golden charm, we can make him well."

Who are these people? Do they really need my pendant to restore his health, or is this another guise to deceive me? Jerry placed his wrists together, and once again death breached his mind. He lowered his aether. "Enough of your deception!"

Without warning, the small child morphed into a grotesque creature with pale white skin and glowing dark eyes. A beard made of living grass and vines draped his face. His arms and legs were tree-like, and he had a tail and horns. The being appeared in his natural form, having failed at making Jerry ill with his potions.

Dumfounded, Jerry realized that all the people he had confronted were the same creature: a shapeshifter.

Frustrated with his effort to obtain the golden shield, Grus released an inhuman screech that tore through the quiet cavern, drilling into Jerry's skull. Jerry dropped his aether and quickly covered his ears. The high-pitched shrill pierced the air like the deafening scream of a banshee, shattering several stalagmites. Like spears, they peppered the ground around him.

Grus paused to take a breath. *Got to stop him now.* Jerry grabbed an exploding stone from his pack and threw the volatile rock toward him. The blast rocked the creature momentarily, allowing Jerry to grab his aether from the ground. But before he could release an impulse wave, Grus shifted into a bird and flew away.

Jerry shook his head, trying to quiet the ringing that lingered. Once again, his impetuous nature had led him astray. How had he allowed this creature to make a fool out of him? *I still have problems with discernment.* He raised his aether. "Mr. G, without the beads of wisdom, I may have fallen short of my goal to reach the portal, and with it Andromeda. Julean was right—I still need to work on my decision-making, but sometimes it helps to have the beads of wisdom."

CHAPTER THIRTY-NINE

CRUX, THE SOUTHERN CROSS

Jerry looked around and sighed. Grus had led him far from the main trail and he was lost, unsure which direction to go. A gust of wind swirled through the sagebrush, spraying dust into his lungs. He coughed until he gagged. He wiped his blurry eyes with the back of his hand. How was he going to find his way back to the main trail?

A dull, dreary silence had seized the area. Then Jerry remembered the compass Circinus had given him. He quickly pulled the medallion from his pack and watched the needle spin around and around until it pointed to the central path. *That was easy.* But now he began to doubt again. He became compulsive about his preparation. I know *I can do this. Even if I can't ... I must.*

Jerry hustled down the trail with new hope of conquering his fears. The cavern's stars brightened, shimmering like diamonds in the sky. Time dwindled, and it wasn't until hours later that Jerry's attention switched to a changing terrain.

Dead leaves, dried and crispy, crunched under his boots on a pathway crowded with strange trees and bushes. Gray crocodile bark covered their thick trunks, and shiny, dark reddish-brown branches shot outward, plagued with scaly erosions. Needle-like leaves resembling sea urchins erupted from the scabby limbs. *I hope these aren't poisonous like the porcupine stones I encountered on the trail to the carina tree.*

Jerry plunged through the dense foliage, pausing to brush away creepy cave spiders with teeth that looked like daggers. Then he stopped. An odd sound flitted through the jumble of trees. *What was that?* He quivered at the sudden danger. Jerry stood in silence, his eyes widening at the emergence of a bizarre creature standing in a large glade-like area. *Holy geode! What in the world is that ... thing?*

Not more than a stone's throw from him stood an intimidating figure he took to be at least ten feet tall. An obscure light bled through a slim opening in the cavern, causing the beast to cast a long ominous shadow. Jerry drew in a nervous breath and felt blood pound his temples.

The man-like creature bore thick gnarly horns like a bull's. Brown frizzy hair covered its body and curled at the ends. Its long corrugated ears twitched and spun, straining to hear. Long warped claws, protruding from giant hairy hands, clutched a heavily carved staff. *Is that the same magic alder wood I have? If so, I certainly don't want to confront this freak of nature.*

A sultry draft stroked Jerry's face. Leaves rustled and twigs broke as he tried to creep past the strange aberration. Jerry froze when he felt its stare upon him, the demon's black eyes tunneling deep into his. Drool had collected in the corner of its mouth, dribbling to the ground. The beast snorted and ground its teeth in rage.

Jerry forced a swallow. Abruptly, the creature rushed toward him. "Holy geode!" His heart plummeted to his feet. He quickly reached into his pack, fumbled for the apus flowers, and ingested them. Instantly, he became invisible and shifted away from the raging beast.

The demon paused, his ears rotating like a radar dish. "I am Crux, the ruler of the Southern Cross. I do not need eyes to see. I can hear your every move."

Jerry stopped. A chill rippled through him. It took intense concentration for him to quell his nerves, subduing a primal fear that lingered in his mind. With his breathing stilled, he wondered, *How am I going to get past this vile creature?*

A strand of hair rested next to his eye, tickling, but he maintained a stillness. *I wish I had a potion that would transport me past this monster.* The heartbeat of the cavern dripped from within its walls, but Jerry's heart pounded louder, beating against his eardrums.

"I can smell the fear that drips from your breath." He snorted air from his flared nostrils. "You have trespassed! You cannot hide. Come out and I will make your death quick!"

Jerry connected to his aether, his trembling hands clamping down tightly. Suddenly, the anuns glowed and a massive lightning bolt shot out from Mr. G's eyes. High voltage erupted, lighting up the beast like a Christmas tree.

"Is that all you have?" Crux shook off the effect. "Surely, you can do better."

Jerry turned and bolted, and Crux followed, breaking and tossing branches. The ground pounded under the southern ruler's heavy feet. He was closing in.

"Aargh!" Jerry seized a pinch of time powder and tossed the concentrate into the air. For a moment, everything stood still, suspended, giving him several seconds to escape. He spied an opening between two boulders and slipped inside. For the time being, Jerry had eluded the grasp of this terrible beast, but now what?

A cold wind moaned throughout the chamber. Jerry struggled to clear his thoughts and think clearly, his mind insisting this could exist only in a horror film. But it was real, and there was no escape from it, no way to avoid it. All he could think to do was to remain pressed between the boulders, fearful to come out. He licked his chapped lips, feeling nauseated. *What am I to do?*

Crux was edging closer, his ears twitching. Jerry's mouth went dry. With only a small amount of time powder left, he dared not chance using any more. What if he needed it later for something more nefarious? Then a thought came to him. *What about the beads of wisdom?*

The instant he placed his quivering wrists together, two winged images formed in his mind. *Dragons?* Never had his thoughts been so clear; never had he felt so connected to his aether. *But ... how? I'm not ready.* He recalled Julean's words:

"This gift will help you through the difficult trials that lie ahead, but you must believe."

As the illusions unfolded in his mind, Jerry raised his aether and launched an assault. Two fire-breathing dragons with long fierce teeth and powerful talons materialized above Crux. Jerry froze, unsure what to do. No doubt, he had produced the illusions, but now what?

The menacing serpents scorched the air above him as if they had a mind of their own. Jerry inhaled an anxious breath, stepped out from the boulders, and blasted the colossal brute with an explosion of pulsed energy, sending him tumbling backward. Crux shook his head, dazed. He seemed tense, and he clenched his jaw so tightly that Jerry could hear his teeth grinding against the palpable screeches that pierced the air.

Spewing yellow and orange flames, the two black dragons dived at the Southern Cross ruler relentlessly. *Now that he's focused on my illusions, maybe I can gain the upper hand.* Jerry released sonic explosions that shattered the air around Crux. He paused to place a few apus petals in his mouth. *If I can remain invisible, I may have an added edge.*

The winged illusions continued to distract the towering beast, but in spite of all the chaos, his rotating ears could still hear and sense movement. Crux threw his head back and roared, letting out a thunderous wail. Then he turned, his eyes narrowed. He lifted his scepter high, snorted, and unleashed a violent force, slamming Jerry against the boulders where he had sought refuge.

Dazed, he lay gasping. Crux came toward him in a frenzied rush. Once again, Jerry seized a pinch of time powder and tossed it into the air. Time froze while he pushed off the ground and ran and pressed himself into the crevice of a rock, holding his aether close. *Holy geode, I feel like a boulder just smashed down on me.* He tried to calm his heartbeat, sure its thumping would alert Crux to his proximity. *No way can I best his power. But maybe I can wear him down.*

Seconds lapsed and Crux spun in confusion. "Where are you?"

Jerry raised his aether and resumed his attack. The dark dragons rained down violent flames of reds, oranges, and yellows, smothering the expanse of shimmering stars and setting the sky ablaze with color. Crux pivoted and hurled a thunderous burst of energy that passed through the aerial illusions. "Curse you!" he growled. "What kind of magic allows you to absorb my thermal storms?"

"Mr. G, this is our chance. Make me proud." Fear gripping his throat, his stomach twisted and his pulse surged. Yet something powerful burned inside him, sending a wave of courage to his heart. Jerry wiped his brow on his upper arm, calmed his breathing, and blasted the ruler of the Southern Cross with sonic compressions of pure energy.

The force hit Crux hard, smashing him into a jagged boulder. He scrambled to his feet in a cloud of dust, shook his head, and retaliated with a fiery burst.

The flash whizzed by Jerry, just missing his face and vaporizing the tree next to him. *Okay, that was too close.*

"Only a coward would hide!" His ears twitched and his eyes darted about. "Do you have no pride? Where is your tongue? Come out where I can see you ... you disgusting maggot." Crux spun in uncertainty, scattering destructive bursts of energy, hoping to find his target.

Jerry remained invisible, quietly changing his position in concert with the vicious assaults from his winged illusions. Sweaty hands gripped his aether as he calculated each attack, sending explosive charges into the beast's flesh, ripping and tearing.

Crux licked his lip, blood dripping from his face. "You're delusional if you think you can destroy me. Only a worm would continue to hide. Show yourself!" Crux lowered his staff and dispersed a black mist from a flaming violet orb.

Got to get away. Jerry beat a fast retreat from the pervasive haze and found cover atop a giant boulder. He clutched his aether tightly and raised it high. Electrical sparks flashed, and the air moaned. An instant later, a thunderous crash of lightning fell upon the frustrated creature, dropping him to his knees. *Incredible! My power ... it's ... it's getting stronger.*

Shredded muscles and lacerations made it difficult for Crux to stand, and he groaned in pain. "Argh! Coward! You're too weak to face me in the open." Blood trickling from his nose, he pushed up from the ground, using his magic staff, choking and coughing.

The putrefying smell of death saturated the air. Crux stumbled forward, groping the air as though everything had become hazy.

Jerry's invisibility wore off and he confronted him. "Courage is not without fear, nor is there valor to give up life so easily. Only a fool would mistake caution for cowardice."

Standing next to the defeated beast, he squared his shoulders. "Respect and fear can cause a person to rise above that in which he is overmatched. It takes more than brawn to win the battle. One must believe in himself to overcome the obstacles placed in his path."

Crux lifted the corner of his mouth, and his eyes glared cold and vindictive. He staggered forward.

Jerry stiffened and released a massive blow that struck him down.

Stained with blood and sweat, the magic alder scepter slipped from his hands. The beast vomited and gurgled before falling.

Jerry lifted his weary eyes and sighed. "Mr. G, we did it!" His voice quivered. "Fear does funny things to a man, forcing him to take a leap of faith. This victory helps ease a lingering doubt, but ..."

Though Jerry had beaten this terrible beast, he didn't feel like celebrating. What other nefarious creatures plagued his path? Would his powers be enough to see him through?

Jerry stared at the star's reflection on the surface of a cave pool and then kicked a stone into the glass-like water, shattering the image into a thousand twinkling eyes. He pulled his nix from his pack and took a long swallow, feeling the cool liquid slide down a dry throat.

Loneliness crept into his heart along with the memories he'd left behind. *Though I've changed, I do miss my friends, but ...*

He pushed the thought away and resumed his quest, hoping to meet with Andromeda.

CHAPTER FORTY

THE OTHER LOVE

The stars showered down their flickering light, bathing the cavern in a warm glow. A musty mist coated his skin and occasionally trickled into his eyes. Jerry traveled for several hours in silence, scanning the area for anything strange, his chest still tight from his encounter with Crux.

The aches and pains had dissipated, but try as he might, he couldn't break the chains of doubt that bound him to indecision, and he found himself jumping at every strange sound. Where was Andromeda? Why hadn't he heard from her? Though he still didn't know much about the daughter of Avela, her presence always seemed to comfort him.

Jerry emerged from dense foliage into an art gallery of speleothems, lit in a dazzling array of colors. *Oh, this is impressive.* Rising from the floor and plunging from the ceiling were rows of blue-green stalagmites and powder-puff pink stalactites, along with a polished, lavender sandstone trail. *Somehow, the combination of copper sulfate and sodium hydroxide must've seeped into this chamber, giving the columns their blue-green color, but I don't know where the pink precipitates came from. Maybe ...*

"Would you like some company?" Clad in a lavender work of wonder, Andromeda, appeared next to him.

"Whoa!" Jerry jumped back. "You startled me."

"I'm sorry. I didn't mean to—"

"No, no. It's a good startle." A smile spread across his face." But, hey, when am I going to learn how to ... you know"—Jerry snapped his fingers—"pop in and out like you?"

"Once you have completed your transcendence, you will go through a process of enlightenment at Zeta Tau. There the wisdom of the ages will direct its life force through your aether into the essence of your very soul." She smiled. "That's where you'll find that a single thought can prove quite powerful.

"Zeta what?" Jerry tilted his head and shrugged. "Wisdom of the ages?"

"Relax. You'll learn more once you have arrived on Enif."

"Well"—Jerry rubbed the back of his neck—"I sure could've used it earlier against Crux. I mean ... you did see my dragons, didn't you?"

"Oh, indeed, and I wasn't the only one watching."

"What do you mean?"

"Your ability to produce such magnificent creatures was amazing." She leaned close and grasped his hand. "The General Council of Overseers were quite impressed with your first illusion. In fact, they have been monitoring your progress and have plans for you when you arrive."

"What do you mean when I arrive?" Jerry squinted his eyes. "What's going to happen to me after I go through the portal?"

"In the seventh chamber, your challenges will be magnified." She squeezed his hand. "All the training and experience you have gathered will come into play. But I know you will prevail, and together we will be united as Enifians."

"I don't know what's scarier, the creatures I've had to face down here or the new life that awaits me." What did he know about Enif other than what he saw in the vision he had at the enchanted wall? What were the people like? What if he hated it?

"Relax, you'll be fine."

"I'm glad you think so, but tell me more about this Zeta Tau."

She placed her finger over his mouth and shushed him. "I can't say any more." Andromeda pointed to the trail. "Don't you think it's time we move on?"

"I guess," Jerry said, scrunching his eyes tightly. "It's just that ..."

"What?"

"I don't know. It's just that ... Never mind."

"No. Tell me what you were going to say."

"It's nothing," he said, reaching into his pack.

She frowned. "Is something wrong?"

"No, it's just that ..." Jerry eyed her, closing the door to his thoughts. "It's just that I don't really know much about you."

"I love you!" Her shoulders sagged. "Isn't that enough?"

"Is it wrong for me to want to know more?"

"I'm not that interesting. My father is Avela, and I am the overseer of illusions."

"And that's all?" His visions at the enchanted wall continued to weary his mind. *Dare I ask about the other love?*

"I'm his only daughter, and"—she blushed—"maybe a little spoiled. Once we are on Enif, I will share my past with you, but for now, you need to stay focused."

"Well then, I think it's time we move on." *Oden was right. She is spoiled, but is it jealousy that taints his attitude?* Perhaps he would someday work up the nerve to ask her about his vision, but now wasn't the time.

The golden shield began to pulse, interrupting his thoughts. "Andromeda! Another power-up." The vibration was faint but distinctive. Jerry lifted the pendant from his chest and rotated it, zeroing in on an isolated stalagmite taller than the rest. "Can you stay with me?" His eyes pleaded.

"My time dwindles, but after your encounter with Crux, I have been granted a brief extension."

A gleam of starlight fell upon her delicate features, shaded by the fullness of her hair. Jerry pulled her close, her scent intoxicating. "It feels like an eternity when I'm without you." He slipped his arms around her waist and held her tightly, his lips pressing against hers.

Their lips parted and she sighed. "No one wants this to be over more than I do, but you need to focus on your goal." She caressed his face, searching his eyes. "Shouldn't you check out your next power-up?"

"I know, I know." He flashed a sheepish grin that showed off his dimples. "It's just that we never have much time together."

The two stood near the sequestered column, and once more a sudden wave of energy shot out from the pendant, burning an image of a shield onto the blue-green stalagmite. He removed the golden charm from the chain and positioned it on the glowing symbol. As before, the charm surged with a blinding light, which then softened. Several slots opened on the glistening column, and etched next to them were the twinkling signs of the constellations.

"Do you see all the symbols and star patterns?" His eyes were wide. "What do they mean?"

"It's hard to explain, but I can tell you the power you receive here is a critical step in your progress."

Jerry passed his aether over the ornate column, causing several precious gems to appear. A potent force emanated from the garnet. The stone sparkled like an opal, and its iridescence screamed power. He rushed to place his aether in its slot and stood back.

Darkness extinguished the chamber's light. The anuns glowed so brightly that it was as though the wooden shaft were ablaze. "I forgot how dark these caverns can get."

Andromeda sighed. "Ahh, but without dark, one cannot appreciate light."

Moments later, the expanse erupted into a heavenly display of shimmering beauty. Galaxies composed of dust, gas, and countless bluish-white stars sprawled above them, surrounded by clouds of pink.

"Oh, my!" Jerry stood motionless. "I've never seen anything so ... so stunning."

"Contrast the darkness with a universe awash in color and light and you have a dazzling beauty that will take your breath away."

After a few moments, the colorful arrangement faded from view, replaced by an unseen radiant light that splashed the chamber with a sunny yellow hue. Jerry grabbed the aether with both hands, and a surge of energy raced through him as though he'd just received a massive injection of adrenaline. His face flushed. "Whew, what was that all about?"

"Julean can explain better, but this is one more step that will place you by my side ... forever." Andromeda beamed.

Jerry circled the pillar, checking to see if he had missed anything. "I guess that's it, but check out my pendant." The second insignia radiated a bluish glow.

"You still need one more before the shield is fully charged."

"That's what Julean said." He took the charm from the column and replaced it around his neck. "But now what?" Andromeda's eyes glowed like embers. Jerry gently touched her face. "How much time do we have left?"

"Never enough!" Andromeda clutched him in her arms and sighed. "I, too, crave more time with you, but the overseers are watching." She gently rested her head on his shoulder. "They're afraid I may interfere after you enter the final chamber," she whispered. "Please focus on your training and remember always to trust in your heart. I'm being summoned, but I will be with you always." Once again, Andromeda vanished, leaving Jerry to ponder his journey.

CHAPTER FORTY-ONE

JADE, THE MOUNTAIN MAN

The ability to create, shape, and manipulate illusions consumed Jerry's thoughts. *Can I cause others to see, hear, or taste something that doesn't actually exist? Is that what Andromeda meant when she said I'd be able to—*

Something in the distance broke his concentration. *Smoke. Could this be the mountain man I've been seeking?* Low hills had popped up and the grade had increased. *Holy geode, this place is huge!* A system of small mountain ranges loomed ahead, void of the usual speleothems. The barren trail was dusty and narrow.

After an hour of tedious hiking, he exhaled a deep breath and began a steep climb. The air was moist and fast to cool. A sticky glaze of perspiration dripped from his brow. He stopped, wiped the sweat from his forehead with the back of his arm, and pulled out his nix. "Time to refresh, Mr. G." He raised the gourd to his lips and felt the cold water rush down his throat, clearing it of dirt and dust. "I guess this is where my Jagged Pitch award is going to come in handy. I hope you're ready." He replaced his nix and resumed his hike. *Man, I wish this ordeal was over!*

Dense brush and numerous barbed threats plagued the path. Poisonous thorns and menacing jumping cacti challenged him at every turn. Strange creatures scurried under his feet, buzzed in his ears, and dived at him relentlessly. The trek was physical, and one mistake could prove dangerous, even fatal!

At last, Jerry arrived at the smoke's source. It was a campsite. Chili with a hint of garlic met his nose. He glanced around and spotted a man whistling next to a cozy campfire, stirring a bubbling pot of beans. Curly brown hair stuck out from a scruffy cowboy hat, and a thick salt-and-pepper stubble covered his face. Quite stout, he rose up as Jerry approached him. Dressed in cowboy boots and the usual wrangler attire, the mountain man extended his hand. "Howdy, pardner. What brings ya way up here?"

Jerry smiled and extended his hand in return. "My name is Jerry, and I'm not really sure." He glanced at a bedroll and a cast-iron Dutch oven next to the fire. "It's kind of a long story, but I followed the smoke to your encampment, hoping to find the person I've been seeking."

The old cowboy gave a nod and invited Jerry to sit down on a wooden bench while he sat in a stained leather saddle that smelled like saddle soap. "What can I do fur ya?"

"I came upon an enchanted wall that gave me explicit warnings and a directive to find you ... I think."

"First things first." His skin had a leathery look, and there was a glint in his eyes and quickness in his glance. "They call me Jade, and I ain't your ordinary cowboy. I make things others can't." He stroked his beard with a heavily callused hand. "I'm not sure why y'all are here either, but tell me, whaddya have in your possession?"

Jerry removed the inventory from his pack while Jade watched silently, his stare intent. When he saw the book, his eyes widened. "Ahh, the Book of Illusions." Jade put a callused finger to his mouth and nodded. "That's it! Now let's see what I can do fur ya."

"I've flipped through the pages, but I don't understand the animation or its role." Jerry handed the leather-bound book to Jade and pulled the opaque lenses from his pack. "The images change when I wear these, but I still don't understand what they mean."

"I do. This book is amazing." His eyes narrowed. "Once on the other side, y'all will be able to implement its illustrations to help with your creations. In the caverns, you can only generate illusions, but after ya pass through the portal, your creations can become real!"

Jerry's pulse quickened. *Now I understand what Andromeda was trying to tell me.* "Can you instruct me on how it works?"

"Well, yes and no. First, you must obtain an enchanted ore from Cygnus's mine. This task is dangerous. He has superhuman strength and can snap ya in half with two fingers. Since he is protected, ya can't kill him. You must find a way to get past him and retrieve the mineral I need."

Jerry frowned. "So why do we need this metal, and how do I find this place?"

"I need it to forge a set of special glasses that will allow your mind to visualize the animations correctly." Jade looked him straight in his eyes. "It's the only way. The ore is bright green with yellow streaks running through it. Y'all will know it when ya see it."

"Is there a way to retrieve the ore without engaging this... this hulk?"

Jade stood up and pointed. "The trail to Cygnus starts here. There's no easy answer. Best be on your way if you're gonna get it done."

Jerry said a hasty good-bye and left to retrieve the green metal.

"Mr. G," he groaned, "how are we going to contend with a creature that's protected? Maybe we'll get a break. Yeah, right. Who are we kidding?"

The dusty trail changed into an ascent straight up the stony mountain. In little time, Jerry found himself standing inside a small encampment of soiled green-canvas tents. The odors of stale coffee and body sweat whipped through the compound. *This must be where the locals live who mine the metal for Cygnus. Maybe I can hit up on someone for help.*

Jerry searched the tents but came up empty. He glanced around and sighed. *Looks like I'm on my own. Figures.* He left the vacant encampment and followed the pathway toward the mine. In the distance, cage doors clanged shut and high-pitched drilling and explosions echoed.

Moments later, an open shaft cut into the side of a hill came into view. Various stone formations surrounded the quarry except for a small clearing in front of the entrance. Jerry set off toward the mine but quickly retreated behind a huge boulder when he spotted a man who seemed forged from muscle and steel—and flaunted it with his sleeveless shirt. *This must be Cygnus.* The creature had a body that would rival the Hulk's. His bare arms rippled with muscles and his veins bulged. He stood at least eight feet tall and had dark green skin and long black hair.

"Mr. G, I never knew the body had that many muscles. He must eat steroids for breakfast. No way can we get into the mineshaft with this Goliath on duty."

With the titan virtually sleeping on top of the depository, only a gnat could get past him. But what about the power of telepathy? *Okay, big guy, is your mind as strong as your brawn?*

Jerry exhaled a slow breath, peeked around the boulder, and invaded Cygnus's mind. The green giant slowly drifted away from his quarry. *It's working!* Bright hope flashed briefly inside him but dimmed fast when Cygnus shook off his incursion and moved back to guard the reservoir of green ore. *Incredible! How does one beat the unbeatable?*

He considered the apus flowers, but turning invisible wouldn't be enough to get him past this mammoth guard. *What about Leo's ring? No. Even if I were to transform into a mouse, slipping by might seem easy, but getting the green metal out would be impossible.* His head spun in confusion. Then a spark flashed in his mind. *What about the time powder?* He could scurry inside as an inconspicuous rodent, acquire the exclusive ore, and activate the time powder to escape. But would the lapse of time be sufficient for him to find safety? That could prove tricky. Jerry looked at Mr. G. and sighed. "I know of no other way."

He sucked in a breath of courage, placed Leo's ring on his finger, and transformed into a gray mouse. Now as a tiny rodent, he slipped around Cygnus and then resumed his usual form far enough inside to avoid notice. *So far so good, but without a hammer and chisel, how am I going to obtain any ore? And just how much do I need?* Clouds of ore dust made him cough and sneeze, but with the noise of the workers, he easily evaded recognition.

Jerry watched his shadow as it danced across the floor, silhouetted by the flickering torches on either side. *Wait a minute.* He bent down and picked up several rocks among the loose debris. *Hey, there may be enough of this enchanted ore just for the picking.*

After stuffing his pockets with the green and yellow mineral, he crept toward the entrance, careful not to make a sound. Then he abruptly stopped. *Holy geode!* The giant stood with his back toward him, blocking his escape. Jerry stood transfixed, his throat tightening. *I thought Crux was intimidating, but this guy is massive! How am I going to get around him?* Jerry rubbed the back of his neck. *Wait a minute—maybe I can still use my telepathy.*

Once again, Jerry invaded Cygnus's mind, drawing him away from the quarry, but before the titan could shake off the incursion, Jerry tossed a pinch of time powder into the air.

Never did his feet move so fast, like lightning! His heartbeat thundered in his ears as he sprinted past the hulking giant, racing behind the boulder where he'd left his pack and aether. Sweat poured down his face and he waited. Several minutes passed, and he'd heard nothing other than the high-pitched sound of drilling and explosions. Sensing no danger, Jerry grabbed his pack and aether and hustled down the mountain, anxious to meet up with Jade.

With the raw material in hand, Jerry entered the campsite. Jade was sitting cross-legged, tending a glowing fire and whistling a tune. The burning embers sent a wavering heat into the air, filling it with the scent of pine.

"That was quick." Jade stood. "How'd ya get the job done so fast?"

"Let's just say that an indomitable will won out over brawn." Jerry emptied his pockets. "So, when will the glasses be ready?"

"Son, y'all are not done yet. I still need sand from the Eridanus River. The ore will construct the frames, but I need the mystic effect from the silica to make the lenses."

A pallor swept across Jerry's face. "Is there more than one Eridanus River down here?"

"No, the same tributary traverses the cavern's entire system except in the last chamber. How'd ya know about the Eridanus?"

"If Lyro hadn't rescued me, I wouldn't be standing here now." Jerry turned away and looked down. "After I had crossed the river, the aquilas attacked me. Lyro came to my rescue and placed them in some sort of altered sleep." His voice quavered. "Is that part of the aquilas nesting area?"

"Unfortunately, the river's banks are part of their lodging, and the sand will be treacherous to obtain. After y'all have gathered enough silica, only then can I melt it into the lenses."

"Figures." Jerry let out a long breath. "How much do I need, and how do I get there?"

"Backtrack halfway down this passage and you'll see a dead tree, except for one branch. Yellow leaves cover the lone limb, and it points to the river. Follow the sandy trail east until ya come to the Eridanus." Jade stoked the bristly stubble on his chin. "A word of caution: beware of the jumping cacti. Those sticky little nuisances grow on the north side, but ya can easily sidestep them. If attacked, it'll be next to impossible to remove their hooked barbs. For what it's worth, they do have a fear of fire." Jade opened his hand. "Once there, fill this pouch and ya should have enough." He sat down and clasped his hands behind his head. "If it's any consolation, I'm sure y'all will succeed."

Jerry closed his eyes and shook his head. *Aquilas. Why does it have to be aquilas? I wonder if I can still call on Lyro. If not, how am I going to survive their attack?*

Jerry hastened his steps, pounding the hard ground beneath him with resolve. He found the dead tree with the trademark yellow leaves and began his hike to the water's edge. Wary of the cacti that sported gigantic prickly needles, he discharged fire from his aether to ward off any attacks. It wasn't long before the Eridanus River came into view, and with it the same grove of colorful trees.

The sense of danger he had felt earlier now grew to trepidation. Anxiety gnawed at his gut. The thought of facing the dreaded aquilas sent a chill down his spine. Every muscle in his body screamed at him to run, but he couldn't, not without obtaining the last ingredient needed to finish his glasses.

Jerry stopped and watched the winding current gracefully tumble over stones, bubbling and gurgling, revealing strange fish-like critters darting about under its glimmering surface. The serenity of the stream acted like a sedative, easing the tension that had built with his previous encounters. A familiar scent of sulfur riffled through the lavender mopped-head blossoms and stroked Jerry's face. But where were the dreaded birds? Could he retrieve the needed sand before being noticed? Had they vacated their nest like the Columba birds?

Slow cautious steps brought him closer to the towering trees. *Hmm, their canopy seems thicker in this part of the river.* He looked up, sensing something. It was as if the cavern were staring at him—like invisible eyes, watching and waiting for him to make one mistake.

Movement stirred within the trees. A sudden burning in his gut shot through his veins. *Great. I knew things were too good to be true.* Jerry quietly pulled out the bag of apus flowers and ingested the remaining few remnants. Instantly, he became invisible. *I need to hurry. These won't last more than a few minutes.*

Jerry crept toward the river's bank, careful with his footsteps, and began filling the bag with the mystical sand, but before he could finish, his invisibility wore off. Within seconds, terrifying screams erupted, and the dreaded birds launched an assault, filling the sky above him.

He panicked.

"Lyro, I need your help now!"

Not knowing if Lyro would show, or could, he tried to run, but the soft sand rolled under his feet, dragging and slowing his pace. Each stride shortened as if he were wading through mud, his feet sinking deeper and deeper.

Jerry dropped and formed a protective shroud around him. The deadly birds cluttered the sky, diving and striking with razor-sharp talons and lethal beaks.

Holy geode, there're too many. No way can I generate any offense. Tension layered the air and his heart pounded. "Lyro!" he continued to call out but was losing hope. *Wait! Leo's ring.* Jerry snatched the magical band from his vest, but before he could put in on, a sweet melody infused the area with a transcendent serenity.

Soothing flute notes sailed through the air like a ship on a gentle sea, settling in the ears of the cold-blooded killers. The melodic tune was quite familiar to Jerry as it moved through him in waves, quieting his anxiety. Within moments, the aquilas ceased their attack. Lyro's music had lulled the deadly birds into a deep slumber.

"I knew you would come!" Jerry shouted. "I just knew it! Once again, you've saved my life."

"Well, to have abandoned you would be rude after you saved my brother's life," Lyro said, appearing next to him.

"Uh, what do you mean?" Jerry feigned puzzlement, remembering his promise to Lyra.

"When I visited my brother, I found fang marks on his neck. He admitted he was trying to outperform me and his pride almost cost him his life. He said if you hadn't killed Serpentius, he would've been his next meal. We owe you a lot, and I'm more than happy to assist. If you are ever in need, please let me know. Oh, I almost forgot." Lyro pulled a plastic bag from his pocket. "I picked a few more apus flowers in case you needed them."

"Uh-huh! Do I ever." Jerry took the bag and stuffed it into his pack. "I ran out and it almost cost me my life."

"The aquilas are one of the most dangerous threats a person can encounter. There's not much you can do, because of their masses. My music has saved many a life. I suppose it's time I assist my brother so that he can acquire the same ability. Our competition has outlived its days. But I ramble."

"As usual, I am indebted. Tell your brother we still make a good team." Jerry lifted his arm and waved, and they parted company. *I hope that's the last time I run into this river. I don't ever want to see those horrid birds again.*

At the campsite, Jade was sitting by a campfire whistling away. In his hand was a set of curious frames fabricated from the glistening enchanted metal. Their appearance varied continually from icy-blue flames to red-hot icicles. They seemed alive and in constant motion.

"See, I knew you'd make the journey back," Jade said, grinning ear to ear. "I spent the last hour forging y'all's antares."

Jerry tilted his head and squinted his eyes. "My what?"

"Your antares." He held out a pair of horn-rimmed settings. "Now all I need is the sand from the Eridanus River."

"How long will it take to finish the glasses?" Jerry handed the pouch of enchanted silica to him and watched his callused hands pour its contents into a red-hot crucible.

"Only a few minutes," Jade boasted with a leathery smirk. He melted and molded the magical silica into a set of clear, thick lenses and then fastened them to their frames. "This'll be the last prescription you'll ever need, pardner."

Jerry placed the glasses on, opened the leather binder, and leafed through the animated pages, inhaling the musty scent of aged paper. Images formed in his mind as though the book had popped open inside of him, sending flashes of creatures he'd never seen before. His heart soared, and he gasped and stuttered. "I ... I can't believe what I'm seeing. Are these real?"

With a wave of his hand, each page turned, delivering a rich, smooth, immersive visual experience. Angelic forms drifted about. Rainbow deer trumpeted odd tunes with their antlers. Horned lizards zapped insects with lasers emitted from their mouths. Mutant bats spawned hordes of deviant winged demons with pointed teeth and hypnotic eyes.

"Oh, my! These images are incredible."

Bubble trees released a colorful effervescence into the sky. Water currents defied gravity, bending up and around without boundaries. Strange-looking birds with long red necks and spoon-shaped beaks flew backward and upside down as though they were confused. Each time he turned a page, another leaf appeared.

The text went on to infinity, as did their animations. The illustrations appeared genuine and vibrant, as though he could reach out and touch them. Whenever he placed his hand on the book, it served to feed his mind. Visions of places and creatures continued to jump off the pages and merge with his consciousness.

"What do I do now? I mean ... now what?"

"Hey, I don't operate 'em. I just make 'em, pardner," Jade said. "If ya want to know how they work, ask Julean." Jade sat back down and started whistling.

Jerry beamed with excitement and waved good-bye, thanking him.

For the next few hours, Jerry traveled back down the dusty trail, his thoughts consumed by the book's images and sounds that had been so vividly burned into his mind. Now more than ever, he wanted to master the ability to perfect his illusions. Something that was far more than a set of tricks. Something so realistic and so powerful it could confuse the senses of anyone or anything he came up against. Something that could give him authority over reality.

He walked down the path, occasionally stopping to merge his mind with the Book of Illusions, allowing its contents to infuse his soul with otherworldly creations. *Huh, and I thought the dragons I used to distract Crux were awesome.* He began to create dark and gruesome creatures. *If only they were real. I could conquer anything that opposed me.* Confidence surged through him. He'd be ready—when the next time came, he'd be waiting.

Maybe.

CHAPTER FORTY-TWO

GROTHAR, THE SPEAR OF LIGHTNING

It wasn't until later that Jerry's concentration switched to the changing terrain. The vast chamber had dwindled into a small cavity. Hexagonal columns of purple and pink basalt, shaped in symmetrical six-sided pillars, made up the interior walls, and wavy sheets of white calcite layered the ceiling along with mineralized yellow forms that twisted this way and that, like curlicue french fries. *The geology here is unlike any other I've seen.*

God's perfume soaked the area with a sweet earthy smell. *Ahh, nothing better than a sage-like fragrance. It makes me want to roll around in its scent.* Towers of purple and pink basalt glowed like alabaster in the moonlight, and the twinkling stars of Pegasus shone down brightly.

A weak vibration from the golden shield caught his attention. Upset, he stopped. *I almost missed this power-up.* Jerry exhaled a deep breath. *Now is not the time to get sloppy.*

Julean's words echoed in his mind. *I'm in the last trials of my journey, and if I lose my concentration, I may lose my life, and with it Andromeda.*

He lifted the pendant from his chest and targeted a brightly lit column only feet away. An unusually hot, dry breeze shot by him and his breath caught. *That was weird.* A sudden wave of energy shot out from the golden charm, burning an image of a shield onto the six-sided pillar.

After unfastening his pendant, he placed it on the glowing symbol, but instead of the usual show of blinding light, it shimmered and fizzled out. *Oh, this is different.* Moments later, the hexagonal column flashed a multitude of colors, and several slots snapped open. *Well, okay.*

Jerry retrieved the charm and placed it around his neck. "Ouch!" Pain seared into his flesh and he yanked the amulet off his chest. "What in the geode was that all about?" He rubbed his skin, trying to ease the pain. "Ugh, it still burns." The skin blistered, reddened, and then healed almost instantly. Emblazoned on his chest was the sign of the shield with its three distinct icons. "Mr. G, I feel like I've just been branded. I don't understand what just happened, but for now, we need to move on."

He passed his aether over the polychromatic column, uncovering several precious gems. *These are gorgeous, but which one?* He focused on each stone, trying to harmonize with its energy. The moonstone pulsed an inner light, emitting a vibrant, flame-blue sheen as if he were looking into a crystal ball. *Aha, this is it!*

No sooner had he inserted his aether than a burst of blinding light erupted from the anuns. A nauseating pain shot through his head. He snapped his eyes shut and shielded them with the back of his hand. It was as though someone had unveiled the sun. He inched forward, waving his right hand in the air, tripping and stumbling until wrenching the beaming staff from the column.

The light calmed and he opened his eyes. "Mr. G, your eyes ... they're bright yellow!" Pain like none he had ever felt before crawled over his skin. "I feel like I have a bad sunburn, but my skin isn't red. Man, do I have a lot of questions for Julean."

A warm feeling infused his soul, and the odor of burned flesh lingered in the air. Jerry circled the pillar several times, trying to harmonize with another gem, but his efforts proved futile. For the moment, he sat on a large rock, gazing at the cavern's twinkling stars, which seemed to gaze back. So much had happened so fast. Almost too fast. *Ever since my experience with the Book of Illusions, something has awakened within me, something deep inside. Something ...*

Weariness overcame him, and he fell asleep on a large flat rock.

Jerry woke an hour later and blinked the sleep from his eyes. He stared at the trail for a moment, unsure how long he'd been out. He'd been dreaming of a faraway place, a strange and beautiful place with tumbling waterfalls sparkling with a supernatural brilliance. Their light was so peaceful, so natural, so carefree. He realized with a start that he'd been dreaming of this place for the past few years, although he had no idea it even existed. Just thinking of this fairy-tale land filled him with a poignant longing, as though he were coming home.

The stars above erupted in force, their glittering brilliance lighting the way. His stomach growled, reminding him it had been a while since he'd eaten. He drew the last of the bright yellow fruit from his pack and ate it. *I hope the next jinan isn't too far away.* He patted his nix. *At least I won't get thirsty.* Jerry grunted, pushed himself up, and continued his trek to the final seal, feeling as though he still had a temperature.

The trail changed into a natural look of stone that jutted out at irregular angles, and not an inch of the chamber was without swirling colors. Water trickled down slick moss-covered walls, and the air was musty. His footsteps squeaked on the moistened floor as he pushed onward, finding spectacular rooms and passages that took his breath away. Enormous deposits of white gypsum hung like frozen sprays. Twig-like helictites dripped mineral-rich water, and yellow gypsum flowers grew along the trail, imparting a vibrant glow. Then he spotted something glistening just off the pathway that shone like a shimmering pearl. *Is that another orb?*

The sphere hovered above a glass-like floor. *Interesting. This looks identical to the place I first met Julean.* Jerry approached the spinning globe, seeking a way to activate it. A sudden burst of multicolored beams shot out in different directions. He paused for a moment as if uncertain what to do and then reached into his pack, pulled out the opaque glasses, and placed them on his face. "Whoa! Mr. G, do you see what I see?"

Seven orbs had materialized around him, each one emitting a colorful spectrum of laser light. One emanated particularly vibrant energy. *Oh, yeah, this is it.* The instant he touched the spinning sphere, a brilliant white light erupted, and with it Julean.

"Am I glad to see you!" Jerry's eyes sparkled with excitement. "I have so many questions."

"It's good to see you again," Julean said, smiling. "How may I assist?"

"I finally found Jade, the mountain man. He made these special glasses to view the Book of Illusions." Jerry held out the anteres. "I think he called them ontaries or something like that."

"Oh, yes, Jade's handiwork. Used correctly, the anteres can open a portal to your mind that will allow you to create many marvelous things, but beware—there is a dark side to the book." His voice grew tense, his stare piercing. "You, my young friend, need to be cautious." Jerry's eyes widened; his lips parted. "You have acquired the power of dissolution, which also has a dark side. Together, they could prove disastrous. That is why I insisted you wait until I could offer proper instruction. Ignorance is no excuse for lack of good knowledge."

Jerry stood silent, trying to sort out his thoughts. *That must've been why I felt so strange with some of the creatures I created. Is this something I should be concerned about?*

"The anteres will help to expand your illusions. When your mind connects with the book's repertoire, you will have the opportunity to create images from your thoughts." Once again, excitement built in Jerry's eyes. "At first, the book will feed ideas to you, but as you progress, your mind will develop an aptitude on its own." Julean leaned forward. "Like everything else, it takes time to master your illusions."

"I understand. I need to be patient, but I do have a few more questions."

"Of course." Julean's shoulders relaxed. "How else may I help?"

"Earlier, I acquired the first of two power-ups from a blue-green column that had the signs of the constellations etched into it. When I grabbed my aether, adrenaline rushed through my body, making me flush." Jerry shook his head. "I'm still not sure what that was all about."

"You have received one of three essential functions required from your aether. Julean stared into Jerry's eyes. "The only way for you to enter your new world is through the Arch of Enif. The power you received will open the gateway and allow transport past the constellations. Without this capacity, you would be lost in space forever. You will receive more instruction at the portal."

"It sounds a little intimidating."

"Only if you had not acquired its power."

"What about my last power-up?" Jerry pointed to his aether. "You should've seen the light that erupted from the anuns." Jerry squinted. "It was as bright as a rising sun. After I'd absorbed the column's energy, it felt like I had a severe sunburn. In fact, I still feel warm. But tell me, is this another function needed to access the portal? I mean—"

"Whoa, slow down," Julean said, extending his arms. "First, what you saw was indeed a simulation of the sun. There may be situations when this blinding offense comes in handy. Not only can its immutable power blind your opponents, but it can also place a burning shield around you as a temporary defense."

"So how do I activate this ... this sun power?"

"It will be part of your repertoire before you leave."

"If you don't mind, I have a few more questions." He pulled his shirt down and exposed the shield's icon on his chest. "This is a result of my last power-up." He rubbed the skin as though it still hurt. "When I replaced the pendant around my neck, it burned like fire, leaving its mark on me, something you failed to inform me about."

"The pendant has bonded to you and is now active. Its protection will remain dynamic through the rest of your journey."

"Bonded to me?"

"When it seared its impression onto your body, it guaranteed its allegiance to you and only you. Whenever you are in danger, the shield will begin to glow, providing a defensive barrier around your body." Julean lifted the pendant and pointed to the icons. "If attacked with fire, the assault will be repelled back to the aggressor. Weak magic will be reciprocated to the assailant, and if caught in an avalanche of rocks or stones, they will be propelled away from you. The pendant is a shield of protection, which means the charm has no offensive advantages other than those of what I speak."

"I have one more question." Jerry dropped his gaze and sighed. "I still have a fear of making bad decisions, and at times I feel alone in my anxiety."

"Don't hang your head, for it is better to look up!" Julean placed his hand on Jerry's shoulder. "The fear of making bad decisions prevents many from doing things that they might be better off doing. Fear is a natural reaction to a perceived threat. Things change fast down here, and you must focus on how to change with them if you are going to survive. Weigh the risks and benefits of each option. Open your mind to your heart and then move boldly. It will not fail you."

Over the next several hours, Julean placed Jerry in an intense training session, offering words of encouragement along the way. At their conclusion, Julean bowed his head and said, "Your power sleeps, but when it awakens, embrace it." He tapped Jerry's heart. "In here. If you believe, your courage will not fail you." With that, Julean vanished.

Jerry stared at his aether, wondering what his words meant. Something stirred inside him, something that was ready to break out. But what?

Alone again, Jerry lifted his head, staring at the cavern's bright twinkling stars. Their light shone throughout the chamber, painting it with a bluish silver that made him feel as if he were frozen in time. He didn't fear the loneliness, though he would have preferred to have Andromeda by his side. Doubt still lurked, raising its ugly head from time to time, making him feel small and insignificant.

Jerry strode down a winding trail, watching for a stealth assault by the nefarious creatures that skulked through the cavern's corridors. A hot breeze blew past him, feathering the strands of hair across his forehead. His gait slowed. The air wobbled and the narrow trail gradually morphed into a mirage, refracting the cavern's light and triggering an illusion of water on the pathway. He stopped and sniffed the air. "Mr. G, what's that smell?"

The sharp, fresh scent of ozone permeated the corridor. His skin tingled and his chest tightened. *Something isn't right.* An assortment of colorful stalagmites and stalactites surrounded him, and in the distance the gateway to the seventh chamber waited.

On either side of the trail, the ground shimmered with unusual rock shards. He crouched down, picked one up, and gently ran his fingers over it. *Hmm, this looks like one of the fulgurites Mr. Stubal shared with me from his French Alps trip, but what could've produced heat intense enough to vitrify the surrounding structures, leaving behind these amorphous glass tubes?*

Something stirred in his heart, a feeling of uneasiness. *Okay, so where's the guardian? Surely, it can't be this easy.* Jerry rose and stared at the trail. "Well, Mr. G, what do you think?" Mr. G's yellow eyes flickered. "Yeah, I know, but we don't have a lot of options?"

Jerry faced forward and eased his way toward the last seal, pushing his fears from his mind. Suddenly, the chamber turned black, and the area was engulfed in a whirlwind of thunder and fury. Lightning crashed down around him as the earth beneath him rumbled.

He stumbled, almost falling to the ground. The air was stifling and sweat poured off his face. *What in the …* Mr. G's eyes were white-hot, ionizing the air around him. *Feeling a bit lightheaded. Not sure how much more of this I can take. Need to get away.*

Jerry backed off, distancing himself from the torrid storm. Seconds later, the lightning stopped, and a silvery light returned from above. In front of him lurked the last guardian, a gelatinous blob discharging electrical sparks across its membranes. *Well, that explains the fried fulgurites. This thing must've generated a billion joules of energy. But how am I going to defeat such a foe?*

The creature had a translucent outer covering that exposed a glistening plasma nucleus. Intense yellow charges branched into small veins of lavender sparks, and frequent bursts of crackling orange alternated with bright magenta flashes. *It looks like a big blob of silicone gel, but I wonder, is this thing a living organism?*

He clenched his jaw. "I demand passage," he said.

"I am Grothar, the spear of lightning." There was no cadence to its speech, no inflection or tone. "You must leave."

Okay, you big heap of electrical gunk, just what is your Achilles' heel? Jerry stepped back beyond its zone to assess his situation. *My aether acted as a conductor, insulating me from his powerful voltage … And Julean did say the diamond's energy provided both offensive and defensive abilities. But has my power matured enough to destroy this evil?*

"Mr. G, this thing sounds like a computer, which means I may not be able to deceive or trick its programming, but if it's organic, it can die. The question is how? What do you think? Can we do this without getting fried?" The geode's eyes had calmed to a soft flickering yellow. Jerry sighed. "I hope you're right."

If I engage this creature recklessly, I may end up like one of Mr. Stubal's fulgurites, burned to a crisp. Jerry paced, running his fingers through his hair. *It's got to have a weakness, but the only way to find out is to test its offensive capacity.*

Once again, Jerry approached the spear of lightning, forming a protective barrier around him, and once again powerful electrical surges zapped him. A faint spark arced from his aether to the liquid nucleus. *That's it! That's his Achilles' heel.*

He hastened back to the safe zone to weigh the risks of his options. None of his amulets would prove effective, nor would his ability to float by or turn invisible. Even the time powder wouldn't provide a sufficient pause. But could he breach its core by creating a short circuit? Maybe he could release one of his arrows to extinguish the gelatinous threat.

The effort would require the ultimate trust in his aether. If he failed to produce the voltage necessary, it would be akin to signing his own death sentence. He sat down and mentally dissected what would be necessary to accomplish the task.

I know that plasma holds a charge and that electrical currents are conducted through the electrons found in it, but does this blob have enough plasma inside? If so, I may be able to create the altered charges using my aether. He scratched his head for a moment. *But what if my power hasn't gained enough intensity? Will I have enough time to release one of my arrows before it reboots?*

Jerry pulled his bow from his pack, loaded it, and hung it from his belt. "Mr. G, I hope you're ready." He sucked in a nervous breath and stepped forward, staring at the high-voltage mass, but then he paused. The air sparked with static electricity. He took a few more steps.

Suddenly, lightning crashed down around him. The earth beneath him growled, and energy surged from his aether, striking the creature. Thunderous flashes blazed back and forth. Matter smoldered between the two combatants, and the smell of ozone grew stronger.

Nausea gripped his gut. His chest tightened and his breath shortened. Sweat poured from his face as he struggled to hold on. Things started to spin and everything became fuzzy. He tried to blink it away as spasms shook his body. His legs buckled and he stumbled to the ground, striving to hold on to his aether. Just as he was about to pass out, the creature lost voltage and sparks flew everywhere.

Jerry rose to his knees, seized the crossbow, and released the arrow. Everything felt like slow motion. The projectile sped forward, punching a hole straight through the arcing nucleus, bursting it like a water balloon. Its viscous contents splattered in all directions. The air cracked against his ear as a hail of sparks rained down on the area. He had delivered the fatal shot.

Jerry crumpled to the ground, exhausted, tasting the joy of having made the right decision. Thirst rippled through his body. He lifted his nix and wet his lips, savoring its sweet taste. *Julean was right. I have the power. I just need to believe in myself.*

Jerry rose and inched his way forward, searching for the symbols that would open the seventh and final entry. Sparks crackled and popped next to the stone gateway. *What's this?* He discharged his aether to illuminate the area. Like a neon light, the electrical energy ignited several hidden symbols, revealing the key to the secured entry.

He glanced around and then touched the glowing images, marveling at ancient designs so intense they seemed to swallow his finger in their hue. The sealed door promptly morphed into a misty blue veil, unlocking the concluding chapter of his odyssey. Jerry hesitated, took a deep breath, and stepped through the shimmering curtain, feeling more confident than he had in a long time.

CHAPTER FORTY-THREE

THE SEVENTH SEAL

Jerry stifled a gasp as he stepped into a highly decorated alcove saturated with a sweet floral scent. A gilded interior featured sculpted golden statues and intricate artwork, reflecting an early Italian Renaissance design. Cherubs, anchored in the luminous walls, held torches that flickered and fluttered, casting a yellow tinge across a white marble floor. *This place is gorgeous, but I feel like I'm in the calm before the storm.*

His gaze shifted to seven pedestals not more than ten feet in front of him and, beyond them, a giant chasm. He stepped cautiously toward the pedestals, which were identical, standing three feet high with strange ciphers encircling them. Each top bore the mark of a blue heptagon, and inside the seven-sided symbol was a riddle. *Interesting. Most of my challenges have been physical up to this point. But now it seems my intellect will be tested.*

With a momentary pause, his thoughts disappeared into the soft echoing of the cavern's dripping pulse. He glanced around and then eased his way to the gulf that separated him from the other side. His skin tingled and his stomach churned. *Great! Another void.* "Mr. G, I sure hope this isn't like the last one. I don't know if my brain could go through that again."

He squatted at its edge and extended his hand into the empty space. Without warning, an ionizing charge zapped him. "Ouch! That really stung." Jerry turned to Mr. G, shaking his hand. "Next time, you go first." The skin on his fingers had eroded and peeled. Although they quickly healed, he shivered at the prospect of going any farther. He glanced once more at the gulf that separated him from his goal. There had to be a way to cross without getting incinerated, but how? If he tried to float across, whatever had zapped his fingers would no doubt reduce him to ashes in seconds. And just what did the puzzles represent? Jerry paused in thought and then walked back to the first pedestal and read the riddle: "You can't see me, and I have no mass, but you can feel me when I race past."

Jerry paced the length of the room, repeating the riddle over and over. But nothing popped into his mind. Absolutely nothing. A cool breeze brushed his face and feathered his hair. He paused. *But of course—it's so simple.* "The wind." His breath came out as little more than a whisper. "The answer is the wind."

The inscription faded and the letter *E* appeared in its place as if drawn by an unseen finger. Instinctively, he touched the vowel, causing it to illuminate. Nothing happened. He looked around. *Okay, so now what?* Jerry shrugged and moved on to the next podium.

"My light shines ever so bright, but it can be viewed only at night. I'm seen running in the sky, but if needed I can fly."

His eyes brightened. "This is too easy. The answer is Pegasus, the flying horse."

Once again, the riddle faded, and this time an *S* formed in its place. *An E and an S. What do these mean?* When Jerry touched the letter, a silvery-blue platform materialized next to the chasm, extending out several feet. He walked over to the suspended segment and placed his foot on it, expecting to get zapped, but nothing happened. *Now I get it. Each puzzle adds a link, forming a bridge to the other side. But why didn't the letter E create a connection?*

Jerry hurried back to the first pedestal and touched the still-glowing *E*. He watched as another silver-blue link appeared. *Awesome! Now all I need to do is solve the remaining teasers.* He shifted to the third podium and read the riddle: "A trial by fire in the furnace of affliction makes this virtue a welcome addition."

"Well, Mr. G, my life has certainly been filled with affliction, but I'm not sure which virtue is in question."

Jerry stared at the riddle, considering his options. "Got any ideas?" His eyes flashed to his wrist as though directed by an unseen force. "Of course, my beads of wisdom." He rested his left hand on the pedestal. "Wisdom. The one virtue I'm in desperate need of."

He leaned over the podium and watched the question fade into an *H*. In excitement, he touched the glowing character, but instead of forming more links, one segment disappeared. *Really?!* His heart sank. *Why did I lose part of the bridge?* Shaking his head, he was in a quandary as to what to do. "Wait a minute." He turned to Mr. G. "This is like *The Wheel of Fortune*, which I used to watch on TV." It was obvious the letters spelled something necessary to crossing the chasm, and once it was exposed, he'd have to solve another puzzle.

Jerry moved to the fourth pedestal, his heart fluttering.

"What comes out at night with a bright shiny face but hides in darkness from the sun's warm embrace?"

Who or what has a bright shiny face that hides from the sun? Jerry stared unblinking, his jaw set. I guess I spoke too soon. I knew things were going way too easy, but I will figure this out. "Well, Mr. G, here we go again." *The only thing that has a shiny face at night is the moon, but how would it hide from the sun? Maybe the beads of wisdom can help.*

The instant he placed his wrists together, an image of a dark planet flashed before him. "Of course! A lunar eclipse." Jerry turned to Mr. G. "Come on, Mr. Bright Eyes, you should've known the moon hides in the Earth's shadow during a lunar eclipse."

Once again the riddle disappeared, and the letter *N* emerged. *Four letters and I still don't have a clue what it's trying to tell me.*

Now at the fifth pedestal, he slowly recited the next riddle: "Journey with this and your destiny you may meet, but too much of it and you may suffer defeat."

My destiny? Just what do I need to secure my destiny? Jerry's thoughts shifted to his past defeats. *I almost lost my life with Promethion and Virga by being overconfident. The only thing that comes to mind is confidence. But what if I am wrong?* Jerry fidgeted about and then released a long-held breath. "Confidence. If you don't believe in yourself, you're bound to fail."

His voice sounded unsure, but when he looked down, the writing faded and the letter V scrolled across the podium's top. "Mr. G, my life has been filled with endless struggles that affected my attitude and belief in myself. No matter how many times I succeeded, doubting myself was just one slip away." Jerry sighed. "Even now I question my abilities." *It's so hard to shake the past, but I am trying.*

At the sixth pedestal, his heart pounded hard, and doubt set in. What if he couldn't answer the remaining riddles? Would he be forever lost, never tasting of the freedom that burned deep inside him? His blood chilled at the thought. *I need to stay focused and believe.* Jerry tilted his head downward, exhaled a deep breath, and read the next question: "What crawls in the morning, sleeps in the afternoon, and flies at night?"

Okay, this is going to take a while. Jerry rubbed the back of his neck, frowning in deep thought. *What crawls in the morning? A baby? Yes, but an infant can't fly. What sleeps in the afternoon and flies at night? Man, these puzzles just keep getting harder and harder. I need some help.*

Sweat dripped down his face as words swarmed in his head. He reviewed the question over and over in his mind, struggling to find the answer. Then he caught sight of the beads of wisdom. *Perhaps they can help.*

Moments after he placed his wrists together, his mind cleared and a vision opened to him—a colorful field of wildflowers filled with a multitude of gorgeous butterflies. "That's it! A caterpillar. The insect crawls first, then sleeps in a cocoon, and then flies away as a butterfly."

Jerry held his breath as the riddle dimmed and the letter *T* emerged. *Yes! Now if I can conquer the last one ... maybe ...*

He moved to the last stand and read the riddle: "What can balance the scales of time and prevent eternity from becoming blind?"

The scales of time? You've got to be kidding! Jerry stared at the question for a long time, his mind cluttered with thoughts. *Time in and of itself is in constant motion. But can it be manipulated beyond the absolute? I have learned that space tends to warp time only in terms of movement. The faster the motion, the slower the time. My physics instructor, Mr. Scott, was convinced the theory of relativity was indisputable, suggesting that if you travel at the speed of light, time will stop. But how can it balance the scales of time?*

Jerry stared at the riddle, willing himself to relax, to breathe. He recalled his experience with Crux and Cygnus. *The erosion of time can't be stopped, but we can punch holes into that tight envelope. I did it with the time powder. Leo proved time can be balanced, but how?*

Pacing, he wrestled with the question, terrified of what would happen if he didn't solve this mystery. Then something inside sparked. "Wait a minute, Mr. G." Jerry's skin tingled. "I've known the answer all the time. Leo had balanced time ... over twelve hundred years and counting, but he still had accountability to his age. The only way to tip the scales of time is to become an Enifian. A person can't escape time, but they can balance it without becoming blind to the consequences of eternity."

Jerry crossed his fingers, his heart pounding hard. What if it wasn't correct? He could hardly bear the thought. He exhaled a nervous breath and stared at the writing inside the seven-sided symbol, watching and waiting.

The words flickered and faded, leaving the letter T in their place. His body went weak and he slumped to the floor. *Julean, you were right. I need to believe in myself and follow my heart.* "Mr. G, if we hadn't met Leo ... well, we probably would've died here. But we did, and I will be forever indebted to him."

With all the letters exposed, he sketched each one on the dusty marble floor, randomly arranging them. "Aha, I should've known ... *Seventh.*" Jerry shook his head. "There must be something significant about the heptagon symbol, but what?"

He rose and positioned himself to solve the final puzzle. Moving from pedestal to pedestal, he proceeded to spell the word *seventh.* With each touch, a silvery-blue platform materialized, linking to the previous segment until the union was completed, allowing access to the other side.

Once across the chasm, Jerry turned and watched as each section vanished, leaving a dark void. "Mr. G, things never seem to get easier." Jerry rubbed the back of his neck. "Like the bridge of life, every trial adds to the strength and stability needed to pass over the gulf of adversity. We are only as strong as our weakest link, and mine ... well, it's still believing in myself."

CHAPTER FORTY-FOUR

THE LAST COMMUNICATION

The pulse of the cavern dripped loudly, like a consistent heartbeat. A cool breeze wandered through the corridor, and a pale light led the way. Jerry tightened his vest around him, savoring its warmth. He recalled the blistering summers in the Arizona desert, hiking the local trails, marveling at the fading sunsets and the spectacular haboobs. Would he ever see the sun again? And if he ever reached Enif, would he truly be happy?

He straightened his backpack and resumed his trek to the portal, his stomach growling and complaining. "Mr. G, I don't know about you, but I'm so hungry I could eat a dragon."

Several hours passed, and his belly continued to groan. The pathway twisted and turned past clumps of dried scrub bushes and barren rock forms, finally emerging into a voluminous chamber. A potpourri of color ricocheted throughout the cavern. Jerry spun in awe. *This is incredible!*

Suspended high above him, translucent stones twinkled like star sapphires, pulsing bright rays of light into the raindrops of seeping water, splashing the rainbow's colors through the misty chamber. Flashes of greens, yellows, and blues created a visual wonderland among the dripping calcite crystals. A distilling spirit brought peace to his soul. *The energy here is strong, and that fragrant smell ...*

Another jinan came into view and his eyes widened. "Mr. G, I knew I sniffed something sweet."

Leaves danced before him on a trail ornamented with rich, vibrant shrubs. The trees were smooth and bluish gray and possessed a hard, muscular fluted trunk. Their leaves dangled like polished gems, reflecting a dazzling array of color—ruby red, amethyst purple, and emerald green. A fruity aroma scented the orchard. His stomach growled, and then he spotted the fruit.

Ugh, not mushrooms. He wrinkled his nose. *I hate mushrooms.* Reluctantly, Jerry plucked one and inhaled its scent. *This looks like a porcini, but it smells kind of citrusy.* He turned it over. *It even has the spongy pore layer on the underside of its cap.* He held his breath and bit off a piece. His eyes sparkled, and he took another, bigger bite.

"Whoa! Mr. G, this isn't a mushroom at all." Stuffing the reddish-brown fruit into his mouth, he savored its sweet flavor. *Mmm, this is really good.* After swallowing the last of it, he smacked his lips. "Mr. G, it's gooey and tastes like a raspberry tart, but what does it offer?"

Jerry waited anxiously while he feasted, expecting something incredible to occur. Minutes went by and nothing happened. *Okay, is this going to be similar to the illumid, or am I doing something wrong?* Still he waited. Nothing.

Just as he was about to leave, he zeroed in on the same lone tree he'd seen in the last few chambers. The illumid. He sprinted to the fruit, plucked the bland morsel, and ate it. *This thing still tastes like cardboard. Not sure how much more of this I can—*

A sudden tingling infused his body, and he began to sweat profusely. His skin burned and then cooled. Confused, he sat down abruptly, dropping his aether and grabbing his head. *Something inside my brain ... surging in my blood ... It feels like I just shifted into hyperdrive and my body's trying to catch up.*

A parched throat sent him running toward the jinan's gurgling stream. He knelt and gulped its water. The flavor was exquisite but not satisfying, and his thirst went unquenched.

Suddenly, his mind exploded with visionary creatures and places he'd viewed in the Book of Illusions. Never did anything feel so real, so tangible, so natural. The smells, sounds, and tastes were more vivid than his waking reality. Was he hallucinating?

Sweat covered his face, and bizarre emotions flashed through him. Strange images continued to inundate his psyche. Creatures with large multicolored eyes darted about, emitting powerful waves of ionizing radiation. Tiny flying insects with mouths wide enough to consume small rodents buzzed above him.

It was as if he could reach out and touch them. He rubbed his eyes fiercely, trying to get a grip on reality. Then all activity ceased. Jerry forced his shoulders to relax and took slow, calm breaths. Exhausted, he lay down, consumed in his thoughts.

I have no idea what just happened, but I feel a sense of power that I've never felt before ... as though a dormant part of my consciousness has awakened to something incredible, but to what ... I don't know.

The sound of trickling water drew his attention to the stream. Jerry rose, dipped his nix into a lagoon of aqua color, and returned the container to his pack. He sat for a moment, immersed in the quiet solitude of the murmuring brook. Peacefulness replaced anxiousness; desire replaced lethargy. He began to relax, and the thought of being united with Andromeda burned deep in his chest.

"Andromeda, are you here?"

"Yes, I'm right here," she said, appearing next to him.

Jerry stood and the two embraced, kissing each other passionately. Andromeda pulled away, gazing into his eyes. "I only have a short window that I can be with you. The overseers have restricted my time with you."

"Why? I don't understand." His eyes desperately searched for an answer.

"You are in the last of your trials, and they are afraid I may try to interfere," Andromeda said, keeping her voice low.

"How—I mean ... I need you."

"Oh, Jerry!" She put her arms around him and lay her head on his shoulder. "You could shake the windows of heaven if you only dared."

"I have no idea of the hazards that still await me, but you do." Jerry lifted her chin. "Am I good enough? You know ... what are my chances of reaching the portal?"

"Obstacles are like hurdles." She squeezed his hand. "Some people see them as impenetrable barriers, impossible to overcome, while others are eager to confront them head-on, strengthened by the experience. There is no obstacle too great, no challenge too hard ... if you believe." She touched his cheek. "And I believe in you."

"They say before you die, your life flashes before your eyes. Well"—he let out a nervous breath—"it seems that I was always hurrying to the next event in my life, thinking things would get easier. But in reality, I was wishing my life away, never taking the time to enjoy those things that mattered most. I felt like a passenger along for the ride. But now it's time I smell the flowers. I just need someone to smell them with."

"I want to be that person, but what you face, you must do alone." Her pupils were the size of golf balls, her chest rising and falling rapidly. "What you're about to encounter is extremely dangerous, but this much I can tell you." Andromeda leaned in and whispered in his ear. "You are going to need the ring of Tauri." With a quick glance upward, she nodded her head. "I am being summoned."

"Wait! I have more questions."

"Trust in your heart. It has yet to fail you!" Andromeda released his hand and vanished.

What does she mean, I'll need the ring of Tauri?

Ever since his experience at the last jinan, Jerry couldn't get the lifelike images out of his mind. Had he imagined it all?

Was it some hallucination from the fruit he'd eaten? The more he thought about the visions, the more real they seemed. A ridiculous thought, he knew. Julean had instructed him only in illusions, not reality. But they did seem real!

With so many thoughts bouncing around in his brain, Jerry walked over, picked up his aether, and resumed his trek to the portal. He looked at Mr. G. "Care to join me?" The geode's eyes flickered a warm gold. "I thought so."

The air was still and warm around his face, and a dimness pervaded the chamber. His eyes darted among the various stone formations in awe of nature's creations. Water seeping through the earth's pores created an unusual capillary action, allowing the water to defy gravity. Large helictite bushes with calcite branches had twisted into contorted trees. Curly fries, butterflies, and other strange helictite formations were scattered about.

His thoughts drifted into the soft sedimentary rocks that dotted the area with incredible scenes of beauty as if magical fairies had shaped them. Strewn among them were smaller stalagmites engulfed in shiny goo that looked like butterscotch syrup.

At the far end of the passage, a forest of stone materialized and the golden shield began to vibrate. As if emerging from a daze, Jerry shook his head and clutched the pulsing amulet to his chest. Now that it had been activated, it seemed to have a life of its own. He squeezed it hard. *Ahh, my next power-up, but where?*

The limestone columns towered around him. Some looked like the head of a shark, teeth included. Jerry lifted the pendant from his chest and rotated it, trying to lock in on his target. In the midst of the towering columns, a short, round crystalline post caught his attention. Light flickered through it. He went right to the structure and studied it. *I don't see the sign of the shield, yet this is where I'm led.* "Mr. G, what do you think? Is this—"

A wave of energy shot out from the golden charm, burning an image of a shield onto the waist-high post. "Well, I guess that answered that question, but the icon is blurred and appears anemic." He studied the image closely. *It's quite vague, but it does have the shape of the shield ... kinda.*

The instant he placed the golden charm on the ill-defined symbol, the small crystalline post extended upward like the antenna of a car. It had a narrow stem, and at the top it unfolded like a blossoming flower, resembling an enormous dandelion. *This is definitely different from all the previous power-ups.* Jerry circled the station, looking for a place to insert his aether. *So how do I activate this thing?*

Only one slot was available, and that was directly in the center at its top. Jerry glanced around, feeling a little unsure, and then placed his aether into the opening and stepped back. "Mr. G, I'm not sensing anything, but I don't seem to have any other choice."

Moments passed and nothing happened. *Great, this isn't working. Maybe there's another slot that I missed.* Just as he reached for his aether, it began to vibrate. *Or maybe not.* With a whoosh, it shot straight up into the air like a skyrocket.

Jerry groaned, "No! Mr. G ..." Instinctively, he stretched his arms upward, his hands grasping the air. Energy wrapped around him and then evaporated, leaving the air charged as if he were near a high-voltage power line. Within a split second, his aether was back in his hands.

Jerry stared up at a crowded ceiling of white calcite crystals. A pale gray light seeped down through narrow, eye-like slits. His gaze dropped to his aether. *Strange, I feel a weird kind of tingle coursing through my body, almost like static electricity.* He caressed the mysterious symbols etched deep into its shaft. *More anuns ... but what do they mean?* He touched each glowing emblem, feeling as though his soul were changing, becoming one with his aether.

With a swift turn, Jerry spun around just in time to see the landscape take on a smooth glass-like appearance. A light fragrance of musk filled the air, lifting Jerry's spirit. Then he spotted the iconic orb spinning off in the distance.

Julean! So soon. I must be getting close to the portal.

At the mirrored surface, the hovering orb emitted a blinding light display, making it difficult to see. Jerry slipped the opaque glasses on, unveiling several spinning spheres. One emanated brilliance beyond that of the others. *Even with the glasses, it's hard to see.* He quickly touched the beaming ball, prompting an array of light to cascade down, and with it Julean. "It's so good to see you." Jerry examined his robe and smiled. "These pink and blue masses ... are they galaxies?"

"You are correct." Julean returned the smile. "These represent a cluster collision with dark matter and hot gases. Galaxies are organized from these materials. This sector is being created for you as we speak."

"So, what will happen if I don't succeed?" Jerry's shoulders slumped. "I mean … what happens to all the events that have taken place? Will they remain?"

"You are now in the last trials of your journey." Julean's face turned solemn, his voice sure. "Your path to Enif culminates at the portal against a fearsome foe. Beyond you lies the scourge of the caverns, Totenkop." He paused, his breath shortened. "He is pure evil. You have no small matter before you. Trust in your heart, but above all … don't doubt."

Jerry grew quiet, pondering Julean's words. *Easy for you to say. I'm the one who must confront this … evil.* He looked down. How terrible was this Totenkop? Would his abilities have matured enough to command the powers of heaven? What would happen to Andromeda if he failed? No, he couldn't think like that. He had to succeed!

"Do you have any questions?"

Jerry had so many but only one that needed answering right now. "What must I do to come off victorious?" As soon as he'd asked the question, he knew the answer. Deep inside, an awareness rushed through him, an awareness that said he alone must defeat this foe, but how?

"You have been given many gifts that will aid in your conquest." Julean placed his hand on Jerry's shoulder. "These gifts from the ancients have made you worthy." He pointed to the heptagon emblem on his aether. "This symbol represents the seven pillars of the ancients, something you will learn more about once you reach Enif. It is your authority to act on their behalf, but if you become complacent in your journey, anything can happen." There was a tense pause. "But surely you must have other questions."

"Well, there are a few." Jerry pulled one of the mushroom-shaped fruit from his pack. "This came from the last jinan, but I felt nothing after eating it."

"Oh, yes, this is similar to the illumid." He took the fruit and turned it around. "Once eaten, the ambrosia's energy will increase slowly until it fully matures, conferring longevity upon whoever consumes it."

"Longevity?" Jerry's eyes opened wide. *So, the ambrosia isn't just a myth.* "Just how long will I live?"

"Hundreds of years, maybe longer."

Jerry's face flashed eagerness and his heart raced. *I can't believe this. It's really going to happen.*

"Young Jerry!" Julean placed his hand on his hip and tilted his head. "Don't get caught up in the dreams of tomorrow until you have completed those of today."

Jerry grinned, his dimples deepening. "I know, but speaking of the illumid, something really incredible happened at the last jinan." His arms shot up, waving as though grasping for words. "After eating one, I began to have hellacious hallucinations I could've sworn were real."

"If you recall, I said the illumid had an accumulation effect and you would have to wait until its essence matured before realizing its power?"

Jerry nodded, looking puzzled.

"Apparently, its quintessence has reached its pinnacle. You now have the ability to create certain things that are not illusions!" Julean's eyes crinkled in delight. "Do you understand what I am saying?"

"I think I do, but all those images in my consciousness ..." Jerry rubbed his eyes. "Were they all real?"

Julean raised a finger as if he were checking the direction of a breeze. "Not everything is real. Some are still illusions. You have the capacity to generate small phenomena right now, but with practice, anything is possible. That, my friend, takes time and patience. A wise old master once said, 'Perfect practice makes perfect.' " Julean leaned in. "Sloppiness can produce disastrous results."

"I don't mean to rush things, but how do I bring the images seen in the Book of Illusions to life?" Jerry leafed through the pages, remaining persistent. "I mean ... it's been fun creating illusions, but now I really have an appetite to produce the real thing."

Julean grasped the book. "Each time you turn a page, two will replace the one, which means the text will go on forever. The most challenging part of managing the book, as well as your capacity to create specific items, is the ability to master control of your mind. Placing your hand on the page will transfer the capability to produce the images you see until they have merged with your subconscious permanently. You have demonstrated that ability, but your technique still needs more discipline.

"What if someone or something confronts me that I'm unable to defeat? *Like this scourge of the caverns.* Will I be able to produce more than illusions—you know, something real that could help turn the tide?"

"Possibly, depending on your level of competence." Julean stroked his chin. "Indeed, you could very well create something real and tangible to influence the outcome."

"And ... will you teach me?"

"But of course." Julean's eyes narrowed. "Are there any other questions before we begin your training?"

"There is one more item." Jerry shuffled his feet.

"Yes, go on."

"My last power-up ... the whole thing was strange."

"Strange?"

"Unlike the previous stations, this one didn't have the usual pizzazz."

"I don't understand. What do you mean *pizzazz*?" Julean stared, puzzled.

"Well, after I placed my aether into the only slot available, it took forever, but then it shook, vibrated, and then shot straight up like a rocket." Jerry rubbed the back of his neck. "Next thing I know, it's back in my hands and the only thing I felt was this strange buzzing shooting through my body."

"You have been given a gift that could very well save your life."

"How's that?" Jerry's eyebrows rose.

"This ability may seem daunting, but you have the power to call for your aether wherever it may be. When you execute your call command, it will instantly materialize in your hands ... as long as they are not bound."

Jerry's gaze dropped to his aether.

"Its energy is also essential in opening the portal ... If you don't have any other questions, I suggest we focus on your training, as we have much to do."

Jerry was thrilled to have acquired his new skills, but after training for several hours, the same question burned within him. "What say you, am I ready? I know I keep asking, but I need to hear it from you."

"If there ever was a person equipped to complete the journey to the portal, it is you! Gold paves the road of the fortunate; blood and sweat pave the road of a leader. And you ... you have left a trail of blood and sweat in your wake." Julean placed his hand on his shoulder. "Courage, my friend. Let your heart guide your path."

Julean bade him farewell and then vanished.

Hidden inside Jerry's heart, a spark of doubt still smoldered, but every pore of his body said he was ready. But what about Andromeda? After his experience at the enchanted wall, he wondered, was it truly his destiny to be united with her?

CHAPTER FORTY-FIVE

THE UNSEEN ASSASSIN

Jerry paused to stretch his back. For a heartbeat, there was a flash of emotion for a world since gone—a glimmer of nostalgia that still flirted with the edges of his dreams—but he blinked and it vanished. His hopes now rested on making it to the portal. He had accepted the reality of his quest and knew matters were going to become more challenging. After what Julean had told him about Totenkop, he knew it was a careful line he had to walk from here on out. He couldn't make hasty decisions or careless choices. To do so would jeopardize his chances of reaching the portal. Now more than ever, the need for increased awareness grew with each step.

He trudged along for the better part of an hour before the corridor opened to a massive expanse that reminded him of Tucson. The curious chamber consisted of a low-elevation valley rimmed by a thin line of mountain ranges that extended for miles. A white light emanated from above, engulfing the cavern in a visible aura. "Incredible!" Jerry shook his head and advanced down the trail. "Mr. G, it's still hard to believe how places like this could evolve in parallel with the world outside."

In the distance, the soft murmur of a desert spring hummed in his ears. Sweat beaded on his forehead, and a hot, humid air bestowed no mercy on him. *I feel like I'm back in the desert, pretending it's a dry heat.* Jerry wiped the dampness from his forehead as he marched forward on a trail that was gritty and dusty, winding his way toward the mountains.

His gait slowed as he neared the gurgling spring that traversed the basin. The air buzzed with a sense of expectation he hadn't felt before. An area dense with boulders and large brown bushes covered with spider webs sprawled out before him. He stopped at the perimeter of the valley and looked around. He was sure someone or something was watching him, although he couldn't see anyone.

The cavern's breath rushed by him, rustling the bushes, making it hard to discern any real physical movement. A flash of light whizzed by him and struck the ground at his feet, scattering debris everywhere. Jerry dropped to the earth and covered his head. *What in the geode was that?* He lay there motionless, not sure what to do.

Heart racing, he lowered his hands from his head and spotted a large boulder. *Got to get to safety.* On trembling legs, he jumped up, sprinted toward the rock, stumbling, and fell behind its protection.

Another explosion detonated next to him, and he jerked his head down, shielding it with his left arm. *Who's attacking me?* From a crouched position, he eased his head up to get a glance at his enemy. A thunderous blast shot past him and shattered a crystal spire. *Whoa, way too close.*

"Show yourself!" Jerry demanded, but the area remained quiet. "Mr. G, they must be invisible. Ugh, how can I fight something I can't see?" Energy surged to his aether, but without a target, he was helpless. He raced toward higher ground but was struck by a powerful blast, flinging him onto his back. Gasping in shock and pain, he quickly rolled behind a jagged boulder just as a loud crack shattered the silence, rattling the air around him. More charges of immense force hurled past him, showering him with loose debris. He covered his face, his heart pounding.

"Enough already!"

Shielded by the boulder, he sat up and watched his body heal. *I need something to even the odds, but what? Something in my pack perhaps?* The instant he unzipped his bag, his eyes shot to the apus flowers. *Of course. They say you fight fire with fire, but in this case, a little invisibility may be just the firepower I need.*

Jerry opened the plastic bag and ate a few of the petals. Within seconds, he turned invisible. Silence flowed to his ears except for the stream's low gurgling hum. "Well, Mr. G, here goes." He exhaled a deep breath and popped his head up. Nothing happened. *So far so good.* He stood and looked in all directions but couldn't see anything. *It seems my aggressor can't see me either, but now what?*

"Mr. G, how am I going to gain access to the trail on the other side of the stream? If I try crossing it, the splashing water will expose my presence." Mr. G's eyes seemed to stare at his pack. "You're right! Maybe there's something else that could help."

When he grabbed his open bag, one of the exploding stones fell out. *Yes, that may just work.* He snatched the volatile rock and threw it in the direction of the assailant. Covering his ears, he watched it explode on contact. Movement in the bushes close to the site of the detonation caught his eye.

Aha, you do have a physical body. But now what?

Jerry surveyed the area and caught sight of a small pocket of black soot. *Hmm, if I can collect enough of this black powder, I may be able to give my assailant a little color.* He crawled around boulders and crept through clusters of dense bushes until he accessed the section of soot. *Now to find a way to scatter this over his body.*

Once again, he searched his pack and pulled out the crumpled roll of plastic sacks. *Just what I need.* Jerry stuffed a few bags with the black powder and attached them to the exploding rocks with rubber bands. *I hope this works. Otherwise, I may be here awhile.*

He grabbed another stone from his pack and threw it in the direction of the last movement. The blast sent debris flying everywhere, but he didn't see anything. Nothing. *Okay, where did you go?* He tossed another one and rubble again flew everywhere, but there was no other movement. *Great, now what am I going to do?*

He watched and waited, searching for the slightest movement. Then a twig snapped. *There you are.* Jerry quickly heaved the explosive combo toward the sound, and the explosion caused a black plume of smoke to form, enabling him to discern a slight tracing of something that resembled a man. Now with a target, he tossed another homemade charge, causing the black soot's dispersal to reveal the true nature of his attacker: a human lizard.

The cunning devil held a sonic cannon and randomly fired short bursts of explosive shockwaves. As the air thundered and rattled, a forceful blast struck Jerry, smashing him into a jagged boulder. Pain shot through his head. Blood oozed.

Jerry released an agonized breath and rolled behind the stone barrier just as another wave of energy shot past him. The percussive discharge fragmented the ground next to him, jolting his body. But a familiar rush of adrenaline surged through his veins, allowing for a quick recovery.

His assailant paused and looked around.

Jerry hesitated before rising and releasing a streaming wave of compressed sonic blasts. Shards of stone splintered, sending deadly arrows of rock toward the creature. Jerry remained relentless, pounding the beast with massive barrages of disintegrating power. Bright flashes of lightning and thunderous explosions battered the area, scattering debris everywhere as though the earth were breaking up.

The force pierced the attacker's flesh, inflicting severe damage and causing his muscles to spasm and collapse. The creature staggered to the stream.

"Mr. G, we can't let him enter the water."

The desperate beast turned and sprayed the area with a fiery blast, striking Jerry. He was protected by his golden shield, though, and the blistering explosion bounced off him and immersed the unknown assailant in a blazing mass. He fell at the water's edge, still trying to get into the stream.

Jerry's pulse hammered in his head. *Got to end this before he washes the marker off.* Energy surged to his scepter, and with a mighty blast he shredded the creature's body.

The beast lay dead.

It was hot and humid, and the smell of burned flesh lingered in the air. Jerry approached the lifeless body. Its invisibility had worn off. Like a horned lizard, the creature had several small bony projections covering its head. Its fierceness caused Jerry to pause. *What other terrors are waiting for me? Will I have the power to conquer them?* He caressed the anuns, drawing on their strength. "Mr. G, Julean was right. I have been given many gifts. I just need to believe." He let out a long sigh. "I suppose it's time to move on."

Jerry turned, pulled his pack over his shoulders, tightened the straps, and splashed his way through the rushing stream, hoping his will would keep him alert to the calamity that lay ahead.

CHAPTER FORTY-SIX

DRACO

Once across the small valley, Jerry stood at the base of a gigantic mountain. A dark cloud of vapor hung over its peak like an Arizona thundercloud. Flashes of light silently rippled through it. He had no clue what lay hidden inside the ominous natural structure, but he had no doubt the rough and rocky trail would push him to the limit.

A quiet breeze lifted his hair while an occasional dust devil scattered dirt in the air. After drinking from his nix, Jerry opened his pack, pulled out an ambrosia, and filled his mouth with its juicy flavor. "Well, Mr. G, I suppose this is my mountain to climb, but will it be my destiny to overcome?" The geode's eyes burned brightly. "I guess I should've said *our* destiny." Jerry closed his pack and slung it around his shoulders. "No matter. What has to be done will be done."

The foreboding mount climbed high above him, rising to a summit shrouded in uncertainty. Jerry's footsteps grated against a ragged path cut through and around walls of massive stone, winding upward into the mountain. In places, the surface was washed out and potholed, making his journey difficult. Chilled wind from the mountain crests blew down the twisting trail, clouding his breath and sapping the warmth from him. Even Mr. G. was cold to the touch.

"What do you say we warm things up a bit?" Jerry discharged a burst of fire from his aether and heated up a small stone until it glowed red-hot. He knelt and rubbed his hands together, taking in the warmth. It took a few minutes for Jerry to thaw out, but then he rose and resumed his hike, tucking his free hand under his arm to keep his fingers warm.

Halfway up the trail he stopped at a clearing next to an enormous hole bored into the mountain. An aroma similar to that of fatty pork on a grill saturated the air. The ground was charcoal-colored like burned toast and crunched beneath his feet. He glanced around. *What lives here, a giant?*

Huge dragonflies with sinister eyes and fierce teeth zigzagged about, along with mutated rats the size of possums. Creepy spiders that looked like big hairy tarantulas were poised to tackle anything that came near them. A sudden rise in temperature made his heart race. *This can't be good.*

"Mr. G, the trail passes right under the threshold of whatever lives there." He ran his hand through his messy hair and tugged on his pack. "I don't know about you, but I think we need to find another way around this place." His breath caught when the foreboding dwelling exhaled a pungent odor, stinging his eyes. *What in the geode ...*

Without warning, a massive scaled head rose above him. Two huge red eyes with black slits stared at Jerry. *Oh, my ...*

An enormous red dragon blocked his path. Like a knife to the gut, he felt everything inside twist and pull.

"I am Draco!" He snorted fire from his nostrils, singeing the hair on Jerry's left arm. "Kneel and pay homage or I will destroy your pitiful existence!"

Jerry staggered back a few steps and nearly fell, all the time staring in awe. Draco looked like a T. rex with twin horns protruding backward and long threatening saber-sharp teeth. Connected at his shoulders were taloned wings that extended outward like a Boeing 747, and its dark red eyes just glared.

To his surprise, Jerry found his voice. "No. It shall be you who pays homage to me!" He slid his hand down the aether, touching each anun as though it were sacred, creating a sense of self-assurance.

"Tell me, puny human, do you really think you can best me?" Draco moved close to study Jerry's face, inhaling his scent as if he were a delicious meal just waiting to be eaten. "You're quite sure of yourself, aren't you?"

Silence fell, and Jerry stood straight as Draco studied him. He reflected on his battle with Ceti, who was dwarfed in comparison with this creature. What hope did he have against this behemoth? Yet he felt the power of the aether surge, strengthening him.

Draco snarled. "You are but a small insignificant gnat." His curious eyes narrowed and his powerful jaws tightened. "I could squash you without even trying." The beast rose and spread his wings. "No. Instead, I think I'll roast you for lunch!"

Draco released a billowing inferno that blanketed Jerry in flames. Protected by his shield, he raised his aether and discharged a barrage of energy that ignited the air around the winged terror. Dazed from the deafening explosions, the monstrous threat continued to berate him.

"You're just a paltry insect!" He shook off the attack and flew high above him. Incensed, and with a painful groan, he seethed with anger. "Do you think my power is only in my breath? You will awake in purgatory after I devour you as my next meal!"

Draco shot toward Jerry, rolling and veering, while a torrent of scorching flames sprayed in wild arcs. The dragon's fierce attack ripped into his leg before he could bolt out of its way. Jerry quickly found refuge behind a large boulder and rubbed his thigh, trying to focus past the pain. A flash of anger rushed through his veins. Raw power surged to his aether, and he stepped out and unleashed a burst of pure energy, lacerating one of Draco's wings.

Blood seeped down the scaly red body, but in his arrogance, the enraged beast assured Jerry, "You cannot win. I *will* destroy you!"

"Your jaws are flapping, but all I feel is a bunch of hot air," Jerry snapped, his pain easing.

"Then with my hot air I will blast you into ashes and spread them among my waste!"

Draco brandished rage to the degree that even the nearby rodents were unnerved and sought refuge from his anger. With a thunderous breath, he plunged Jerry into a roaring inferno and tried to smash him like a bug.

Jerry's shield repelled the fiery discharge as he spun away from the crushing jaws of death. *That was way too close. He's almost as fast as the griffin.*

"You annoying little pest. Dragons dominated the Earth long before your pathetic kind showed up and ruined everything." Draco hung in the air, flapping his wings. "You're a stupid person if you think you can defeat me."

"Get ready! You're about to become extinct again."

"We'll see about that." Draco swooped down with lightning quickness and bashed Jerry against the rocky ground, his claws digging deep into his flesh and knocking the aether from his grasp.

A wave of pain shot through his body. "Mr. G, come back!" he moaned. Within a split second, his trusted companion appeared in his outstretched hands just as Draco struck again. Jerry fell with a hard thud, hitting his head on the unforgiving ground. He got to his knees, his spinning vision correcting, and formed a protective shroud around him. *Can't afford to get careless now.*

The air was thick with smoke and sweat and Jerry's pulse pounded in his ears. Droplets of blood dripped into his eyes. A thunderous shriek filled the air as the red dragon swooped down, clawing and biting. Jerry fought for balance while his boots slipped on the crunchy black ground. Muscles flexed and strained to stay upright with the constant pounding.

Smashed into a jagged boulder, Jerry rolled, twisted, and blasted the beast with a sonic surge that slashed the unprotected area beneath his exposed neck. He rose and shook his head, trying to regain his focus from the pain that shot across his temple.

Blood spilled down the dragon's neck, fixing his eyes on Jerry, waiting to feast on his prey. He grunted, flared his nostrils, and plunged downward.

Before the beast was upon him, a rush of energy coursed to Jerry's scepter, and the anuns glowed with an intense radiance. In a flash, his aether erupted with a mighty blast that knocked Draco out of the air, severing part of his winged talon.

"Any fool can get lucky!" Stunned, Draco bellowed hate. "No quick death for you. Your lifeblood will ooze into my sacred ground." Though Draco spoke with arrogance, his features were grave, and his entire demeanor seemed tense.

"Enough, you worthless vermin!" Like a man possessed, words rushed through Jerry with a force he couldn't stop. "I just became your worst nightmare." The anuns surged under his grip. "It's time to end this!"

Sputtering profanities, Draco met his stare and lifted his chin in defiance. Streams of smoke gushed from his nostrils and his ember-like eyes burned like fire. He leaned forward in a sudden fit of rage and rushed Jerry.

Jerry backed up, assessing his opponent, and then leaped sideways, shifting away from the deadly creature. He retaliated with a barrage of devastating lightning bolts, engulfing the infuriated beast in a cloud of sizzling voltage. Like a limp rag, Draco collapsed, tumbling into a contorted knot, gasping for air.

Fueled by a breath of courage, Jerry approached the dying beast. *Julean, my heart has not let me down.* With a dramatic exhale, he delivered the final blow, immersing Draco in an electrical display that ignited the heavens in a shower of thunderbolts. The indignant brute lay gasping for breath, his chest heaving. His gaze shifted to Jerry. "Curse you!" His eyes rolled back into his head and he exhaled the last puff of life.

Exhausted, Jerry plopped down on a large flat rock. He opened his pack and ate a needed stimulant, rinsing each bite down with a gulp of fresh spring water. Within moments, he was refreshed, ready to resume his quest to the portal.

He picked up his pack and slung it over his shoulder, but before he left, he glanced down at the dragon's lifeless body and grimaced. Things still didn't seem real to him, but Draco was proof, a reminder that in this dreadful place, nightmares were real, so real they could devour a person whole.

Jerry heard a distant cry. He stopped and tilted his ear. There it was again, coming from inside the dragon's lair. *Great. Now what?* He crept into the den and glanced around, seeking the source of the whimper. Inside was a treasure surpassing that of a king's fortune. Gold, silver, rubies, and exquisite diamonds abounded everywhere. Apparently, paying homage to Draco meant giving up all your wealth.

Greed and power continue as a dominant theme on Earth. How ironic. I entered the caverns due to my hunger for riches, but now I have come full circle with my evolution. That's the one thing I won't miss when I leave this planet. I look forward to living a life without the conflicts those factions cause. I don't understand all my feelings yet, but I'm sure there'll come a time when I do.

Once again, a faint whimpering echoed throughout the lair, interrupting his thoughts. Movement behind a large golden vase caught his eye. "Who's there?" A cold shiver shot through him. Had he become oversensitive, seeing things that weren't really there, or had the vase really moved? Warily, he crept in the direction of the weak voice, his aether pulsing. He inhaled a deep breath and pushed the vessel aside.

"Oh, my." He was astonished to see a small child huddled in a ball, trembling. He set his aether down, picked her up, and held her in his arms. She couldn't have been more than six years old, and she was so cute. Her short, curly blond hair matched her ruffled yellow nightgown, but she wasn't wearing any shoes.

She wiped her big brown eyes and sniffed, trying to compose herself. "Mister ... who are you?"

"My name is Jerry, and you're safe now. But who are you, and how in the geode did you get in here?"

"I'm Ori." Rubbing her eyes, she continued to sniffle. "I was with my dad when Draco swept down and grabbed me. That ol' dragon was demanding our treasure before you came."

"Ori," Jerry said, setting her down. "It's a pleasure to meet you."

"Mister Jerry, thanks for saving me. I thought I was going to die." Her voice was soft and respectful. "How can I ever repay you?"

"I seek no payment, only advice." Jerry squatted down at her level and stared into her eyes. "I'm traveling to the portal and am searching for the best route."

"Oh, that's easy," She said, her eyes now clear and bright. "Stay on this path until it makes two."

"What do you mean *two*?" His head tilted and his eyes narrowed. "Does it split into different directions?"

"Yes. Both are dangerous, but if you stay to the right, you won't run into Sagittar, the archer." She bent down and, with her finger, she drew the route in the dirt. "He has poison arrows and can see far." She looked up, worried. "I don't know if anyone has survived his attack."

"You've helped much, but what about you?" Jerry stood, leaning on his aether. "How do we get you back to your father?"

"Oh, my dad will be here soon."

"How do you know this?"

She made a face. "Silly, because he's Orion."

Jerry gave her a concerned look. "Are you sure?"

"I've already called for him. It won't be long."

Jerry was about to leave when Ori's eyes grew big. A polite facial expression gave way to frank fear. "Oh ..." She paused and glanced around as though someone were listening. "Watch out for Totenkop. He has many eyes and ears."

"What do you mean?" Jerry recalled Julean's warning.

"All those eyes and ears ... they come from the shadows. They look for people to kill."

"He must be a strange-looking character." Jerry raised his left eyebrow.

"No, no." She shook her head. "I mean he has lots of bad guys that act as his eyes and ears."

"Tell me more about this ... Totenkop." *Mom used to say, "Out of the mouths of babes came pure knowledge," and right now I'll take all the help I can get.*

"My dad says the mortar in the walls of his fortress is made with human blood, his army is evil, and they like to kill and torture people." She looked around. "I'm not even supposed to say his name."

"What does he look like?" Jerry leaned forward, his eyes narrowed.

"I've never seen him, but I've heard he's really ugly." Her hands gestured in the air. "His face is covered with dead skin, and he has nasty looking-veins that pop out when he talks. Mister Jerry"—she paused and put her fingers in her mouth—"Nobody ever comes back alive. Please be careful."

Jerry leaned back. *Just who is this person whose name strikes fear into the hearts of those around here? Are these the scared thoughts of a little girl, or is this scourge of the caverns indeed that fearsome?*

CHAPTER FORTY-SEVEN

THE RACE THAT CAN'T BE WON

Jerry looked up toward the silvery light spilling into the cavern, the stars shining brightly. Turning to Mr. G, he paused long enough to take a breath. "We have to be flawless going forward. Our thoughts must be disciplined and channeled." He touched the anuns, drawing strength from their energy. He knew he had no choice, no other way out of his situation, but just maybe he could get lucky and avoid a confrontation with this Totenkop.

With Ori safe, Jerry adjusted his pack and began a steep ascent up the mountain. Shallow and uneven steps marked a trail plagued by traps and shadowy movements. *Must be cautious. Too many places for an ambush.*

He came to the split in the lane and stopped. Both paths made him uneasy. *Ori did warn against Sagittar, the archer, but I wonder ...* Jerry dug into his pack and pulled out the compass Circinus had given him. "Mr. G, let's see what this says." The needle spun until it pointed in the direction Ori had said was the safest. "Right it is." He threw the compass back into his pack and was off.

Minutes up the trail, he crouched at the sight of a sudden haze that seemed to be moving toward him. *Only a mirage. Another test of my senses, but this time I knew.* Uneasiness journeyed with him, a companion of value, one to keep him alert.

The narrow lane stretched upward, snaking a path to the unknown, a path so sheer and unyielding that a simple misstep was all it would have taken to send Jerry plummeting hundreds of feet. Out of the shadows, a giant bat swept soundlessly past him, grasping a small rodent in its claws. His heart leaped. *I needed that reminder.*

Near the peak, his pulse quickened when a small plateau came into view. The rocky ground grated beneath his feet as he forced his way through a thick undergrowth of dangly bushes. He paused at a small clearing devoid of flora and fauna. A strong odor hung in the air. "Mr. G, something here is familiar yet foreign."

A cool, moist breeze brought a chill to his bones. The stillness was unnerving. Erosion had carved out a dark, dense volcanic rock that encapsulated the arena. The warmth Jerry had felt slipped away, replaced by a dull gnawing dread.

Footsteps rustled behind him, breaking the silence. Jerry spun, his anuns glowing. *What in the geode?* There, in front of him, stood something he couldn't have ever imagined: his clone!

Jerry didn't blink for at least thirty seconds. It was like looking in the mirror. Finally, he released a jagged breath. "Are you for real?"

"As real as you."

The two exchanged daunting glares.

"And just what do you want?" Jerry's eyes narrowed.

"I am the voice inside of you." He smirked. "I am you."

"Oh, really!" Jerry's lips formed a tight line. "I need to pass?"

"Only if you win."

"Win what?"

The clone remained silent, his stare penetrating so deeply into Jerry's eyes that he felt him digging around in his psyche. Though he tried to block his thoughts, it was as if a twin were seeing into his mind, his memories, his very soul, perhaps even further. Somehow they were linked, mind to mind. A chill shot through him.

"I don't understand," Jerry said.

"I am the race that you will never win."

Confused, Jerry paced while his double matched his actions. *What race is he talking about?* He stopped and glared. "Let's not deceive ourselves. You are but a fictitious character, one conceived from my mind." Jerry dropped his eyes in anger and frustration. *I can't let my emotions cloud my reasoning, but what do I do?* His gaze shifted back to his clone. *Maybe ...*

Jerry formed a defensive buffer and lowered his aether. His replica mirrored his actions. *Is he really going to attack me?* The anuns glowed brightly as he released a mild burst of energy, his twin reciprocating, but both were protected by their shields. *Well, that was pointless.*

Jerry tried to slip by his clone but was met with matching movements. "You will be forever chasing but never catching," his clone said.

"Just what am I trying to catch?" Jerry's jaw tightened.

"Your eyes will always see poverty, and misfortune will always be your mistress."

Jerry shook his head. "We're definitely not on the same page."

"It's not failure you fear but success."

"Failure? I've succeeded in most things."

"Have you now?" His clone sneered.

"Absolutely. You have no idea of what I've had to overcome."

"Long ago, you programmed yourself to fail."

"I still don't know what you are talking about," Jerry said, his eyebrows smashed together.

"Think about it. Every time you held success in your hand, your subconscious sabotaged the outcome."

"That's ludicrous. I graduated with honors with a degree in geology and have my own business."

"When you were ten, you opened up a street-side stand and sold cold sodas to the construction workers who installed a water line in your neighborhood. Then you raised your prices so high that no one could afford it and you folded."

"I was a little kid." Jerry threw his hands in the air. "I didn't understand business then."

"You bought a thriving geology business only to narrow your vision to a geothermal market that was not sustainable with your debt."

Jerry stood silent, feeling the rebuke as if he had just been struck.

"You took risk you knew would fail. Go ahead—deny it. In your subconscious, you've never felt deserving."

Still, Jerry remained silent. He did not move. The indictment seemed to have turned him to stone.

"You bind the drive inside that prevents you from rising. You've played the victim card your whole life."

Jerry's face went blank, for he knew it was true. He contemplated his past, his weaknesses, and the lie he had lived. He reflected on his experience at the pathway of memories and realized he had not exposed the whole truth.

"These fears are what keep you limited and stagnant, perpetuating the illusion of winning." His clone stared. "You've carried these beliefs so long that they have become part of your being and will continue to distort your worth and deny your greatness."

In an instant, Jerry's heart opened. It was as if a light had turned on inside him. God wasn't against him. It was he who placed the stumbling stones in his path, and it was he who accepted his failures as fate. But now, like a raging fire, the truth burned within him.

"Your heart remains heavy, burdened. You have guarded your heart and have built a wall around it, with only a tiny door to enter." He rolled his eyes and laughed. "You will be forever chasing but never catching because you are programmed to fail."

"We'll see about that!" His twin's laughter stabbed like an ice pick to the heart. Jerry grimaced. "I may not be able to change the actions of others, but I certainly can change myself."

Silence fell between them as his clone continued to mimic Jerry's movements. *Can I cast off my past as easily as taking off a burdening coat?* He paced restlessly, eyeing his counterpart. *Is this actually me? How well does he know me?* Jerry hung his head, his shoulders hunched. *How am I to get past someone who knows my weaknesses and strengths?*

Jerry meditated on his rival but was surprised to find that his mind was being invaded. At once, he halted his probe. *Hmm, perhaps a few apus petals.* He unzipped his pack and pulled out the bag of blossoms but only ate one, hoping to preserve his stash for a time when he needed it more.

Within moments, he became invisible, but his unseen double quickly halted him. *Aargh, unbelievable. This guy is like a flea on a dog's back. How am I to shake him?* While Jerry pondered his options, both he and his clone's invisibility wore off. *Wait! What about stopping time?* He took a pinch of time powder from his pack and tossed the magic dust into the air.

Mimicking Jerry's action, his twin did the same. With time halted, each stood frozen until the effect wore off.

Jerry closed his eyes, deep in thought. *So far, he's copied everything I've done. If I try to destroy him with the power of my aether, the effects may lead to my demise. But there's got to be a way past this impostor.*

His mind shifted to Leo's ring, and he slipped the coveted band onto his finger. Instantly, he transformed into a gray dove and tried to fly away, but another dove rendered the path impassable.

With the ring off, Jerry resumed his usual form. *I'm running out of options.* His gaze darted about as though he were looking for something. *Maybe my illusions could help.* He sucked in a desperate breath, closed his eyes, and summoned the images he had garnered from the Book of Illusions.

The area became inundated with all sorts of creatures: fire-breathing dragons, horned beasts, and an assortment of supernatural beings. When he opened his eyes, his creations were all met with their doubles.

"No, not again," Jerry groaned and stopped summoning the illusions. He clenched and unclenched his fist. His brain felt like scrambled eggs, and he was completely out of ideas, even bad ones. He couldn't even make sense of the clue that his clone continued to taunt him with. Unsure what to do, he sat down, his thoughts flowing toward his true love.

"Andromeda, are you here?" Nothing. His pulse throbbed in his throat. "Andromeda, please answer." Still nothing. Threads of panic surged through him. *Is she ... gone?* He felt lost, drifting in a world he knew little about. It was as if he were treading water without a lifeline. He had to force himself to move, to allow himself to gain a sense of direction, a sense of confidence. Jerry had always tried to keep a tight rein on everything but now felt out of control. What if he failed? Andromeda would be lost forever, and so would his dreams.

His thoughts faded to the life he had before entering the cavern. Had he been running from his past or even himself? He stood silent, gazing at his double. A future full of happiness lay beyond this challenge. He had changed and had accepted his fate, shutting the door behind him. But now what?

After a long while, Jerry wiped his brow and sighed in frustration. He fidgeted around while his clone smirked, mirroring his every move. Jerry's gaze swung to his hands. *What about the beads of wisdom?*

He placed his wrists together and cleared his mind of all distractions. As he squeezed his eyes shut, his thoughts shifted. *What am I chasing that I can't catch?* His mind zeroed in on his fears and phobias. *Can I turn my fear into power?*

"That's it!" Jerry jumped up. "Mr. G, I have it!" He recalled his encounters in the Canyon of Fears and reasoned, *If I can reproduce those same fears, only real, I may have the advantage. It's time to see if I can generate something more than just a set of tricks.*

Jerry raised his aether. His anuns burned so brightly that it was as if his staff were on fire. A ripple of energy shot through him, probing his mind, and with a muttered chant, he summoned an enormous cloud of angry bees—real bees.

The terrifying stinging insects swarmed the air, triggering memories from his childhood.

I can't let my fears cripple me. Today, I gain control.

In the midst of his creations, he remained calm, but his clone panicked, sputtering disgust and threatening to destroy him. He frantically flung his arms and swatted the air, trying to fend off the attacking masses. Jerry gripped his aether and fired off a fiery blast, but just as the air ignited around his clone, the impostor vanished.

Jerry's face beamed with conviction. "Mr. G, running away from my fears was the race I would've never won. Not only did I need to chase my fears, but I had to catch and conquer them. Something my clone wasn't programmed to do. Today, I chose reality over an illusion and won."

Even with the new enlightenment, Jerry's quest continued to weigh heavily on his mind. Would he be able to endure his trials? What about Andromeda? Was this heaven's punishment, giving him someone to love and then taking her away? Would his fate ever change?

"Andromeda!" He waited, glancing around, hoping she would show. "Andromeda, please answer."

Nothing!

A single thread of hope tethered Jerry to his journey, the hope of joining Andromeda in a life without worries and wants. Without her, his life would be meaningless. But her voice had fallen silent. Was it his fault? The thought nauseated him, giving him a sense of guilt. Now only one dream burned deep within his chest: to reach Enif, wherever that was.

CHAPTER FORTY-EIGHT

THE SCOURGE OF THE CAVERNS

After gathering his gear, Jerry ascended a mountain trail of barren rock and blowing dust that led through a dry wasteland, perhaps scattered with creatures of death. His heart remained troubled. Did he have the necessary abilities to conquer the challenges that lay ahead, or would he become just another human to mingle his flesh with the trampled dirt, never to be remembered? Why hadn't Andromeda responded to his petition? So many questions pinged in his mind. He knew he had to press forward. He had no choice but to follow the path before him.

Hours dragged on, and the air began to heat up. *Why is it so warm?* Then, ahead of him, an entrance appeared abruptly. The trail turned sharply, leading deep into the heart of the mountain. Jerry moved forward in a void of thought, stroking his anuns, seeking strength and support.

Intense heat and a noxious odor hit him at once, causing him to choke on a hot, bitter breath. He coughed and wiped his eyes on his arm. He stopped and his gaze darted about. Red-hot lava flowed beneath him like a river of fire, bubbling and popping in an enormous chasm that interrupted the path, separating him from the other side.

Jerry stood at its edge with one hand in a pocket of his Levi's and the other on his aether. Lava waterfalls emitted an orange glow like a pulsing night-light, illuminating the area with an eerie aura. Magma solidified in mid-drip, dangling like strings. Lavacicles hung in thick clusters from the ceiling like stalactites, taking on a variety of weird shapes, from long threatening alien teeth to twisted, hollow soda straws that oozed a black goo.

He closed his eyes and tried to become weightless, but nothing happened. *Okay, what am I doing wrong?* He tried again, but nothing. His breath shortened and his pulse raced. "Mr. G, this isn't good. Without my ability to rise and float over this deadly gulf, we may be in trouble." Then he spotted a tiny ledge of protruding rock that sloped upward, traversing the molten river. "I hope your balance is up to snuff."

Jerry exhaled a nervous breath and stepped onto the narrow shelf, pressing himself against the jagged wall to keep from falling. He moved tentatively upward, his hand clutching the rough hot limestone and his feet testing the narrow ledge.

Amid the popping and crackling, vents of hot volcanic gas spewed through fissures in the walls, releasing a horrible stench that stung his eyes. Hydrothermal explosions thundered throughout the chamber. Sweat poured off Jerry's brow as an unsettling light shifted the chamber into a mystical place filled with shadows.

Suddenly, it was as if the flaming pillars of hell had been ignited beneath him, their wrath raging wild, engulfing the entire chasm. As the earth trembled, Jerry wobbled. *I feel like I'm walking on a jiggling bowl of Jell-O.*

He pushed forward through the flaming storm, the fire icon glowing brightly. His aether helped maintain his balance on a stone walkway that swayed and shook, threatening to collapse under his feet and hurl him into the roaring abyss.

Hope flashed across his face when he spotted the other side. "Mr. G, hang in there. It's not much farther."

No sooner had he spoken than the ledge crumbled beneath his feet and he fell. Quick reflexes enabled him to grab an edge, but he lost the grip on his aether and it plunged into the fiery abyss. "No! Ugh, Mr. G."

Dread filled his lungs and his breath quickened. Jerry dangled from the narrow shelf, his arms quivering and his trembling fingers digging into its slippery surface. The rising heat was becoming critical and the air unstable. A shudder went through him as he glanced at the river of molten lava. *If I'm to get back on the walkway, it's now or never.* He gritted his teeth and heaved his body upward, flipping onto the ledge and twirling his arms to keep his balance. With an outstretched arm, he beckoned to his aether. Instantly, it was back in his hands. Jerry sighed. "Mr. G, I thought I had lost you, but now what do we do?"

The earth's trembling had subsided, but most of the stone walkway had collapsed, leaving a massive gap between him and the other side. His heart sank. *Without my ability to float across, I'm dead!*

What was he to do? Jerry had known he would be tried to the extent of his abilities, but this was ridiculous. He squeezed his aether tight. *Maybe I should use Leo's ring and transform into a dove. No, the noxious gases and intense heat could be lethal. But what other choice do I have?*

Jerry felt nauseated and faint. Toxic amounts of carbon dioxide and sulfur dioxide had reached a critical level, and the oppressive heat was getting worse. He wiped the wetness from his forehead, puffing short breaths and pushing past the nausea. *Ugh, if only I could fly.*

Once again, he closed his eyes and tried to lift off. Abruptly, he felt weightless energy flow through him. He opened his eyes to see the barriers of nature lifted, freeing him from this horrid nightmare. His face twitched and his body tingled as he became airborne and floated over the fiery furnace, the scorching flames licking his feet.

Moments later, he crouched in the twinkling light at the base of a large column. He gazed into the fiery abyss. *I don't get it. Why now? What changed? And where's Andromeda?* With his heart still racing, he stood up. "Andromeda! Are you here? Did you see what happened? Please, say something!"

Again, a lonely silence filled the cavern except for the crackling and popping of the molten river of lava. A sudden warm breeze rushed by. He raised his eyes toward the flickering stars, his face becoming grave. *Mom used to tell me I needed to be refined in the furnace of affliction. Today, I think I met that and then some.*

He alone was responsible for his own fate and had to focus on his quest if he was to ever see Andromeda again.

Jerry finished the last bite of his ambrosia and washed it down with a long gulp. Toward the end of the passageway, the trail had thinned and an exit appeared, exposing another path that led to the mountain's peak. *The portal must be at the top, but I wonder what else awaits me.* He adjusted the straps on his pack and headed off, using caution as his guide.

An hour later, Jerry entered a flat barren region marked by erosion and deep ruts. A subdued light filled the chamber. *Finally, I'm at the top, but now what?* He continued his march, the hard-baked ground crackling under his feet. Then he stopped at a sign that read "Territory of the Skull."

He hesitated. *Is this the place of Totenkop?* A chill ran down his spine. *If so, I hope Julean was right.*

Moments into the plateau, his eyes began to water. *What's that stench? It smells like something died.* Jerry ventured forward, covering his nose, his eyes darting about. He stopped for a drink. *What's this?* His water supply had mysteriously dwindled to only a mouthful. *I thought my water would never run out. But then, I never thought I'd lose my ability to become weightless.*

It wasn't long before he came upon a walled fortification with the warning "The Fortress of Totenkop. A place of death!"

His heart chilled. *So this is it.*

A menacing black cloud churned over the macabre edifice. A hot penetrating breath of wind shot past him, whipping a lone pennant that displayed the death scythe. Graffiti, drawn in blood, marred the external walls. Suspended around the fortified nightmare were the carcasses of animals, along with the heads of many unfortunate victims. Tombstones dotted the landscape near the stronghold, serving as a warning to uninvited guests.

The smell of death and rot was so thick he could taste it coursing down his throat, and Jerry burrowed his face in his vest. It took every ounce of effort to thread his way between the mangled bodies, breathing through his mouth to keep from gagging.

Strange voices he couldn't understand echoed from within the walled fortress. He glanced around and spotted a weakness in its structure, a gap that appeared to be booby-trapped. Upon reaching the breach, he turned and gasped at a corpse hanging from a dead withered tree. His heart stopped! "Oh, no, not Lyra!" Grief and fear paralyzed him. His gut seized, and he heaved. This obviously was the work of Totenkop!

Doubt swept over him, and his past resurfaced like a tidal wave. What if his clone was right? Had he set himself up for failure again? A catatonic fear engulfed him. His brain cramped. He couldn't think, and he shrank from his goal. Jerry shuddered at the thought of going on, but he knew he had to. Everything seemed to be in slow motion as he stared stunned at Lyra's mangled body. He clung to his aether to steady himself. "Mr. G, I don't know if I can do this."

Then hope filled his soul when Julean's counsel crept into his mind: "Success is not measured by your past failures but by the hurdles you have overcome against overwhelming odds. One man with courage can prevail even when things seem darkest."

Jerry took a deep breath. *Am I enough?* His glance shifted toward Lyra. He yearned for revenge, for being free from this place, but he would never achieve his goal unless he believed in himself. The words of Julean continued to burn in his mind.

Suddenly, the thrill of danger sparked his heart. Who was this Totenkop? He'd beaten the cavern's best, and Julean said that if anyone was ready, he was. No one could stop him. And those who tried, well, they would taste the agony of death. Rage replaced fear as he squeezed his way through a barbed opening just large enough for him to sneak through.

Inside the compound, birds of prey perched over victims, ripping slivers of bloody flesh from the lifeless bodies and plucking their eyes out. Jerry inched his way to a spot where he could raise his head without being seen. He worked his head back and forth, trying to take everything in. That's when a city of strange beings came into view, a city surrounded by massive towers and walls. *Incredible! Never have I seen such a vile place or such a disgusting population.*

Hundreds of Totenkop's misfits milled about like ants crawling on a piece of meat. Strange-looking beings in long hooded robes paced the grounds, their faces shadowed by the hanging hoods. Coupled with these creatures were ashen, bloodless, cadaverous beasts emanating violet auras. Their emaciated frames were little more than skin stretched over their bones, and shapeless clothes hung from their bodies. They were casting spells of magic while sitting around embers of timber.

In the midst of the chaotic scenes, he caught sight of an elaborate stairway. *This must be the place Ori warned me about.* He searched for the portal, the stench of rotting flesh stinging his eyes. Then he spotted a natural stone arch at the top of the stairs sculpted from harlequin opal. It flashed brilliant patches of color in the shape of rectangles and diamonds. Jerry paused—a sudden urge to hurry came over him. But no, he mustn't be hasty. Too many stood between him and his goal. He would be mad to try to rush the portal. *Maybe if I were invisible, I could sneak past the guards.*

While the creatures busied themselves with tussles of sport, Jerry quickly ingested the apus flowers, and once invisible, he took slow steps, gulping breaths through his mouth and wiping tears from his burning eyes. *My concealment should allow easy access to the threshold if...*

Caught off guard, he was seized. Bony fingers clamped down on his arms and legs. "Ugh, no, no, no! Not now!" The emaciated creatures he'd seen earlier possessed extreme sensitivity, giving them the ability to perceive auras. Like ghosts in the night, they sensed his movements and quickly surrounded him.

Jerry's breath came hard and fast. He trembled with as much rage as fear and struggled to maintain his focus. He strained to get away, but their vise-like grip locked onto his muscles. Restrained and stripped of his aether and pack, he was helpless. Totenkop's entourage chained his hands to a post next to a half-eaten carcass. He watched the concourse overflow with uncouth and raunchy creatures clamoring for his death.

Numb with fear, Jerry tried to swallow. Dehydrated and vexed with a parched mouth, his throat felt like cotton.

Chapped lips and a tongue that felt like sandpaper made it hard to speak. His voice was hoarse and shaky. In desperation, Jerry called out for Andromeda, but still no response.

Images of Lyra's mangled body flooded his mind. Was there no hope? Was this God's plan for him—to die alone, never to have tasted the true pleasures of life? His mother had always taught him to accept his fate, for God was in control. But Jerry didn't want to accept it. A glimmer of hope still flickered inside. He wasn't dead yet. *In this darkest hour, I remain a man of courage.* But without his aether, he stood helpless. More than anything, he yearned to hold it again, to summon its power.

Jerry fought back panic, but everywhere he looked, repulsive creatures shouted for his death, causing his chest to tighten as though someone were squeezing his heart, gripping it hard. He groaned as the mob stomped their feet and pushed each other aside, making room for their ruler.

Their leader approached Jerry, who was still invisible, and ran his gnarled pointed fingers over him, trying to get a sense of his physical being. Crimson blood dripped from his hands. Lyra's blood!

"I am Totenkop, ruler of this region!" he announced in a raspy tone.

Jerry's ears pricked when he heard his gruff voice. Suddenly, his knees wobbled, and his heart pounded. He hadn't tasted fear like this since he first entered the cave.

"Did you not see the warning about entering the Territory of the Skull?" A casual air of brutality emanated from him, a sense of toughness and poise that sent a shiver through Jerry.

"What is it you seek?" Thick muscles girded his neck, and with the head of a dragon, his prognathic jaws seemed more suited for devouring his prey than socializing. The unnerving stillness in his eyes gave Jerry chills, and when he smiled, a putrid odor escaped between his bloodstained teeth. He was quite different from the description Ori had given.

Jerry recalled what Julean had told him—that Totenkop had been the most trusted of all the universe's legends when he was known as Karkino of Beta Cancri. He guarded the sacred emblem of immortality at Altaf's northern gate on the star Kut. In a devious attempt to steal the emblem's immortality and live forever, he collaborated with the demon Algol. In the twelfth hour of the night, he betrayed Sarandiel, the ruling regent over Kut, and killed him. However, before he could engage the emblem's power, Sarandiel's sentinels captured him. In a plea agreement with the Grand Council, they exiled him to Earth to live out his days. That is when he changed his name to Totenkop, a symbol of defiance, a symbol of death. His narcissism did not stop there. Consumed with rage, he'd organized a band of mutants and terrorized those who traveled the subterranean chambers of Earth. His murderous mantle brought fear even to the most courageous.

"I thought I would pay tribute to the great Totenkop." Jerry said, trying to pacify him. "I wanted to meet you, but I may have made a mistake coming here. If the almighty Totenkop will let me go, I'll leave immediately."

The cold, cruel tyrant laughed and asked his army of mutants, "Should we let this weak, pathetic victim go?" Encouraging his band of followers to clamor for his death, he roared, "Or should we entertain him with our hospitality? Maybe we should skin him alive or, better yet, boil him in a pot and have him for dinner!"

"Slice 'im up!" an impulsive insurgent yelled.

"Nay, let's cut 'im up into little pieces and feed 'im to da grackal," another one said, cackling.

"Me wants to see 'im roasted!"

Angry voices shouted around him, chanting for his death. Things looked hopeless. What could he do now? Where was Andromeda? Jerry could feel the chains around his wrist, the ache of muscles, the taste of thirst settling in his throat. The only thing he saw was death, staring across the fortress with crazed eyes, sent to harass the desperate and terrorize the innocent.

Holy geode! With Totenkop's minions in a frenzy, Jerry shuddered. *Without my aether, there is no hope.*

While they continued to heckle and intimidate him, his invisibility wore off. The light of desperation reflected in his eyes. Jerry felt abandoned and alone, fed by a fierce spirit of survival. He now faced an opponent more devious and cunning than any he had encountered before.

Totenkop gave a cold stare, and his tone was coarse and cruel. He raised his arm and turned to the crowd of mutants. "Are his looks not daunting? Even his appearance commands terror in my heart." Then he waved his hand. "Take him and do what you will."

Yes, he was going to die. There was no hope. Jerry winced in pain as the horde of underworld creatures dragged him across the rocky ground, yanking and kicking him on the way toward their sacrificial altar, arguing over who could torture him.

Pain shot through his head as they slammed him onto the ensanguined stone slab, fresh blood still dripping. His wrists were loosed and placed at his side. His heart ached with hopelessness.

He expected to feel his flesh being ripped to shreds at any moment. Then he remembered that he could call for his aether if his hands weren't bound. Before they could bind his wrists again, he raised his arms and beckoned to his aether. Instantly, it appeared in his grasp. He squeezed his eyes shut and unleashed the power of the sun, catching Totenkop and his contentious factions off guard.

The light blinded them momentarily, allowing time for him to flee. Jerry sprinted up the stairs to the portal and prepared to do battle against an invincible army.

At the arch, he turned and formed a protective shield. A stunned expression seared his face. Hundreds of thundering steps charged toward him. Fear gripped his throat. His stomach burned while his pulse surged. "Unbelievable! Mr. G, how are we going to contend with something like this?"

Outnumbered and outgunned, Jerry blasted the area with massive bursts of explosive shockwaves, tearing into their emaciated flesh and knocking several off their feet. "Mr. G, there're too many!" The vermin fought like starved wolves on their way to a feast. *I feel like I'm trying to win a war with a slingshot.*

He struggled under the sheer weight of their numbers, falling back, inch by inch, fighting for his life! Death was a breath away, but a thin thread of hope remained when the words whispered from Andromeda came back to him.

You will need to activate the ring of Tauri.

Stumbling back, he grabbed the ring from his pocket and slipped it onto his finger. A sensation of power shot through him, giving him courage. *Got to align it with the constellation of Taurus.* Jerry struggled to raise his hand high, fighting the onslaught of bony fingers grabbing and pulling at his arms.

Finally, the ring's emblem united with the stars of Taurus. Within moments, the band's icon burst into an intense radiance, causing the heavens to open. Jerry gasped. "Holy geode! They're everywhere."

Part bull and part man, the legion of Tauri descended from above.

Totenkop's deviants waved their magical swords and glowing lances, chanting and screaming. Jerry slipped away as the sadistic crowd jumped up and down in a frenzy, crying out like a pack of wild animals.

Draped in the garments of barbarians and riding on the backs of dragons, Tauri's warriors swooped down in a grunting rage, their animal skins whipping in the wind as they cut through the melee of swishing and flashing blades. Armed with flaming swords and bolts of lightning, they littered the sky. Chaos had erupted into a battle to the death.

Massive flames shot out from the dragons' mouths, accompanied by sonic bursts. With a blast from the serpents' nostrils, a blaze of hellfire spewed forth, engulfing the mutant beasts.

Weapons clashed and clanged. Blades whizzed and slashed through flesh. Totenkop's predators squealed as lightning sabers seared deep into their marrow. Shadowy figures fell everywhere.

Jerry stood dumbfounded at the frenzied sights and sounds. Anger turned to fear, and the palace of vagabonds turned and ran, but mercy wasn't shown. Frantic screams fractured the air. The barbarians' might raged, desolation ensued, and screeches of pain resonated within the fortification.

Inspired by Tauri's warriors, Jerry fought with a strength he'd never felt before. He shook the terror from his heart and released a force so terrible that the creatures began to flee from him. His aether bathed him in a warm glow as violent bursts of destruction hailed down upon the hideous underlings. Desperate gasps for air reverberated throughout the chamber, and a sick acrid smell of burning flesh filtered through the fortress.

Try as they might, Totenkop's gang was no match for the barbarians. His minions were slaughtered in a display of grandeur until finally, the last degenerate fell, and Tauri's legion vanished as if it had never been there.

A certain staleness lingered in the air, and the putrid stench of decay hung in a dark haze. Nauseating fumes of rotting corpses riddled the fortification's interior. Jerry wiped his eyes with the back of his hand, the traumatic taste of death lodging deep in his throat.

Suddenly, an unstable cloud vortex canopied the stronghold. *Now what?* The swirling gray manifestation filtered its way into the compound. Winds thrashed and auras hummed.

Amid the dead, Totenkop appeared, his lips pulled back from his bloodstained teeth in a snarl. "This isn't over." Blood dripped from his nose. "Give up and your death will be swift and painless."

Jerry raised his head slowly toward Totenkop until their eyes met. A cold flush raced through his body, followed by a burning heat. He could feel him searching, seeking for a weakness, any weakness. Could he see what lay beyond his mind? Just how powerful was this creature of death? Had Jerry's power progressed sufficiently to end this once and forever? If he lost—

No, don't even go there.

His throat tightened. Now wasn't the time for this. He had to focus on this scourge and secure his fate.

Totenkop stood alone, holding a scepter like no other. Its golden shaft shimmered, and on top, entwined in roots, a purple sphere cast an eerie aura. There was a coldness in his eyes, dark and foreign, his face pale. Like the Grim Reaper, he personified death! Draped in the ancient magical armor of Chandra, the ruthless butcher rocked his head from left to right, cracking his neck. Face to face, the two glared at each other.

"Where is your fearsome army now?" Jerry gritted his teeth. His words were like the flames of fury, a fury ignited by passionate energy, an awakening waiting to explode inside him. "You ... butcher! I will avenge Lyra's death."

Totenkop laughed. "The savagery of the kill is what I enjoy. After I finish with you, I'll hang you next to your friend and we'll see who squirms more."

Jerry could feel Totenkop's eyes on him, judging, weighing, and wondering. Anger smoldered like smoke rising in an upward spiral.

They shouted, their voices cutting sharply through the air. He tried to swallow, but his mouth was dry. *My name is Jerry Humphreys. I shall not fail.* Jerry stood silent, his eyes flashing fire.

"Few can be as cold-blooded as I," Totenkop ranted. His wide mouth twisted into an arrogant smirk, and the scars slashed across his face seemed to move with a life of their own. "You know, you were meant to fail. You cannot win." The vicious beast sneered, a frothy drool dribbling from his mouth. "It's death that you must prepare for. When I'm finished with you, I will dissect you like a rat."

Jerry studied the way he balanced his weight, shifting from side to side. Calming his breathing, Jerry wiped his brow with his upper arm and channeled his thoughts toward Totenkop. "Wrong! It's you who must prepare to die. You will be counted among your dead," Jerry said tersely, his muscles tensing.

"I'll see you in hell first!" Totenkop raged, releasing a powerful sonic beam.

The force hit Jerry hard, smashing him against a stone wall. He scrambled to his feet in a cloud of dust and retaliated with a burst of pure energy.

Totenkop leaped, rolled, and struck back.

The ground ripped open and Jerry's legs buckled. Off balance, he fell within the crevice's grasp. But before the deep fissure could close and seal his fate, he became weightless and rose above it.

A blazing inferno met Jerry and his shield pulsed brightly. The fiery mass exploded backward, engulfing Totenkop.

The gruesome creature blinked and shook his head. Screaming insults, he rushed up the stairs. At the mount's top, he threatened to destroy the portal.

"Let's see how far you get without your precious transport!"

Spitting blood, Jerry remained focused. He stormed the portal's stairs, gravel crunching beneath his feet. Before the fiend could execute his magical mace, Jerry released a blistering firestorm. Energy blazed between the two rivals, the air igniting around them and sparks flying, lighting up the sky.

Totenkop's precise movements, the swiftness of reflex, rendered him a powerful adversary. Anything could tip the scales of destiny—a shadow, a variation of light, a deceptive illusion. Blood and sweat dripped from Jerry's face. In despair, he felt his energy wane. He clenched his aether until his knuckles turned white. Though he was outmatched in power and experience, his desire to survive and live with Andromeda gave strength.

Totenkop hammered him with forceful sonic waves and explosive blasts. Jerry tried to counter with an ionizing ray but was struck again. The piercing pain tore through his chest and he stumbled backward and fell down the stairs. He tried to suck in a breath, but the pain splintered throughout his body, making it difficult to breathe. It was all he could do to keep from passing out. He couldn't fail now—not now.

"You're making this too easy," Totenkop said, snickering. "Even Lyra did better."

With a fear of dying and losing Andromeda, Jerry fought for his life as never before. He recalled his encounter with Crux. *My illusions helped defeat that giant. What about now?*

Suddenly, two winged serpents appeared. Gigantic fire-breathing dragons with long, fierce teeth and powerful talons surrounded Totenkop. Distracted by the fiery terrors, the scourge lost his focus.

With a momentary pause, Jerry unzipped his pack, his knees buckling and his fingers trembling. He fumbled, grabbing the last morsel of food and bit into it.

"Your tricks can't fool me." Totenkop turned to Jerry and pinned him to the spot with his stare. "What you have done is of no consequence. I will rebuild my army stronger than ever. My wrath will rage again." He tilted his head. "And you ... you shall be its first casualty."

"Hold your tongue." Jerry straightened, his chin rising. "I am not afraid of your wretched face or your empty threats." For the first time in a while, his words felt strong and sure. He stood silent. His eyes flashed confidence that made Totenkop take notice.

Jerry released a thunderous bolt of lightning that crashed down upon Totenkop. The air popped and boomed.

Stunned, the despicable monster struck back with an electrical mass of sizzling voltage.

Jerry rolled to the side, narrowly missing the devastating force, and unleashed a wall of fire.

Totenkop stumbled back. "Nice try." The tyrant laughed as he waved his scepter, vanquishing the roaring blaze. Raising his staff to the sky, he threw his head back and screamed. It was a sound so horrifying it defied description. In a flash, he released a sonic blast that slammed Jerry into a jagged boulder, tearing his flesh and sending blood spilling from his nose.

Kneeling on the ground, Jerry gasped for breath, everything spinning. *Mustn't give up.*

Just as Jerry rose, a thunderous explosion struck his body, engulfing him in a burst of electrical carnage and sending him backward in a shower of sparks and blood. He licked his chapped lips, feeling nauseated. The burning in his gut spread to his head. *His power—it's too strong.*

"Pathetic," Totenkop said, his shadow falling over Jerry. A glare of death emanated from the tense, menacing fiend. "I expected better."

"Shut your mouth," Jerry said, his words muffled as he fought the pain. Still weak, he struggled to clear his mind and think clearly. Tightening his grip on his aether, he tried to get to his feet but was struck again. Stabbing pain shot through his head and his vision blurred. With the constant thrashing, his body had no time to recover.

"Where's your courage now?" It was as if Totenkop were toying with him, like a cat playing with its meal before killing it.

Jerry lay on the ground gasping for breath. This couldn't be happening—not after all he'd been through. Searing pain surged from his gut and up his throat, and he gagged. He slumped forward, squeezing his eyes shut as nausea swept through him again. Andromeda's face flashed before him. *No! It can't end like this. It just can't.*

Jerry felt life slipping from his grasp, extinguishing any dreams he may have had for real happiness. Where was Andromeda? Why had she abandoned him? He was hanging by the last, frayed thread of hope. Darkness surrounded him, his destiny cut short.

"Enough! You waste my time," Totenkop said as Jerry crawled into a kneeling position, still clutching his aether. The pounding in his ears had drowned out his thoughts and any hope of survival. He panted through his mouth, blood dripping from his lips. His legs could barely support him, but he clenched his teeth and rose.

Totenkop let out a sadistic laugh. "Now, you die!" He stepped toward Jerry and raised his staff, his violet orb glowing brightly.

Suddenly, a hot flush seized Jerry and a wave of pure light pierced his innermost soul. His face turned as white as snow. His body felt like it was on fire. Jerry stood with a transcendent glow. The pain and lightheadedness eased. Air rushed down his throat and his ragged breathing calmed.

My sanctuary is in my mind! My mind is the one place I cannot be beaten. Courage is uncovered when fear is buried. Whether I live or die, this day shall be remembered. This day, I shall fulfill my destiny and become as the stars of heaven.

For a split second, both Totenkop and Jerry stared at each other. Unsure of what had just happened, Totenkop stopped dead and blinked a few times. His nostrils flared. "I tire of this nonsense. You no longer amuse me."

For a heartbeat, Jerry saw through Totenkop with stark clarity. He was a disgusting beast—a beast without followers. And in that one heartbeat, he didn't fear him. "I will see my destiny through," he vowed, gripping his aether tighter.

Totenkop bared his teeth in a savage growl and released an explosive sonic burst.

Jerry's synaptic reflexes were sharp and quick, enabling him to leap away from Totenkop's destructive forces. Something had awakened inside him as if he had been reborn. Each step was calculated, lethal, and he never broke his stare. The world quieted into nothing, his focus intent.

Jerry bombarded the sadistic tyrant with explosive waves of energy, igniting the air around him. Each time he extended his power, energy rushed inside him. Their weapons blazed back and forth until Jerry felt something he had not experienced before. Like a volcano ready to explode, his power surged and the anuns glowed white-hot. Endowed with a lethal force almost too hard to handle, he summoned all his strength, and with a mighty blast, he obliterated Totenkop's magical armor.

Stripped of his defensive shielding, Totenkop stood vulnerable, his face pale against the drab gray backdrop. Infuriated, he refused to accept defeat. Moved by vain arrogance, he rushed Jerry only to encounter a final surge of force.

Like a giant capacitor in the sky, an ominous storm cloud formed. Charged with the energy of the regal star, Jerry summoned the universe's omnipotent power. On his command, he unleashed the most destructive force nature could provide.

Totenkop stood immersed in a stunning array of pure lightning. The area lit up like a Fourth of July fireworks. Explosions of flesh and bones ruptured within his body. His skin smoldered and popped from the sizzling electrical discharges. Bloody and disfigured, he lifted his gaze. With one last agonized breath, he gave a vile curse and collapsed, his eyes rolled back into his head.

Motionless, Totenkop lay dead!

A hot wind blustered against Jerry's battered face, his eyes resting on the massacre. With the conflict over, the dismal vortex slowly dispersed and a cool breeze replaced the harsh, gloomy haze. The turbulence grew silent as time stood still. Jerry's story had unfolded, one event leading to another, woven in a way no one would understand or could have imagined. For the first time in his life, he was awake, his lie exposed and conquered.

Weary and exhausted, he collapsed next to the arch, the air settling around him. He had done it! He had beaten the scourge of the caverns. The moment played over and over in his mind, but without the help of Julean and Andromeda, he would have failed.

Elation filled him but then dimmed. What about Andromeda? His heart sank. Had he lost her through his hesitancy and neglect? A need to understand ached in his heart—a need that tugged at his very soul with such fierceness it pained him. Jerry stood and called out in a weak voice. "Andromeda, are you here? Please answer!"

"Yes!" She appeared next to him, falling into his arms. The seductive fragrance of sweet orchids hovered in the air. She lifted her head, tears flowing down her cheeks. "And now we will be together forever!"

Jerry stared, taking her in, her face so delicately sculpted, her raven-black hair splashing down around her shoulders like a waterfall of waves. A stunning golden circlet sloped to a *V* shape on her forehead. Silver ivy leaves laced with flashes of star-like diamonds embellished the sides, and an elegant sapphire rested in the center, radiating an enchanting array of colored light.

He wove his fingers between hers, her hand feeling warm and alive. His heart thrashed and his temperature rose as they passionately embraced. Their bodies pressed together, her heart throbbed against his. In the heat of desire, their lips touched.

Suddenly, the cavern ruptured into a shimmering curtain of immense color. Once again, the aurora borealis was immersing them in a swirl of passion. It was a magical love, a sweet passionate love. They longed for each other. It seemed like an eternity before they came up for air. Free from Totenkop's tyranny, Jerry lifted his head and gazed into her eyes.

"At last, it's over!" Jerry squeezed her tight. "I called out to you several times. I was concerned something had happened to you ... to us! Why didn't you answer?"

"You don't understand." She spoke with anguish and remorse, tears streaming from her eyes. "In your last conflict, I was constrained from helping you. The overseers were in complete control. You are my heart and soul. My dreams are with you and only you!"

"*Ahem.*" Julean materialized and interrupted their impassioned embrace. "Are you ready to continue your journey?"

Giggling like two kids, they both shouted, "Absolutely!"

Jerry's gaze shifted to Julean. "I couldn't have defeated Totenkop without your help. Your instruction was invaluable, but it was your belief in me that made the difference. Your words gave me the courage and confidence to persevere." Jerry's smile widened, touching his dimples. "And now, here we are!"

"You trusted your heart, and it saw you through." Julean placed his hand on Jerry's shoulder. "At first you struggled to survive, but then, like a dying star striving to become a supernova, you were able to shed your shell of despair and discover your potential."

"Without the confrontations, without the challenges ... I wouldn't have survived my final battle. I would have perished. Now I understand. It took everything I had to defeat Totenkop. I can't thank you enough for the patience given to such a hardheaded person like me."

"Your transformation is almost complete, but you still need to visit one more jinan." Julean pointed to his next destination at the base of the portal. "Three steps are required to open the door to your next world. Ingesting this last fruit will complete your conversion. Once finalized, return and I will give you further instruction."

"Oh, if I may ask." Jerry cleared his throat. "Why did I lose my ability to levitate?"

"Ahh, good question," Julean said, his eyebrows raised. "Once you entered the zeta sector, an ionizing field neutralized your capacity to become weightless. The phenomenon is linked to a mysterious zone haunted by adverse storms of aberrant energy, rendering most helpless." Julean stoked his chin. "Unfortunately, there is no way to stay clear of the anomaly."

"And I thought you had control of everything."

"Not everything. Certain laws of nature can't be altered, only manipulated."

"But I can defy gravity. Isn't that altering nature's law?"

"Not at all. Once you understand the physics behind the law, you can use that knowledge to your benefit."

"I guess I still have much to learn." Jerry started to leave but hesitated. "Oh, one more question, if you don't mind."

Julean nodded. "What might that be?"

"My battle with Totenkop ..." Jerry paused in reflection. "Just when I thought all was lost, I was consumed by intense energy. What was that about?"

"Do you remember when you received the 'teardrops from the gods'?"

"But of course."

"What you experienced was the maturation of that power. Without it, you would not have beaten Totenkop. In the end, you succeeded where many have failed."

"Indeed I did!" Jerry clutched Andromeda's waiting hand and they raced to the small grove.

One tree stood alone. Its bark was smooth and reddish-brown. The stems twisted and corkscrewed. Nodding white bells with a hint of green crowded their tips. Lilac scent made for a charming wonderland display.

"So, what's this last one all about?" Jerry asked, sniffing the flowers.

"This is an essential power that will cause the constellations to alter their alignment when you activate the portal. Without it, you might collide with a star or some other space debris."

"Sounds dangerous!"

"Only if you don't complete your transformation."

"Then what happens?"

"Once the constellations are arranged correctly, you'll be transported."

"You mean *we'll* be transported."

Andromeda nodded. "Yes. Now hurry and pick the last fruit you'll ever eat on Earth."

Jerry lifted the twisted branches and plucked something that resembled a red banana. He passed it under his nose and bit into its soft center.

"This is delicious." His eyes narrowed. "So ... what kind of food will we eat on Enif?"

"You'll have to wait to find out, but it is literally out of this world." Andromeda poked him in the side, and Jerry chuckled, flicking her hand away.

"Ooh, how odd." The corner of his mouth raised. "I feel ... strange ... as though my organs just shrank."

"Yes." She giggled. "Now you can breathe without oxygen!"

Jerry shook his head. "Who would've thought? Me—anaerobic."

Hand in hand, they hustled back to the portal, anxious to move on. "Julean, are you here?" Jerry turned, searching. "I'm ready."

Julean appeared near the threshold, emanating a golden hue. His robe had a surreal visual depth exposing the movement of planets, stars, and other celestial notables among a bright red cloud of interstellar dust.

"Wow! You look amazing." With his eyes wide open, Jerry stared. "And your vestments ... I've never seen anything so vivid or detailed. Are they real?"

"These are a window into your future. You have completed your journey. It is time for your next adventure to begin. This is the only way to Enif. The way it has always been ... the way it will always be."

Julean positioned Jerry at the arch. "First, holding your aether high will command the lightning to generate the thermogenesis needed to ignite the turret. Once you have triggered the turret, then, under your directive, the anuns must align the constellations in the correct order, enabling you to travel unharmed. The final component is to open the portal for transport. This is done by placing your aether in the area marked with the bright blue star."

"Even though my eyes were fixed on the minerals of the ground, my heart yearned for the stars." Giddy, Jerry smiled, his dimples deepening. "I never realized how important they were, but I always knew we were not alone in the universe."

"Are you ready?" Julean's eyes were wide.

"Oh, wait." Jerry hustled down the steps to the stone altar that had almost taken his life. He paused for a moment of reflection and then grabbed his pack, strapped it around his shoulders, and sprinted back. "Okay, now I'm ready."

Jerry's heart pounded as he came one step closer to fulfilling his destiny. He turned to Andromeda, exhaled a long breath, and raised his aether high. The anuns glowed like they were on fire. Flashes of lightning crashed down, sparking the turret. Thunderous explosions shattered the air. Mr. G's eyes burned brightly.

Stars shifted and coalesced. It was as if a window of heaven had opened, exposing the universe above. It was dark, not a cloud in the sky. Jerry looked up and pointed. "What's that?" A new and strange constellation had formed.

"That, my young friend, is a sign of your accomplishment." Julean's smile widened. "You are now ready to transport, to join countless others who have made the transition, to wield an authority of power."

Standing on the step that would change his life forever, he placed his aether in the starburst slot, causing the constellations to illuminate. As the portal shimmered, the celestial stars reorganized. With Andromeda in his arms, they stepped into the arched entry, and—*whoosh*—they were sucked into the vacuum of transport, leaving behind them a cloud of stardust.

In the quiet void of space, traveling faster than the speed of light, they beamed toward Enif, passing a spectacular array of divine stellar manifestations. Jerry gasped. "All of this, right in front of my face." Thousands of star clusters and colorful spiral galaxies saturated the cosmos. Each constellation presented a panoramic view, flaunting its majesty and nobility. For the first time, he felt connected to the universe, having become part of its essence.

CHAPTER FORTY-NINE

ENIF, THE FINAL ADVENTURE

Jerry had come to the end of his quest. After spending what seemed like an eternity in the caverns on Earth, he was finally free—free from the cares and adversities that had plagued his life.

"We're home," Andromeda announced with excitement. "This is a special place." She leaned forward, her breath quickened. "When it touches your soul, you'll never forget that feeling—it binds and ties you to its heart."

Home—the word filled him with images of Tucson, but they felt so distant now, as though it had all been a dream. Enif was his home now.

"Are you okay?"

"Yeah, I think." Jerry hadn't given much thought to how his life would change, only that it would. What did he know about Enif? Absolutely nothing. Now that he was here, how would he proceed? He didn't understand its laws or its ways. What if he did something wrong?

Andromeda took his hand and smiled. "Relax. I know what you're thinking, and you have nothing to fear. All of Enif will support you and aid in your assimilation. You need not worry. You've made it!"

"I hope so," Jerry said hesitantly. *There's that déjà vu again, but ...*

He felt overwhelmed and knew there was still much to learn and realized it would take time. But, hey, he had a lot of time—hundreds of years if need be. He smiled. "I feel like I'm living a fairy tale. Someone needs to pinch me so I know it's real."

Andromeda reached over and tweaked him.

"Ouch!"

"Convinced?" she said, wrapping her arms around him. "Now it's time to meet the General Council of Overseers."

After exiting the portal, the two were escorted from the receiving room and taken to the main holding station. Jerry's breath caught when he stepped outside and gazed at the magnificent skyline. "Oh, my!"

Majestic mountain ranges showed their wrinkles, and pastel colors adorned their polished slopes. He stared at the glistening waterfalls, their twinkling reminding him of the crystals in the cavern where his journey first started. Sculpted from the physical geography, natural dwellings represented unique structures that housed its population.

Jerry closed his eyes. He could hear a soft melodic tune drifting on the breeze, filling his soul, touching a chord in his heart. His eyes lit upon Andromeda. She, too, pulsed with a harmony all her own as though she drew every breath from Enif's spirit.

"So, tell me, where does Enif reside in the galaxy?"

"It's anchored in the constellation Pegasus." As she spoke, a planet that looked similar to Jupiter loomed behind her, filling half the sky, its colorful body turning slowly. Atmospheric swirls formed a vibrant spectrum of color. Violet crescent clouds created magical islands in the sky against a whispering yellow backdrop.

Utterly humbled, Jerry turned in all directions, reveling in the sweet calm that had filled his soul. "So, this is Enif? Words can't describe what I feel." He turned toward Andromeda, tears pooling in his eyes. "Now I understand."

His heart pounded so hard he thought it would burst. This is what he had dreamed of his entire life. Never had he felt so alive! Never had he felt so much joy and happiness. Enif's aura seeped past his mind and burned deep into his heart. To think that a place like this existed all the time he had struggled for peace and contentment on Earth.

"Hey, I thought you said the sky was always blue?" Jerry said, teasing.

Andromeda winked. "It was only a figure of speech to help you understand how beautiful our world actually was."

"Back on Earth, Enif is listed as a star, yet here we stand, admiring scenery that defies mortal description." Jerry splayed his arms. "Aren't all stars hot balls of glowing plasma undergoing nuclear fusion? I mean ... how is this possible?"

"Just like the caverns, not all is as it seems. Enif produces an intense aura that others in the universe perceive as a blazing star. It protects our anonymity from unwanted eyes."

The sounds were full but different. Jerry stopped and listened to the tranquil ambience of a gentle breeze and a gurgling spring so clear and clean that he wanted to cup his hands and drink from it.

The thoroughfares glistened with gold. The streets hummed with activity. People shifted about, popping in and out. The city incorporated utilities, but again, not the type Jerry was accustomed to seeing. Underground conduits assimilated their power from solar conductors concealed within the buildings in which the inhabitants lived.

"What about these structures built right into nature?" Jerry asked, pointing to the cliff-side dwellings. "I've never seen such marvelous creations."

"These underground mountainside homes are mostly hidden, adding to the natural charm of the surrounding landscape. We will live and commute from a place similar to what you see here." She beamed with excitement. "We have found that when we reciprocate with our environment, nature provides us with the necessary items to live on as well as providing shelter. In return, we focus our efforts on nurturing and protecting these natural resources. You'll soon learn that it is the power and force of nature that give life to all matter."

Beneath him, Enif felt alive, rich with unbelievable things. Jerry also felt alive, like a seedling struggling to push through the soil, waiting to take his first breath of air, opening his eyes to a new way of life. He couldn't wait!

"I still can't believe my ordeal is over," Jerry said, releasing a deep sigh of relief. "But, hey, where's the taxi service?"

"You're staring at it." Andromeda flashed a wide smile. "It's called the starlift."

In front of him was a string of hovering seats arranged in tandem. They reminded him of a roller-coaster ride without the track and safety bars.

"How does one get into this—thingamajig?"

"Oh, it's simple. Take one foot and place it on the rung. Then ease yourself into the seat. Watch me," Andromeda said as she swiftly boarded the starlift.

The individual seats looked as though they were made out of stone, but when Jerry sat down, he exclaimed, "Wow! I've never experienced anything this soft and comfortable."

"Don't forget to buckle in. We still need to practice safety. I would hate to lose you now," Andromeda chuckled as she helped him into his seat.

The stateliness and beauty of Enif left him breathless as they rode the starlift past countless homes and buildings that blended seamlessly into the landscape. He marveled at how everything seemed so perfect. He felt so insignificant yet worthy of such a place.

"So, what is this thing?" Jerry leaned over the edge of his seat and looked down. "It feels like we're traveling on a wave of air."

"You're riding on a beam of electromagnetic energy, invisible to the naked eye and detectable only to the technicians who care for it. Our system of transport removes the gravitational pull from the body, thus providing a fast and smooth passage. See, we're already at the Grand Hall."

Jerry stepped out of the starlift and stood silent, staring at a massive manor made from foliated marble. It reminded him of the Pantheon back on Earth. He marched up several ornate steps toward a massive pair of opulent doors that sparkled like the sun on a rippling stream. A sharp hum sounded when they slid open, allowing access to a hallway that led to the Great Assembly Room.

The corridor was warm and glowing. Stunning shades of color with visual elegance and artistry decorated the hallway. Pure natural light shining through high arched windows bounced off a polished white floor. Vibrant opal statues honoring former Enifian leaders illuminated the long walkway.

"Wow!" Jerry slowed his gait. "These are incredible."

"The best is yet to come, but first you must dress accordingly for your interview," Andromeda said.

She escorted Jerry into a small cubicle. Images of fashionable apparel materialized. Like a hologram, they flashed before him. After viewing several, he decided on an emerald-green banyan that glimmered like sunrays on a glistening pool. Since he was new to Enif, the silk vestment had only a few adornments resembling the Milky Way galaxy from whence he came.

"What do you think?" Stepping out of the dressing room, Jerry spun around, admiring his hooded robe. "Do you like the green or should I have chosen the blue?"

"Oh, I like the green. It matches my eyes."

"Okay, so how do I pay?"

"Don't be silly," Andromeda said as she touched his face. "Remember, I told you money has no place on Enif."

"Ahh, yes, but now what?"

"It's time you meet the overseers."

Now was the moment when Jerry would learn his fate. From the beginning, he had been molded, forged, and tempered. Jerry's life had been interrupted, uprooted, and thrust into the refining fire of transformation. Each chamber provided experiences. Each step allowed progressive changes. He entered the caverns as an infant but emerged as a refined Enifian.

With his conquest over, his adventures had just begun. Jerry remained at the helm of his destiny, and now equipped with power and authority, he stood ready to take on the universe's challenges. Clothed as an Enifian and holding the hand of his love, a staff member ushered them into the Main Hall to meet with Enif's General Council.

The doors to the overseers' chamber parted, giving access to a room that glistened like polished silver. Large crystal chandeliers with elegant sparkles hung gracefully, illuminating the chamber with a bright prismatic effect.

Three ornate podiums stood in the middle of the assembly room. Large winged cherubs and gold lion heads adorned each elaborate lectern. Opposite them, a line of chairs hewed from pure Enif quartz—bright yellow as though imbued with the touch of a god—radiated grace and elegance.

Jerry waited to hear his fate.

"I'm more nervous about meeting the overseers than some of my confrontations back in the caverns," Jerry said sitting down.

"I'm with you now. You have nothing to fear," Andromeda whispered.

Jerry glanced over his shoulders while he thrummed his fingers on the arm of his chair.

"Relax."

"I am." Jerry continued to glance around.

"You're going to do fine."

"I feel like the main course and I'm about to be grilled."

"Jerry." Andromeda seized his hand. "Calm down. This is the easy part."

"Feels hard to me."

"Jerry—"

She was cut off when the members of the General Body of Overseers materialized behind their podiums, introducing themselves as Avela, Volan, and Triangu.

"This day marks a new beginning for you ... and Andromeda." Avela shot a quick glance at his daughter and smiled. "A day you will remember forever. We've watched your journey with particular interest and have monitored your tenacity and ability to overcome adversity."

Volan cut in. "The way you incorporated your insight and experience to endure the cavern's trials was impressive."

"Your skills at conceiving illusions have been impressive, to say the least," Triangu said with wide eyes. "We feel your talents in this area will be a welcome addition to our community, and once you have acclimated to our city, you will continue your training. Until then, Andromeda will be your guide."

"We've provided a sector for you to train and to learn." Avela pointed to a three-dimensional hologram detailing Enif's position in the universe. "In due time, you will be transported to an area where you will create not illusions but real masterpieces within the ever-expanding cosmos. Just as an artist wields his brush, you will paint with your aether, using the universe as your canvas." Avela smiled. "You will become not only a painter of light but a poet of creation."

"Do you have any questions?" Volan asked.

"Yes, one in particular." Jerry rubbed the back of his neck. "I still don't quite understand why I had to go through so much pain and suffering to qualify for this position."

"Only through adversity can one overcome the weakness of the flesh," Avela said. "With much power comes much responsibility."

"And accountability," Volan interjected.

"Yes, indeed. Reckless authority creates turmoil that can be difficult to change." Jerry shook his head. "I still don't know if I totally get it, but—"

"Patience. In time you will. For now, my daughter will show you the inner workings of Enif. You are now one of us, an Enifian!"

Afterward, Jerry and Andromeda met with her father in private. She squeezed Jerry's hand. "I want you to meet my dad, Avela," she said proudly. "Without his understanding, I might not be here. He was the one who intervened when I saved your life with Virga. Nature governs our rules, and when we ignore the natural rubrics, we place everything we have in jeopardy. I was lucky in receiving only a warning." She grinned. "I'm fortunate my father is the primary overseer, and he has wholeheartedly endorsed our union."

"I'm impressed with your abilities." Avela reached out and embraced Jerry, welcoming him to their family. "You have surpassed many who have made the journey to our world. But you ... you're a real star!" Avela beamed with pride. "We have big plans for you, and someday we hope to see you as one of our leaders." He turned to Andromeda. "I am especially excited about your relationship with my daughter, and I can't wait for your consummation to occur in the Tower of Enif. Now go ... go and enjoy the amenities our planet has to offer."

Jerry shook her father's hand, offering his thanks and gratitude, and then left with Andromeda.

"Well, that was exhilarating and a little frightening," Jerry said.

"Ditto, but I told you, the best part is yet to come."

"Okay, boss, what's first on the agenda?"

"We're off to the mines." Andromeda giggled.

"That reminds me ... what's to eat?" Jerry's culinary desires had kicked in after having a restricted diet of fruit and water in the caverns.

She playfully punched his shoulder. "It's bread and water for you."

"Oh, no." He laughed but then exhaled a deep breath and fixed his eyes on hers. "I feel like I just woke from a dream. Never have I felt so free. This feeling ... it's strange. It's wonderful."

"It's Enif, and you are home." She squeezed his hand, hard. "First, we find our place of residence. Then I will take you on a tour of your new world. Food comes later."

Enif wasn't like Earth, but it was his home now, the home of his people, a home where he would be known as an Enifian. Hand in hand and with burning love, they were off to discover Jerry's innovative environment.

Jerry's eyes shifted about as he and Andromeda toured Enif's homeland. The sights were intoxicating to his senses. Excitement built and questions formed. *How long must I wait before I can start creating real, physical things?* He recalled the celestial bodies on Julean's robe. *What about all those planets and galaxies? When will I be able to—*

"Relax." Andromeda had perceived his thoughts. "You've come a long way. Now is not the time to become impatient. Once we find a residence, you will be assigned an overseer who will instruct and assist you in your progress. Until then, let's enjoy each other's company."

"Sorry. I'm just eager to get started." Jerry's face reddened. "So, where are we to live?"

"I think I found a place you'd approve of." Andromeda bubbled with excitement. "The dwelling has easy access to everything we'd need and lies within the central mountain corridor."

"Hey, I'm all yours." He held up his hands. "Lead on." Jerry smiled. He felt peace, the peace he had waited so long for. What was a few more days or, for that matter, a few more weeks?

CHAPTER FIFTY

TRITIUM, THE NATIONAL PASTIME

Several days later, Jerry Humphreys rose to a crisp Enif morning. Strong solar winds whistled through the architectural fantasy he called home, and he ran to the glassless window and gazed out at a set of pink puffy clouds drifting across a fiery orange sky. His lips spread into a smile. Then he looked down at a turquoise lagoon, the transparent water revealing shadows of large fish darting about, and Jerry felt jubilant, almost giddy with excitement.

He turned to see his wardrobe. He loved his new clothes, the way they moved with him as if they knew his every action. And the best thing: he never had to buy anything again.

Jerry had reached a point of assimilation, and his heart thumped in anticipation of the training that had been scheduled. That evening, he met with his sweetheart at her dwelling to celebrate the date of his departure.

"I can't wait to turn my illusions into reality." Jerry's eyes met Andromeda's. "What's going to happen once I'm there?"

"You will have an overseer assigned to you." She pointed to the Algar system on a three-dimensional map. "You'll take the starlift to this sector, and once there, you will go through training similar to Julean's. The most difficult task you'll have is learning how to organize and create larger objects. You know, designing smaller forms, especially illusions, is easy compared to generating an assemblage of a nebula to form a galaxy." She paused. "It's going to take some time before you'll become a master. I only wish I could go with you, but ... I'm forbidden."

She gently rested her head on his shoulder. Her breath was warm on his neck, and she sighed as he put his arm around her and cupped her shoulder. They were silent for a while, content to be together.

"How would you like to attend our national pastime?" she finally said.

"Our national pastime?" He lifted his eyebrows. "As in an athletic event pastime?"

"Oh, come on." She hooked Jerry's elbow in hers and tugged on his arm. "You'd love the competition. It's held at Rinea Stadium, named after the greatest player ever to play the game, and the arena is only a few clicks away."

Jerry, who was getting comfortable with the local jargon, joked, "Does that mean we should just click on down?"

"No, I'm serious. I think you would enjoy the tournament."

"Okay, what's it like?"

Andromeda gazed at him with those sparkling emerald eyes. "Did you ever wonder about those shooting stars that streaked across the sky at night?"

"You mean I was wishing on a game?" He laughed as though he'd been tickled. "All this time I thought they were meteors zipping through the galaxy."

"Don't be silly." She smacked him on the shoulder. "The first one to release five flaming stars into space wins the game. Of course, you can still wish upon them, but I don't know how much good it'll do you."

"Sure, all right, tell me more about our national pastime."

"The sport is called tritium, and only the best enter the arena." Gesturing with her hands, Andromeda tried to explain the game's goal and strategy. "Automated orbs pop in and out, appearing and disappearing at random. They zip around, zigzagging throughout the stadium while the contestants try to blast them with their aether's. But that's not all. They have to stay alert if they expect to dodge the biotitens."

"Biotitens?"

"Oh, yes. They're small stones, like tiny asteroids whizzing about. Though the participants wear protection, it still hurts if they get hit."

"Now, let me get this right." Jerry pointed his aether in the air. "You have two opponents standing in a sports arena shooting at floating orbs."

"The game isn't that easy." Andromeda was a bit frustrated but continued to explain. "The competition is harder than what you think. The players employ strategies to confuse their opponents by creating illusions that cause distractions while targeting the elusive orbs and dodging the biotitens. It can be quite confusing."

Jerry tried to form a mental image while Andromeda continued.

"One orb is worth twice as much as the others. It appears less frequently and is tough to discern, especially while trying to sidestep the biotitens."

"I suppose it means you don't want to take the stones for granite!" Jerry chuckled.

Andromeda rolled her eyes. "You need incredible reflexes and super-keen vision to hit the coveted prize ... and maybe a little luck. However, when destroyed, the player gains two points. And with only a few safety barriers to hide behind, the game can become quite demanding and dangerous. The first one to release five flaming stars wins."

"Let me get this right. The contestant with the quickest and deadliest aim wins the battle."

"I suppose you're right to a certain degree. You must be quick with your decision-making and accurate with your shot, but even more, you need awareness."

"Well, then, let's go win one for the Gipper!" Jerry shouted with his fist raised in the air.

"Who's the Gipper?"

"Oh, he was a famous football player back on Earth who fell ill and died. It became a phrase people said to inspire their team. Nowadays, I'm sure most people have forgotten him."

And with that, they left.

It was getting dark when they arrived at Rinea Stadium. The outdoor arena was nestled in a valley surrounded by a sea of yellow and lavender blooms. As the two stepped out of the starlift an attendant appeared and escorted them up a series of black marble steps carved into the hillside.

"This place is gorgeous!" Jerry's eyes were wide with excitement.

"I think you'll find all the facilities on Enif are quite impressive," Andromeda said as they took their seats behind a transparent shield similar to those in hockey arenas.

"Why the protection?"

"They shelter the fans from rogue biotitens or missed shots."

"Oookay, I guess it's more dangerous than I thought."

Jerry turned his attention to the sky and marveled at the regal sight. It was as if a thousand pinpricks of light illuminated the heavens, stretching across the immensity of space, each one a celestial being, a spiritual force, a synaptic link in the universe's divinity.

"The views here are so much better than anything we have back home." Jerry's gaze shifted to Andromeda. "But I wonder … do the people here really appreciate Enif's beauty?"

"It's unfortunate, but when you see something on a routine basis, you have a tendency to take it for granted. I suppose that happens no matter where you live."

Jerry sighed. "Yeah, I know, but—"

An announcer cut him off. "Welcome! Welcome!" the voice boomed. "Tonight's match involves two of our most celebrated victors. Making his way into the arena is the reigning and defending tritium champion, Enif's own Icarius!"

The crowd jumped to their feet and cheered loudly. There was a short pause while the fans calmed.

"Introducing the challenger from Kikutu and the holder of the prestigious Vega Award, please welcome ... Liberius."

Andromeda leaned toward Jerry. "Oh, I forgot to tell you, the players can change their positions instantly, seeking to gain an advantage over their opponent. You need to pay attention or you might miss something."

Icarius wore a uniform decorated with numerous celestial bodies that changed colors with every movement.

"So, what are they wearing?"

"It's called a jenuva."

"A jenuva?"

"Yes, the more wins, the more adornments on their jacket."

"Oh, like the athletes on Earth, strutting their medals."

Andromeda nodded. "Exactly."

Icarius came into the game as a class M player, the highest recognition possible. Jerry stared at his jenuva. It was as if a 3-D video game were being played, showing nebulae exploding into galaxies, stars bursting into orbital debris, and fierce creatures devouring their opponents. *No medals on Earth ever looked like this.*

Meanwhile, Liberius wore a black jenuva that flashed ghastly images while he held his arms up high, demanding praise from the crowd.

"Why is his so different?" Jerry said.

"What do you mean?"

"Check out Liberius. His vestments are not that of an Enifian, and he possesses a faint aura unlike any I have ever seen. He has a darkness about him, something unnerving. Even his eyes are deceptive."

"Well..." Andromeda squirmed in her seat, and her voice quavered. "Liberius is from another sector in the universe which is separate and independent from our governing system."

"Whoa, wait a minute!" Jerry stiffened and pulled away. "What do you mean, separate and independent from our governing system?"

"I guess now is as good a time as any to inform you. The governing factions of Enif do not have dominion over the entire universe. We have to coexist with diverse beings with whom we have agreements, similar to what you would call treaties. We are at peace with our neighbors and interact with many of them."

Jerry nodded, though he could see the worry in her eyes. He looked at Liberius and felt a dreariness. He recalled Julean's warning about the power of dissolution. *You have acquired a malicious power many try to avoid.*

"You know ..." Jerry hesitated, his stare shifting back to Andromeda. "I came upon a disintegrating column where I received a transference of power. Julean told me the structure transferred the ability to destroy matter after its creation—that it had a dark side. Are there malicious forces we have to contend with outside of Enif?"

"I was going to tell you more about your life as an Enifian a little at a time, allowing you to acclimate to its culture."

Andromeda squeezed his hand. "Look around you." She pointed toward the sky. "You need to understand—we aren't alone. The universe is forever expanding, and plenty of space exists, which means seldom is there any conflict." Her gaze drifted back to Jerry. "Most of our neighbors are like us and have the same laws and values."

Questions roared through him, along with a sense of dread. "I never learned how to execute the power of dissolution, but now I wonder, does everyone here possess this potential?"

"No!" Andromeda became uneasy. "Most have shunned its devastating ability, but there have been a few."

Jerry sighed. "After battling the creatures in the caverns on Earth, I thought my confrontations were over. I was thrilled with the idea of living a life full of joy and love ... destined to be with you. Everyone led me to believe I would live a life of bliss." He crossed his arms, still grasping his aether. "Tell me I wasn't lied to, please!"

"We haven't had a conflict in eons. But there will always be a need to defend, or place deterrents against those who would do us harm." There was a panicky look in her eyes. "This power you speak of has a dark side, and from time to time these evil forces can be alluring, drawing those who already have a nefarious side into its grasp, but you need not worry."

"Tell me, when did the last conflict occur?" Jerry demanded.

"The last skirmish was with the Jatas from the ninth realm. They live on the celestial star, Kikutu, in the ninth sector." Her voice tensed. "They were arrogant, vicious, and cruel. Even with the continued expansion of space and time, they wanted to control everything. Their strength and power made them cold and callous to the suffering of their surrounding neighbors, and they killed as easily and thoughtlessly as one swatting a fly."

Jerry's face went pale.

"But that was a long time ago." She squeezed his hand tighter. "Really, things are fine now."

"How can you say that?"

"It's been almost a millennium since we fought the war." She gave a sheepish smile. "That's when we divided into sectors and formed an agreement with the overseers of Kikutu. Not only have we enjoyed peace, but we've become partners in several of our efforts to support the natural development of all planets."

Jerry shrugged, "I don't know about you, but every time I try to count my chickens before they hatch, more eggs break."

"What?" She shook her head, her face blank.

"Oh, nothing."

Jerry sank silently back in his seat and watched the players compete, but he still had concerns about the disturbing information. With his tensions eased, he started to take an interest in the game.

Each player produced some surprising distractive illusions. Icarius created massive explosions above his competitor, while Liberius generated dark, gruesome manifestations that engulfed Icarius. Images of creatures attacking the opponent were intriguing and daunting at times. Playing on the weakness of each other's thoughts produced some very intense moments.

Suddenly, the ground ripped open and an enormous worm reeled forth with gaping jaws and shark-like teeth. It devoured

Icarius before dissipating into a fine mist. In retaliation, a thunderous explosion rocked Liberius, causing him to lose focus, missing another opportunity to dispose of an elusive orb.

Jerry became engrossed in the game's strategies and the players' techniques. He was surprised at the athleticism and quickness of Icarius and understood why he was the crowd favorite. The two jumped and spun around to avoid being struck by space debris while taking aim at the speedy orbs. The action was fast. If you blinked, you might have missed an impressive moment.

Andromeda bounced around, cheering on Icarius. Jerry smiled, seeing a side of her he hadn't seen before, one that helped to excite him as the event unfolded. The noise from the crowd brought back the few glimpses he had as a youth when he patronized the local baseball games. The players even trash-talked similar to the athletes on Earth, and the game's announcers entertained the fans by providing play-by-play analysis.

"Liberius is down, hit by a biotiten!" one of them bellowed. "But wait, he's up shaking his head, sprinting back to the arena's center."

"Icarius scoooorred!" the other announcer screamed.

Andromeda jumped up chanting his name as another shooting star rocketed into space.

"Icarius! Icarius! Icarius!" the crowd roared.

Jerry watched the sky light up every time a shooting star streaked across the firmament. And as the game progressed, he felt something different, something he hadn't experienced since his time in the caverns. A feeling of despair shot through him similar to what he'd felt when he assimilated the power of dissolution.

His vision was drawn to Liberius. A dark, malicious aura continued to surround the player, and just before the event ended, Liberius fixed his eyes on him. "Who is Liberius and where does he live?" Jerry asked, rubbing the back of his neck.

"I don't know, but we can check the records at the Resource Department." Her forehead crinkled. "Is something wrong?"

"No ... no. I was just wondering." *Something's not right here.* Jerry's eyes lingered on him, probing, determined. For a heartbeat, something touched his soul. But then he blinked and it was gone. *I bet he possesses the power of dissolution. Still, something else is pulling at me ... I'm not sure what, but—*

"Wasn't that awesome?" Andromeda said. "Our games are so much better than anything on Earth. Don't you think?"

"I suppose," Jerry said with a worried intonation.

"Something is bothering you." She spoke hesitantly. "Are you still worried about the Jatas?"

"I'm anxious to start my training, and I have a lot on my mind." Jerry sensed her escalating anxiety and touched her face. "How about something to eat?"

"Well ... only if you're sure nothing is wrong," she said, tilting her head.

"I'm good, but my stomach is complaining."

"Let's go to the Mineshaft." She flashed her gorgeous smile and tapped on his stomach. "They have a delectable dish that is out of this star system."

"What is it?"

"I know how much you fantasize about chocolate, and they specialize in a delicious dessert that will make your palate tingle and ache for more."

Maybe something sweet is just what I need to clear my head, Jerry thought, still not able to shake the feeling he'd experienced at the game. "Sounds good to me. So how do we get there?"

"It's but moments away."

Hand in hand, the two boarded the starlift and headed off.

That night, Jerry strove to comprehend everything she had explained to him but struggled with the thought that not all would necessarily be bliss. *Ever since I connected with Liberius, something happened inside of me that isn't right. I can't shake this feeling. But the last thing I want right now is to upset Andromeda.*

CHAPTER FIFTY-ONE

A MASTER OF REALITY

Jerry continued to practice the illusions Julean had taught him until the morning he was to report at the guidance center. Just as he was about to leave, Andromeda appeared.

"Are you supposed to be here?" He found himself putting his arms around her waist.

"Not really, but I had to sneak a last kiss before you left." She ran her fingers through his thick brown hair, pulling his face close. Their lips brushed and they kissed.

Jerry lifted his head and sighed. "I can't believe how fast things have progressed."

"Nor I." Andromeda's eyes gleamed. "I'm going to miss you while you're away, but I know your departure is another step toward being together forever."

"I'm a little nervous. I mean ... what if I make a mistake? Can they ban me from training?"

"You're Julean's protégée. They wouldn't dare. Besides"— her eyes twinkled—"you're engaged to Avela's daughter."

"I will think of you constantly until my return," he said, squeezing her tighter.

"It's time," she said softly. "You need to go."

With an emotional sendoff, he proceeded to sector seven.

The learning compound was located on the ghost star in the Pandora cluster. Like the cooling embers of a fire, the climate was quite lovely. Craters and crowds of loose rocks plagued the surface. For the most part, the environment was barren other than an occasional sandstorm, which made it the perfect place to train.

At first Jerry struggled. He couldn't comprehend how to organize and develop small planets, let alone place viable life forms on them. Frustrated and unable to progress as fast as he thought he should, he made several mistakes. But with time and patience, his techniques and abilities improved.

The universe was all about time and space, from the smallest subatomic particles to the largest galaxies and planets. His knowledge had expanded beyond the imaginable. Ionized hydrogen and plasma, containing electrons and protons, didn't have the same meaning as they did before. Using the Book of Illusions, he created celestial formations, drawing from the powers of his mind and turning them into reality.

Tiny bits of matter expanded, displacing chaos and darkness with light. Intense energy poured into the emptiness of space, igniting it with fiery clouds of hydrogen. Colliding galaxies ruptured into a cosmic kaleidoscope of pink, purple, and blue, giving form to an ever-expanding universe. Norvos, his instructor, marveled at the power Jerry possessed and expanded his training.

The overseers took a keen interest in the birth of Jerry's creations. Colorful nebulae, combined with various gases, exploded into a majestic provenance of intricate designs never seen before. Fairy-tale creatures of beauty and detail eluded any human rendering. The phenomena created from the thoughts of his mind were beyond anyone's comprehension.

His work was becoming famous, to the point where many came to watch his conceptual dreams become absolute masterpieces. Being able to transcend his desires and dreams consumed his life. His talents did not go unnoticed. Not only did Jerry achieve the recognition of being the best at creating illusions, but he became a master of reality!

CHAPTER FIFTY-TWO

THE FORGOTTEN LOVE

Back on Earth, life had turned doleful and joyless for Mandy after Jerry's disappearance. More than three months had passed since he had vanished and was listed as a missing person. He had become one of those stories of unexplained disappearances. Her heart rebelled at the thought of living a life without him, and she vehemently protested when the local authorities said they'd run out of clues. Deep inside, she knew he was still alive. She just knew it. Every fiber of her body told her so. She remained resolute, refusing to give up the search when everyone else had written him off.

Mandy recalled his fascination with a remote region where unusual events had occurred. *I know the authorities said they searched that area, but what about all the back roads?* He'd promised her he wouldn't go, but now she wondered. Mandy's mind spun. *Surely, he wouldn't have tried to take his truck down one of those primitive trails. I don't even know if my Jeep could make it.*

With so many strange reports related to that particular sector, she was reluctant to pursue it, but what choice did she have? It was her last hope. Unaware of what she might encounter, she prepared for the worst, assembling a full pack of gear needed for camping and hiking. Dressed in a pair of black jeans and an old sweatshirt with a faded University of Arizona logo across the chest, Mandy left the following morning in search of her beloved soul mate, hoping to do what the local authorities couldn't do.

Summer had given way to an Arizona winter of mild temperatures. Cooler weather had vanquished the scorching days. Mandy yawned as she merged onto southbound I-10. *What a lousy night of sleep. I must be crazy, but I don't know what else to do.* After a few hours of driving, she spotted the 186 milepost and eased her Jeep onto a back road. She crept over a neglected, dried-up washboard trail until arriving near the site they'd discussed on their last night together.

Mandy's heart leaped when she saw his '56 Chevy truck. I knew it. *I just knew it. They didn't check all the back roads.* She jumped out of her Jeep and sprinted to the faded-green Chevy. Cold crisp air met her face, and her nose wrinkled at the rotten-egg smell rising from the sulfur spring. *This is his truck, but where could he be?* "Jerry!" she shouted. "Please answer if you can hear me."

Nothing.

She remembered their last night together, the argument they had, the look in his eyes, and the things left unsaid. *What if he's dead?!* Her heart lurched at the thought of Jerry missing from her life. Tears threatened at the back of her eyes, making her blink faster in hopes of restraining a waterfall of emotion. She tensed for a moment but relaxed. *Stop it. Stop it now. He's not dead.*

She paced until she spotted a partially surveyed trail. *He must've gone this way.* She grabbed her gear and followed the route to an abandoned site near the mountain's base, avoiding the assortment of thorny bushes and prickly pear cactus along the way.

Within an hour, she arrived at an abandoned site near the mountain's base, elated to find Jerry's campsite. "Yes!" She spun in excitement. "Jerry! Are you here?"

Again, nothing. Everything was as he had left it—his faded brown tent with the flap still pulled open, his sleeping bag unzipped and tossed to the side, loose notebook papers that described symbols, constellations, and ... a cave.

Mandy inspected his records and began to understand why he was there. Her heart surged every time she turned a page. *Jerry, what have you discovered?* With a background in astronomy, she was able to piece together the puzzle that gave Jerry so much trouble. Mandy's heart hummed, and her first inclination was to locate the cave's entrance, but she hesitated. *Should I go back and ask for help, or should I try to find more evidence first?*

The lack of commitment from the local law enforcement had upset her. Who knew if they would take her seriously? And how long would it take for them to start an investigation if they did believe her? Now more than ever, time was of the essence, and she couldn't wait.

She placed his notes in her pack and patrolled the area, hunting for a strange group of rocks that possessed a powerful magnetic pull. *Maybe if I use the same method he did ...*

Mandy pulled the keys from her pocket and marched around. Within seconds, she was drawn to an area that stood out from the surrounding terrain. *I don't know if my imagination is playing tricks on me or not, but I feel an electric current in the air. Even my hair is lifting.*

Suddenly, her keys jingled, and then they flew out of her hand and attached to a set of strange-looking rocks. Seven magnetic stones, oblong-shaped like a football, were positioned in a circle on a mysterious blue-crystal platform. *Amazing, just like his notes.* She touched their smooth, shiny surfaces. *Wow, they are cold.*

She knew she had to duplicate his procedure perfectly if she was to gain entrance to the mysterious cave. Mandy took a deep breath and exhaled slowly. *Here goes.* Once all the elliptical rocks had been removed, she replaced them, one at a time, in the same order in which she'd taken them, purposely misplacing one particular stone in the opposite direction. She stepped back and watched as the rocks began to spin simultaneously.

The ground quaked and the entrance to a cave materialized. Her breath caught. *Unbelievable! This must be the cavern he referred to in his notes.* Curiosity mounted, and like Jerry, she entered the dark ominous chamber.

Mandy wiped the beaded moisture from her forehead with the back of her hand and waved her flashlight's beam back and forth. Inscribed on its walls were several engravings. A few were unique symbols she had never seen before. *I know all the constellations in our universe, but some of these are unknown. To find a new star system is unfathomable. Obviously, Jerry was on to something extraordinary.*

Further examination of his log suggested that a series of supernatural events had occurred later that night. In preparation, she went back to Jerry's tent and reviewed his notes, waiting for darkness to descend. Tired from a lack of sleep, she dozed off and woke hours later with a jolt. *Oh, no, I hope I didn't miss anything.*

The sun had dipped into a gorgeous sunset, painting the sky in hues of fiery red and crimson. She blinked when a shimmering curtain of light materialized near the cave's mouth, not more than twenty feet from her. It burned sapphire blue at its center and white at the edges—just as Jerry had noted.

The soothing fantasy of color seemed to call to her, pulling her close. She froze at the sudden emergence of a frightening mountain lion. Even though she anticipated the threat of a grizzly bear or lion, her legs wobbled, and her eyes opened wide.

Mandy remained motionless, her heart pounding out of her chest. *Jerry, I hope you're right.* The terrifying lion leaped into the air and she squeezed her eyes shut and clenched her teeth. Its warm, moist breath tickled against her neck, and just as she was about to be devoured, the wild beast dissipated into a gentle mist.

When she opened her eyes, a veil had materialized. She tried to move, but her legs felt like mush. After a few moments, she staggered to the shimmering blue mist and eased her trembling hand into it. *Okay, that wasn't too bad.* Her heart racing, she exhaled a deep breath and penetrated the intimidating curtain, tingling as she passed through.

Mandy stared wide-eyed, gasping at the magnificence of space as it pulsed with life. "Incredible!" It was as if she were drifting among the stars. *Jerry, what did you stumble on to?* She grabbed her phone and quickly snapped several photographs before everything faded from view. Then, like Jerry, she was left standing near the entrance as though nothing had ever happened.

A cool breeze brushed against her face and her pulse raced with excitement. *Wow, that was like a dream.* Mandy shook her head in disbelief. *I can see why some people would question their sanity about now.* The stars shone bright, and the ambient sounds of the desert echoed around her. She gazed upward and sighed. "Jerry, please be alive."

She swiftly gathered her gear and made her way back into the cave, hoping to correlate the celestial symbols with those on the wall. She paused to pull out her flashlight. *This is where Jerry's notes end, but maybe I can do this on my own.*

One at a time, she touched the inscriptions on the cave's interior, tracing them slowly with her finger, each one glowing and pulsing with a bluish tone. Her body tingled, her heart racing again.

Suddenly, a blinding blue light erupted from the symbols, projecting a three-dimensional holographic image suspended in midair. Her mouth gaped open. *Never have I seen anything like this.* She leaned forward and studied the glowing sphere.

It looks like a map of underground channels that run deep into the earth. Mandy straightened. *Jerry, tell me you didn't pursue this without help.*

She pulled her phone from her pocket and took several pictures. *Hmm, there are seven levels of corridors, each associated with a different constellation ... concluding with Pegasus. But I don't get it. What's the connection?*

It was time for Mandy to decide. Should she go forward or go back home for help? She wavered. If she asked for help, who would believe her story? She could hardly believe it herself. If she did persuade the authorities to investigate, would she be able to duplicate the events as they had unfolded? No, she couldn't take that chance. She had to go forward, at least for now.

Mandy stuffed her flashlight into her pack, pulled out her headlamp, and adjusted it to fit snugly around her forehead. Her heart filled with hope as she made her descent, going deep into the cave. Loose rocks skittered under her feet and the ground became uneven, making it hard to traverse at times. A sudden foul odor of organic decay filled the passage. *Please, don't let that be Jerry.* Her heart tugged. Then she saw a decomposing raccoon. *Ugh, how'd that get in here?*

Like Jerry, she found herself scrambling up and over broken piles of loose rock, squeezing between large blocks of stone, trying to remain alert for loose debris that might shift, causing her to slip and fall. Her anxiety built the farther she traveled, waiting for something, anything, that would give her hope.

It wasn't long before her hike came to an abrupt halt, terminating at a solid wall of weathered rock. Mandy's headlamp extended into the darkness, flickering off the damp stone and evoking a feeling of apprehension. A light breeze brushed her cheek as she focused on a set of symmetrical spiral lines. *These symbols ... they're the same as those on the pedestal outside. But what do they mean?*

Instinctively, she touched the engravings with both hands, her fingers, tracing the two spirals in unison. "Whoa!" Electricity shot through her as though she had stuck her fingers into an electrical outlet. Moments later, the images emanated a bluish hue, revealing a misty blue archway. *No way!* Mandy stood motionless, her brain teeming with questions. *Is this like the veil that appeared outside? If so, dare I go inside?*

She placed her hand through the shrouded entrance, and it caused the same tingling sensation she had experienced before. Another choice now confronted Mandy: whether to proceed. She pulled her phone out and tried to call out. Just as she expected—no service.

Mandy's head swarmed with indecision. *Is Jerry lost inside? What if I get lost? And who's going to believe me if I go for help? What if, what if, what if ... The least I should do is check inside. If I don't see anything, I can always go back for help.* Mandy stood on the precipice of making the most important decision of her life. Should she or shouldn't she?

On Enif, Jerry had become a master at his craft, turning illusions into reality. But before he could consummate his union with Andromeda, he had to demonstrate a willingness to serve. At the Main Hall, he nervously sat while he interviewed with Avela, who had the authority to appoint him to his first station.

"I have given this much consideration," Avela said. "With the aptitude you've demonstrated, I feel your first assignment should be involved with your greatest talent." He looked Jerry straight in the eyes. "I am recommending you serve as the primary overseer of illusions in the caverns on Earth, the same assignment my daughter filled when she met you. How do you feel about this?"

At first Jerry was disappointed when he learned about this trivial responsibility. He had become the greatest of all time at turning illusions into reality and thought he should have a higher calling. But then it occurred to him that the assignment might be easy to complete, which in turn would allow him to consummate his union with Andromeda sooner rather than later.

"Well, initially I was discouraged. I excelled in all my training and thought I should have the opportunity to do greater things." Jerry forced a smile. "Who knows? Maybe I'll get the chance to visit some of my old friends like Leo. In fact, I welcome the chance to show what I have learned and to help others make the transition."

Jerry had embraced the magical beginnings of his new life, one of knowledge, one of adventure, one of imagination. He had conquered his fears. He had changed. No longer a victim of circumstance, he controlled his destiny.

Even though Jerry felt invigorated and alive, something still troubled him. But for now, he was excited about the prospect of meeting the weary travelers brave enough to traverse the caverns of Earth. He was ready to help those who became trapped in a journey that would forever change their lives ... even his forgotten love, Mandy!

www.ingramcontent.com/pod-product-compliance
Lightning Source LLC
Chambersburg PA
CBHW020626020726
47494CB00001B/74